THE WOO[

Praise for *The Woodcutter*:

'An outstanding novel of force and beauty [which shows] Hill's elegant writing, erudition and imagination' *The Times*

'He quickly proves he's lost none of his sardonic wit, punch and complexity . . . You'll be hard pushed to find another crime writer with his verve . . . Hill uses every trick in his arsenal to elucidate. The result is an epic, unbeatable mystery' *Financial Times*

'A big, fat mystery which has the enduring power of a myth . . . Hill proves once again that the driving force of a successful crime novel is character, not incident . . . The heights of the Dalziel & Pascoe series aside, Hill has never written a better book' *Evening Standard*

'Reginald Hill's books are as good as crime fiction gets and this one is as good as he gets . . . A tragic, funny standalone mystery . . . History is rewritten with brilliant originality and verve. The combination of wit and humanity is characteristic of this most inventive of crime novelists – warmly recommended' *Literary Review*

'Hill's plotting is brilliant, the jokes first-rate, the prose supple: it's his humble awe at the English language that enables him to be a minor master of it' *Daily Telegraph*

'To give any more of the plot would be to destroy the great pleasure this complex and accomplished novel offers . . . Added to his colourful prose and involving narrative are acute psychological insights, beautifully realized characters and landscapes, an examination of the nature of justice, political rage, humour and enough word games to keep any bookish crossword-puzzler happy for hours . . . *The Woodcutter* combines romance, fairy tale and tragedy in one of the most gripping crime novels of the past few years'   *TLS*

Praise for Reginald Hill:

'Reginald Hill's novels are really dances to the music of time, his heroes and villains interconnecting, their stories entwining'   Ian Rankin

'Reginald Hill is one of the finest crime writers ever'
Sunday Telegraph

'Probably the best living male crime writer in the English-speaking world'   *Independent*

'The fertility of Hill's imagination, the range of his power, the sheer quality of his literary style never cease to delight'
Val McDermid

'His energy, wit and erudition are astonishing . . . he can still see off most of his rivals'   *Daily Telegraph*

'Few writers in the genre today have Hill's gifts: formidable intelligence, quick humour, compassion and a prose style that blends elegance and grace'   *Sunday Times*

'Hill's ingenuity continues to dazzle'   *Guardian*

'Hill is a masterful writer, quirky and intelligent, and his characters are drawn with a depth rare in crime fiction'
The Times

THE WOODCUTTER

Reginald Hill is a native of Cumbria and former resident of Yorkshire, the setting for his novels featuring Superintendent Dalziel and DCI Pascoe. Their appearances have won him numerous awards including a CWA Gold Dagger, the Diamond Dagger for Lifetime Achievement and the Theakstons Old Peculier Outstanding Contribution to Crime Fiction Award. They have also been adapted into a hugely popular BBC TV series.

Also by Reginald Hill

Dalziel and Pascoe novels
A CLUBBABLE WOMAN
AN ADVANCEMENT OF LEARNING
RULING PASSION
AN APRIL SHROUD
A PINCH OF SNUFF
A KILLING KINDNESS
DEADHEADS
EXIT LINES
CHILD'S PLAY
UNDER WORLD
BONES AND SILENCE
ONE SMALL STEP
RECALLED TO LIFE
PICTURES OF PERFECTION
ASKING FOR THE MOON
THE WOOD BEYOND
ON BEULAH HEIGHT
ARMS AND THE WOMEN
DIALOGUES OF THE DEAD
DEATH'S JEST-BOOK
GOOD MORNING, MIDNIGHT
THE DEATH OF DALZIEL
A CURE FOR ALL DISEASES
MIDNIGHT FUGUE

Joe Sixsmith novels
BLOOD SYMPATHY
BORN GUILTY
KILLING THE LAWYERS
SINGING THE SADNESS
THE ROAR OF THE BUTTERFLIES

THE COLLABORATORS
FELL OF DARK
THE LONG KILL
DEATH OF A DORMOUSE
DREAM OF DARKNESS
THE ONLY GAME
THE STRANGER HOUSE

REGINALD HILL

The Woodcutter

HARPER

Harper
An imprint of HarperCollins*Publishers*
77–85 Fulham Palace Road,
Hammersmith, London W6 8JB

www.harpercollins.co.uk

This paperback edition 2011
3

First published in Great Britain by
HarperCollins*Publishers* 2010

Back cover painting *The Woodcutter*, 1891 (watercolour over graphite) by Winslow Homer
(1836–1910)/Fayez Sarofim Collection

A catalogue record for this book is
available from the British Library

ISBN: 978 0 00 734390 4

Set in Meridien Roman by Palimpsest Book Production Ltd,
Falkirk, Stirlingshire

Printed and bound in Great Britain by Clays Ltd, St Ives plc

Mixed Sources
Product group from well-managed
forests and other controlled sources
www.fsc.org Cert no. SW-COC-001806
© 1996 Forest Stewardship Council

FSC is a non-profit international organisation established
to promote the responsible management of the world's forests.
Products carrying the FSC label are independently certified
to assure consumers that they come from forests that are managed
to meet the social, economic and ecological needs
of present and future generations.

Find out more about HarperCollins and the environment at
www.harpercollins.co.uk/green

For John Lennard
a poet among critics
a true friend to writers
and a fountain of knowledge
who by imagining what he knows
helps us to know what we imagine

'Insensé, dit-il, le jour où j'avais résolu de me venger, de ne pas m'être arraché le coeur!'*

Alexander Dumas: *Le Comte de Monte-Cristo*

---

*'I must have been mad,' he said, 'the day I started planning revenge, not to have ripped my heart out!'

PROLOGUE

necessity

I am sworn brother, sweet,
To grim Necessity, and he and I
Will keep a league till death.

Shakespeare: *Richard II* (v.i)

1

Summer 1963; Profumo disgraced; Ward dead; The Beatles' *Please please me* top album; Luther King having his dream; JFK fast approaching the end of his; the Cold War at its chilliest; the Wind of Change blowing ever more strongly through Colonial Africa, with its rising blasts already being felt across the Gate of Tears in British-controlled Aden.

But the threat of terrorist activity is not yet so great that an eleven-year-old English boy cannot enjoy his summer holiday there before returning to school.

There are restrictions, however. His diplomat father, aware of the growing threat from the National Liberation Front, no longer lets him roam free, but sets strict boundaries and insists he is always accompanied by Ahmed, a young Yemeni gardener cum handyman who has become very attached to the boy.

In Ahmed's company he feels perfectly safe, so when a scarred and dusty Morris Oxford pulls up alongside them with its rear door invitingly open, he feels surprise but no alarm as his friend urges him inside.

There are already two people on the back seat. The boy finds himself crushed not too comfortably between Ahmed and a stout bald man who smells of sweat and cheap tobacco.

The car roars away. Soon they reach one of the boundaries laid down by his father. The boy looks at Ahmed queryingly, but already they are moving into one of the less salubrious areas of the city.

Oddly this isn't his first visit. The previous year, in safer times, having overheard one of the British clerks refer smirkingly to its main thoroughfare as *The Street of a Thousand Arseholes*, he had persuaded Ahmed to bring him here. The street in question had been something of a disappointment, offering the boy little clue as to the origin of its entertaining name. Ahmed had responded to his questioning by saying with a grin, 'Too young. Later maybe, when you are older!'

Now the Morris turns into this very street, slows down, and almost before it has come to a halt the boy finds himself bundled out by the bald man and pushed through a doorway.

But he is not yet so frightened that he does not observe the number 19 painted on the wall beside the door.

He is almost carried up some stairs and taken into a room empty of furniture but full of men. Here he is dumped on the floor in a corner. He tries to speak to Ahmed. The young man shakes his head impatiently, and after that will not meet his gaze.

After ten minutes or so a new man arrives, this one wearing a European suit and exuding authority. The others fall silent.

The newcomer stands over the boy and stoops to peer into his face.

'So, boy,' he says. 'You are the son of the British spymaster.'

'No, sir,' he replies. 'My father is the British commercial attaché.'

The man laughs.

'When I was your age, I knew what my father was,' he

4

says. 'Come, let us speak to him and see how much he values you.'

He is dragged to his feet by the bald man and marched into another room where there is a telephone.

The man in the suit dials a number, the boy hears him speak his father's name, there is a pause, then the man says, 'Say nothing. I speak for the Front for the Liberation of South Yemen. We have your son. He will speak to you so that you know I do not lie.'

He makes a gesture and the boy is forced forward.

The man says, 'Speak to your father so he may know it is you,' and puts the phone to the boy's mouth.

The boy chants, '*Mille ani undeviginti.*'

The man snatches the phone away and grabs the boy by the throat.

'What did you say?' he screams.

'You said he had to know it was me,' gabbles the boy. 'It's a song we sing together about Paddy McGinty's Goat. Ask him, he'll tell you.'

The man speaks into the phone: 'What is this Ginty goat?'

Whatever is said to him seems to satisfy him and, at a nod from the man, the boy is dragged back to the first room.

Here he lies in the corner, ignored. Men come and go. There is an atmosphere of excitement as though everything is going well. Ahmed, who receives many congratulatory slaps and embraces, still refuses to look at him. He grows increasingly fearful and sinks towards despair.

Then from below comes a sudden outburst of noise.

First the splintering of wood as though a locked door is being broken down, then a tumult of upraised voices followed almost instantly by the rattle of small-arms fire.

All the men rush out. Left alone, the boy looks for a place to hide but there is nowhere. The room's one window is too small for even a small eleven-year-old to wriggle through.

The din is getting louder, nearer. The door bursts open. The bald man rushes in with a pistol in his hand. The boy falls to the floor. The man screams something unintelligible and aims the weapon. Before he can fire, Ahmed comes in behind and jumps on his back. The gun goes off. The bullet hits the floor between the boy's splayed legs.

The two men wrestle briefly. The gun explodes again.

And the bald man slumps against the wall, his hands holding his stomach. Blood seeps through his fingers.

Ahmed stands over him, clutching the pistol. Now at last his eyes meet the boy's and he tries to smile, but it doesn't quite work. Then he turns to the door that has been slammed shut in the struggle.

The boy cries, 'Ahmed, wait!'

But the young Yemeni is already opening the door.

He hardly takes one pace over the threshold before he is driven back into the room by a hail of bullets that shatter his chest.

Their eyes meet once more as he lies on the floor. This time the smile makes it to his lips. Then he dies.

Folded in his father's arms, the boy finally lets himself cry.

His father says, 'You did well, you kept your head; the apple doesn't fall far from the tree, eh? And didn't I tell you that doing your Latin homework would come in useful some day!'

Two years later his father will be killed when his car is blown up by a FLOSY bomb, so the boy never has the chance to sit down with him as an adult and ask what the subversives wanted him to do as the price of his son's safety.

Nor what his answer would have been if his own young wits had not been quick enough to reveal the street and the building number where he was being held.

But before he went back to school he did ask how it was

that his friend Ahmed, who had loved him enough to save his life and give up his own in the process, could have put him in that perilous position in the first place.

And his father had answered, 'When love is in opposition to grim necessity, there is usually only one winner.'

He had not understood then what he meant. But he was to understand later.

2

Autumn 1989; the world in turmoil; the Berlin Wall crumbling; Chris Rea's *The Road to Hell* top album; Western civilization watching with bated breath the chain of events that will lead to the freeing of Eastern Europe and the end of the Cold War.

In a Cumbrian forest in a glade dappled by the midday sun, a man sits slumped against a twisted rowan, his weathered face more deeply scored by the thoughts grinding through his bowed head, his eyes fixed upon but not seeing the unopened flask and sandwich box between his feet. A little way apart, a second man stands and watches, his long brown hair edged wolf-grey, his troubled face full of a compassion he knows it is vain to express, while at his back a young girl too regards the sitting man with unblinking gaze, though her expression is much harder to read. And over the wide woodland tract, so rarely free of the wind's soughing music above, and the pizzicato of cracking twigs below, a silence falls as if trees and sky and surrounding mountains too were bating their breath for fear of intruding on grief.

Three hundred miles to the south in an East London multi-storey car park, five hoodies who probably wouldn't bate a breath if Jesus Christ crash-landed on St Paul's in a chariot of fire are breaking into a car.

But they've done it once too often, and suddenly cops spring up all around as if someone had been sowing dragon's teeth. The hoodies scatter and run, only to find there's no place to run to.

Except for one. He heads for a ten-foot concrete wall with a one-foot gap at the top. To the cops' amazement, he goes up the wall like a lizard. Then, to their horror, he rolls through the gap and vanishes.

They are on the fifth level and there's nothing beyond that gap but a sixty-foot drop to the street below.

The cops radio down to ask their waiting colleagues to go round the back of the multi-storey and pick up the corpse.

A few minutes later word comes back – no corpse at the foot of the wall, just a young hoodie who tried to run off as soon as he spotted them.

At the station he tells them he is John Smith, age eighteen, no fixed abode.

After that he shuts up and stays shut up.

They print him. He's not in the records.

His fellow hoodies claim never to have seen him before. They also claim never to have seen each other before. One of them is so doped up he's uncertain whether he's ever seen himself before.

Two are clearly juveniles. A social worker is summoned to sit in on their questioning. The other two have police records. One is eighteen, the other nineteen. The duty solicitor deals with them.

John Smith's age they're still not sure about, and something about the youth, some intangible aura of likeability, makes them share their doubts with the duty solicitor.

He starts his interview by pointing out to Smith that as a juvenile he would be dealt with differently, probably getting a light, non-custodial sentence. Smith sticks to his story, refusing to add details about his background though his accent is clearly northern.

The solicitor guesses he's lying about his age and name to keep his family out of the picture. Hoping to scare the boy into honesty by over-egging the adult consequences of his crime, he turns his attention to the case against him and quickly perceives it isn't all that strong. Identification via the grainy CCTV tape in the dimly lit multi-storey is a long way this side of reasonable doubt. And could anyone really have shinned down the sheer outer wall in under a minute as the police evidence claims?

As they talk, the boy relaxes as long as no questions are asked about his origins, and the solicitor finds himself warming to his young client. On his way home he diverts to take a photo of the outer wall of the multi-storey to show just how sheer it is. Next day he shows it to the boy, who is clearly touched by this sign of concern, but becomes panicky when told he has to appear before a magistrate that same morning. The solicitor assures him this is just a committal hearing, not a trial, but warns him that as he is officially an adult of no fixed abode, he will almost certainly be remanded in custody.

This is what happens. As the boy is led away, the solicitor tells him not to worry, he will call round at the Remand Centre later in the day. But he has other work to deal with that keeps him busy well into the evening. He remembers the boy as he makes his way home and eases his guilt with the thought that a night in a Remand Centre without sight of a friendly face might be just the thing Smith needs to make him see sense.

He talks to his wife about the boy. She regards him with surprise. He is not in the habit of getting attached to the low-life criminals who form his customary clientele.

He goes to bed early, exhausted. In the small hours when

his wife awakens him, whispering she thinks someone is trying to break in through the living-room window, he reckons she must be having a nightmare as their flat is on the tenth floor of a high rise.

But when they go into the living room and switch on the light, there perched on the narrow window box outside the window is the figure of a man.

Not a man. A boy. John Smith.

The solicitor tells his wife it's OK, opens the window and lets Smith in.

You said you would come, says the boy, half tearfully, half accusingly.

How did you get out of the Centre? asks the solicitor. *And how did you find me?*

Through a window, says the boy. *And your office address was on that card you gave me, so I got in through a skylight and rooted around till I found your home address. I tidied up after, I didn't leave a mess.*

His wife, who has been listening to this exchange with interest, lowers the bread knife she is carrying and says, *I'll make a cup of tea.*

She returns with a pot of tea and a large sponge cake which Smith demolishes over the next hour. During this time she gets more out of the boy than the combined efforts of her husband and the police managed in two days.

When she's satisfied she's got all she can, she says, *Now we'd better get you back.*

The boy looks alarmed and she reassures him, *My husband's going to get you off this charge, no problem. But absconding from custody's another matter, so you need to be back in the Remand Centre before reveille.*

We can't just knock at the door, protests her husband.

Of course not. You'll get back in the way you came out, won't you, ducks?

11

The boy nods, and half an hour later the couple sit in their car distantly watching a shadow running up the outer wall of the Remand Centre.

Nice lad, says the wife. *You always did have good judgment. When you get him off you'd better bring him back home till we decide what to do with him.*

Home! exclaims the solicitor. *Our home?*

Who else's?

Look, I like the lad, but I wasn't planning to adopt him!

Me neither, says his wife. *But we've got to do something with him. Otherwise what does he do? Goes back to thieving, or ends up flogging his arsehole round King's Cross.*

So when the case is dismissed, Smith takes possession of the solicitor's spare room.

But not for long.

The wife says, *I've mentioned him at the Chapel. JC says he'd like to meet him.*

The solicitor pulls a face and says, *King's Cross might be a better bet.*

The wife says, *No, you're wrong. None of that with a kid he takes under his wing. In any case, the boy needs a job and who else can we talk to?*

The meeting takes place in a pub after the lunchtime crush has thinned out. To start with the boy doesn't say much, but under the influence of a couple of halves of lager and the man, JC's, relaxed undemanding manner he becomes quite voluble. Voluble enough to make it clear he's not too big on hymn-singing, collection-box rattling or any of the other activities conjured up in his mind by references to the Chapel.

The man says, *I expect you'd prefer something more active and out of doors, eh? So tell me, apart from running up and down vertical walls, what else is it that you do?*

The boy thinks, then replies, *I can chop down trees.*

JC laughs.

12

A woodcutter! Well, curiously at the Chapel we do have an extensive garden to tend and occasionally a nimble woodcutter might come in handy. I'll see what I can do.

The boy and the woman look at each other and exchange smiles.

And the man, JC, looks on and smiles benevolently too.

3

Winter 1991; Terry Waite freed; 264 Croats massacred at Vukovar; Freddy Mercury dies of AIDS; Michael Jackson's *Dangerous* top album; the Soviet Union dissolved; Gorbachev resigns.

And in a quiet side street in the 20th arrondissement of Paris, a man with a saintly smile relaxes in the comfortable rear seat of a Citroën CX. Through the swirling mist above the trees on the far side of a small park he can just make out the top three storeys of a six-storey apartment block. He imagines he sees a shadow moving rapidly down the side of the building, but it is soon out of sight, and in any case he is long used to the deceptions of the imagination on such a night as this. He returns his attention to Quintus Curtius's account of the fall of Tyre, and is soon so immersed that he is taken by surprise a few minutes later when the car door opens and the boy slips inside.

'Oh hello,' he says, closing the book. 'Everything all right?'

'Piece of cake,' says the boy. 'Bit chilly on the fingers though.'

'You ought to wear gloves,' says the man, passing over a thermos flask.

'Can't feel the holds the same with gloves,' replies the boy, drinking directly from the flask.

The man regards him fondly and says, 'You're a good little woodcutter.'

In the front of the car a phone rings. The driver answers it, speaking in French. After a while, he turns and says, 'He's on his way, JC. But there's a problem. He diverted to the Gare d'Est. He picked up a woman and a child. They think it's his wife and daughter. They're in the car with him.'

Without any change of expression or tone the man says softly, '*Parles Français, idiot!*'

But his warning is too late.

The boy says, 'What's that about a wife and daughter? You said he lived by himself.'

'So he does,' reassures the man. 'As you doubtless observed, it's a very small flat. Also he's estranged from his family. If it is his wife and daughter, and that's not definite, he is almost certainly taking them to a hotel. Would you like something to eat? I have some chocolate.'

The boy shakes his head and drinks again from the flask. His face is troubled.

The man says quietly, 'This is a véry wicked person, I mean wicked in himself as well as a dangerous enemy of our country.'

The boy says, 'Yeah, I know that, you explained that. But that doesn't mean his wife and kid are wicked, does it?'

'Of course it doesn't. And we do everything in our power not to hurt the innocent; I explained that too, didn't I?'

'Yes,' agrees the boy.

'Well then.'

They sit in silence for some minutes. The phone sounds again.

The driver answers, listens, turns his head and says, '*Ils sont arrivés. La femme et l'enfant aussi. Il demande, que voudrais-vous?*'

The man said, *'Dites-lui, vas'y.'*

The boy's face is screwed up as if by sheer concentration he can make sense of what's being said. On the far side of the park the mist above the trees clears for a moment and the apartment block is visible silhouetted against a brightly starred sky.

A light comes on in one of the uppermost chambers. At first it is an ordinary light, amber against an uncurtained window.

And then it turns red. It is too distant for any sound to reach inside the well-insulated car, but in that moment they see the glass dissolve and smoke and debris come streaming towards them like the fingers of a reaching hand.

Then the mist swirls back and the man says, 'Go.'

Back in their apartment, the boy goes to his room and the man sits by a gently hissing gas fire, encoding his report. When it is finished, he pours himself a drink and opens his *History of Alexander the Great.*

Suddenly the door opens and the boy, naked except for his brief underpants, bursts into the room.

He says in a voice so choked with emotion he can hardly get the words out, 'You lied to me, you fucking bastard! They were still with him, both of them, it's on the news, it's so fucking terrible it's on the British news. You lied! Why?'

The man says, 'It had to be done tonight. Tomorrow would have been too late.'

The boy comes nearer. The man is very aware of the young muscular body so close he can feel the heat off it.

The boy says, 'Why did you make me do it? You said you'd never ask me to do anything I didn't want to do. But you tricked me. Why?'

The man for once is not smiling. He says quietly, 'My father once said to me, when love and grim necessity meet, there is only one winner. You probably don't understand

16

that now any more than I did then. But you will. In the meantime all I can say is I'm very sorry. I'll find a way to make it up to you, I promise.'

'How? How can you possibly make it up to me?' screams the boy. 'You've made me a murderer. What can you do that can ever make up for that! There's nothing! Nothing!'

And the man says, rather sadly, like one who pronounces a sentence rather than makes a gift, 'I shall give you your heart's desire.'

BOOK ONE

wolf and elf

After the hunters trapped the wolf, they put him in a cage where he lay for many years, suffering grievously, till one day a curious elf, to whom iron bars were no more obstacle than the shadows of grasses on a sunlit meadow, took pity on his plight, and asked, 'What can I bring you that will ease your pain, Wolf?'

And the wolf replied, 'My foes to play with.'

Charles Underhill (tr): *Folk Tales of Scandinavia*

Wolf

Once upon a time I was living happily ever after.

That's right. Like in a fairy tale.

How else to describe my life up till that bright autumn morning back in 2008?

I was the lowly woodcutter who fell in love with a beautiful princess glimpsed dancing on the castle lawn, knew she was so far above him that even his fantasies could get his head chopped off, nonetheless when three seemingly impossible tasks were set as the price of her hand in marriage threw his cap into the ring and after many perilous adventures returned triumphant to claim his heart's desire.

Here began the *happily ever after*, the precise extent of which is nowhere defined in fairy literature. In my case it lasted fourteen years.

During this time I acquired a fortune of several millions, a private jet, residences in Holland Park, Devon, New York, Barbados and Umbria, my lovely daughter, Ginny, and a knighthood for services to commerce.

Over the same period my wife Imogen turned from a

21

fragrant young princess into an elegant, sophisticated woman. She ran our social life with easy efficiency, made no demands on me that I could not afford, and always had an appropriate welcome waiting in whichever of our homes I returned to after my often extensive business trips.

Sometimes I looked at her and found it hard to understand how I could deserve such beauty, such happiness. She was my piece of perfection, my heart's desire, and whenever the stresses and strains of my hugely active life began to make themselves felt, I just had to think of my princess to know that, whatever fate brought me, I was the most blessed of men.

Then on that autumn day – by one of those coincidences that only a wicked fairy can contrive, our wedding anniversary – everything changed.

At half past six in the morning we were woken in our Holland Park house by an extended ringing of the doorbell. I got up and went to the window. My first thought when I saw the police uniforms was that some joker had sent us an anniversary strip-aubade. But they didn't look as if they were about to rip off their uniforms and burst into song, and suddenly my heart contracted at the thought that something could have happened to Ginny. She was away at school – not by my choice, but when the lowly woodcutter marries the princess, there are some ancestral customs he meekly goes along with.

Then it occurred to me they'd hardly need a whole posse of plods to convey such a message.

Nor would they bring a bunch of press photographers and a TV crew.

Imogen was sitting up in bed by this time. Even in these fraught circumstances I was distracted by the sight of her perfect breasts.

She said, 'Wolf, what is it?' in her usual calm manner.

'I don't know,' I said. 'I'll go and see.'

She said, 'Perhaps you should put some clothes on.'

I grabbed my dressing gown and was still pulling it round my shoulders as I started down the stairs. I could hear voices below. Among them I recognized the Cockney accent of Mrs Roper, our housekeeper. She was crying out in protest and I saw why as I reached the half landing. She must have opened the front door and policemen were thrusting past her without ceremony. Jogging up the stairs towards me was a short fleshy man in a creased blue suit flanked by two uniformed constables.

He came to a halt a couple of steps below me and said breathlessly, 'Wolf Hadda? *Sorry*. Sir *Wilfred* Hadda. Detective Inspector Medler. I have a warrant to search these premises.'

He reached up to hand me a sheet of paper. Below I could hear people moving, doors opening and shutting, Mrs Roper still protesting.

I said, 'What the hell's going on?'

His gaze went down to my crotch. His lips twitched. Then his eyes ran up my body and focused beyond me.

He said, 'Maybe you should make yourself decent, unless you fancy posing for Page Three.'

I turned to see what he was looking at. Through the half-landing window overlooking the garden, I could see the old rowan tree I'd transplanted from Cumbria when I bought the house. It was incandescent with berries at this time of year, and I was incandescent with rage at the sight of a *paparazzo* clinging to its branches, pointing a camera at me. Even at this distance I could see the damage caused by his ascent.

I turned back to Medler.

'How did he get there? What are the press doing here anyway? Did you bring them?'

'Now why on earth should I do that, sir?' he said. 'Maybe they just happened to be passing.'

He didn't even bother to try to sound convincing.

He had an insinuating voice and one of those mouths which looks as if it's holding back a knowing sneer. I've always had a short fuse. At six thirty in the morning, confronted by a bunch of heavy-handed plods tearing my home to pieces and a paparazzo desecrating my lovely rowan, it was very short indeed. I punched the little bastard right in his smug mouth and he went backwards down the stairs, taking one of his constables with him. The other produced his baton and whacked me on the leg. The pain was excruciating and I collapsed in a heap on the landing.

After that things got confused. As I was half dragged, half carried out of the house, I screamed at Imogen, who'd appeared fully dressed on the stairs, 'Ring Toby!'

She looked very calm, very much in control. Princesses don't panic. The thought was a comfort to me.

Cameras clicked and journalists yelled inanities as I was thrust into a car. As it sped away, I twisted round to look back. Cops were already coming down the steps carrying loaded bin bags that they tossed into the back of a van. The house, gleaming in the morning sunlight, seemed to look down on them with disdain. Then we turned a corner and it vanished from sight.

I did not realize – how could I? – that I was never to enter it again.

ii

My arrival at the police station seemed to take them by surprise. My arrest at that stage can't have been anticipated. Once the pain in my leg subsided and my brain started functioning again, I'd worked out that I must be the subject of

24

a Fraud Office investigation. Personal equity companies rise on the back of other companies' failures and Woodcutter Enterprises had left a lot of unhappy people in its wake. Also the atmosphere on the markets was full of foreboding and when nerves are on edge, malicious tongues soon start wagging.

So being banged up was my own fault. If I hadn't lost my temper, I would probably be sitting in my own drawing room, refusing to answer any of Medler's impertinent questions till Toby Estover, my solicitor, arrived. I would have liked to see Medler's expression when he heard the name. *Mr Itsover* his colleagues call him, because that's what the prosecution says when they hear Toby's acting for the defence. Barristers may get the glory but there are many dodgy characters walking free because they were wise enough and rich enough to hire Toby Estover when the law came calling.

I was treated courteously – I even thought I detected the ghost of a smile on the custody sergeant's lips when told I'd been arrested for thumping Medler – then put in a cell. Pretty minimalist, but stick a couple of Vettriano prints on the wall and it could have passed for a standard single in a lot of boutique hotels.

I don't know how long I sat there. I hadn't been wearing my watch when they arrested me. In fact I hadn't been wearing anything but my dressing gown. They'd taken that and given me an off-white cotton overall and a pair of plastic flip-flops.

I was just wondering whether to start banging on the door and making a fuss when it opened and Toby came in. It was good to see him, in every sense. As well as having one of the smartest minds I've ever known, he dresses to match. Same age as me but slim and elegant. Me, I can make a Savile Row three-piece look like a boiler suit in twenty minutes; Toby would look good in army fatigues. In his Henry

Poole threads and John Lobb shoes he looked smooth enough to talk Jesus off the Cross which, had he been in Jerusalem at the time, I daresay he would have done.

I said, 'Toby, thank God. Have you brought me some clothes?'

He looked surprised and said, 'No, sorry, old boy. Never crossed my mind.'

'Damn,' I said. 'I thought Imo might have chucked a few things together.'

'I think she may have other things to occupy her,' he observed. 'Let's sit down and have a chat.'

'Here?' I said.

'Here,' he said firmly, sitting on the narrow bed. 'Less chance of being overheard than in an interview room.'

The idea that the police might try to eavesdrop on a client/lawyer conversation troubled me less than the implication that it could contain something damaging to me.

I said, 'Frankly, I don't give a damn what they hear. I've got nothing to hide.'

'It's certainly true that by now you're unlikely to have anything you think may be hidden,' he said sardonically. 'I understand they are still searching the house. But it's your computers we need to concentrate on. Wolf, we won't have much time so let's cut to the chase. I've had a word with DI Medler . . . is it true you hit him, by the way?'

'Oh yes,' I said with some satisfaction. 'You'll probably see the picture in the tabloids. I'd like to buy the negative and have it blown up for my office wall, if you can fix that. Did Imogen tell you the media were all over the place? There must have been a tip-off from the police. I want you to chase that up vigorously, Toby. There's been far too much of that kind of thing recently and no one's ever called to account . . .'

'Wolf, for fuck's sake, shut up.'

I stopped talking. Toby was normally the most courteous of men. OK, he'd heard me on one of my favourite hobby horses before, but there was an urgency in his tone that went far beyond mere exasperation. For the first time I started to feel worried.

I said, 'Toby, what's going on? What are the bastards looking for? For God's sake, I may have cut a few corners in my time, but the business is sound, believe me. Does Johnny Nutbrown know about this? I think we ought to give him a call . . .'

Nutbrown was my closest friend and finance director at Woodcutter. He was mathematically eidetic. If Johnny and a computer calculation differed, I'd back Johnny every time.

Toby said, 'Johnny's not going to be any use here. Medler's not Fraud. He's on what used to be called the Vice Squad. Specifically his area is paedophilia. Kiddy porn.'

I laughed in relief. I really did.

I said, 'In that case, the only reason I'm banged up here is because I hit the smarmy bastard. They've had plenty of time to realize they've made a huge booboo, and they're just hoping the media will get tired and go away before I emerge. No chance! I'll have my say if I've got to rent space on TV!'

I stopped talking again, not because of anything Toby said to me but because of the way he was looking at me. Assessingly. That was the word for it. Like a man looking for reassurance and not being convinced he'd found it.

He said, 'From what Medler said, they feel they have enough evidence to proceed.'

I shook my head in exasperation.

I said, 'But they'll have squeezed my hard drive dry by now. What's the problem? Some encryptions they haven't been able to break? God, I'm happy to let them in for a quick glance at anything, so long as I'm there . . .'

Toby said, 'He spoke as if they'd found . . . stuff.'

That stopped me in my tracks.

'Stuff?' I echoed. 'You mean kiddy porn? Impossible!'

He just looked at me for a long moment. When he spoke, his voice had taken on its forensic colouring.

'Wolf, I need to be clear so that I know how to proceed. You are assuring me there is nothing of this nature, no images involving paedophilia, to be found on any computer belonging to you?'

I felt a surge of anger but quickly controlled it. A friend wouldn't have needed to ask, but Toby was more than my friend, he was my solicitor, and that was how I had to regard him now, in the same way that he was clearly looking at me purely as a client.

I said, 'Nothing.'

He said, 'OK,' stood up and went to the door.

'So let's go and see what DI Medler has to say,' he said.

So hell begins.

iii

I'll say this for Medler, he didn't mess around.

He showed me some credit-card statements covering the past year, asked me to confirm they were mine. I said that as they had my name and a selection of my addresses on them, I supposed they must be. He asked me to check them more closely. I glanced over them, identified a couple of large items on each – hotel bills, that kind of thing – and said yes, they were definitely mine. He then drew my attention to a series of payments – mainly to an Internet company called InArcadia – and asked me if I could recall what these were for. I said I couldn't offhand, which wasn't surprising as I paid for just about everything in my extremely busy life by one of the vast selection of cards I'd managed to accumulate, but no doubt if I sat down with my secretary we could work out exactly what each and every payment covered.

He shuffled the statements together, put them in a folder, and smiled. His split lip must have hurt but it didn't stop his smile from being as slyly insinuating as ever.

'Don't think we'll need to involve your secretary, Sir Wilfred,' he said. 'We can give your memory a jog by showing you some of the stuff you were paying for.'

Then he opened a laptop resting on the table between us, pressed a key and turned it towards me.

There were stills to start with, then some snatches of video. All involved girls on the cusp of puberty, some displaying themselves provocatively, some being assaulted by men. Years later those images still haunt me.

Thirty seconds was enough. I slammed the laptop lid shut. For a moment I couldn't speak. I looked towards Toby. Our gazes met. Then he looked away.

I said, 'Toby, for God's sake, you don't think . . .'

Then I pulled myself together. Whatever was going off here, getting into a public and recorded row with my solicitor wasn't going to help things.

I said to Medler, 'Why the hell are you showing me this filth?'

He said, 'Because we found it on a computer belonging to you, Sir Wilfred. On a computer protected by your password, in an encrypted program accessed by entering a twenty-five digit code and answering three personal questions. Personal to you, I mean. Also, the images in question, and many more, both still and moving, were acquired from the Internet company InArcadia and paid for with various of your credit cards, details of which you have just confirmed.'

The rest of the interview was brief and farcical. Medler made no effort to be subtle. Perhaps the little bastard disliked me so much he didn't want me to cooperate! He simply fired a fusillade of increasingly offensive questions at me – How

29

long had I been doing this? How deeply involved was I with the people behind InArcadia? Had I ever personally taken part in any of the video sessions? and so on, and so on – never paying the slightest heed to my increasingly vehement denials.

Toby sat there silent as a statue during all this and in the end I forgot my resolve not to have a public row and screamed, 'For fuck's sake, man, say something! What the hell do you think I'm paying you for?'

He didn't reply. I saw him glance at Medler. Maybe I was so wrought up I started imagining things but it seemed to me Toby was looking almost apologetic as if to say, I really don't want to be here doing this, and Medler gave him a little sympathetic smile as if to reply, yes, I can see how tough it must be for you.

I was at the end of my admittedly short tether. It was a toss up whether I took a swing at my lawyer or the cop. If I had to rationalize I'd say it made more sense to opt for the latter on the grounds that my relationship with him was clearly beyond hope whereas I was still going to need Toby.

Whatever, I gave Medler a busted nose to add to his split lip.

And that brought the interview to a close.

iv

My second journey to my cell was handled less courteously than the first.

The two cops who dragged me there then followed me inside were experts. I lay on the floor, racked with pain for a good half hour after the door crashed shut behind them. But when I recovered enough to examine my body, I realized there was precious little visual evidence of police brutality.

I banged at the door till a constable appeared and told me to shut up. I demanded to see Toby. He went away and came back a few minutes later to say that Mr Estover had left the station. I then said I wanted to make the phone call I was entitled to. How entitled I was, I'd no idea. Like most people my knowledge of criminal law was garnered mainly from TV and movies. The cop went away again and nothing happened for what felt like an hour. I was just about to launch another assault on the door when it opened to reveal Medler. His nose was swollen and he had a couple of stitches in his lip. In his hand was a grip that I recognized as mine. He tossed it towards me and said, 'Get yourself dressed, Sir Wilfred.'

I opened the bag to see it contained clothing.

I said, 'Did my wife bring this? Is she here?'

He said, 'No. She's gone to stay with a Mrs Nutbrown at her house, Poynters, is it? Out near Saffron Walden.'

I sat down on the bed. OK, so Johnny Nutbrown's wife, Pippa, was Imogen's best friend, but the notion that she was running for cover without even attempting to contact me filled me with dismay. And disappointment.

It must have showed, for Medler said roughly, as though he hated offering me any consolation, 'She had to go. Your daughter was being taken there. The press would have been sniffing round her school in no time. They're already camped outside your house.'

'Yes, and whose fault is that?' I demanded.

'Yours, I think,' he said shortly.

I didn't argue. What was the point? And if Imo and Ginny needed to seek refuge, there were few better places than Poynters. Johnny had bought the half-timbered Elizabethan mansion a couple of years earlier. It must have cost him a fortune. I recall saying to him at the time, *I'm obviously paying you too much!* He claimed it had once belonged to the

31

Nutbrowns back in the eighteenth century and he'd always known it would come back. The great thing in the present situation was that it was pretty remote and Pippa, who was a bit of a hi-tech nerd, had installed a state-of-the-art security system.

I tipped the clothes he'd brought on to the bed. The jacket trousers and shirt weren't a great match, which meant they hadn't been selected by Imogen. Presumably Medler or one of his minions had flung them together. I ripped off the paper overall.

Medler stood watching me.

'Looking for bruises?' I said.

He didn't reply and I turned my back on him. As I pulled on my underpants, there was a brief flash of light. I looked round to see Medler holding a mobile phone.

'Did you just take a photo?' I demanded incredulously.

I got that knowing smirk, then he said, 'That's a nasty scar you've got on your back, Sir Wilfred.'

'So I believe,' I said, controlling my temper again. 'I don't see a lot of it.'

A man doesn't spend much time watching his back. Perhaps he ought to. The scar in question dated from when I was thirteen and running wild in the Cumbrian fells. I slipped on an icy rock on Red Pike and tobogganed three hundred feet down into Mosedale. By the time I came to a halt, my clothing had been ripped to shreds and my spine was clearly visible through the torn flesh on my back. Fortunately my fall was seen and the mountain rescue boys stretchered me out to hospital in a relatively short time.

First assessment of the damage offered little hope I would ever walk again. But gradually as they worked on me over several days, their bulletins grew cautiously more optimistic, till finally, much to their amazement, they declared that, while the damage was serious, I had a fair chance of recovery.

Six months later, I was back on the fells with nothing to show for my adventure other than a firm conviction of my personal immortality and a lightning-jag scar from between my shoulder blades to the tip of my coccyx.

Was it legal for Medler to take a photo of my naked body without my permission? I wondered.

Whatever, I was determined not to let him think he had worried me, so I carried on dressing and when I was finished I said, 'Right, now I'd like to phone my wife.'

'First things first. Sergeant, bring Sir Wilfred along to the charge room.'

Things were moving quickly. Too quickly, perhaps. Arrest, questioning, police custody, these were stages a man could come out of with his reputation intact. There were time limits that applied. Eventually that moment so beloved of TV dramatists would arrive when a solicitor says, 'Either charge my client or let him go, Inspector.'

But Medler was pre-empting all that.

Foolishly when I realized I was being charged with assault on a police officer in the execution of his duty, I felt relieved. I took this to mean they were still uncertain about their child pornography case. I'd passed through disbelief and outrage to indignation. Either the cops had made a huge mistake or someone was trying to drop me in the shit. Either way, I felt certain I could get it sorted. After all, wasn't I rich and powerful? I could pay for the best investigators, the best advisors, the best lawyers, and once they got on the case I felt confident that all these obscene allegations would quickly be shown for the nonsense they were.

After the formalities were over, I was about to re-assert my right to call Imogen when Medler took the wind out of my sails by saying, 'Right, Sir Wilfred, let's get you to a phone.'

He took me to a small windowless room containing a chair and a table with a phone on it.

'This is linked to a recorder, I take it?' I said mockingly.

'Why? Are you going to say something you don't want us to hear?' he asked.

He always slipped away from my questions, I realized.

But what did I expect him to say anyway?

I sat down and Medler went out of the door. It took a few seconds for me to recall the Nutbrowns' Essex number. I dialled. After six or seven rings, a woman's voice said cautiously, 'Yes?'

'Pippa? Is that you? It's Wolf.'

She didn't reply but I heard her call, 'Imo, it's him.'

A moment later I heard Imogen's voice saying, 'Wolf, how are you?'

She sounded so unworried, so normal that my spirits lifted several degrees. This was not the least of her many qualities, the ability to provide an area of calm in the midst of turbulence. She was always at the eye of the storm.

I said, 'I'm fine. Don't worry, we'll soon get this nonsense sorted out. How about you? Is Ginny with you? How is she?'

'Yes, she's here. She's fine. We're all fine. Pippa's being marvellous. There've been a couple of calls from the papers. I think that once they realized I'd gone, and Ginny had been taken out of school, they started checking out all possible contacts. They really are most assiduous, aren't they?'

She sounded almost admiring. I was alarmed.

'Jesus! What did Pippa say?'

'She was great. Pretended not to have heard anything about the business, then drove them to distraction by asking them endless silly questions till finally they were glad to ring off.'

'Good. But it means you'll have to keep your heads down in case they send someone to take a look for themselves. I blame that little shit Medler for this, he obviously alerted the press in the first place . . .'

She said, 'Perhaps. But it was Mr Medler who suggested

34

I got Ginny out of school, then helped smuggle me out of the house without the press noticing.'

This got a mixed reaction from me. Naturally I was pleased my family were safe, but I didn't like having to feel grateful to Medler. Still, I comforted myself, it was good to know that Imogen's powers of organization included the police.

I said, 'I'm glad to hear Medler's got a conscience. And if the media turn up mob-handed at Pippa's door, we'll definitely know who to blame, won't we?'

'Yes,' she said. 'We'll know who to blame. Wolf, I need to ring off now. I'm expecting a call. I rang home to let them know what was going on. I didn't want them to start hearing things through the media. I spoke to Daddy but Mummy was out. She's expected back for lunch, so Daddy said he'd get her to ring me then.'

I bet she'll enjoy that! I thought savagely. My mother-in-law, Lady Kira Ulphingstone, had never been my greatest fan, though things improved slightly after the birth of Ginny. I suspect she vowed to herself that her granddaughter wasn't going to make the same ghastly mistake as her mother, and she was clever enough to know that pissing me off all the time might put Ginny outside her sphere of influence. So superficially she thawed a little, but underneath I knew it was the same impenetrable permafrost.

My father-in-law, Sir Leon, on the other hand, though he was a Cumbrian landowner of the old school with political views that erred towards the feudal, had demonstrated the pragmatism of his class by making the best of a bad job. Unlike my own father, Fred. He and Sir Leon had been united in absolute opposition to the marriage, the difference being that Fred's disapproval survived the ceremony. I can't blame Dad. After putting him through the wringer by vanishing for five years with only the most minimal attempt at contact, I'd returned, and while he was still trying to get his head round that, I had once more set my will in opposition to his. Any hope of getting back to our old relationship had died then and things had never been the same between us since. That had been the highest price I paid for my fairy-tale happy ending. For fourteen years I had judged it a price worth paying. I was wrong. And though I didn't know it yet, I was never going to get the chance to tell him so.

I said, 'Well, we can't have Mummy getting the engaged signal, can we? But if the journalists start bothering them up there, do try to stop Leon setting the dogs on them. Listen, you couldn't give Fred a ring, could you? The bastards are likely to have him in their sights too. I'd do it myself soon as I get out of here, but I'm not sure how long that will take.'

'I asked Daddy to make sure Fred knows,' she said.

God, she was efficient, I thought admiringly. Even at moments of crisis, she took care of all the details.

She went on, 'You're expecting to be out . . . when?'

'I don't know exactly, but it can't be long,' I said confidently. 'You know Toby. He's helped get serial killers, billion-dollar fraudsters and al-Qaeda terrorists off. I'm sure he can sort out my bit of bother.'

I was exaggerating a bit, less about Toby's CV than my confidence in his ability to sort out my problem. I recalled the way he'd looked at me. Perhaps he was just too high powered for something like this.

'Is he there with you now?' said Imogen.

'No, he left after . . . after my interview.'

I hesitated to tell Imogen that I'd assaulted Medler a second time. She'd find out soon enough, but no need to give her extra worry now.

'Then I'll hear from you later,' she said.

'Of course. Listen, don't ring off, I'd like a quick word with Ginny.'

There was a pause then she said, 'I don't think that would

be a good idea. She's very bewildered by everything that's happened, naturally. So I gave her a mild sedative and she's having a rest now.'

I said, 'OK. Then give her my love and tell her I'll see her very soon.'

'Of course,' she said. 'Goodbye, Wolf.'

'Bye,' I said. 'I love you.'

But she'd already rung off.

I put the phone down. The fact that Imogen hadn't felt it necessary to refer to the monstrous allegations being made against me should have been a comfort. But somehow I didn't feel comforted.

Medler came into the room a moment later, confirming my suspicion he'd probably been listening in.

I said, 'Look, I need to get Mr Estover back here so that he can speed up whatever rigmarole you people put me through before my release.'

He said, 'We've kept Mr Estover in the picture. He'll be waiting at the court.'

I said, 'The court? Which court?'

He said, 'The magistrate's court. The hearing's in half an hour.'

And again, I was relieved!

Magistrate's court, assault charge, slap on the wrist, hefty fine, I could be out in a couple of hours organizing my own super-investigation into what the fuck was going on here.

'So what are we hanging about for?' I said. 'Let's go!'

v

When we reached West End Magistrates Court, the media were already there in force.

I looked at Medler and said, 'I expect they were just passing, huh?'

37

He said wearily, 'You'd better get used to it. You're in the system now and the system is accessible. Wherever you're headed, there'll always be someone ready to make a quick buck by tipping the mob.'

Curiously, this time I believed him.

Inside I was shown into a small windowless room furnished with two chairs and a table. Toby was waiting there. He quickly disabused me of my notion that I'd be in and out in the time it took to sign a cheque.

He said, 'You're being charged with assaulting a police officer in the execution of his duty and occasioning actual bodily harm. The magistrate can deal with this himself or decide it's serious enough to commit you to the Crown Court for a jury trial.'

I said, 'Which is best for me? I mean, which will get me on my way home quickest?'

He regarded me gloomily and said, 'There are problems either way. The magistrate has the power to jail you for six months . . .'

'Six months for hitting a cop?' I interrupted. 'There's people murder their mothers and get less than that, especially when they've got you on a retainer!'

He ignored the flattery and said. 'If on the other hand the beak decides you're a Crown Court job, then the question of bail arises. Medler would certainly oppose it.'

'On what grounds?' I demanded.

'On the grounds that you are being investigated on more serious charges and that, with your wealth and international connections, there's a serious risk you might abscond.'

This incensed me as much as anything I'd heard on this increasingly surreal day.

'Abscond? Why would I? From what, for God's sake? From these ludicrous kiddy-porn allegations? Give me twenty-four hours to have those properly investigated and they'll vanish like snow off a dyke. And how the hell can Medler claim they're more serious anyhow? You said I could get six months for punching his stupid face. That pop singer they sent down for having child abuse images on his computer only got three months, didn't he?'

Toby said, 'There have been developments. I'm far from sure exactly what's going on, but they've raided your offices. Also we're getting word that simultaneous raids are being carried out on your other premises worldwide, domestic and commercial.'

I think that was the moment when I first felt a chill of fear beneath the volcano of anger and indignation that had been simmering inside me since I met Medler coming up my stairs.

I sank heavily on to a chair.

'Toby,' I said, 'what the fuck's going on?'

Before he could answer, the door opened and Medler's face appeared.

'Nearly done, Mr Estover?' he said.

'Give us another minute,' said Toby.

Medler glanced at me. What he saw in my face seemed to please him.

He gave me one of his smug smiles and said, 'OK. One minute.'

It was the smile that provoked me to my next bit of stupidity. To me it seemed to say, Now you're starting to realize we've really got you by the short and curlies!

I said to Toby, 'Give me your mobile.'

He said, 'Why?'

I said, 'For fuck's sake, just give it to me!'

In the *Observer* profile when I got my knighthood, they talked about what they called my in-your-face abrasive manner. When I read the draft, I rang up to request, politely I thought, that this phrase should be modified. After I'd been talking to the feature writer for a few minutes, he said, 'Hang on. Something I'd like you to listen to.' And he played me back a tape of what I'd just been saying.

When it finished, I said, 'Jesus. Print your piece the way it is. And send me a copy of that tape.'

I made a genuine effort to tone down my manner after that, but it wasn't easy. I paid my employees top dollar and I didn't expect to have to repeat anything I said to them. That included solicitors, even if they happened to be friends.

I thrust my hand out towards Toby. It took him a second or two, but in the end he put his mobile into my palm.

I thumbed in 999.

When the operator asked, 'Which service?' I said, 'Police.'

Toby's eyes widened.

When he heard what I said next, it was a wonder they didn't pop right out of their sockets.

'The Supreme Council of the People's Jihad has spoken. There is a bomb in West End Magistrate's Court. In three and a half minutes all the infidel gathered there will be joining their accursed ancestors in the fires of Hell. *Allahu Akbar!*'

Toby's face was grey.

'For God's sake, Wolf, you can't . . .'

'Shut up,' I said, putting the phone in my pocket. 'Now we'll see just how efficient all these new anti-terrorist strategies really are.'

They were pretty good, I have to admit.

Within less than a minute I heard the first sounds of activity outside the door.

Toby said, 'This is madness. We've got to tell them . . .'

I poked him hard in the stomach.

It served a double purpose. It shut him up and when the door opened and Medler said, 'Come on, we've got to get out of here,' I was able to reply, 'Mr Estover's not feeling well. I think we ought to get a doctor.'

'Not here, outside!' commanded Medler.

I got one of Toby's arms over my shoulder and began moving him through the door. I looked appealingly at Medler. He didn't look happy, but to give him credit he didn't hesitate. He hooked Toby's other arm over his shoulder and we joined the flood of people pouring down the corridor towards the exit.

To create urgency without causing panic is no easy task and I think the police and court officers did pretty well. But of course the last people to get the message are very aware that there's a large crowd between them and safety, and they want it to move a lot faster than it seems to be doing. Two men dragging a third along between them forms a pretty effective bung and all I had to do as the lobby came in sight was to cease resisting the growing pressure behind me and let myself be swept towards the exit on the tide.

I don't know at what point Medler realized I was no longer with him. I didn't look back but burst out of the building into the sunlight to be confronted by a uniformed constable who shouted at me. For a second I thought my escape was going to be very short lived. Then I realized that what he was shouting was, 'Get away from the building! Run!'

I ran. Everyone was running. I felt a surge of exhilaration. It must feel like this to start a marathon, I thought. All those months of training and now the moment was here to put your fitness to the test.

My marathon lasted about a quarter of a mile, firstly because I was now far enough away from the court for a running man to attract attention and secondly because I was knackered. I still tried to keep reasonably fit but clearly the days when I could roam twenty miles across the Cumbrian fells without breaking sweat were long past.

I was beginning to feel anything but exhilarated. My sense of self-congratulation at getting away was being replaced by serious self-doubt. What did I imagine I was going to do with my freedom? Head up to Poynters to see Imogen and Ginny? That would be the first place Medler would set his dogs to watch. Or was my plan to set about proving my innocence like they do all the time in the movies? I'd need professional help to do that and no legitimate investigator was going to risk his licence aiding and abetting a fugitive. OK, the promise of large sums of money might make one or two of them bend the rules a little, but only if they believed I still had easy access to large sums of money.

And now I came to think about it, I didn't even have access to small sums of money. In fact, I had absolutely nothing in my pockets except for Toby's phone. I was an idiot. I should have made him hand over his wallet as well!

My horizons had shrunk. Without money I wasn't going anywhere I couldn't reach on my own two feet. The obvious places to lay my hands on cash – home in Holland Park, my offices in the City – were out because they were so obvious.

Well, as my Great Aunt Carrie was fond of saying, if the mountain won't come to Mohammed, Mohammed must go to the mountain. Probably saying that would get you stuck on the pointed end of a fatwa nowadays. But Carrie lived all her life in Cumberland where they knew a lot about the intractability of mountains and bugger all about the intractability of Islam.

I took out Toby's phone and rang Johnny Nutbrown on his mobile.

When he answered I said, 'Johnny, it's me. Meet me in twenty minutes at the Black Widow.'

I thought I was being clever when I said that. No reason why anybody should be listening in to Johnny, but even if they were, unless the Met was recruiting Smart Young Things, even less reason for them to know this was how habitués referred to The Victoria pub in Chelsea. Not that I was ever a Smart Young Thing, but Johnny had taken me there once and been greeted as an old chum by the swarming Dysons, i.e. vacuums so empty they don't even contain a bag. I'd committed the place to my memory as somewhere I'd no intention of visiting again.

Circumstances change cases. It's being nimble on your feet that keeps you ahead of the game in business and in life.

I soon realized that I was going to need to be exceedingly nimble on my feet if I was going to make the Widow in twenty minutes. Being chauffeured around in an S-class Merc tends to make you insensitive to distances. Might have done it if I'd started running again but neither my legs nor my need for discretion permitted that. Not that it mattered. Johnny would wait. In fact, come to think of it, he too would be hard pushed to make it through the lunchtime traffic in much under half an hour.

I took thirty-five minutes. As I entered the crowded bar my first thought was that we were going to have to find somewhere a lot quieter to have a chat. I couldn't see Johnny. At six feet seven, he was usually pretty easy to spot, even in a crowd, but I pushed a little further into the room just to make sure.

No sign, but I did notice a man at the bar, not because he was tall, though he was; nor because he had the kind of face that defies you to make it smile, though he did. No, it was just that somehow he looked out of place. That is, he looked like an ordinary guy who'd just dropped in for a quick half in his lunch break. Except that this was the kind of bar that ordinary guys in search of a quick half reversed out of at speed. He was raising a bottle of Pils to his mouth. As he did so his gaze met mine for a moment and registered . . . something. Maybe he'd just realized how much he'd had to pay for the Pils. He drank, lowered his head, and I saw his lips move. Nowadays everyone knows what men speaking into their lapels are doing.

I didn't turn back to the main door. If I'd got it right, the guys he was talking to would be coming in through there pretty quickly. Instead I followed a sign reading Toilets and found myself in a dead-end corridor. I peered into the Gents. Windowless. I pushed open the door of the Ladies. That looked better. A frosted-glass pane about eighteen inches square. There was a bin for the receipt of towels. I stood on it and examined the catch. It didn't look as if it had been opened in years and the frame was firmly painted in place. I stepped down, picked up the bin and hit the glass hard. Cheap stuff, it shattered easily. Behind me I heard a door open. I swung round but it was only a woman coming out of one of the cubicles. I'll say this for the Dysons, they don't do swoons or hysterics.

She said, 'About time they aired this place out.'

I rattled the bin around the frame to dislodge the residual shards, put the bin on the floor once more, stood on it and launched myself through the window. As I did so, I heard another door open and male voices shouting.

I felt my trousers tear, then my leg, so my clear-up technique hadn't been all that successful. I hit the ground awkwardly, doing something to my shoulder. I was dazed but able to see that I was in a narrow alley. One way it ran into a brick wall, the other on to a busy street. I staggered towards the street.

Behind me, voices. Ahead, a crowded pavement. I could vanish into the crowd, I told myself. I glanced back. Two men coming very quick. I commanded my legs to move faster and the old in-your-face-abrasive technique worked.

I erupted on to the pavement at a fair rate of knots, decided that turning left or right would slow me down, so kept on going.

The thing about London buses is you can wait forever when you want one in a hurry, but if you don't want one . . .

I saw it coming, even saw the driver's shocked face, almost saw the number . . .

Then I saw no more.

Elf

'It's . . . interesting,' said Alva Ozigbo cautiously.

Wolf Hadda smiled. It was like a pale ray of winter sunshine momentarily touching a dark mountain. In all the months she'd been treating him, this was only the second time she'd seen his smile, but even this limited observation had hinted at its power to distract attention from the sinister sunglasses and the corrugated scars, inviting you instead to relate to the still charming man beneath.

Charm was perhaps the most potent weapon a pederast could possess.

But it was a weapon Hadda could hardly be conscious of possessing or surely he would have brought it out before now to reinforce his lies?

He said, 'I remember interesting. That's the word they use out there to describe things they don't understand, don't approve of, or don't like, without appearing ignorant, judgmental or lacking in taste.'

She noted the intensity of *out there*.

She said, 'In here I use it to describe things I find interesting.'

They sat and looked at each other across the narrow table for a while. At least she presumed he was looking at her; his wrap-around glasses made it difficult to be certain. She could see herself reflected in the mirrored lenses, a narrow ebon face, its colouring inherited from her Nigerian father, its bone structure from her Swedish mother. Also her hair, straight and pale as bone. Many people assumed it was a wig, worn for effect. She was dressed in black jeans and a white short-sleeved sweater that neither obscured nor drew attention to her breasts. *Don't be provocative in your dress,* the Director had advised her when she started the job. *But no point in over-compensating. If you turned up in a burka, they'd still mentally undress you.*

Did Hadda mentally undress her? she wondered. Up to their last session she'd have judged not. But what had happened then had stayed with her for the whole of the intervening seven days.

It had started in the usual way. She was already seated at her side of the bare wooden table when the door on the secure side of the interview room opened. Prison Officer Lindale, young and compassionate, had smiled and nodded his head at her, then stood aside to let Wilfred Hadda enter.

He limped laboriously into the room and sat down on the basic wooden chair that always seemed too small for him. Her fanciful notion that his rare smile was like wintry sunshine on a mountain probably rose from the sense of mountainous stillness he exuded. A craggy mountain, its face bearing the scars of ancient storms, its brow streaked with the greyish white of old snows.

It was well over a year since their first meeting, and despite her own extensive research that had been added to the file inherited from Joe Ruskin, her predecessor at Parkleigh, she did not feel she knew much more about Hadda. Ruskin's file was in Alva's eyes a simple admission of failure. All his attempts to open a dialogue were simply ignored and in the end the psychiatrist had set down his assessment that in his view the prisoner was depressed but stable, and enforced medication would only be an option if his behaviour changed markedly.

Alva Ozigbo had read the file with growing exasperation. The system it seemed to her had abandoned Hadda to deal with his past himself, and the way he was choosing to do it was to treat his sentence as a kind of hibernation.

The trouble with hibernation was when the bat or the hedgehog or the polar bear woke up, it was itself again.

Hadda, she read, had never admitted any of his crimes, but unlike many prisoners he did not make a thing of protesting his innocence either. According to his prison record, verbal abuse simply bounced off his monumental indifference. Isolation in the Special Unit had meant that there was little opportunity for other prisoners to attack him physically, but on the couple of occasions when, hopefully by accident, the warders let their guard down and an assault had been launched, his response had been so immediate and violent, it was the attackers who ended up in hospital.

But that had been in the early days. For five years until Alva's appointment in January 2015 he had been from the viewpoint of that most traditional of turnkeys, Chief Officer George Proctor, a model prisoner, troubling no one and doing exactly what he was told.

The Chief Officer, a well-fleshed man with a round and rubicund face that gave a deceptive impression of Pickwickian good humour, was by no means devoid of humanity, but in his list of penal priorities it came a long way behind good order and discipline. So when he concluded his verdict on Hadda by saying, 'Can't understand what he's doing in here,' Alva was puzzled.

'But he was found guilty of very serious crimes,' she said.

'Yeah, and the bugger should be locked up for ever,' said Proctor. 'But look around you, miss. We got terrorists and subversives and serial killers, the bloody lot. That's what this place is for. Hadda never done any serious harm to no one.'

It was a point Alva would usually have debated fiercely, but she had already wasted too much time beating her fists against Proctor's rock-hard shell of received wisdom and in-herited certainties. Also she knew how easy it would be for him to make her job even harder than it was, though in fairness he had never done anything to block or disrupt what he called her *tête-à-têtes*, which he pronounced *tit-a-tits* with a face so blank it defied correction.

After a year in post, she wasn't sure how much good she'd done in relation to the killers and terrorists, but as far as Hadda was concerned, she felt she'd made no impression whatsoever. They brought him along to see her, but he simply refused to talk. After a while she found that her earlier exas-peration with what she had judged to be her predecessor's too easy abandonment of his efforts was modifying into a reluctant understanding.

And then one day when she turned up at Parkleigh, the Director had sent for her.

'Terrible news,' he said. 'It's Hadda's daughter. She's dead.'

Alva had studied the man's file so closely she did not need reminding of the facts. The girl, Virginia, had been thirteen when her father was sentenced. She had never visited him in prison. A careful check was kept of prisoners' mail in and out. He had written letters to her c/o his ex-wife in the early days. There had been no known reply and the letters out had ceased though he persevered with birthday and Christmas cards.

Joe Ruskin had recorded that Hadda's reaction to any attempt to bring up the subject of his relationship with his daughter had been to stand up and head for the door. Grief or guilt? the psychiatrist speculated. Hadda's predilection for pubescent girls had led the more prurient tabloids to speculate whether she might have been an object of his abuse, but there had been no suggestion of this either in the police investigation nor in the case for the prosecution. Ruskin had demanded full disclosure of all information relevant to the man's state of mind and crimes, but nowhere had he found anything to indicate that details had been kept secret to protect the child.

Now the Director filled in the details of Ginny's life after her father's downfall.

'Her mother sent her to finish her education abroad, out of the reach of the tabloids. Her grandmother, that's Lady Kira Ulphingstone, has family connections in Paris, and that's where the girl seems to have settled. She was, by all accounts, pretty wild.'

'With her background, why wouldn't she be?' said Alva. 'How did she die?'

'The worst way,' said the Director. 'There was a party in a friend's flat, drugs, sex, the usual. She was found early this morning in an alley behind the apartment block. She'd passed out, choked on her own vomit. Nineteen years old. What a waste! Alva, he's got to be told. It's my job, I know, but I'd like you to be there.'

She'd watched Hadda's face as he heard the news. There'd been no reaction that a camera could have recorded, but she had felt a reaction the way you feel a change of pressure as a plane swoops down to land, and you swallow, and it's gone.

He hadn't been wearing his sunglasses and his monoptic gaze had met hers for a moment. For the first time in their silent encounters, she felt her presence was registered.

Then he had turned his back on them and stood there till the Director nodded at the escorting officer and he opened the door and ushered the prisoner out.

'I've put him on watch,' said the Director. 'It's procedure in such circumstances.'

'Of course,' she said. 'Procedure.'

He looked at her curiously.

'You don't think he's a risk?'

'To himself, you mean? No. But there has to be some sort of reaction.'

There was, but its nature surprised her.

He started talking.

Or at least he started responding to her questions. He was always reactive, never proactive. Only once did he ask a question.

He looked up at the CCTV camera in the interview room and said, 'Can they hear us?'

She replied, 'No. As I told you when we first met, the cameras are on for obvious security reasons, but the sound is switched off. This is a condition of my work here.'

The question had raised hopes that in the weeks that followed were consistently disappointed. He began to talk more but he never said anything that came close to the confessional. References to his daughter were met by the old blankness. She asked why he hadn't applied to go to the funeral. He said he wouldn't see his daughter there but he would see people he didn't want to see. What people? she asked. The people who put me here, he said. But he didn't even assert his innocence with any particular passion. Again the mountain image came into her mind. Climbers talk of conquering mountains. They don't. Sometimes the mountain changes them, but they never change the mountain.

But she persevered and after a few more months of this, there came a session when, as soon as he came into the room, she had felt something different in him. As the door closed behind Prison Officer Lindale, she got a visual clue as to what it was.

Usually when he sat down, he placed his hands palm up on the table, the right one black gloved, the left bare, its life and fate lines deep etched, as though he expected his fortune to be read.

This day his hands were out of sight, as though placed on his knees.

She said, 'Good morning, Mr Hadda. How are you today?'

He said in his customary quiet, level tone, 'Listen, you black bitch, and listen carefully. I have a shiv in my hand. Show any sign of alarm and I'll have one of your eyes out before they can open the door.'

Shock kept her brave. Only once had she been attacked, shortly after she'd started work here. A client (she refused to talk of them as prisoners), a mild-mannered little man who hadn't even come close to the kind of innuendo by which some of the men tried to imply a sexual relationship with her, suddenly lunged across the table, desperate to get his hands on some part of her, *any* part of her. The best he'd managed was to brush her left wrist before the door slid open and a warder gave him a short burst with a taser.

Since then there'd been no trouble. Only Alva knew how frightened she'd been. When Parliament passed the Act a year ago permitting prison officers to carry tasers after the great Pentonville riot of 2014 she had been one of those who protested strongly against it. Now her certainty that if she pushed back her chair and screamed, the taser would be pumping 50kV into Hadda's back long before the shiv could get anywhere near her eyes, gave her the strength to respond calmly, 'What is it you want, Mr Hadda?'

He said, 'What I want is to fuck you till you faint, but we don't have time for that. So I'll have to make do with you kicking your left shoe off, stretching your leg under the table, placing your bare foot against my crotch, and rubbing it up and down till I come.'

The part of her mind not still in shock thought, You poor sad bastard! You're banged up with all the other deviants. Can't you find someone in there to service you?

She was still wondering if she could bring this situation to a conclusion without testing what level of voltage was necessary to subdue a mountain when Hadda smiled – that was the first time – and placed his empty hands palm up on the table and said, 'I think if they were going to come they'd have been here by now, don't you agree?'

It took a second or two to get it. He'd been testing her assurance that the watching officers could not hear what was being said. Her mind was already exploring the implications of this, and she did not realize that her body was shaking in reaction until the door slid open and Officer Lindale said, 'You OK, miss?'

'Yes, thank you,' she said. 'Just got something stuck in my throat.' And subsumed her trembling into a bout of coughing.

He said, 'Like some water, miss?'

She shook her head and said, 'No thanks. I'll be OK.'

When the door was closed again, Hadda said, 'Sorry about my little charade. What you need is a stiff brandy. I suggest we cut this session short so you can go and get one.'

She was still struggling with the after-effects of the shock and now she had to adjust to the new tone of voice in which he was addressing her.

Somehow she managed to keep her own voice level as she replied, 'No, if you're so keen to be sure we're not being listened to, I presume that means you've got something you'd like to say.'

'Not now,' he said. 'What I've got is something for you to read. OK, I'm convinced you're telling the truth when you say there's nobody listening to us. Now I'd like your re-assurance that nobody else will read this or anything else I give to you.'

As he spoke, he pulled from his prison blouse a blue school exercise book.

This was a shock different in nature from the threat of a shiv attack but in its way almost as extreme.

With many of her clients, she suggested that if they felt like putting any of their feelings or thoughts down on paper before their next meeting, this could only be to the good. Nobody but herself would see what they wrote, she assured them, an assurance some took advantage of to lay before her in graphic detail their sexual fantasies.

Hadda had simply blanked her out when she first suggested he might like to write something. She'd repeated the suggestion over several weeks, then at last she had given up.

So this came completely out of the blue. It should have felt like a breakthrough, but she didn't have the energy to exult.

She realized Hadda was right. What she wanted to do now was get away to somewhere quiet and have a stiff drink.

She said, 'I promise you. No one will read anything of yours, unless you give permission. All right?'

'It will have to be,' he said, handing her the book.

She took it and held it without attempting to open it.

'And this is . . .?' she said.

'You keep saying you want to understand how I ended up in here. Well, this is the story. First instalment anyway.'

She stood up, glanced at one of the cameras, and said as the door opened, 'I look forward to reading it.'

Then she'd headed straight back to her flat, had the longed-for stiff drink after which, rather to her surprise, she was violently sick.

When she was done, she had a very hot shower. Dried and wrapped in a heavy white bathrobe, she sat at her dressing table and stared back at herself out of the mirror.

Behind her, through the open door into the living room,

she could see the exercise book lying on a table where she'd thrown it on entering the flat.

Opening it was going to be the first step on a journey that could take her to some very dark places. No darker, she guessed, than many others she'd visited already. But somehow going there in the company of Wilfred Hadda seemed particularly unappealing.

Why was that? she asked herself.

Not because of any horrors that might possibly be revealed. They came with the territory. So it must have something to do with the man they would be revealed about.

This was a measure of his power. This was why she must be on her guard at all times, not against the physical threat which he had used to test her assurance of confidentiality, but against a much more insinuating mental and emotional onslaught.

She recalled her father's words when she told him about the job offer.

'Elf,' he had boomed, 'you sure you're not biting off more than you can chew?'

'Trust me,' she had replied. 'I'm a psychiatrist.'

And they had shared one of those outbursts of helpless laughter that had her mother looking at them in affectionate bewilderment.

But now, alone, in her mind's eye she conjured up an image of the menacing bulk of Parkleigh Prison printed against the eastern sky and shuddered at the thought of driving towards it in the morning.

ii

Parkleigh Prison was built in the 1850s on a marshy green-field site in Essex just outside London. As if determined that it would be to penology what cathedrals were to religion, its architect incorporated into the design a single massive tower, visible for miles around in that flat landscape, a reassurance to the virtuous and a warning to the sinful.

Rapidly overtaken by the capital's urban sprawl, it continued pretty well unchanged until the 1980s when even the Thatcher hardliners had to accept it was no longer fit for purpose. Closed, it languished as a menacing monument to Victorian values for a decade or more. Everyone expected that eventually the building would be demolished and the site redeveloped for housing, but then it was announced, in the face of considerable but unavailing local protest, that under the Private Finance Initiative, Parkleigh was going to be refurbished as a maximum-security category A private prison.

It would be a prison for all seasons, enthused the developers. Outside dark and forbidding enough to please the floggers and hangers, inside well ahead of the game in its rehabilitatory structures and facilities.

Its clientele was to be category A prisoners, those whom society needed to be certain stayed locked up until they had served out their usually lengthy sentences. In 2010 Wolf Hadda was sent there to popular acclaim. Five years later he was joined by Alva Ozigbo, to far from popular acclaim.

There were two main strikes against her.

As a psychiatrist, she was too young.

And as a woman, she was a woman.

Outwardly Alva treated such objections with the contempt they deserved.

Inwardly she acknowledged that both had some merit.

At twenty-eight she was certainly a rising star, a rise commenced when she'd worked up her PhD thesis on the causes and treatment of deviant behaviour into a book with the catchy title of *Curing Souls*. This attracted attention, mainly complimentary, though the word *precocious* did occur rather frequently in the reviews. But it was a chance meeting that brought her to Parkleigh.

Giles Nevinson, a lawyer friend who hoped by persistence to become more, had invited her to a formal dinner in the Middle Temple. While she had no intention of ever becoming more, she liked Giles. Also, through his job with the Crown Prosecution Service, he was a useful source of free legal advice and information. So she accepted.

Giles spent much of the dinner deep in conversation about the breeding of Persian cats with the rather grand-looking woman on his left. As he explained later, it was ambition rather than ailurophilia that caused him to neglect his guest. The other woman was Isa Toplady, the appropriately named wife of a High Court judge rumoured to be much influenced by his spouse's personal opinions.

Alva, obliged to turn to her right for conversational nourishment, found herself confronted by a slightly built man in his sixties, with wispy blond hair, pale blue eyes, and that expression of rather vapid benevolence with which some painters have attempted to indicate the indifference of saints to the scourges they are being scourged with, arrows they are being pierced with, or flames they are being roasted with.

He introduced himself as John Childs and when he heard her name, he said, 'Ah, yes. *Curing Souls.* A stimulating read.'

Suspecting that, for whatever reason, he might have simply done a little basic pre-prandial homework, she tried him out with a few leading questions and was flattered to discover that not only had he actually read the book but he did indeed seem to have been stimulated by it.

Some explanation of his interest came when he told her that he had a godson, Harry, who was doing A-level psychology and hoping to pursue his studies at university. Childs then set himself to pick Alva's brain about the best way forward for the boy. It is always flattering to be consulted as an expert and it wasn't till well through the dinner that she managed to turn the conversation from herself to her interlocutor.

His own job he described as *a sort of Home Office advisor, I suppose*, a vagueness that from any other nationality Alva would have read as an attempt to conceal unimportance, but which from this kind of Englishman probably meant he was very important indeed.

When they parted he said how much he'd enjoyed her company, and she replied that the feeling was mutual, realizing, slightly to her surprise that this was no more than the truth. He was certainly very good to talk to, meaning, of course, that he was an excellent listener!

Next morning she was surprised but not taken aback when he rang to invite her to take tea with him in Claridge's. Curious as to his motives, and also (she always tried to confront her own motivations honestly) because she'd never before been invited to take tea at Claridge's, she accepted. The hotel lived up to her expectations. Childs couldn't because she had none. They chatted easily, moving from the weather through the ghastliness of politicians to more personal matters. She learned that he came from Norfolk yeoman stock, lived alone in London, and was very fond of his godson, whose parents, alas, had separated. Childs had clearly done all he could to minimize the damage done to the boy. He seemed keen to get her approval for the way he'd responded to the situation, and once again Alva enjoyed the pleasure of being deferred to.

Later she also had a vague feeling with no traceable source that she was being assessed.

But for what? The notion that this might be an early stage of some rather old-fashioned seduction technique occurred and was dismissed.

Then a couple of days later he asked her to lunch at a

Soho restaurant she didn't know. When on arrival she found she had to knock to get admittance, the seduction theory suddenly presented itself again. Might this be the kind of place where elderly gentlemen entertained their lights-of-love in small private rooms decorated in high Edwardian kitsch? If so, what might the menu consist of?

She knocked and entered, and didn't know whether to be pleased or disappointed when she was escorted into an airy dining room with very well spaced tables. Any residual suspicions were finally dissipated by the sight of a second man at the table she was led towards.

Childs said, 'Dr Ozigbo, hope you don't mind, I invited Simon Homewood along. Homewood, this is Alva Ozigbo that I was telling you about.'

'Dr Ozigbo,' said the newcomer, reaching out his hand. 'Delighted to meet you.'

Not as delighted as me, she thought as they shook hands. This had to be the Simon Homewood, Director of Parkleigh Prison, whose liberal views on the treatment of prisoners, widely aired when appointed to the job six years earlier, had met with scornful laughter or enthusiastic applause, depending on which paper you read.

Or maybe, she deflated herself as she took her seat, maybe it was *another* Simon Homewood, the Childs family trouble-shooter, come to cast an assessing eye over this weird young woman bumbling old John had taken a fancy to.

One way to settle that.

'How are things at Parkleigh, Mr Homewood?' she enquired.

He smiled broadly and said, 'Depends whether you're looking in or out, I suppose.'

The contrast with Childs couldn't have been stronger. There was nothing that you could call retiring or self-effacing about Homewood. In his late thirties with a square, determined face

59

topped by a thatch of vigorous brown hair, he fixed her with an unblinking and very unmoist gaze as he talked to her. He asked her about her book, prompted her to expatiate on her ideas, outlined some of the problems he was experiencing in the management of long-term prisoners, and invited her opinion.

Am I being interviewed? she asked herself. Unlikely, because if she were, it could only be for one job. Ten days previously, the chief psychiatrist at Parkleigh Prison, Joe Ruskin, had died in a pile-up on the M5. She'd had only a slight acquaintance with the man, so her distress at the news was correspondingly slight and soon displaced by the thought that, if this had happened four or five years later, she might well have applied to fill the vacancy. Parkleigh held many of the most fascinating criminals of the age. For someone with her areas of interest, it was a job to die for.

But at twenty-eight, she was far too young and inexperienced to be a candidate. And they'd want another man anyway. But she enjoyed the conversation, in which Childs took little part, simply sitting, watching, with a faintly proprietorial smile on his lips.

At the end of lunch she excused herself and made for the Ladies. Away from the two men, her absurdity in even considering the possibility seemed crystal clear.

'Idiot,' she told her reflection in the mirror.

As she returned to the table she saw the two men in deep conversation. It stopped as she sat down.

Then Homewood fixed her with that gaze which probably declared to everyone he spoke to, *You are the most interesting person in the room*, and as if enquiring where she was spending her holidays this year, he said, 'So how would you like to work at Parkleigh, Dr Ozigbo?'

Fortified with a large scotch and water accompanied by a bowl of bacon-flavoured crisps, Alva at last felt up to opening Hadda's exercise book.

She went through the narrative three times, the first time swiftly, to get the feel of it; the second slowly, taking notes; the third intermittently, giving herself plenty of time for reflection and analysis.

She was as disappointed at the end of the third reading as she had been by the first.

The narrative had panache, it was presented with great clarity of detail and emphatic certainty of recollection, it rang true.

All of which meant only one thing: Wilfred Hadda was still in complete denial.

This was not going to be easy, but surely she'd never expected it would be?

She knew from both professional experience and wide study how hard it was to lead some men to the point where they could confront their own crimes. When child abuse was involved, the journey was understandably long and tortuous. At its end was a moment of such self-revulsion that the subconscious decided the cure was worse than the disease and performed gymnastics of Olympic standard to avoid it.

This was why the narrative rang so true. Hadda wasn't trying to deceive her. He'd had years to convince himself he was telling the truth. Plus, of course, so far as the events described were concerned, she knew from her close reading of all the trial and associated media material, he never deviated from the known facts. Only the implied motivation had changed. He was a man of wealth and power, used to getting his own way, and while he clearly had a very sharp mind, he was a man whose physical responses were sometimes so urgent and immediate that reason lagged behind. It wasn't outraged innocence that made him assault Medler but the challenge to his authority. And once he realized that, by doing this, he had provided the police with an excuse for keeping him in custody while they delved into his private business at their leisure, he had made a desperate bid to get within reach of the sources of wealth and influence he felt could protect him.

The important thing was that her relationship with Hadda had advanced to the point where he clearly wanted to get her on his side. She knew she had to proceed very carefully from here on in. To let him see how little credit she gave to his account would almost certainly inhibit him from writing any more. There was still much to be learned even from evasions and downright lies.

As she drove towards Parkleigh next morning, she found herself wondering as she did most mornings why she wasn't feeling a lot happier at the prospect of going to work. Was it cause or effect that, when she met older, more experienced colleagues, particularly those who had been close to her predecessor, Joe Ruskin, she had to bite back words of explanation and apology? What had she to feel sorry for? She hadn't been responsible for the lousy driving that killed him!

As for explanation, she still hadn't explained things satisfactorily to herself. Had she been deliberately sought out or was she just lucky enough to be in the right place at the right time? After the euphoria of being offered the post died down, she'd asked Giles very casually who'd invited John Childs to the dinner. Not casually enough, it seemed. His barrister sensors had detected instantly the thought behind the question and he had teased her unmercifully about her alleged egotism in imagining she might have been head-hunted. Next day he had renewed the attack when he rang to say that Childs had been the guest of the uxorious Mr Justice Toplady, whose cat-loving wife was always on the lookout for elderly bachelors to partner her unmarried sister.

'Though that might be described as the triumph of hope over experience,' he concluded.

'That sounds rather sexist even for a dedicated male chauvinist like yourself,' said Alva.

'Why so? I refer not to the sister's unattractiveness, although it is great, but Childs' predilections.'

'You mean he's gay?'

'Very likely, though in his case he seems to get his kicks out of moulding and mentoring personable young men, then sitting back to watch them prosper in their adult careers. Geoff Toplady was one such, I believe, and he's certainly prospered. Word is that he'll be lording it in the Court of Appeal by Christmas. Oh yes. Hitch your wagon to John Childs and the sky's the limit.'

'Meaning what? That he's buying their silence?'

'Good Lord, what a mind you have! Still, if you spend your time dabbling in dirt, I suppose some of it must stick. No, on the whole Childs' young men seem to be very positively heterosexual types, and the fact that most of them seem perfectly happy to continue the relationship in adult life suggests that he never tried to initiate them into the joys of buggery as boys. A form of sublimation, I expect you'd call it.'

'Giles, if you don't try any analysis, I won't try any cases,' said Alva acidly, stung more than she cared to show by the dabbling-in-dirt crack. 'Would Simon Homewood have been one of his mentored boys?'

'I believe he was. Of course, it could be Childs is going blind and mistook you for a testosteronic young man in need of a helping hand. Whatever, you simply hit lucky, Alva. No subtle conspiracy to take a closer look at you. Even the seating plan at these do's is purely a random thing so you don't get all the nobs clumping together.'

Alva didn't believe the last – nothing lawyers did was ever random – but she more or less accepted that fate alone had been responsible for her advancement. Which, she assured herself, she didn't mind. The world was full of excellent young psychiatrists; far better to be one of the lucky ones!

Still it would have been nice to be headhunted! Or perhaps she meant it would have made her feel more confident that she was the right person in the right job.

She met Chief Officer Proctor as she went through the gate. He greeted her with his usual breezy friendliness, but as always she felt those sharp eyes were probing in search of the weakness that would justify his belief that this wasn't a suitable job for a woman.

She put all these negative thoughts out of her mind as she sat and waited for Hadda to be brought into the interview room.

His face was expressionless as he sat down, placing his hands on the table before him with perhaps a little over emphasis.

Then he let his gaze fall slowly to the exercise book she'd laid before her and said, 'Well?'

And she said, with a brightness that set her own teeth on edge, 'It's very interesting.'

And this led to the brief exchange that ended with them trying to outstare each other.

This was not how she'd planned to control the session.

She said abruptly, 'Tell me about Woodcutter Enterprises.'

Her intention was to distract him by focusing not on his paedophilia, which was her principal concern, but on the fraudulent business activities that had got him the other half of his long sentence.

He looked at her with an expression that suggested he

64

saw through her efforts at dissimulation as easily as she saw through his, but he answered, 'You know what a private equity company is?'

She nodded and he went on, 'That's what Woodcutter was to start with. We identified businesses that needed restructuring because of poor management and organization which often made them vulnerable to take-over as well. When we took charge, we restructured by identifying the healthy profit-making elements and getting rid of the rest. And eventually we'd move on, leaving behind a leaner, healthier, much more viable business.'

'So, a sort of social service?' she said, smiling.

'No need to take the piss,' he said shortly. 'The aim of business is to make profits and that's what Woodcutter did very successfully and completely legitimately.'

She said, 'And you called yourselves Woodcutter Enterprises because you saw your job as pruning away dead-wood from potentially healthy business growth?'

He smiled, not the attractive face-lightening smile she had already remarked upon but a teeth-baring grimace that reminded her that his nickname was Wolf.

'That's it, you're right, as usual. And eventually as time went by with some of our more striking successes we retained a long-term interest, so anyone saying we were in for a quick buck then off without a backward glance ought to check the history.'

Interesting, she thought. His indignation at accusation of business malpractice seems at least as fervent as in relation to the sexual charges.

She said, 'I think the relevant government department has done all the checking necessary, don't you?'

For a moment she thought she might have provoked him into another outburst, but he controlled himself and said quietly, 'So where are we now, Dr Ozigbo? I've done what you asked and started putting things down on paper. I've told you how things happened, the way they happened. I thought someone in your job would have an open mind, but it seems to me you've made as many prejudgments as the rest of them!'

The reaction didn't surprise her. The written word gave fantasy a physical existence and, to start with, the act of writing things down nearly always reinforced denial.

'This isn't about me, it's about you,' she said gently. 'I said it was very interesting, and I really meant that. But you said it was just the first instalment. Perhaps we'd better wait till I've had the whole oeuvre before I venture any further comment. How does that sound, Wilfred? May I call you Wilfred? Or do you prefer Wilf? Or Wolf? That was your nickname, wasn't it?'

She had never moved beyond the formality of Mr Hadda. To use any other form of address when she was getting no or very little response would have sounded painfully patronizing. But she needed to do something to mark this small advance in their relationship.

He said, '*Wolf*. Yes, I used to get Wolf. Press made a lot of that, I recall. I was named after my dad. Wilfred. He got Fred. And I got Wilf till . . . But that's old history. Call me what you like. But what about you? I'm tired of saying *Doctor*. Sounds a bit clinical, doesn't it? And you want to be my friend, don't you? So let me see . . . Your name's Alva, isn't it? Where does that come from?'

'It's Swedish. My mother's Swedish. It means *elf* or something.'

The genuine non-lupine smile again. That made three times. It was good he doled it out so sparingly. Forewarned was forearmed.

'Wolf and elf, not a million miles apart,' he said. 'You call me Wolf, I'll call you Elf, OK?'

66

Elf. This had been her father's pet name for her since childhood. No one else ever used it. She wished she hadn't mentioned the meaning, but thought she'd hidden her reaction till Hadda said, 'Sure you're OK with that? I can call you madam, if you prefer.'

'No, *Elf* will be fine,' she said.

'Great. And elves perform magic, don't they?'

He reached into his tunic and pulled out another exercise book.

'So let's see you perform yours, Elf,' he said, handing it over. 'Here's Instalment Two.'

Wolf

You open your eye.

The light is so dazzling, you close it instantly.

Then you try again, this time very cautiously. The process takes two or three minutes and even then you don't open it fully but squint into the brightness through your lashes.

You are in bed. You have wires and tubes attached to your body, so it must be a hospital bed. Unless you've been kidnapped by aliens.

You close your eye once more to consider whether that is a joke or a serious option.

Surely you ought to know that?

It occurs to you that somehow you are both experiencing this and at the same time observing yourself experiencing it.

Neither the observer nor the experiencer is as yet worried.

You open your eye again.

You're getting used to the brightness. In fact the observer notes that it's nothing more than whatever daylight is managing to enter the room through the slats of a Venetian blind on the single window.

The only sound you can hear is a regular beep.

This is reassuring to both of your entities as they know from the hospital soaps it means you're alive.

Then you hear another sound, a door opening.

You close your eye and wait.

Someone enters the room and approaches the bed. Everything goes quiet again. The suspense is too much. You need to take a look.

A nurse is standing by the bedside, writing on a clipboard. Her gaze moves down to your face and registers the open eye. Hers round in surprise.

It is only then that it occurs to you that they usually come in pairs.

You say, 'Where's my other eye?'

At least that's your intention. To the observer and presumably to the nurse what comes out sounds like a rusty hinge on a long unopened door.

She steps back, takes a mobile out of her pocket, presses a button and says, 'Tell Dr Jekyll he's awake.'

Dr Jekyll? That doesn't sound like good news.

You close your eye again. Until you get a full report on the spare situation, it seems wise not to overtax it.

You hear the door open and then the nurse's voice as she assures the newcomer that your eye was open and you'd tried to talk. A somewhat superior male voice says, 'Well, let's see, shall we?'

A Doubting Thomas, you think. Feeling indignant on the nurse's behalf you give him a repeat performance. He responds by producing a pencil torch and shining it straight into your precious eye.

Bastard!

Then he asks, 'Do you know who you are?'

You could have done with notice of this question.

Does it mean he has no idea who you are?

Or is he merely wanting to check on your state of awareness?

You need time to think. Not just about how you should respond tactically, but simply how you should respond.

You are beginning to realize you're far from certain if you know who you are or not.

You check with your split personality.

The observer declares his best bet is that you're someone called Wilfred Hadda, that you've been in an accident, that leading up to the accident you'd been in some kind of trouble, but no need to worry about that just now as it will probably all come back to you eventually.

The experiencer ignores all this intellectual stuff. You're a one-eyed man in a hospital bed, he says, and all that matters is finding out just how much of the rest of you is missing.

You make a few more rusty hinge noises and Dr Jekyll demonstrates that the tens of thousands spent on his training have not been altogether misused by saying, 'Nurse, I think he needs some water.'

He presses a button that raises the top half of the bed up to an angle of forty-five degrees. For a moment the change of viewpoint is vertiginous and you feel like you're about to tumble off the edge of a cliff.

Then your head clears and the nurse puts a beaker of water to your lips.

'Careful,' says Jekyll. 'Not too much.'

Bastard! He's probably one of those mean gits who put optics on spirit bottles so they know exactly how much booze they're giving their dinner guests.

When at last you get enough liquid down your throat to ease your clogged vocal cords, you don't try to speak straight away. First you need a body check.

You try to waggle fingers and toes and feel pleased to get a reaction. But that means nothing. You've read about people still having pain from a limb that was amputated years ago. With a great effort you raise your head to get a one-eyed view of your arms.

First the left. That looks fine. Then the right. Something wrong there. You're sure you used to have more than two fingers. But a man can get by on two fingers. Missing toes would be more problematical.

You say, 'Feet.'

Jekyll looks blank but the nurse catches on quickly.

'He wants to see his feet,' she says.

Jekyll still looks puzzled. Perhaps he had a hangover when they did feet on his course. But the nurse slowly draws back the sheet and reveals your lower body.

The Boy David it isn't, but at least everything seems to be there even if your left leg does look like it's been badly assembled by a sculptor who felt that Giacometti was a bit too profligate with his materials. There's a tube coming out of your cock and someone's been shaving your pubic hair. So far as you can see, your scrotum's still intact.

You try for something a little more complicated than wiggling your toes but an attempt to bend your knees produces nothing more than a slow twitch and you give up.

You say, 'Mirror.'

Nurse and doctor exchange glances over your body.

They're both wearing name tags. The nurse is called Jane Duggan.

The doctor claims to be Jacklin, not Jekyll. A misprint, you decide.

Jekyll shrugs as if to say he doesn't care one way or the other, mirrors are a nurse thing.

Nurse Duggan leaves the room. Jekyll takes your pulse and does a couple of other doctorly things you're too weak to stop him from doing. Then Jane comes back in carrying a small shaving mirror.

She holds it up before your face.

You look into it and observer and experiencer unite in a memory of what you used to look like.

You never were classically handsome; more an out-of-doors, rough-hewn type.

Rough-hewn falls a long way short now. You look as if you've been worked over by a drunken chain-saw operator.

Where your right eye used to be is a hollow you could sink a long putt in.

Out of your left eye something liquid is oozing.

You realize you are starting to cry.

You say, 'Fuck off.'

And to give Nurse Duggan and Dr Jekyll their due, off they fuck.

ii

It turns out you have been in a coma for nearly nine months.

During the next nine you come to regard that as a blessed state.

There is some good news. You've slept through another lousy winter.

Your memories are as fragmented as your body. You've little recall of the accident, but someone must have described it in detail for later you know exactly what happened.

It seems you'd been very unlucky.

Normally in the middle of the day Central London traffic proceeds at a crawl. Occasionally, however, there occur sudden pockets of space, stretches of open road extending for as much as a hundred metres. Most drivers respond by standing on the accelerator in their eagerness to reconnect with the back of the crawl.

You'd emerged in the middle of one of these pockets. The bus had lumbered up to close on thirty miles an hour. You were flung through the air diagonally on to the bonnet of an oncoming Range Rover whose superior acceleration had got him up to near sixty. From there you bounced on to a table set on the pavement outside a coffee shop, and from there through the shop's plate-glass window.

By this time your body was in such a mess that it wasn't till they got you into an ambulance that someone noticed there was a coffee spoon sticking out of your right eye.

Both your legs were fractured, the left one in several places. You also broke your left arm, your collarbone, your pelvis and most of your ribs. You suffered severe head trauma and fractured your skull. And you'd left half of your right hand somewhere in the coffee shop, but unfortunately no one handed it in to Lost Property.

As for your internal organs, you get the impression the medics crossed their fingers and hoped.

Not that it can seem to have mattered all that much. Until you opened your eye, the smart prognosis was that sooner or later you'd have to be switched off.

At first you have almost as little concept of the passage of time as in your coma. You exist in a no-man's land between waking and sleeping, and the pain of treatment and the pain of dreams merge indistinguishably. Brief intervals of lucidity are occupied with trying to come to terms with your physical state. You are totally self-centred with your mental faculties so fragmented that information comes in fluorescent flashes, making it impossible to distinguish between memory and nightmare. So you do what non-nerds do when a computer goes on the blink: you switch off and hope it will have put itself right by the time you switch on again.

But though you have no sense of progress, progress there must be for eventually in one of the lucid intervals you find that you're certain you have a wife and family.

But no one comes visiting. Your room is not bedecked

with get-well cards, you receive no bouquets of flowers or bottles of bubbly to mark your return to life. *Perhaps the nursing staff are hoarding them,* is your last lucid thought before drifting off into no-man's land once more.

Next time you awake, you have a visitor. Or a vision.

He stands at the end of your bed, a fleshy little man wearing a beach shirt with the kind of pattern you make on the wall after a bad chicken tikka. You think you recognize his sun-reddened face but no name goes with it.

He doesn't speak, just stands there looking at you.

You close your eye for a second. Or a minute. Or longer.

When you open it again, he's gone.

But the space he occupied, in reality or in your mind, retains an after-image.

Or rather an after-impression.

Though still unable to separate memory from nightmare, you've always had a vague sense of some unpleasantness in the circumstances leading up to your accident. But even if real, you don't feel that this is anything to worry about. It's as if a deadline had passed. OK, you regret not being able to meet it, but once it has actually passed, your initial reaction is simply huge relief that you no longer have to worry about it!

But the appearance of Medler destroyed this foolish illusion.

Medler!

There, you remember the name without trying, or perhaps because you didn't try.

And with the name come other definite memories.

Medler, with his sly insinuating manner.

Medler whose mealy-mouth you punched. Twice.

Medler who raided your house, drove your wife and child into hiding, accused you of being a paedophile.

That at least must be sorted out by now, you reckon. Even

the slow creaky mills of the Met must have ground the truth out of that ludicrous allegation after all these months.

Nurse Duggan comes in. You ask her how long since you came out of your coma.

She says, 'Nearly a fortnight.'

'A fortnight!' you echo, looking round at the flowerless, cardless room.

She takes your point instantly and smiles sympathetically. She is, you come to realize, a truly kind woman. And she's not alone. OK, a couple of the nurses treat you like dogshit, but most are thoroughly professional, even compassionate. Good old NHS!

Nurse Duggan now tries to soothe your disappointment with an explanation.

'It's not policy to make a general announcement until they think it's time.'

Meaning until they're sure your resurgence hasn't just been a fleeting visit before you slip back under for ever. But surely your nearest and dearest, Imogen and Ginny, would have been kept informed of every change in your condition? Why weren't they here by your bedside?

You take a drink of water, using your left hand. The two fingers remaining on the right come in useful when words fail you in conversation with Dr Jekyll, but you're a long way from trusting a glass to their tender care.

Your vocal cords seem to be getting back to full flexibility, though your voice now has a sort of permanent hoarseness.

You say, 'Any phone calls for me? Any messages?'

Nurse Duggan says, 'I think you need to talk to Mr McLucky. I'll have a word.'

She leaves the room. Mr McLucky, you assume, is part of the hospital bureaucracy and you settle back for a long wait while he is summoned from his palatial office. But after only a few seconds, the door opens and a tall, lean man in tight

75

jeans and a grey sweatshirt comes in. About thirty, with a mouthful of nicotine-stained teeth in a long lugubrious face, he doesn't look like your idea of a hospital administrator.

You say, 'Mr McLucky?'

He says, 'Detective Constable McLucky.'

You stare at him. You feel you've seen him before, not like Medler, much more briefly . . . across a crowded room? Later you'll work out this was the out-of-place drinker in the Black Widow who alerted you to the fact that the police were waiting for you.

You say, 'What the hell are you doing here?'

He says, 'My job.'

You say, 'And what is your job, Detective Constable McLucky?'

He says, 'Making sure you don't bugger off again, Sir Wilfred.'

You would have laughed if you knew which muscles to use.

You say, 'You mean you're sitting outside the door, guarding me? How long have you been there?'

'Since you decided to wake,' he says. 'The nurse said you wanted to talk to me.'

He has a rough Glasgow accent and a manner to go with it.

You say, 'I wanted to know if there's been any messages for me. Or any visitors. But I'm not clear why this information should come through you.'

He says, 'Maybe it's something to do with you being in police custody, facing serious charges.'

It comes as a shock to hear confirmed what Medler's visit has made you suspect, that nothing has changed in the time you've spent out of things.

You are wrong there, of course. A hell of a lot of things have changed.

You feel mad but you're not in a position to lose your rag, so you say, 'Messages?'

76

He shrugs and says, 'Sorry, none.'

That's enough excitement for one day. Or one week. Or whatever period of time it is that elapses before you feel strong enough to make a decision.

You get Nurse Duggan to summon DC McLucky again.

You say, 'I'd like to make a phone call. Several phone calls.'

He purses his lips doubtfully, an expression his friends must find very irritating. You want to respond with some kind of legalistic threat, but a man not yet able to wipe his own arse is not in a position to be threatening. The best you can manage is, 'Go ask DI Medler if you must. That will give him time to make sure all his bugs are working.'

He says laconically, 'Medler? No use asking him. Early retirement back in January. Bad health.'

That confirms what you suspected. You were hallucinating. Funny thing, the subconscious. Can't have been much of an effort for it to have conjured up Imo in all her naked glory, but instead it opted for that little shit.

You squint up at McLucky, difficult as that is with one eye. He still looks real.

You say, 'Please,' resenting sounding so childish. But it does the trick.

McLucky leaves the room. You hear his voice distantly. You presume he is ringing for instructions.

Then a silence so long that you slip back into no-man's land. As you come out of it again, you wouldn't be surprised to find you'd imagined DC McLucky too.

But there he is, sitting at the bedside. Has he been there for a minute or for an hour? Seeing your eye open, he picks up a phone from the floor and places it on the bed.

'Can you manage?' he asks.

'Yes,' you say. It might be a lie.

He goes out of the room.

You pick up the phone with difficulty, then realize you

can't recall a single number. Except, thank God, Directory Enquiries. Asking for your own home number seems a sad admission of failure, so you say, 'Estover, Mast and Turbery. Solicitors in Holborn.'

They get the number and put you through. You give your name and ask for Toby. After a delay a woman's voice says, 'Hello, Sir Wilfred. It's Leila. How can I help you?'

Leila. The name conjures up a picture of a big blonde girl with a lovely bum. Rumour has it that when Toby enters his office in the morning, his mail and Leila are both lying open on his desk. You've always got on well with Leila.

'Hi, Leila,' you say. 'Could you put me through to Toby.'

'I'm sorry, Sir Wilfred, but I can't do that,' she says.

'Why not, for God's sake? Isn't he there?' you say.

'I mean I've consulted Mr Estover and he does not think it would be appropriate to talk with you,' she says, sounding very formal, as if she's quoting verbatim.

'Not appropriate?' You can't raise a bellow yet, but you manage a menacing croak. 'So when did sodding lawyers start thinking it wasn't appropriate to talk to their clients?'

She says, still formal, 'I'm sorry, Sir Wilfred, I assumed it had been made clear to you that you are no longer Mr Estover's client.'

Then her voice changes and she reverts to her usual chatty tone, this time tinged with a certain worrying sympathy.

'In the circumstances, it wouldn't really be appropriate, you must see that.'

You get very close to a bellow now.

'What circumstances, for fuck's sake?'

'Oh hell. Look, I'm sorry,' she says, now sounding really concerned. 'I just assumed you'd know. It shouldn't be me who's telling you this, but the thing is, Toby's acting for your wife in the divorce.'

Elf

Now this really *was* interesting, thought Alva Ozigbo.

He'd moved from the first person past to the second person present.

Did this bring him closer or move him further away?

Closer in a sense. The first instalment had been a pretty straightforward piece of storytelling. The detail he recalled, the emotional colouring he injected, all suggested this was a version of that distant morning frequently rehearsed in his mind. In fact, *rehearsed* was the *mot juste*. Like a dedicated actor, he had immersed himself so deeply in his role of innocent victim that he was actually living the part.

She'd done some serious research since she took over Hadda's case. In fact, when she looked at her records, she was surprised to see just how much research she'd done. She'd turned her eye inwards to seek out the reason for this special interest. Like her analysis of Hadda, that too was still work in progress.

She recalled Simon Homewood's advice when she had

started here on that dark January day in 2015. It had surprised her.

'Many of them will tell you they are innocent. Believe them. Carry on believing them as you study their cases. Examine all the evidence against them with an open, even a sceptical mind. You understand what I'm saying?'

'Yes, but I don't understand why you're saying it,' she'd said.

He smiled and said, 'Because that's what I do with every prisoner who comes into my care at Parkleigh. Until I'm absolutely convinced of their guilt, I cannot help them. I want it to be the same for you.'

'And how often have you not been convinced?' she'd asked boldly.

'Twice,' he said. 'One was freed on appeal. The other killed himself before anything could be done. I am determined that will never happen again.'

So she'd gone over the evidence against Hadda in the paedophile case with a fine-tooth comb. And she'd persuaded Giles Nevinson of the prosecutor's office to do the same. 'Tight as a duck's arse,' he'd declared cheerfully. 'And that's water-tight. Why so interested in this fellow?'

'Because he's . . . interesting,' was all she could reply. 'Psychologically, I mean.'

Why did she need to add that? How else could she be interested in a man like this, a convicted sexual predator and fraudster with a penchant for violence? It was on record that in his early days at Parkleigh he'd come close enough to 'normal' prisoners for them to attempt physical assault. His crippling leg injury limited his speed of movement, but he retained tremendous upper body strength and he had hospitalized one assailant. Transfer to the Special Wing had put him out of reach of physical attack, and verbal abuse he treated with the same massive indifference as he displayed to all other attempts to make contact with him. In the end a kind of contract was established with the prison management. He made no trouble, he got no trouble.

He also got no treatment. While he wasn't one of those prisoners who staged roof-top demonstrations to protest their innocence or had outside support groups mounting appeals, he never took the smallest step towards acknowledging his guilt. Perhaps it was this sheer intractability that caught her attention.

With the Director's permission, she had visited Hadda's cell at a time he and all the other prisoners were in the dining hall. Even by prison standards it was bare. A reasonable amount of personalization was allowed, but all that Hadda seemed to have done to mark his occupancy was to Blu-Tack to the wall a copy of a painting that looked as if it had been torn out of a colour supplement. It showed a tall upright figure, his right hand resting on a lumberjack's axe, standing under a turbulent sky, looking out over a wide landscape of mountains and lakes. Alva studied it for several minutes.

'Like paintings, do you, miss?' enquired Chief Officer Proctor, who'd escorted her into the cell.

'I like what they tell me about the people who like them,' said Alva. 'And of course the people who paint them.'

If there were a signature on the painting, the reproduction wasn't good enough to show it. She made a note to check and turned her attention to the rest of the cell. Only its emptiness said anything about the personality of its inmate. It was as if Hadda had resolved to leave no trace of his passing. She did find one book, a dog-eared paperback copy of *The Count of Monte-Cristo*. Seeing her looking at it, Proctor said sardonically, 'It's all right, miss. We check regularly under the bed for tunnels.'

Later in the prison library she asked for a record of Hadda's borrowings and found there were none. Years of imprisonment with little but his own thoughts for company. He was either a man of great inner resources or of no inner life whatsoever.

Giles Nevinson during his trawl through the case files on her behalf had come up with an inventory of all the material removed from Hadda's house at the time of the initial raid. It was the books and DVDs confiscated that she was interested in. There was nothing here that the prosecution had been able to use to support their case, but they suggested that, pre-accident, Hadda's taste had been for the kind of story in which a tough, hard-bitten protagonist fought his way through to some kind of rough justice despite the fiendish plots and furious onslaughts of powerful enemies.

This could account for his choosing to present the police raid and its sequel in the form of the opening chapters of a thriller with himself as the much put-upon hero.

But in Alva's estimate the form disguised its true function.

For Hadda this wasn't fiction, it was revelation, it was Holy Writ! If ever any doubts about the rightness of his cause crept into his consciousness, all he had to do was refer back to this ur-text and all became simple and straightforward again.

But he hadn't been able to keep it up when it came to writing about his emergence from the coma. Here the tight narrative control was gone. Even after the passage of so many years, that sense of confusion on waking into a new and alien landscape remained with him. His account of it was immediate, not historical. Hindsight usually allows us to order experience, but here it was still possible to feel him straining to make sense of blurred images, broken lines, shifting foci.

There was some shape. Each of the two sections climaxed

at a moment of violent shock. The first, his recognition of physical change; the second, his discovery of his wife's defection. Nowhere in his account of his waking confusion, nor in the aftermath of these systemic shocks, was there the slightest indication that he was moving out of denial towards recognition.

But these were early days. She was pretty certain she now had every scrap of available information about Wolf Hadda, but what did it add up to? Very little. The significant narrative of the mental and emotional journey that had brought him to Parkleigh could only come from within.

Her hope had to be that, by coaxing him to provide it, she might be able to lead him to a moment of self-knowledge when, like a mountain walker confronted by a Brocken Spectre, he would draw back in horror from the monstrous apparition before him, then recognize it as a projection of himself.

She liked that image, and it was particularly apt in Hadda's case. From her study of his background she knew he'd grown up in the Lake District where his father had been head forester on the estate of his father-in-law, Sir Leon Ulphingstone. Lots of fascinating possibilities there. Perhaps the almost idealized figure in the painting on his cell wall was saying something about his relationship with his father. Or perhaps it was there as a reminder to himself of what he had been and what he now was.

With the help of an artistic friend, she'd identified the artist as the American, Winslow Homer. The painting was called *The Woodcutter*. She'd tracked down an image on her computer. It was accompanied by an old catalogue blurb.

In Winslow Homer's painting, the Woodcutter stands looking out on a panorama of mountains and lakes and virgin forest. He is tall and muscular, brimful of youthful confidence that he can see no peak too high to climb, no river too wide to cross, no tree too tall to fell. This land is his to shape, and shape it he will, or die in the attempt.

She could see what the writer meant. And of course Woodcutter had been the name of Hadda's business organization. Significant?

Everything is significant, her tutor used to reiterate. You cannot know too much.

I'm certainly still a long way from knowing too much about you, Wolf Hadda, she thought as she watched him limp slowly into the interview room. She'd wondered in George Proctor's presence if it might not be possible to equip him with a walking stick. The Chief Officer had laughed and said, 'Yeah, and I'll put in a requisition for a supply of shillelaghs and assegais while I'm at it!'

He seemed even slower than usual today. As he settled on to his chair, she looked for signs that he was impatient to discuss the second episode. That would have been indicative; she wasn't sure of what. But there were no signs, which was also indicative, though again she wasn't sure what of.

His face was expressionless, the dark glasses blanking out his good eye. For all she knew, it could be closed and he could be asleep.

She said loudly, 'How do you feel now about your disfigurement?'

If she'd thought to startle him by her sudden bluntness, she was disappointed.

He said reflectively, 'Now let me see. Do you mean the Long John Silver limp, or the Cyclopean stare, or the fact that I'll never play the violin again?'

She nodded and said, 'Thank you,' and made a note on her pad.

'What for? I didn't answer your question.'

'I think you did. By hyperbole in respect of your leg and your eye. Silver was a murderous cutthroat who'd lost his

84

entire leg, and the Cyclops were vile cannibalistic monsters. As for your hand, nothing in your file suggests you ever could play the violin, so that was a dismissive joke.'

'Indicating?'

'That you're really pissed off by being lame and one-eyed, but you've managed to adapt to the finger loss.'

'Maybe that's because I don't get the chance to play much golf in this place. Mind you, I'll be able to cap Sammy Davis Junior's answer when asked what his handicap was.'

'I'm sorry, I'm not into golf.'

'He said, "I'm a black, one-eyed Jew." I'd be able to say, I'm a one-eyed, one-handed, lame, paedophiliac fraudster.'

'And how much of that would be true?'

He frowned and said, 'You don't give up, do you? Eighty per cent at most. The physical stuff is undeniable. As for the fraud, I walked some lines that seemed to get re-drawn after the big crash and I'm willing to accept that maybe I ended up on the wrong side of the new line. But I'm not in word or thought or deed a paedophile.'

She decided to let it alone. Accepting he might have been guilty of fraud had to be some kind of advance, though from her reading of the trial transcripts, the evidence against him here had looked far from conclusive. Perhaps his lawyer had got it right when he tried to argue that the huge publicity surrounding his conviction on the paedophilia charges made it impossible for him to get a fair hearing at the fraud trial. The judge had slapped him down, saying that in his court he would be the arbiter of fairness. But by all accounts Hadda had cut such an unattractive and non-responsive figure in the dock, if they'd accused him of membership of al-Qaeda, too, he'd probably have been convicted.

She knew how the jury felt. He had made no effort to project a positive image of himself. Even after he started talking to her, all she got was a sense of massive indifference.

This in itself did not bother her. It was a psychiatrist's job to inspire trust, not affection. But it did puzzle her if only because in jail her clients usually fell into two categories – those who resented and feared her, and those who saw her as a potential ally in their campaigns for parole.

Hadda was different. Though he had by now served enough time to be eligible for parole he had made no application nor shown the slightest interest in doing so.

Not of course that there was much point. A conviction like his made it very hard to persuade the parole board to release you back into the community, particularly when your application was unsupported by any admission of guilt or acceptance of treatment.

But at least he had started writing these narratives. That had to be progress.

And there was something about him today, something only detectable once he'd started talking. An undercurrent of restlessness; or, if that was too strong, at least a sense of strain in his self-control.

She said, 'Wilfred . . . Wilf . . .'

Both versions of his name felt awkward on her lips, smacking of the enforced familiarity of the hospital ward or the nursing home. His expression suggested he was enjoying her problem.

She said, '. . . Wolf.'

He nodded as if she'd done well and said, 'Yes, Elf?'

Her sobriquet came off his tongue easily, almost eagerly, as though she were an old friend whose words he was anxious to hear.

She said, 'How do you feel about Imogen now?'

He frowned as if this wasn't the question he'd been looking for.

'About the fact that she divorced me? Or the fact that she

subsequently married my former solicitor and friend, Toby Estover? Wonder how that worked out?'

He spoke casually, almost mockingly. A front, she guessed. And she also guessed he might have a pretty good idea how it had worked out. Modern prisons had come a long way from the Bastille and the Chateau d'If, where a man could linger, forgotten and forgetting, oblivious to the march of history outside. She'd checked on the happy pair, telling herself she had a professional interest. Estover was now, if not a household name, at least a name recognized in many households. He was so sought after he could pick and choose his clients, and the fact that he seemed to pick those involved in cases that attracted maximum publicity could hardly be held against him.

As for the lovely Imogen, she was certainly as lovely as ever. Alva had seen a recent photo of her in the Cumbrian churchyard where her daughter's ashes were being placed in the family tomb. Not an event that drew the world's press, but a local reporter had been there and taken a snap on his mobile. By chance he'd got a combination of light, angle, and background that lent the picture a kind of dark, brooding Brontë-esque quality, and the *Observer* had printed it for its atmospheric impact rather than its news value.

She said, 'I just wondered what you feel when I mention her name?'

'Hate,' he said.

This took her aback.

He said, 'You look surprised. That I should feel it, or that I should say it?'

'Both. It's such an absolute concept . . .'

'It's not a bloody concept!' he interrupted. 'It has nothing to do with intellectual organization. You asked what I felt. What else should I reply? Contempt? Revulsion? Anger? Dismay? A bit of all of those, I suppose. But hate does it, I think. Hate folds them all neatly into a single package.'

'But what has she done to deserve this?' she asked.

'She has believed the lies they told about me,' he said. 'And because she believed them, my lovely daughter is dead.'

All Alva's previous attempts to get him to talk about his daughter had been met with his mountainous blankness, but now for a moment she saw the agony that seethed beneath the rocky surface.

She said in her most neutral tone, 'You blame her for Ginny's death?'

He was back in control but within his apparent calm she sensed a tension like that intense stillness of air when an electric storm is close to breaking.

'Maybe,' he said. 'But not so much as I blame her bitch of a mother.'

She noted that, despite the intensity of the negative feelings he'd expressed about Imogen, he was reluctant to lay full responsibility for the girl's death upon her. Whatever bonds there had been between him and his wife must have been unusually strong for this ambiguity of feeling to have survived.

'You hold Lady Kira responsible?'

'Oh yes. Everything tracks back to her. She never wanted me to have her daughter. And now she has helped deprive me of mine.'

'And she did this, how? By helping with the arrangements for her to finish her education in France, out of reach of our prurient press?'

She deliberately let a trace of doubt seep into her voice, hoping to provoke further revelation of what was going on inside his mind, but all she succeeded in doing was bring down the defences even further.

He said indifferently, 'If you'd ever met her, you'd understand.'

This for the moment was a dead end. Leave the mother-in-law, get back to the wife, she told herself.

She said, 'If, as you claim, you are innocent, then someone must have framed you. Do you have any idea who?'

The question seemed to amuse him.

'I have a short list of possibilities, yes.'

'Is Imogen on it?'

The question seemed to surprise him. Or perhaps he simply didn't like it. She really must find a way to get into this key relationship.

'What does it matter?' he demanded. 'Which is worse? That she went along with a plot to frame me? Or that she actually believed I was guilty as charged?'

'Be fair,' said Alva. 'The evidence was overwhelming; the jury took twenty minutes to find you guilty . . .'

'Twelve strangers!' he interrupted. 'Twelve citizens picked off the street! In this world we're unfortunate enough to live in, and especially in this septic isle we live on, where squalid politicians conspire with a squalid press to feed a half-educated and wholly complacent public on a diet of meretricious trivia, I'm sure it would be possible to concoct enough evidence to persuade twelve strangers that Nelson Mandela was a cannibal.'

Wow! she thought as she studied him closely. That rolled off your tongue so easily, it's clearly been picking up momentum in your mind for years!

His voice was still controlled, but his single eye sparkled with passion. What was it he said he felt about his ex-wife's behaviour?

Contempt.

Revulsion.

Anger.

Dismay.

These were all necessary elements of that condition of

89

self-awareness she was trying to draw him to. Perhaps by transferring these emotions away from himself to his ex-wife, he was showing her he was closer than she'd thought. His strained parallel with Mandela was also significant. A man of dignity and probity, imprisoned by a warped regime, and finally released and vindicated after long years to become a symbol of peace and reconciliation. It was as if Hadda's denial could only be sustained by going to the furthermost extreme in search of supportive self-images.

Hopefully, if he continued far enough in that direction, he would eventually come upon himself unawares. And then it would be up to her to direct him away from self-hatred into more positively remedial channels.

Meanwhile it would be good if she could nudge him into a memory of Imogen in her fairy-tale princess phase. It was possible that by reliving that period when she had become the unique and obsessive object of his adoration, he might come to wonder whether it was in fact his idol that had fallen or himself.

Even if that admittedly ideal outcome didn't materialize, this was the part of his life she had least information about, for there were few living sources but himself.

Now the passion had faded and he was looking at her assessingly.

He's got something else for me, she thought. She knew how habit-forming this business of writing about your past could be. In many clients, it went beyond habit into compulsion. So of course since their last meeting he'd carried on writing.

But as what he wrote came closer to the most intimate details of his being, he naturally became less and less sure of sharing it with her.

So, show no eagerness. Do not press.

She said, 'Wolf, time's nearly up. I was wondering, is there anything I can get for you? Books, journals, that sort of thing? I should have asked before. Or something more personal. Something in the food line? Or proper linen handkerchiefs, silk socks, perhaps?'

He shook his head as if impatient at her change of subject, or perhaps at the silly notion that there could be something he might enjoy receiving, and said, 'We were talking about Imo. I got to thinking about her after I wrote that last piece.'

She said, 'Yes?'

He said, 'That stuff about feeling hate, I mean it. Or part of me means it. But there's also a part of me that hates me for feeling it. Does that make sense?'

She nodded and said gravely, 'What wouldn't make sense is for you not to feel it.'

That was the right answer. He pulled another exercise book out of his blouson.

'You might like to see this,' he said.

'Thank you,' she said, taking the book. She opened it and glanced at the first page.

And she knew at once she'd got what she wanted.

Wolf

i

I was a wild boy, in just about every sense.

My mam, God bless her, died when I was only six. Brain fever, they called it locally. Probably some form of meningitis, spotted too late.

We had my dad's Aunt Carrie living with us. Or rather we were living with her in her farmhouse, Birkstane. Up there in Cumbria they still expect the young to take care of the old. Not that Carrie can have been all that old when we moved in with her. Birkstane was all that remained, plus a couple of small fields, of her husband's farm. Widowed in her mid forties, already in her early fifties she was getting a bit forgetful. Also she had arthritis which gave her mobility problems. Normally up there supportive neighbours would have kept her going quite happily till her dotage, but she was a bit isolated, several miles from Mireton, the nearest village, right on the edge of the Ulphingstone estate.

Dad was her only living relative so when word reached him that there was a social worker snooping around, he knew something had to be done. I was still in nappies at the time, so I can only speculate, but I suspect it suited him to move into Birkstane. As head forester to Sir Leon, Dad had a tied cottage on the estate but as I often heard him say later, only a fool lives in a house another fool can throw him out of any time he likes. Not that he thought Sir Leon was a fool. In fact they got on pretty well, and far from dividing them, my liaison with Leon's daughter only brought them closer together.

They both thought it was a lousy idea.

But that was a long way in the future.

Everything seems to have worked fine to start with. Birkstane was almost as handy for Dad's work as the tied cottage had been. Mam got to work on the old farmhouse and dragged it back from the edge of dereliction, while Carrie, in familiar surroundings with someone constantly present to keep an eye on her, got a new lease of life.

All this I picked up later. Like I say, I was so young that my memory of those early years in Birkstane is generally non-specific, but I know how blissfully happy I must have been, for I recall all too clearly how I felt when they told me Mam was dead. No, not when they told me; I mean when it finally got through to me that being dead meant gone for good, meant I would never ever see her again.

I was in my second year at school. It had taken a whole year for me to come to terms with the daily separation from Mam; this new and permanent separation was a loss beyond all reach of consolation. I was far too young and far too immersed in my own pain to observe what this blow did to my father, but as I have no recollection of him finding the strength to try and comfort me, I'd guess he too was rendered completely helpless by the loss. I suppose if I'd drawn attention to myself, someone might have tried to do something about me, but I think I must have moved in a bubble of grief through which everyone could see and hear me behaving apparently normally – in fact I suspect that many people observed what a blessing it was that I was clearly too young to take it all in and the best thing was for everyone to treat me as if nothing important had happened.

What they didn't realize was that within that bubble I too was as good as dead, and as I slowly came back to life, I think I unconsciously resolved that never again would I be in a position where the loss of any single individual could cause me such pain.

Because there was still a woman in the house, no thought was given to the need to make any special arrangements for me. And because of Carrie's apparent return to her old self during the five years of having us to live with her, nobody doubted that she was a fit guardian and housekeeper.

The reality was very different. Her mobility problems made it hard for her to keep up with a wild young boy, and without my mam's corrective presence, the old memory lapses (the result, it was later diagnosed, of early-onset Alzheimer's) now became much more significant. As for Fred, my dad, he went out to work and rarely came home till it was time for his tea. This is the generic term we gave to the early evening meal. As Carrie got more forgetful, the combinations of food offered to us grew increasingly eccentric, but neither of us took much notice – me because I was too young to make comparisons, Dad because he prefaced the meal with a couple of bottles of strong ale and washed it down with another two before driving down to the Black Dog in Mireton. He successfully avoided the attention of the local constabulary by driving his old Defender along the forest tracks, which he knew like the back of his hand, and leaving it on the edge of the estate and walking the last quarter mile to the Dog.

Sorry, I've gone on a lot more than I intended about all this early trauma stuff and I know all you really wanted was an account of how me and Imogen got together. But I started off trying to explain the kind of youngster I was, and to understand that, you need to know the rest.

To cut a long story short, because of my instinctive reluctance to get close to anybody and because of the almost total lack of any meaningful supervision at home, I ran wild. Literally. Every free moment I had I spent roaming the countryside. Some streak of natural cunning made me realize the dangers of too much truancy, and I trod a line between being an internal nuisance and an external problem. But I usually turned up late and when I could I bunked off early. As I said, Aunt Carrie was ill-equipped physically or mentally to cope with me. Indeed, as I grew older and wiser, if that's the right word, a combination of self-interest and I hope fondness for the old lady made me cover up for her as best I could.

Of course my behaviour did not go unremarked, but unlike in the towns where suspicion of child neglect prompts people either to look the other way or at best to ring Social Services anonymously, in the countryside they deal with such problems in-house, so to speak. Looking back, I see that I was probably watched over much more carefully than I understood then. The postman was the eyes and ears of the district, the vicar dropped by a couple of times a week, and there was a steady stream of local ladies who found a reason to call on Carrie, and help with a bit of tidying up. Also for some reason I never really understood, everyone, teachers and locals alike, seemed ready to show a remarkable degree of tolerance towards my aberrant behaviour.

Maybe I'd have turned out better if someone had been ready to skelp my ear a bit more frequently!

Sir Leon was another one who missed the chance to sort me out. I remember when I was eight or nine I got caught by his gamekeeper. I was never a serious poacher, though if the odd trout or rabbit came my way, I regarded it as the peasant's tithe. The day I got caught peering into Sir Leon's newly stocked tarn, it was the fact that I had no criminal intent that made me vulnerable. I was stretched out on the bank, raptly viewing the tiny fry at their play, when a heavy hand landed on my shoulder and I was hauled upright by Sir Leon's head keeper.

When he realized who he'd got, he threw me into his pick-up and drove me through the forest to where my father was supervising a gang of loggers. Sir Leon was there too, and after the situation had been explained, he stared down at me and said, 'This your brat then, Fred? What's your name, boy?'

'Wilf,' I blurted.

'Wilf?'

Then he squatted down beside me, ran his fingers through my hair, opened my mouth and peered in like he was checking out a horse, then winked at me and said, 'Sure you don't mean Wolf? Looks to me like you've been suckled by wolves. That might explain things! Suckled by wolves, and here's me thinking they were all dead.'

He stood up, laughing at his own joke, and everyone else laughed, except me and Dad.

Thereafter every time Sir Leon saw me he called me Wolf and gradually the name stuck. I rather like the notion of being suckled by wolves, maybe because Sir Leon with his long nose and great mane of grey-brown hair looked like he might have a bit of wolf in him too. His name, Ulphingstone, certainly did.

Dad, however, hadn't cared to be shown up in front of his workers and his boss. That night he stayed home and paid me more attention than I think he had since Mam died, and he didn't much like what he saw. When I responded surlily to his remonstrations, he skelped me round the left ear, and when I responded angrily to that, he skelped me round the right.

After that I was obliged to mend my ways for a while, but as well as developing a taste for the wild life, I was already well grounded in the art of deception, and I continued on my independent way pretty much as before, only taking a little more care.

I suppose I was a bit of a loner, but that was through choice. At junior school I never had any problem getting on with the other boys; in fact most of them seemed keen to be friends with me, but I always felt myself apart from them. Maybe it was because I didn't give a toss about who was going to win the Premier League, maybe it was something deeper than that. A lot of the girls were keen to be friendly too, but I reckoned they were a waste of space. At least with the boys you could run around and jump on top of each other and have a bit of a wrestle. It was a long time before I realized you could do that with girls too.

Then came secondary school. There was the usual bullying, but I've always had a short fuse. Neither size nor number made any difference – if you messed with me, I lived up to my name and reacted like a wild beast, wading in with fists, feet, teeth, and head till someone lay bleeding on the school-yard floor. Eventually the physical bullying stopped, but there were still scores to settle. One day, aged about twelve, I found someone had broken into my locker and sprayed car paint all over the stuff I kept there. I had a good idea who it was. Next morning I smuggled in the cut-down lumber axe my dad was teaching me to use and I demolished my chief suspect's locker and everything in it. All the kids thought I'd be expelled or at least excluded for that, but the Head just settled for giving me a long lecture and getting Dad to pay for the damage.

I didn't get a lecture from Fred, but an ear-ringing slap

which he made clear wasn't for damaging the other boy's gear but for ruining a perfectly good axe!

After that, helped by the fact that I got bigger and stronger every month, I was left strictly alone by the would-be bullies. I wasn't thick, I did enough work to keep my head above water, and for some reason the teachers cut me a lot of slack. I never sucked up to any of them but most of them seemed to like me and I suspect I got away with stuff another kid might have been pulled up for. I never made any particular friends because the kind of thing I liked to do away from school, I liked to do alone. But I was always one of the first to get picked when my class was split up for schoolyard games.

The only significant contacts I made was age thirteen when I had my accident. You must have heard about my accident, Elf, the one that left me with the scars on my back that the bastards at my trial tried to claim established I was in those filthy videos. It was a real accident, not carelessness or anything on my part. A boulder that had been firmly anchored for a couple of thousand years decided to give way the same moment I put my weight on it. I fell off on to a sheet of ice and went bouncing and slithering down the fell-side for a couple of hundred feet, and when the mountain rescue team reached me, they reckoned I was a goner. Didn't I mention this in one of my other scribblings? I think I did, so you'll know that fortunately there was no permanent damage and a few months later I was back on the fells with nothing worse than a heavily scarred back.

But what the experience did do was let me see close-up what a great bunch of guys the mountain rescue team was. They were really good to me. I was too young to join officially, but none of them objected when I started hanging out with them, and a couple of them really took me under their wing and taught me all about proper climbing.

Mind you, I did sometimes have a quiet laugh when they

roped me up to do some relatively easy ascent that I'd been scampering up like a monkey all by myself for years, but I was learning sense and kept my gob shut.

Now at last we're getting to Imogen.

I was fifteen when I first saw her, she was – is – a year younger.

I knew Sir Leon had a daughter and I daresay I'd glimpsed her before, but this was the first time I really noticed her.

Like I said, after that first encounter with Sir Leon, whenever our paths crossed he greeted me as Wolf and always asked very seriously how the rest of the pack was getting on. I'd grunt some response, the way boys do. Once when Dad told me to speak proper, Sir Leon said, 'No need for that, Fred. The boy's talking wolf and I understand him perfectly,' then he grunted something back at me, and smiled so broadly I had to smile back as if I'd understood him. After that he always greeted me with a grunt and a grin.

There was of course no socialization between us peasants and the castle, not even in the old feudal sense: no Christmas parties for the estate staff, no village fêtes in the castle grounds, nothing like that. Sir Leon was a good and fair employer, but his wife, Lady Kira, my dear ma-in-law, called the shots at home.

Scion of a White Russian émigré family, Kira was more tsarist than her ancestors in her social attitudes. She believed servants were serfs, and anything that encouraged familiarity diminished efficiency. For her the term servant covered everyone in the locality. In her eyes we all belonged to the same sub-class, related by frequently incestuous intermarriage, and united in a determination to cheat, rob and, if the opportunity rose, rape our superiors.

I don't think anyone actually doffed their cap and tugged their forelock as she passed, but she made you feel you ought to.

So when Sir Leon suggested to my dad I might like to come up to the castle one summer day to 'play with the young 'uns' as he put it, we were both flabbergasted.

It turned out they had some house guests who between them had five daughters and one son, a boy of my own age, and Sir Leon felt he needed some male company to prevent his spirit being crushed by the 'monstrous regiment' (Sir Leon's phrase again).

I didn't want to go, but Dad dug his heels in and said that it was time I learnt some manners and Sir Leon had always been good to me and if for once I didn't do what he wanted, he'd make bloody sure I didn't do what I wanted for the rest of the summer holidays and lots of stuff like that, so one bright sunny afternoon I clambered over the boundary wall behind Birkstane and walked through the forest to the castle.

As castles go, it's not much to write home about, no battlements or towers, not even a moat. It had been a proper castle once, way back in the Middle Ages, I think, but somewhere along the line it got bashed about a bit, whether by cannon balls or just general neglect and decay I don't know, and when the family started rebuilding, they downsized and what they ended up with was a big house.

But that's adult me talking. As I emerged from the trees that day, the building loomed ahead as formidable and as huge as Windsor!

Everyone was scattered around the lawn in front of the house. With each step I took, it became more apparent that the Sunday-best outfit that Dad had forced me to wear was entirely the wrong choice. Shorts, jeans, T-shirts abounded, not a hot tweed suit in sight. I almost turned and ran away, but Sir Leon had spotted me and advanced to meet me.

'Uggh grrr,' he said in his pretended wolf-speak. 'Wolf, my boy, so glad you could make it. You look like you could do with a nice cold lemonade. And why don't you take your jacket and tie off – bit too hot for them on a day like this.'

Thus he managed to get me looking slightly less ridiculous by the time he introduced me to the 'kids'.

The girls, ranging from eleven to fifteen, more or less ignored me. The boy, stretched out on the grass apparently asleep, rolled over as Sir Leon prodded him with his foot, raised himself on one elbow, and smiled at me.

'Johnny,' said Leon, 'this is Wolf Hadda. Wolf, this is Johnny Nutbrown. Johnny, why don't you get Wolf a glass of lemonade?'

Then he left us.

Johnny said, 'Is your name really Wolf?'

'No. Wilf,' I said. 'Sir Leon calls me Wolf.'

'Then that's what I'll call you, if that's all right,' he said with a smile.

Then he went and got me a lemonade.

I got no real impression of Johnny from that first encounter. The way he looked, and moved, and talked, he might have been a creature from another planet. As for him, I think even then he was as unperturbed by everything, present, past or future, as I was to find him in later life. He took the arrival of this inarticulate peasant in his stride. I think he was totally unaware that I'd been brought along to keep him company. I can't believe that being the sole boy among all those girls had troubled him for a moment. That was Sir Leon imagining how he might have felt in the same circumstances.

A tall woman, slim and athletic with a lovely figure and a face whose features were almost too perfect to be beautiful came and looked at me for a second or two with ice-cold eyes, then moved away. That was Lady Kira. The ice-cold look and the accompanying silence set the pattern for most of our future encounters.

I've little recollection of any of the other adults. As for the girls, they were just a blur of bright colours and shrill noises. Except for Imogen. Not that I knew it was Sir Leon's daughter to start with. She was just part of the blur until they started dancing.

Most of the adults had moved off somewhere. Johnny, after two or three attempts at conversation, had given up on me and gone back to sleep. The girls had got hold of a radio or it might have been a portable cassette player, I don't know. Anyway it was beating out the pop songs of the time and they started dancing. Disco dancing, I suppose it was – it could have been classical ballet for all it meant to me – the music scene, as they term it, was an area of teenage life that entirely passed me by.

But presently as they went through their weird gyrations, one figure began to stand out from the half-dozen, not because she was particularly shapely or anything – in fact she was the skinniest of the lot – but because while the others were very aware of this as a competitive group activity, she was totally absorbed in the music. You got the feeling she would have been doing this if she'd been completely alone in the middle of a desert.

The difference eventually made itself felt even among her fellow dancers, and one by one they slowed down and stopped, till only this single figure still moved, rhythmically, sinuously, as though in perfect harmony not only with the music but with the grass beneath her feet and the blue sky above, and the gently shimmering trees of the distant woodland that formed the backdrop from my viewpoint. Unlike the others, she was wearing a white summer dress of some flimsy material that floated around her as she danced, and her long golden hair wreathed about her head like a halo of sunbeams.

I was entranced, in the strictest sense of the word; drawn into her trance; totally absorbed. I didn't know what it meant, only that it meant something hugely significant to me. I didn't want it to stop. I wanted to sit here and watch this small and still totally anonymous figure dancing forever.

Then Johnny who, unseen by me, had woken and sat up, said, 'Oh God, there goes Imo again. Turn on the music and it sets her off like a monkey on a stick!'

His tone was totally non-malicious, but that didn't save him.

I punched him on the nose. I didn't even think about it. I just punched him.

Blood fountained out; one of the remaining adults – maybe it was Johnny's mother – had been looking our way, and she screamed. Johnny sat there, stock-still, staring down at his cupped hand as it filled with blood.

I just wanted to be as far away from all this as I could get.

Again without thought, I found myself on my feet and heading as fast as I could run towards the welcome shelter of the distant woodland.

My shortest line took me past Imogen. She had stopped dancing and her eyes tracked me towards her and past her and I imagined I could feel them on me still as I covered the couple of hundred yards or so to the sanctuary of the trees.

That is my first memory of Imogen. I think even then, uncouth and untutored though I was, I knew I was hers and she was mine forever.

Just shows how wrong you can be, eh, Elf?

ii

I've just read over what I've written.

It strikes me this is just the kind of stuff you want, Elf. Childhood trauma, all that crap.

Except maybe I haven't made it clear: I *enjoyed* my

childhood. It was a magical time. Do you read poetry? I don't. Rhyme or reason, isn't that what they say? Well, I'm a reason man. At school I learnt some stuff by rote to keep the teachers happy but I also learnt the trick of instant deletion the minute I'd spouted it. The only bit that's stuck doesn't come from my schooldays but from my daughter, Ginny's.

It was some time in that last summer, '08 I mean, it was raining most of the time I recall, perhaps that's why Ginny got stuck into her holiday assignments early.

At her posh school, they reckoned poetry was important, and one of the things she had to do was write a paraphrase of some lines of Wordsworth. She assumed because I was a Cumbrian lad, I'd know all about him. A father doesn't like to disappoint his daughter, so I glanced at the passage. A lot of the language was daft and he went all round the houses to say something, but to my amazement I found myself thinking, this bugger's writing about me!

He was talking about himself as a kid, the things he got up to, climbing steep cliffs, moonlight poaching, going out on the lake, but the lines that stuck were the ones that summed it all up for him.

> *Fair seed-time had my soul and I grew up*
> *Fostered alike by beauty and by fear.*

That was me. I don't mean fear of being clouted or abused, anything like that. I mean the kind of fear you feel when you're hanging over a hundred-foot drop by your fingernails or when the night's so black you can't see your hand in front of your face and you hear something snuffling in the dark, the fear that makes your sense of being alive so much sharper, that lets you feel the life-blood pounding through your heart, that makes you want to dance and shout when you beat it and survive!

Do you know what I'm talking about, Elf? Or are you stuck in all that Freudian clart, where everything's to do with sex, even if you're dealing with kids before they know what sex is all about?

Me, I was never much interested in sex, not even after my balls dropped. Maybe I was leading such a physical life, I was just too knackered. Of course my cock stood up from time to time and I'd give it a pull and I enjoyed the spasm of pleasure that eventually ensued. But I didn't have much time for the dirty jokes and mucky books and boasting about what they'd done with girls that most of my schoolmates went in for.

Not that I didn't have the chance to learn on the job, so to speak. Despite me ignoring them as much as I could, most of the girls seemed more than willing to be friendly, but I couldn't see any point in wasting time with them that I could have spent scrambling up a wet rock face!

So what you'd likely call significant sexual experience didn't come my way until . . . well, let me tell you about it.

Or rather, let me tell myself. I'm not at all sure I shall ever let you see this, Elf, which means I can be completely frank as I'm reserving the right to tear it all to pieces, if that's what I decide.

So let's go back to me taking off into the woods, leaving Imogen staring after me, Johnny Nutbrown bleeding from the nose, his parents puce with indignation, Sir Leon hugely disappointed and Lady Kira flaring her nostrils in her favourite *what-did-you-expect* expression.

Of course I'm just guessing at most of that, apart from Johnny's nose. What I'm certain I left behind was the jacket and tie I'd taken off at Sir Leon's suggestion.

He came round to Birkstane with them that evening.

I was in my bedroom. Naturally I'd said nothing about the events of the day to either Dad or Aunt Carrie, just

105

muttered something in reply to their question as to whether I'd had a good time.

I heard the car pull up outside and when I looked out and recognized Sir Leon's Range Rover, I thought of climbing out of the window and doing a bunk.

Then I saw there was still someone in the car after Sir Leon had climbed out of the driver's seat.

It was Imogen, her pale face pressed against the window, staring up at me.

For a moment our gazes locked. I don't know what my face showed but hers showed nothing.

Then Dad roared, 'Wilf! Get yourself down here!'

The time for flight was past. I went down and met my fate.

It wasn't as bad as I'd feared. Sir Leon was very laid back about things. He said boys always fight, it's in their genes, and he was sure my blow had been more in sport than in earnest, and Johnny's nose wasn't broken, and he was sure a little note of apology would set all things well.

Dad stood over me while I wrote it.

Dear Johnny, I'm really sorry I made your nose bleed, I didn't mean to, it was an accident. Yours sincerely Wilfred Hadda.

Dad also wanted me to write to Lady Kira, but Sir Leon said that wouldn't be necessary, he'd pass on my verbal apologies.

As he left, he punched me lightly on the arm and said, 'Us wolves need to pick our moments to growl, eh?'

I expected Dad to really whale into me after Sir Leon had gone, but he just looked at me and said, 'So that's a lesson to us both, lad, one I thought I'd learned a long time back. My fault. Folks like us and folks like the Ulphingstones don't mix.'

'Because they're better than us?' I asked.

'Nay!' he said sharply. 'The Haddas are as good as any

106

bugger. But if you put banties in with turtle doves, you're going to get ructions!'

And that was it. He obviously felt in part responsible. Me, I suppose I should have been delighted to get off so lightly, but as I lay in bed that night, all I could think of was Imogen, and why she'd accompanied her father to Birkstane.

I found out the next day. She wanted to be sure she knew how to get there by herself. I left the house as usual straight after breakfast, i.e. about seven a.m. Dad got up at six and so did Aunt Carrie. Breakfast was the one meal of the day she could be relied on for, so long as you were happy to have porridge followed by scrambled egg, sausage and black pudding all the year round. If I decided to have a lie-in, the penalty was I had to make my own, so usually I got up.

It was a beautiful late July morning. The sun had been up for a good hour and a half and the morning mists were being sucked up the wooded fellside behind the house, clinging on to the tall pines like the last gauzy garments of a teasing stripper.

I hadn't any definite plan, it might well turn into a pleasant pottering-about, basking kind of day with a dip in the lake at the end of it, but in case I got the urge to do a bit of serious scrambling, I looped a shortish length of rope over my rucksack and clipped a couple of karabiners and slings to my belt.

I hadn't gone a hundred yards before Imogen stepped out from behind a tree and blocked my path.

I didn't know what to say so said nothing.

She was wearing a T-shirt, shorts and trainers. On her back was a small pack, on her head a huge sunhat that shaded her face so I could not see her expression.

She said, 'Johnny says you punched him 'cos he was rude about my dancing. He said if I saw you to tell you he's OK and it was a jolly good punch.'

107

I remember feeling surprise. In Nutbrown's shoes I don't think I'd have been anywhere near as gracious. In fact I know bloody well I wouldn't!

I said, 'Is that what you've come to tell us? Grand. Then I'll be off.'

I pushed by her rudely and strode away. I thought I'd left her standing but after a moment I heard her voice behind me saying, 'So where are we going?'

I spun round to face her and snapped, 'I'm going climbing. Don't know where you're going. Don't care either.'

In case you're wondering, Elf, how come I was talking like this to the same girl I'd fallen for so utterly and irreversibly just the day before, you should recall I was a fifteen-year-old lad, uncouth as they came, with even fewer communication skills than most of the breed because there were so very few people I wanted to communicate with.

Also, let's be honest, standing still in shorts and trainers with her golden hair hidden beneath that stupid hat, it was hard to believe this was the visionary creature I'd seen dancing on the lawn.

My mind was in a whirl so I set off again because that seemed the only alternative to standing there, looking at her.

She fell into step beside me when the terrain permitted, a yard behind me when it didn't. I set a cracking pace, a lot faster than I would have done if I'd been by myself, but it didn't seem to trouble her. When I got to the lake, that's Wastwater, I deliberately headed along the path on the southeast side, the one at the foot of what they call the Screes, a thousand feet or so of steep, unstable rock that only an idiot would mess with. Even the so-called path that tracks the lake's edge is a penance, involving a tedious mile or so of scrambling across awkwardly placed boulders. I thought that would soon shake her off, but she was still there at the far end. So now I crossed the valley and went up by the inn at

Wasdale Head into Mosedale, not stopping until I reached Black Sail Pass between Kirk Fell and Pillar.

This was a good six miles over some pretty rough ground and she was still with me, no more out of breath than I was. Now I found I had a dilemma. The further I went, particularly if as usual I wandered off the main well-trodden paths, the more I'd be stuck with her. But she could easily retrace the path we'd come by back to the valley road, and on a day like this, there would be plenty of walkers tracking across Black Sail, so I felt I could dump her here without too much trouble to my conscience.

I sat down and took a drink from the bottle of water I carried in my sack. She produced a can of cola and drank from that.

I said, 'That's stupid.'

'Why's that?' she said, not sounding offended but genuinely interested.

'Because you can't seal it up again like a bottle. You've got to drink the lot.'

'So I'll drink the lot.'

'What happens when you get thirsty again?'

'I'll open another one,' she said, grinning and shaking her rucksack till I could hear several cans rattling against each other. 'Like a drink?'

She offered me the can. I shook my head. I wouldn't have minded, but drinking out of a can that had touched her mouth seemed a bit too intimate when I was planning to dump her.

I said, 'Won't your mam and dad be worrying about you?'

She said, 'No. They think I'm out walking up Greendale with Jules and Pippa.'

These it emerged were two of the other girls I'd seen the previous day. Imogen had proposed they all went out walking today, but when she revealed her plan involved getting up really early, two of them had dropped out. It said much for her powers of persuasion that she'd persuaded the other two to go along with her. It said even more that she'd got them to agree to cover up for her when she announced she was taking off on her own the moment they were out of sight of the castle.

'I've arranged to meet them at five,' she said, 'so that gives us plenty of time.'

'To do what?' I was foolish enough to ask.

'Whatever you're going to do,' she said expectantly. 'Sounds like it could be fun. A lot better than anything that was likely to happen with Jules and Pippa.'

It turned out she'd made enquiries about me, of Sir Leon and also of some of the locals who worked at the castle.

From them she'd learned that I spent most of my spare time roaming the countryside, 'getting up to God knows what kind of mischief'. She heard the story of my accident, my miraculous survival, and my subsequent exploits with some of the mountain rescue team. She'd also learned that I was usually up with the lark, so when she resolved to tag along with me, she knew she had to contrive an early start.

The trouble was, in letting her explain all this to me, I had taken a significant step towards the role of fellow conspirator. If I tried to dump her, I could now see that she was quite capable of following at a distance. I could have tried to take her back to the castle, but I had no way to compel her. And one thing I knew for certain, if ever it became known that she hadn't spent the day with her friends, no way would my pleas of complete innocence cut any ice with Lady Kira.

So I was stuck with her. The best plan looked to be to keep her occupied a couple of hours and above all make sure that she kept her rendezvous with the other two girls.

'Right,' I said. 'Time to move.'

We stood up. I noticed she just left her Coke can lying on the ground. I gave it a kick. She looked down at it, looked up at me, thought for a moment, then grinned and picked it up and stuffed it into her sack.

Daft, but somehow that acknowledgement that I was the boss gave me a thrill, so rather than simply lead her up the main track on to Pillar, I decided to take her round by the High Level route that winds above Ennerdale and eventually leads to the summit by a steep scramble at the back of Pillar Rock.

It was a bad mistake. It turned out she'd heard of Pillar Rock because a friend's brother had had a fall there in the spring and broken both his legs.

'Yeah,' I said. 'I remember. I know a couple of the guys who brought him down. They said him and his mates were real wankers, didn't know what they were doing.'

'My friend said her brother had been climbing in the Alps,' she protested.

'Oh yeah? Can't have been all that good if he managed to come off the Slab and Notch,' I declared, annoyed that my mountain rescue friends' verdict should be called in doubt. 'It's nowt but a scramble. Don't even need a rope.'

This was laying it on a bit thick. OK, in terms of climbing difficulty, this most popular route up the Rock really is classed as a Grade-3 scramble. But it's got tremendous exposure. If you come off, you fall a long way. Only real climbers, or real idiots, go up there without a rope. The guy they brought down in the spring was lucky to get away with nothing worse than a couple of smashed legs.

She said, 'You've been up it then?'

'Couple of times.'

'By yourself?'

'Yeah.'

It was true. The first time I'd been ten and back then I

suppose I was a real idiot. I was like a spider, scuttling up rock faces that give me vertigo now just thinking about them. How the hell I never got cragfast, I don't know.

I'd got a bit more sense since my close encounter with the mountain rescue, but I still liked climbing by myself. The second time I went up Pillar Rock had been the previous spring. After I heard my mountain rescue friends talking about the accident, some ghoulish subconscious impulse took me back there. I remember pausing in the Notch and looking down and picturing the guy tumbling through the air. I wondered what it must feel like. All I had to do to find out was let go.

Don't worry, it wasn't a serious thought. If I was going to fall, it would be off something that would impress my rescue mates! But dismissing the Slab and Notch as a 'mere' scramble now got me into more bother.

'Let's go up there then,' she said.

'With you? No way!'

'Why not? You just said it was dead easy.'

'Yeah, but not for someone like you.'

'What do you mean, like me? We do climbing at my school. I've been on the wall at the sports centre.'

This was true, though, as I learned later, Imogen's desire to take up rock climbing seriously had provoked a loud and unified negative from her parents, and the school had been instructed to make sure she didn't get near the wall again.

Well, her parents might have got their way, but with me it was no contest.

In my defence, she did make it clear that she was going to have a go with or without me, and by going along with her at least I could make sure she was on the end of my rope.

And to tell the truth, this readiness of hers to go spidering up a rock face the way I'd been doing for years had an effect on me like the sight of her dancing on the lawn.

So up we went, me first, then Imogen after I'd got her belayed. There were no problems, and she clearly wasn't in the slightest fazed by having several hundred feet of air beneath her at the most exposed points.

It was worth it just to see her face as she stood on the top of the rock.

It's a marvellous place to be, beautifully airy in three directions with the huge bulk of Pillar Fell itself looming behind.

She drank it all in then she turned towards me, a wide smile on her face.

'Thanks,' she said, pulling her hat off so that her golden hair once more floated in the gentle breeze.

Then in one fluid movement she pulled her T-shirt over her head, kicked off her trainers, pushed down her shorts and stepped out of them.

'Would you like to fuck me?' she said.

I stood staring at her, dumbfounded.

Part of me was thinking that anyone on their way up the path to the summit of Pillar has a perfect view of the top of the rock.

Another part was thinking there was next to nothing of her! She was so skinny her ribs showed, her breasts looked like they'd just begun to form, she looked more like ten than fourteen. She was as far as you could get from those pneumatic images in the porn mags that got passed around at school.

But despite the danger of being overlooked, despite her lack of any obvious feminine attractiveness, my heart and my soul and, yes, my body was crying out in answer to her question: Oh yes, I'd like to fuck you very much!

And I did.

What was it like? It was a first for me, and for her too. I knew that because I ended up with blood on my cock. So, a pair of raw virgins, but we meshed like we'd been doing it for years, and unless they ran lessons in faking it at that expensive boarding school of hers, she enjoyed it every bit as much as I did. I can't take any credit for that. While it was happening I was totally absorbed in my own feelings. But afterwards as we lay wrapped in each other's arms, I knew I wanted this to be for ever.

In the end it was her who pushed me away and stood up.

'Mustn't be late,' she said, 'or those two will run scared and give the game away.'

She got dressed as quickly as she'd stripped, but not through any modest need to cover up. I've never met anyone as unself-conscious as Imogen.

I lay there and watched her, then followed suit. She would have done the descent unroped, but I wouldn't let her.

On the long walk back I don't think we exchanged more than half a dozen words. There was lots I wanted to say but, like I told you, communication wasn't my thing.

With about a quarter mile to go she halted and put her hand on my chest.

'I'm OK from now on,' she said.

I said, 'Yeah. When . . . how . . .?'

'Don't worry,' she said. 'I'll find you when I want you.'

And she was gone.

So there you have it, Elf. Sex, rites of passage, teenage trauma, all the steamy stuff you people like to paddle your inquisitive little fingers in.

Watch out that you don't find yourself touching something nasty!

But that's what turns you on, isn't it?

That's what turns you on!

Elf

i

When she was thirteen Alva Ozigbo's English teacher had asked her class to write about what they wanted to be when they grew up.

That night Alva sat so long over the assignment that both her parents asked if there was something they could help with.

She regarded them long and assessingly before shaking her head.

Her father, Ike, big, black and ebullient, was a consultant cardiologist at the Greater Manchester Teaching Hospital. Her mother, Elvira, slender, blonde and self-contained, had been an actress. She'd left her native Sweden in her teens to study in London in the belief that the English-speaking world would offer far greater opportunities. For a while her Scandinavian looks had got her parts that required Scandinavian looks, but it soon became clear that her best future lay on the stage. The nearest she got to a film career was being screen-tested for a Bergman movie. She still talked of it as a missed opportunity but the truth was the camera didn't love her. On screen she became almost transparent, and by her mid-twenties she was resigned to a career of secondary roles in the theatre. She was Dina in *The Pillars of the Community* at the Royal Exchange when she met Ike Ozigbo. When they married six months later, she made a rare joke as they walked down the aisle together after the ceremony.

'I always knew I'd get a starring role one day.'

To which he'd romantically replied, 'And it's going to be a record-breaking run!'

So it had proved.

Thirteen-year-old Alva was proud of her father, but it had always been her mother she pestered for stories of her life on the stage. Now, after vacillating for a good hour between the two main exemplars in her life, it was not without a small twinge of disloyalty that she finally wrote that what she wanted to be was an actress.

At the time she meant it. But somewhere over the next few years that urge to get inside the skin of a character had changed from interpretation to analysis. She discovered that wanting to understand was not the same as wanting to be. The actress had to lose herself in the part; Alva found that she wanted to preserve herself, to remain the detached observer even as all the intricate wirings of personality and motivation were laid bare.

Psychiatry gave her that option, but she soon discovered that the observer had to be an actor too. When she read Hadda's account of his first encounters with Imogen, she felt a great surge of excitement. To be sure, there was a deal of hyperbole here. The bolder the picture he painted of himself as the victim of a grand passion for one woman, the dimmer his sense of that other degrading and disgusting passion became. But in his effort to stress that his love for Imogen was based on some collision of mind and spirit rather than simply a natural adolescent lust, he had fallen into a trap of his own setting.

What did he say? Here it was . . . *there was next to nothing of her! She was so skinny her ribs showed, her breasts looked like they'd just begun to form, she looked more like ten than fourteen.* . . Yet he'd been sexually roused by this prepubescent figure, and sexually satisfied too. This was probably what he saw in his fantasies thereafter, this was the source of those desires that had brought about his downfall.

She recalled a passage in the first piece he'd written for her, when he was in his best hard-nosed thriller mode.

Imogen was sitting up in bed by this time. Even in these fraught circumstances I was distracted by sight of her perfect breasts.

Stressing his red-blooded maleness, trying to distract her attention, and his own, away from the fact that it was unformed new-budding bosoms that really turned him on.

And now she knew she would need to call upon her acting skills when next she saw him. She must give no hint that she saw in this narrative anything more than an honest and moving account of first love. Indeed, it might be well to give him a quick glimpse of that Freudian prurience he was accusing her of. He was, she judged, a man who liked to be right, who was used to having his assessments of people and policies confirmed. No way could she hope to drive such a man to that final climactic confrontation with his own dark inner self, but with care and patience she might eventually lead him there.

Another spur to caution was the fact that he'd obviously got the writing bug. She'd seen this happen in other cases. The people she dealt with were more often than not obsessive characters and this was something she liked to use to her advantage. Her guess was that he'd have another exercise book ready for her, but if she annoyed him, he'd punish her by not handing it over.

That was his weapon.

Hers of course was his desire that what he wrote should be read! Withholding it might punish her, but only at the expense of punishing himself.

So she prepared for her next session with more than usual care.

ii

'Wolf,' she said. 'Tell me about your father.'

'What?'

She'd wrong-footed him, she could tell. He'd expected her to home in on that first sexual engagement on top of Pillar Rock.

'Fred, your father. Is he still alive?'

'Ah. I see where we're going. Oedipus stuff, right? No, I didn't blame him for my mother's death; no, I didn't want to kill him; and no, just in case you're too shy to ask, he never abused me in any way. Unless you count the odd clip around the ear, that is.'

'In some circumstances, I might indeed count that,' she said, smiling. 'I was just wondering about his attitude to what's happened, that's all. You do indicate that when it came to your marriage with Imogen, he wasn't all that keen.'

That got the flicker of a smile. The smiles, though hardly regular, came more frequently now. She took that as a sign of progress, though, paradoxically, in physical terms her goal was tears, not smiling.

'That's putting it mildly,' he said. 'He was even more opposed than Sir Leon. He at least in the end gave his daughter away. Dad wouldn't even come to the wedding.'

'Did that hurt you very much?'

'Of course it bloody hurt me,' he said angrily. 'But I was ready for it, I suppose. He wasn't exactly supportive when

118

I started bettering myself. I thought he'd be proud of me, but he made it quite clear that he thought I'd have done better to follow in his footsteps and become a forester.'

'Did he have any reason to think that was what you were going to do?'

Hadda shrugged and said, 'Yeah, I suppose so. I'd always gone along with the assumption that I'd leave school as soon as I could and start working under him on the estate. I mean, why wouldn't I? I loved working with him, I'd been wielding an axe almost since I was big enough to pick up a teddy bear without falling over. And working outdoors in the countryside I loved seemed the best way of carrying on the way I was.'

'So what changed?'

'Don't act stupid. You know what changed. I met Imogen.'

'You carried on meeting after that first time?'

'Obviously. All that summer, whenever we could. She needed to keep quiet about it of course. Me too. It was easier in my case, I just went on as normal, taking off in the morning with my walking and climbing gear. She had to make excuses. She was good at that, I guess. She couldn't manage every day, but if three days went by without her showing up, I started getting seriously frustrated.'

'You continued having sex?'

'Why wouldn't we?'

'She was under age. And the danger of pregnancy. Did you start using condoms?'

'No, she said she'd taken care of all that. As for her age, I suppose I was under age too to start with. Anyway, it never crossed my mind. We were at it all the time. Always out of doors and in all weathers. On the fellside, in the forest.'

He smiled reminiscently.

'There was this old rowan tree that had survived among all the conifers that had been planted commercially on the estate. We often used to meet there early morning or late

119

evening if one of us couldn't manage to get away for the whole day. Imo would slip out of the castle and I would go over the wall behind Birkstane, and be there in twenty minutes or so. We didn't even have to make a special arrangement. It was like we both knew the other would be there under the tree.'

'This was the rowan you had dug up and transplanted to your London garden?'

He said, 'You remembered! Yes, the very same. They were harvesting the conifers in that part of the forest and it looked as if the rowan would simply be mowed down to give the big machines access. So I saved it. A romantic gesture, don't you think?'

'More sentimental, I'd say. Men in particular look back fondly on their adolescent encounters. Pleasure without responsibility, I can see its attraction. So you'd meet under this tree, have a quick bang, then go home?'

This was a deliberate provocation. The clue to what he'd become had to lie in this first significant sexual relationship.

He looked at her coldly.

'It wasn't like that. We drew each other like magnets. I felt her presence wherever I was, whatever I was doing. She was always with me. Under the rowan we were in total union, but no matter how far apart physically, she was always with me.'

She was tempted to probe how he felt now, whether he still believed that Imogen had genuinely shared that intensity of feeling. But she judged this wasn't the right moment. Concentrate on getting the facts.

'So when did it end?'

'How do you know it ended?'

'Because it had to. From what you say of Lady Kira, she wasn't going to be fooled for ever. Also that first piece you wrote, the one about living in a fairy tale, in it you talk

120

about the woodcutter's son being given three impossible tasks and going away and performing them. That implies an ending – and a new beginning, of course.'

'Did I write that? Yes, I did, didn't I? It seems a long time ago, somehow.'

'Three weeks,' she said.

'Is that all? We've come a long way.'

He spoke neutrally and she was tempted to probe but decided against it. The more progress you made, the more dangerous the ground became.

'So, the end,' she said.

'It was in the Christmas holidays,' he said slowly. 'We'd both gone back to school in the autumn, her to her fancy ladies' college in the south, me to the comp. I couldn't wait for the term to finish.'

'You didn't think she might have had second thoughts about your relationship during those months apart?'

'Never crossed my mind,' he said wearily. 'Not vanity, if that's what you're thinking. It was just a certainty, like knowing the sun would rise. But when we met in December, it was harder for us to get whole days together when the weather was bad. I mean, a teenage girl wanting to go for a solitary stroll in the summer sunshine is one thing. In a winter gale it's much more suspicious. We met more and more often under the rowan tree. A blizzard blew up, it was practically a white-out. We sheltered among the trees till things improved a bit, then I insisted on accompanying her back through the grounds till the castle was in sight. Sir Leon had got worried and organized a little search party that included my dad. We met them on the estate drive. I'd have tried to bluff it out, say I'd run into Imogen somewhere and offered to see her home, but she didn't bother. I think she was right. They weren't going to believe us. I went home with Fred, she went home with Sir Leon to face her mother.'

121

'What did Fred say?'

'He asked me what I thought I was doing. I told him we were in love, that I was going to marry her as soon as I legally could. He said, "Forget the law, there's no law ever passed that'll let you marry that lass!" I said, "Why not? There's nowt anyone can say that'll make a difference." And he laughed, more snarl than a laugh, and he said that up at the castle the difference had been made a long time back. I didn't know what he meant, not until the next day.'

'You saw Imogen again?' guessed Alva.

'Oh yes. Sir Leon brought her down to Birkstane. They left us alone together. I grabbed hold of her and began gabbling about it making no difference, we could still do what we planned, we could run away together, and so on, lots of callow adolescent stuff. She pushed me away and said, sort of puzzled, "Wolf, don't talk silly. We never planned anything." And she was right, I realized later. All the plans had been in my head.'

'And was this when she set you the three impossible tasks?' asked Alva.

'Who's a clever little shrink then?' he mocked. 'Yes, suddenly this girl every bit of whose body I knew as well as my own turned into something as cold and distant as the North Pole. She said she was sorry, it had been great fun, but she'd assumed I knew as well as she did that it would have to come to an end eventually. I managed to stutter, "Why?" And she told me. With brutal frankness.'

His face darkened at the memory, still potent after all these years.

Alva prompted, 'What did she say?'

'She said surely I could see how impossible it would be for her to marry someone who couldn't speak properly, had neither manners nor education, and was likely to remain on a working man's wage all his life.'

Jesus! thought Alva. They really do bring their princesses up differently!

'So these were the three impossible tasks?' she said. 'Get elocution lessons, get educated, get rich. And you resolved you would amaze everyone by performing them?'

'Don't be silly. I had a short fuse, remember? I went into a right strop, told her she was a stuck-up little cow just like her mam, that I weren't ashamed to talk the way everyone else round here talked, that a Hadda were as good as an Ulphingstone any day of the week, and that my dad said all a man needs is enough money to buy what's necessary for him to live. She smiled and said, "Clearly you don't put me in that category. That's good. I'll see you around." And she went.'

'She sounds very self-contained for a fourteen-year-old,' said Alva.

'She was fifteen by then,' he said, as if this made a difference. 'And I was sixteen.'

'What did you do?'

'I moped all over Christmas. Must have been unliveable with. Dad headed off to the Dog as often as he could. Then New Year came. Time for resolutions about changing your life, according to the guys on the telly. I started fantasizing about leaving home, having lots of adventures, striking it rich by finding a gold mine or something, then returning, all suave and sexy like one of them TV presenters, to woo Imogen. Only she wouldn't know it was me till she'd been overcome by my manly charms. Pathetic, eh?'

'We all have our dreams,' said Alva, recalling her teenage fantasies of collecting a best actress Oscar.

'Yeah. I'd like to say I set off to chase mine, but it wouldn't be true. I just knew that, whatever I wanted, I wasn't going to get it hanging around in Cumbria. So I set off to school one morning with everything I owned in my sports bag and

123

all the money I could raise in my pocket. And I just kept on going. The rest as they say is history.'

'I'd still like to hear it,' said Alva.

'Come on!' he said. 'You strike me as a conscientious little researcher. The meteoric rise of Wilfred Hadda from uncouth Cumbrian peasant to multi-millionaire master of the universe has been charted so often you must have got it by heart!'

'Indeed,' she said, reaching into her document case. 'I've got copies of most of the articles here. There's general agreement on events after your return. But their guesses at what you did between running away as a poor woodcutter's son and coming back with your rough edges smoothed and enough money in the bank to launch your business career make speculation about Lord Lucan read like a Noddy story. Anyone get close?'

'How would I know? I never read them. Which looks best to you?'

'Well, I'm torn between the South American diamond mine and the Mexican lottery. But on the whole I'd go for the *Observer* writer, who reckons you probably got kidnapped by the fairies, like True Thomas in the ballad.'

That made him laugh, a rare sound, the kind of laugh that made you want to join in.

'Yeah, go with that one,' he said. 'Away with the fairies, that's about right. Did he have a good time, this Thomas fellow?'

'It was a strange place they took him too,' said Alva. 'Hang on, he quotes from the ballad in his article. You'll have to excuse my Scots accent.'

She opened the file and began to read.

> *'It was mirk mirk night, there was nae stern light,*
> *And they waded through red blude to the knee;*
> *For a' the blude that's shed on earth*
> *Rins through the springs o' that countrie.'*

When she finished he nodded vigorously and said, 'Oh yes, that guy knows what he's talking about. So how did Thomas make out when he got back?'

'Well, he had a bit of a problem, Wolf,' she said. 'The one condition of his return was that thereafter he was never able to tell a lie.'

Their gazes locked. Then he smiled, not his attractive winning smile this time, but something a lot more knowing, almost mocking.

'Just like me then, Elf,' he said. 'That old lie-detector mind of yours must have spotted long ago that you're getting nothing but gospel truth from me!'

'Gospel? Somehow I doubt if your runaway years had much of religion in them!'

'You're so wrong, Elf,' he said with a grin. 'I was a regular attender at chapel.'

'Chapel?' she said. 'Not church? That's interesting. None of the speculation in the papers suggested a religious dimension to your disappearance.'

'For God's sake,' he said, suddenly irritated. 'Can we get away from what those fantasists dream up? Look, Elf, I'm trying to be honest with you, but if I say there's something I don't want to talk about, you've got to accept it, OK?'

'OK, OK,' she said making a note. 'Let's cut to the chase. Age twenty-one, you're back with a suitcase full of cash, talking like a gent, no longer sucking your peas off your knife, and able to tell a hawk from a handsaw. How did Imogen greet you?'

'She asked me to dinner at the castle. There were two or three other guests. Sir Leon was very polite to me. Lady Kira watched me like the Ice Queen but hardly spoke. I joined in the conversation, managed to use the right cutlery and didn't knock over any wine glasses. After dinner Imogen took me out into the garden, allegedly to cast my so-called expert eye over a new magnolia planted to replace one that hadn't made it through the winter. Out of sight of the house she stopped and turned to face me. "Well, will I do?" I asked. "Let's see," she said. And stepped out of her dress with the same ease that she'd stepped out of her shorts and trainers on Pillar Rock all those years ago. When we finished, she said, "You'll do." Couple of months later we married.'

'Despite all the family objections?'

'We had a trump card by then. Imo was pregnant. With Ginny. Made no difference to Dad and Sir Leon. They still stood out against the marriage. But Lady Kira seemed to see it made sense and that was enough. She calls the shots at the castle. Always did. So poor Leon had no choice but to give his blessing, and shake the mothballs out of his morning dress to give the bride away.'

'Poor Leon?' she echoed. 'You sound as if you have some sympathy for him.'

'Why not? He's married to the Ice Queen, isn't he? No, fair do's, he may not have wanted me for his son-in-law, but I always got on well with Leon. And he went out of his way to try to make things right between me and my dad. Just about managed it the first two times. Third time was beyond human help.'

'I'm sorry . . .?'

Hadda said bleakly, 'Think about it. They say things come in threes, don't they? They certainly did for Fred. One, I disappeared for five years. Two, I came back and married Imogen against his wish and his judgment. Three, I got sent down for fraud and messing with young girls. Three times I broke his heart. The last time it didn't mend.'

And who do you blame for that? wondered Alva. But this wasn't the time to get aggressive, not when she'd got him talking about what had to be one of the most significant relationships in his life.

She said, 'But the first two times, you say Leon tried to help?'

'Oh yes. I think he recognized Dad and me were carved from the same rock. Left to our own devices, we'd probably never have spoken again! Don't know what he said to Fred about me, but he told me that, after I vanished, often he'd go into the forest with Imogen, and they'd find Dad just sitting slumped against the old rowan, staring into space, completely out of it. Sometimes there'd be tears on his cheeks. It cracked me up, just hearing about it. So whenever I felt like telling Dad that if he wanted to be a stubborn old fool, he could just get on with it, I'd think of what Leon had told me and try to bite my tongue. Gradually things got better between us. And when Ginny was born . . .'

He stopped abruptly and glared at her as if defying her to question him further about his daughter.

She said, 'So did Fred attend the wedding?'

'Oh no,' said Wolf, relaxing. 'That would have been too much. I hoped right up till the ceremony started he'd show up. Then, once it started, I was scared he might!'

'Why?'

'That bit when the vicar asks if anyone knows of any impediment, I imagined the church door bursting open and Fred coming in with his axe and yelling, "How's this for an impediment?" I remember, after the vicar asked the question he seemed to pause for ever. Then Johnny glanced round to the back of the church and shouted, "Speak up then" and that set everyone laughing.'

'Johnny . . .?'

'Johnny Nutbrown. He was my best man.'

'A large step from being the nose-bleeding object of your anger,' she said. 'How did that come about?'

'You mean, how come I didn't have any old friends of my own to take on the job? Simple. I was always a loner and

127

the few half friendships I formed at school didn't survive my transformation, as you call it.'

'But didn't you make any new ones during this transformation period?' she asked. 'Even lowly woodcutters on a quest to perform three impossible tasks probably need a bit of human contact on the way.'

'I don't know, I didn't meet any others,' he said shortly.

Then he pushed back his chair and stood up, reaching into his blouson as he did so.

'You're curious about me and Johnny Nutbrown?' he said. 'Well, I think you'll find all you need to know in here.'

And there it was, the next exercise book just as she'd hypothesized.

But by producing it he had once again stepped aside from talking about those missing years, so as she took the book, she felt it less as a triumph than an evasion.

Wolf

i

Let's move on from our little diversion into childhood trauma and adolescent sexuality, shall we? Where was I before you nudged me down that fascinating side road?

Oh yes.

I'd been in a coma for the best part of nine months.

During the early stages of my so-called recovery, I've no idea what proportion of my time I spent out of things. All I do know is that every period of full lucidity seemed to provide the opportunity for a new piece of shit to be hurled at me.

I rapidly came to see that, far from things going away while I lay unconscious, they had got immeasurably and by now irrecoverably worse.

Let me lay them out, not in any particular order.

The charges against me had multiplied and intensified.

It seems that during the panic caused by my false terrorist attack warning to the Magistrates Court, several people had been injured and one had died. Didn't matter that like me he was a prisoner waiting to face committal proceedings, that he too tried to escape in the panic, slipped on the stairs, and suffered a heart attack from a long-standing condition, the bastards still added a charge of manslaughter to the offence of making a hoax terrorist call which was worth a long jail sentence in itself.

In addition, the bus driver had been severely traumatized, several of his passengers had been hurt, two patrons of the pavement café had been hospitalized, and the driver of the Range Rover turned out to be a barrister, and he was orchestrating a whole battery of civil claims against me.

But these were the least of my troubles. In face of these charges there was nothing to do but put my hand up and plead guilty, only offering in mitigation the tremendous strain the manifestly ludicrous allegations of paedophilia had put me under.

Except they were no longer manifestly ludicrous. In fact they had moved on from the passive downloading of pornographic images to devastating accusations that I was actively involved in the whole revolting business, both as commercial organizer and active participant.

The InArcadia website, it was alleged, had been set up and maintained by money channelled through one of my off-shore companies. Some of the video footage obtained from InArcadia was identified as having been shot at various of my overseas properties. And in several scenes of a particularly revolting nature, there were glimpses of a naked back that bore a scar similar to mine.

There had been a steady leak of much of this material into the public domain and I'd already been tried, judged and condemned by the media, a verdict that must have seemed confirmed by the news that Imogen had started divorce proceedings.

And was this the end?

No, Elf, you bet your sweet life it wasn't!

Back in 2008 we could all hear the rumblings of the approaching economic storm. I admit I was rather smug about it and arrogantly assumed Woodcutter was soundly enough rigged to ride it out. When I woke from my trance, I found the tempest had struck with even greater force than anyone had anticipated and the economies of the Western world were in tatters.

Had I been around, I might have been able to do something to limit the damage to Woodcutter.

Or, as the *Financial Times* put it, 'Possibly if Sir Wilfred's grubby paw had still been on the helm, he might have been able to steer the most seaworthy of his piratical fleet into some extrajudicial haven, but left unmanned in those desperate seas, they either sank with all hands or were boarded and taken in tow by the local excise men.'

In times of crisis, journalists often erupt in flowery excrescence.

To continue in the same vein, as far as I could make out many of my old shipmates had leapt overboard clutching whatever portable pillage they could, while others had surrendered to the invading officers and saved their own worthless carcases from the yard-arm by offering them mine!

My initial assumption had been that the morning raid on my house was part of a Fraud Office investigation, and I recalled my airy reassurance to Toby that there was nothing for them to find.

Now I had the Fraud Office crawling all over my affairs and finding all kinds of crap! The worst of it was that I couldn't remember in most instances whether I knew it was there or not. The trauma of the accident had left so many gaps both physical and mental that my degree of recovery was always in doubt. But *I can't remember* is not a line of defence that wins much sympathy from a stony-faced financial investigator.

But none of these events and accusations hit me like the news that Imogen was planning to divorce me. And even that wasn't the end of the trauma. The very next day they broke the news to me that Fred had suffered a serious stroke and while I had been lying in my coma, he'd been lying in the twilight state of the stroke victim.

I was desperate to see him, but I wasn't fit to travel even if the authorities had given me permission. DC McLucky was very helpful here, bringing me the phone and getting me connected to the Northern hospital where Dad was a patient. According to the consultant I spoke to, Dad's condition was still extremely serious. He wasn't willing to even estimate just how far any recovery process might take him.

Fred and I had slowly moved back towards each other after the rift over my marriage. Ginny made the difference. In a way I'm glad he wasn't around to hear of her death.

Back then I was devastated by the prospect that I might never see him again.

McLucky did his best to reassure me in his forthright Glaswegian way. He it was who ran a check on the hospital and discovered that it had possibly the best stroke unit in the north of England, and that Fred was there as a private patient funded by no less a person than my dear old father-in-law, Sir Leon! It was a strange irony that their shared opposition to a Hadda–Ulphingstone marriage had turned their strong employer/employee bond into something like friendship and ultimately Fred had graduated from being the estate's head forester to more of an overall estate manager.

For several days, I could think about nothing else but my sick father and my estranged wife. I had plenty of time for thinking as, apart from the medical staff and DC McLucky, I saw no one.

As I've said, I'd never been a particularly sociable man and as I became rich and powerful, I put little faith in the pretensions of new acquaintance to genuine affection. But people seemed to like me and I did form a small circle of friends to whom I would once have applied the old-fashioned designation of *faithful and true*.

Not one of the faithful and the true made an effort to contact me or turned up to see me in hospital. Wankers! I thought. But why should any of them prove more faithful and true than my own wife and my good friend and solicitor, Toby Estover?

The only one I felt confident would show me some loyalty was Johnny Nutbrown.

As I've already told you, my first encounter with Johnny age fifteen was far from auspicious. On my return after my years away with the fairies, I was rather surprised to find him still around. While Johnny is always at ease everywhere, he never gives an impression of actually belonging anywhere. Of course he'd been to the same school as some of the others, including Estover, and also he had a bad case of the hots for Imo's best friend, Pippa Thursby. So they were good enough reasons for him to be on the fringe of their magic little circle.

But I never counted him as being truly in it, which was a plus for me.

I'm sure Imogen had to put up with a lot of crap from her friends when she announced she was going to marry me. She never passed any of it on, and it wouldn't have bothered me if she had. Frankly, I thought most of them were a waste of space that could have been more usefully occupied by a flock of Herdwicks. All the interest most of them showed in me was a prurient curiosity about the parameters of the sexual performance they were sure must be the basis of Imogen's interest. I think I could probably have shagged the lot of them, men and women, if I'd been so inclined.

But Johnny saw me differently. Later, when we got close

enough for honesty, he told me with that cynical grin of his, 'The others looked at you and thought *big fucks;* I looked at you and thought *big bucks.* This guy is going where the money is.'

I couldn't complain about this economic basis for our relationship as initially I only became interested in him when I realized he'd got the sharpest mind for figures of anyone I'd ever met. If it had been allied to an entrepreneurial spirit, he would have been a master of the commercial universe in his own right.

I soon realized we were made for each other.

The thing was that Johnny could do just about anything, so long as someone told him what to do.

An old schoolmate of his – in fact, Toby Estover my former solicitor, and former friend – told me about Johnny's first appearance on a rugby field. As he evinced neither interest nor talent, they stuck him on the wing for a practice game. The first time the ball was passed to him, he caught it one-handed and was standing still, examining it with mild curiosity, when most of the opposing team jumped on top of him. When he'd got back on his feet, the games master expostulated, 'For heaven's sake, Nutbrown, I don't expect you to do much when you get the ball, but I do expect you to do *something*!'

'Yes, sir. What exactly?' replied Johnny.

'Well, ideally I'd like to see you run forward as fast as you can, not letting anyone touch you, until you reach those two tall posts sticking out of the ground, and then place the ball gently between them. Failing that, as I'm sure you will, just kick it as far as you can!'

'Yes, sir,' said Johnny.

And next time he received the ball, he jinked and side-stepped his way the length of the field without anyone laying a hand upon him and touched down between the posts. The only trouble was the *next* time he took a pass he chose the alternative instruction and kicked it as far as he could, this being sideways over the line of poplars separating the ground from a river into which the ball plopped, never to be seen again.

That was the thing about Johnny. You had to tell him what to do, you had to be clear what you were telling him, and you had to tell him every time. We suited each other perfectly. I had the ambition, the energy and the imagination; and he had a mind that could run over my proposals, detect flaws, point out short-cuts, and calculate risks, often in the time it took to down the two large vodka martinis that were the inevitable precursor to lunch and dinner.

Without Johnny, I don't doubt I would have still managed to become stinking rich, but with him, the sweet stink of success came a lot quicker.

Without me, Johnny might well have degenerated into a sort of old-fashioned lounge-lizard, charming enough money to get by on out of a succession of susceptible women. I took some pride in having saved him from this fate, but rather less in having been responsible for his marriage.

Pippa Thursby, like many best friends, was all the things that Imogen wasn't.

While Imogen defied friends and family to marry the man she loved, Pippa never made any secret of the fact that though she found Johnny to be hugely attractive, highly entertaining, and a maestro of the mattress, he was merely (as she put it) stopping her gap until she could get her hands on some seriously wealthy old guy who would set her up for life by either death or divorce. She had her sights set on the MD of the advertising company for which she worked. Pippa was no featherbrain, she had excellent IT skills and could have carved out a successful career for herself, but she saw no reason to catch a train into work every day when she could get somebody else to do that on her behalf.

So Johnny was fun but marriage to someone so feckless simply wasn't an option. Then he and I got together, and things changed as it dawned on Pippa that my eruption towards the financial stratosphere was dragging Johnny in its wake.

Johnny himself was more than happy with his long-standing no-strings relationship, but he was dead meat once Pippa decided that life as Mrs Nutbrown could be a five-star arrangement after all. So three years after my own wedding, I was standing as best man at Johnny's.

As my closest colleague and my closest friend, I had hoped, nay I had believed, he would stand by me in turn.

I put it to the back of my mind as I set about trying to make sense of what was happening in my marriage.

DC McLucky had proved to be a rough diamond with a heart of gold. He even apologized obliquely for not being allowed to leave the phone permanently plugged in by my bedside, but he fetched it without demur whenever I asked for it. I tried without success to talk with Imogen. I rang Pippa but she told me bluntly that she couldn't help me and put the phone down. I rang my office and found the number was disconnected. When I got on to BT to complain, there was a long silence then I found myself connected to a DI in the Fraud Squad. I told him all the money was buried in a dead man's chest on a South Sea island but I'd lost the map, which wasn't very clever but I was getting beyond clever. I rang just about everyone I knew and found they were either uncommunicative or unavailable. A call from me clearly sounded like the tinkle of a leper's bell.

But I made no attempt to contact Johnny Nutbrown. I didn't mention him even when I spoke to his wife. I think it was superstition. If Johnny deserted me, then I was truly fucked. He would surely come to see me of his own accord. And in his own time, of course, for one thing you soon found out about Johnny was that his own time was not as other people's time.

But as the days passed and he didn't appear, I was ready to sink into despair.

Then one afternoon I woke up from yet another involuntary nap to find a lean, rangy figure sitting by my bed. His face was hidden behind a copy of the *Racing Times* but I didn't need to see his face to know who it was.

I felt a huge surge of happiness.

If you're interested in drawing a detailed map of my emotional progress, Elf, here is a significant moment to sketch in.

That is the last time I can recall feeling happy. I mean, what the fuck have I had to be happy about in the last seven years?

But, moron that I was, I felt happy then.

Johnny had come at last.

ii

As I fixed my one eye on Johnny, a second emotion came to join happiness.

It was relief.

The thing was he looked so relaxed, so completely unchanged from the man I had last seen many months earlier, or indeed from the elegant figure who'd winked at me as I passed him his wedding ring all those years ago, that it seemed impossible there could be anything seriously wrong with my life or my business.

'My dear old Wolf,' he said. 'So glad you've decided to join us.'

I pressed the button that raised the top end of the bed.

'Johnny, good to see you,' I croaked. 'Have you been here long?'

'Ten minutes or so. Chap in the corridor with a speech defect wanted to stop me, but I managed to talk him round.'

It was a comfort to know that not even DC McLucky was immune to the Nutbrown charm.

He said, 'Brought you a bunch of grapes. Could only get them processed, I'm afraid.'

He was wearing what he called his poacher's jacket. I don't think it was altogether a joke. Johnny would much rather help himself to a neighbour's birds than accept an invitation to an organized shoot. From one of the deep internal pockets he drew a bottle of red wine and from the other two goblets.

'Thank God for screw tops, eh?' he said, opening the bottle and filling the glasses. 'Bottoms up.'

We drank. It was my first alcohol and it tasted foul, but symbolically it was nectar. Despite everything I found myself thinking, with Johnny here, things must be on the up.

I said, 'So how're things looking, Johnny?'

For a moment my heart leapt as he said, 'Not so bad if you like lots of blue sky.'

Then he added with a grin, 'Of course, not much else to see when you've gone belly-up.'

It was then I recalled that never in any crisis situation, professional or personal, had I seen Johnny anything but relaxed! Here was a mind that could make sense of a vast acreage of figures at a glance but had no more concept of tomorrow than a gadfly.

'It can't be as bad as that, surely?' I said, still scrabbling for some scrap of hope.

'You weren't there,' he said. 'Might have been different if you had been. Did what I could but it was *sauve qui peut* with the rest of them. That arse Massie in charge of Off-shore just vanished. Even helped himself to those rather nice Gillray prints from his office wall. Then those awful Fraud Squad people started crawling all over the place. I stopped

138

going in after that. Nothing to do and they've got absolutely no conversation.'

I was genuinely bewildered by this indication of just how serious my business worries were.

I said, 'What the hell's going on, Johnny? Hell, we pushed the boundaries like everyone else, but we didn't step over them, or at least not very far.'

He shrugged and said, 'You know what they say, Wolf. When the tide goes out, that's when all the crap shows up on the beach. Not a lot of sympathy around for anyone just now, and with this other business, you are pretty well at the bottom of the list.'

'You mean the kiddy-porn stuff? For God's sake, Johnny, they can't make that stick.'

'No? Well, if anyone can beat the rap, I'd back you, Wolf.'

I didn't like the way he phrased that.

I said sharply, 'Johnny, you don't believe any of that crap, do you? I shouldn't need to tell you that it's just not true!'

He shrugged again and said, 'Whatever you say. Doesn't matter what I think, does it? Like my great uncle Nigel. Had this thing about sheep, no one in the family gave a damn, they were his sheep, weren't they? But when it hit the papers, that was different. Had to resign from his clubs. What the papers are saying about you, Wolf, well, all I can say is, if you can prove it's not true, no need to worry about the business. You'll be able to live like a lord on your profits from libel actions!'

I looked at him aghast. I'd always known Johnny lived in a different world from the rest of us, now I saw he lived in another dimension.

At least if he was giving me the truth as he saw it here, he was my best bet to get the truth about what took pride of place at the top of my mountain of worries.

I said, 'Is Imogen still staying with you?'

'Good lord, no. Moved out a few months back. Went up to Cumbria, easier to set mantraps for the press boys up there.'

'And Ginny?'

'Went with her, I think. Some talk of sending her off to this school in Paris, all the top people have their kids there so they've got better security than the Pentagon. Don't know whether she's gone yet or not, though.'

'Have you talked to her at all – Imogen, I mean? About the divorce?'

I don't know what I was looking for. Perhaps I had some faint hope that what Imogen was doing was in some way tactical, a legal move to put herself and some of our fortune beyond the reach of the circling sharks while I lay in a coma.

I wanted truth from Johnny. I got it.

'Yes, I had a chat when Pippa told me that was the way Imo was thinking. Nothing else for her to do really. I mean, it's a no-brainer. I expect Toby told her the same. Husband either a vegetable, or if he wakes, a convicted kiddy-fucker and fraudster. Either way, no point hanging about, get out quick as you can with as much as you can. Though the way things are looking, you've really got to be sorry for the poor old girl.'

'*Poor old girl . . .!* You've lost me, Johnny,' I said tightly.

'Think about it. If she'd divorced you, say, a year ago, she'd have scooped the pot! Kind of settlements our courts have been giving, even the Yanks were flocking here from Reno. She'd have walked away with God knows how many millions. Now . . . well . . .'

He made a wry face.

I said bitterly, 'If you see her, tell her I'm really sorry about that, Johnny.'

'Yes, I will,' he said. 'She'll appreciate that. Here, let me top you up.'

I shook my head. As we talked my initial euphoria had wilted and died, leaving me in a worse state than before. Johnny, I realized, had been my last best hope of relief, the only basket left for me to place my eggs in. Not his fault for not being able to give me what I wanted. My need had bulled him up to saviour status. And in any case the eggs were probably cracked and addled already. There was nothing he could do for me, I realized. All I wanted now was to be left alone.

'No thanks,' I said. 'Actually, I'm feeling a bit tired. I suppose I'm not used to visitors. Sorry.'

'No, it's me who should be sorry. Should have known better than to overtire you. I'll leave the bottle in your locker here. Don't want the nurses taking a swig, do we?'

He disposed of the bottle and stood up. At six foot seven, he'd always had a good four inches on me. Now he seemed to tower like some visitor to Lilliput, free from malicious intent but unable to avoid giving the tiny figures around his ankles the occasional painful kick.

I said, 'If you get a chance to talk to Ginny, tell her I love her.'

'Of course I will,' he said. 'I'll be in touch when you're feeling a bit more up to snuff. Take care now.'

He left. Before the door could swing shut, DC McLucky came through.

'Enjoy your wine, did you?' he said.

This for him was a subtle way of letting me know he'd been listening in on our conversation. Curiously the sight of his lugubrious face and the sound of his aggressive voice raised my spirits a bit. To say his manner had softened would be going too far – I don't think he did soft – but at least he seemed to regard me as a human being, unlike some of the medical staff who could hardly conceal their distaste. I realized later this was because as news of my recovery circulated, the papers had decided this was too good a story to

141

miss. 'The Kraken Wakes' was an *Observer* headline. 'IT'S BACK!' was the *Sun*'s.

But DC McLucky treated me, if not like a man innocent till proven guilty, at least like a PoW under the protection of the Geneva Convention.

I said, 'Not a lot. Help yourself, if you fancy a glass. Won't keep now it's opened.'

'Thanks,' he said, taking the bottle out of the locker and filling my water tumbler. 'Cheers. Very nice.'

'This mean you're not on duty?' I asked.

He said, 'Read a lot of detective stories, do you? But I suppose you're right. I'm on my break. Till I finish this anyway.'

He was regarding me with an expression I couldn't quite identify.

He said, 'Buddy of yours, that Mr Nutbrown?'

I said, 'Yes, he is. A close friend and business colleague. Why?'

He drank some more wine then said, 'No reason. Must be a comfort to have such a close friend and colleague walking around free and watching your back.'

He finished the wine as I let the implications of what he was saying sink in.

If the Fraud Squad investigation was probing so deep, why wasn't my closest business associate at its heart?

It was at this point another bubble of memory floated to the surface of my mind.

Before my accident, I'd been rendezvousing with Johnny at the Black Widow, but it was the cops who were waiting for me there.

McLucky was at the door.

I said, 'Mr McLucky.'

He said warningly, 'I'm back on duty now.'

I said, 'I'd just like the telephone, if I could. I think I should get myself a lawyer.'

He nodded, and it came to me that the elusive expression was not a million miles from pity.

He said, 'First good idea you've had since you woke up, Sir Wilfred.'

iii

It was six months from my awakening before I was fit enough to stand trial and even then I entered court leaning heavily on a stick. I'd been told I would have a permanent limp, by which I think they meant stagger. Add to that my scarred face, black eye-patch, and the leather glove on my right hand, and you'd think that perhaps the change from what I used to be might have provoked some pangs of sympathy in the great British public.

No chance. The abuse and catcalls, not to mention stones and spit that were hurled my way by the crowd gathered for my first appearance, indicated that to a man and woman they'd taken their lead from the tabloids. The *Mirror* described me as lower than vermin while the *Mail* had photos of me before and after the accident with the headline 'Now We See Him as He Really Is!'

The so-called quality press weren't much better. The *Guardian* developed the *Mail*'s theme in a cartoon showing two policemen struggling up the steps of the Bailey with an ornate picture frame containing what was obviously a painting of me with the caption 'Dorian Gray Comes Down from the Attic'. The *Telegraph*, not to be outdone in the literary stakes, published a photo that could have been a still from a Frankenstein movie accompanied by the tag-line 'He must be wicked to deserve such pain'. They didn't, however, trust their readers sufficiently not to give chapter and verse of the quotation's source.

Meant nothing to me, but I'd guess a well-educated girl like you didn't need to be told, Elf.

143

But worst of all was the way they treated Dad's stroke. Responsibility was laid entirely at my door. The sins of the child being visited on the father was the burden of every reference to Fred. My pleas to be allowed to visit him continued to be disregarded on the grounds that (a) his condition was not presently life-threatening and (b) such a visit might cause public unrest if not disorder. When I pressed my solicitor to make waves, he said laconically, 'Not worth the bother. Even if we did get permission, they'd leak it to the press and the whole fucking thing would turn into a circus parade with you as the main attraction.'

Getting a new solicitor hadn't been as easy as I envisaged. Toby Estover's defection had dropped me in the mire and none of the other legal firms I knew proved keen to dig me out. I quickly realized the problem wasn't moral repugnance but money. What the financial crash had left of my fortune, the divorce courts took, and it was soon made clear to me that there was a mile-long queue of investors with writs in their hands, all eager to sue me for the pittance I was likely to earn sewing mailbags or whatever gainful employment was available in HM Prisons these days. In the end I would have had to take pot luck with the legal aid system if I hadn't remembered Edgar Trapp, a small-time solicitor with an East End practice, who I'd once done a favour for. He had two great merits, one was availability, the other was frankness. Not once either in the run-up to or during the course of my trials did he hold out any hope of an acquittal.

I had to fall back on Legal Aid for a barrister and when I heard that the court had appointed Andrew Stoller QC, my spirits lifted for a moment. Stoller was a radical crusading lawyer with a growing reputation for taking on lost causes and sometimes winning them. But Trapp shook his head and said gloomily, 'It just means the CPS are so sure of their case, they've pulled strings to make sure you get the best defence possible so there'll be no leeway for an appeal.'

I said, 'For Christ's sake, Ed! If I were paying you, I'd sack you!'

He gave one of his rare smiles and said, 'If you were paying me, I'd have probably resigned long since.'

It was a joke, but I knew it couldn't be easy for someone like Ed Trapp to be my legal representative. I was the perfect hate figure. The high-flying bankers who'd brought the country to the edge of ruin were on the whole still flying high, some of them buoyed up by the kind of pension packet that would have kept a dozen or more families out of the dole queue. No way to touch them. But I was in the public's sights and in their reach, a ruthless financial fraudster with a taste for molesting children. I suspect the general public gave Ed a pretty rough time. Not that they'd get much change if Ed's wife and assistant, Doll, was around. Only a very brave or very stupid man messed with Doll!

These were the thoughts that I consoled myself with when I thought of the trouble I might be bringing Ed. Not that I thought of it all that much. To be honest, I had little emotional energy left to worry about anyone else's woes. As the months rolled by, my physical improvement was matched by a mental deterioration. My early confident belief that nobody could place any credence in any of these accusations, sexual or financial, was worn away by the unremitting drip of evidence from the investigators. After a couple of months it was plain they had enough to drown me in. Trapp said they were showing their hand so clearly because it would save time and money if I pleaded guilty on all charges. This was particularly true in the fraud case, which recent experience had shown could run on for months.

'Let it run!' was my first reaction. 'They'll run out of steam before I do.'

Ed shook his head and said lugubriously, 'Doubt it. Anyway, you'll almost certainly be in jail by then. That's why they've scheduled the other thing first.'

He usually referred to the kiddy-porn case as *the other thing*.

It soon became clear Stoller, my brief, was as pessimistic as Trapp about my chances in the porn case. He asked me how I was thinking of pleading.

I exploded, 'Not guilty, of course!'

He drew in his breath like a plumber you've asked for a quote and said, 'Let's not be too hasty. Not before we examine the options . . .'

I said, 'The only option for me is not guilty, because that's what I am. No one who's known me for any length of time could possibly think I'd get off on this filth. And if you don't believe that, maybe I should look for another lawyer.'

He smiled and said, 'Of course I believe everything you tell me, Sir Wilfred. I could not function else. But the evidence appears strong. And I fear that by now the Great British Public has grown so accustomed to the notion that sexual deviancy may lurk behind even the most respectable façade that Jesus Christ himself at the second coming might be well advised to drop that *suffer the little children to come unto me* stuff.'

I got the message. He'd studied the prosecution case and what he'd found there had left him a long way short of absolute faith in my innocence.

I think that was when the fight began to go out of me. As long as I'd been able to think that, no matter what evidence the cops dug up or what kind of crap the papers printed, most people who actually knew me, even those who didn't like me much, would find the porn charges impossible to believe, I'd had something to cling to.

Now, looking at myself through Stoller's eyes, I saw that

most of my acquaintance, far from declaring, *Wolf Hadda? No way he could be into that stuff!* were probably saying, *Hadda, eh? Who'd have thought it? Mind you, there was always something* . . .

And, as I've indicated earlier, that readiness to believe the worst of people which has been the inevitable consequence of the downward spiral of modern standards was only reinforced by the change in my appearance.

Stoller was looking to do a deal with the CPS. He reckoned that in return for a plea of guilty to the charge of possessing illegal downloaded images he could persuade them to shelve the related charges of helping to finance InArcadia, the pornographic website, and of taking part in one of its videos.

'Their evidence is much shakier here,' he said. 'And on the surface there would be some illogicality in your downloading stuff from the site if you were not only one of its organizers but also an active participant in its videos.'

I jumped on this eagerly, saying that as my defence was that this was all a set-up, surely this looked like a weakness we could exploit.

He said patiently, 'It's a very small weakness and we could only attempt to exploit it by encouraging them to bring the more serious charges. As it is, you could get away with a relatively short period of jail time for the downloading, particularly if you put your hand up for it and promised to sign up for the aversion course. But if they throw the book at you, then we could be talking five or six years.'

I wouldn't listen. Whatever else happened, no way was I going to admit to being into that filth.

It's a matter of history now that I got found guilty on all counts. I can't even say I went down fighting. I was deeply depressed on the eve of the trial but still deluded myself that when I stepped out into the spotlight and the directors called *Action!* I'd be up for it.

Then, at the end of our last pre-trial consultation, Stoller and Trapp looked at each other and exchanged what seemed to me a reluctant nod of agreement.

I said, 'What?'

Stoller said, 'There's something you need to know, Sir Wilfred. Better you hear it from us than from someone shouting it out during the trial. It's your wife, I mean your former wife . . .'

I remember feeling a real shock of fear that he was going to tell me something bad had happened to Imogen. Instead, and even more shocking, that was the first time I learned that Imo was going to remarry, and the intended groom was my ex-solicitor and ex-friend, Toby Estover.

Stoller and Trapp tried to play down the implications of the news. What concerned them of course was that to the Great British Public, including the twelve on my jury, my beloved wife and my dear friend might as well have put out an advert on prime-time television declaring that they knew beyond all doubt that I was guilty as charged.

But I was way beyond such practical forensic concerns. Somewhere deep down beyond the reach of reason I must have nursed a hope that the divorce was tactical, a temporary measure devised by Toby to put Imo out of reach of the media and my creditors. Now I was unable to ignore the full enormity of their betrayal.

After a sleepless night retreading every inch of the past till my heavy feet must have obliterated all traces of truth, I turned up at court like a zombie. My face and bearing spoke guilt, and in the end Stoller didn't even bother to put me on the witness stand.

In prison, I was put in the relative safety of the exclusion wing from the start, but that didn't stop me being viciously abused whenever the so-called normal prisoners got within shouting and spitting distance. When the time of my second trial arrived, I was past caring about its outcome. I wouldn't plead guilty, but I couldn't be bothered to make much effort to prove I wasn't guilty. No surprise then that they found me guilty.

So that's how it ended, my fairy tale.

A year after I came out of the coma, I was locked up for a total of twelve years.

That feels like forever after in anyone's language.

Like that guy Thomas in the poem, I told nothing but the truth. Those fairies knew a thing or two. The truth doesn't set you free, it gets you banged up for ever!

I had no friends. Johnny never came back. The only time I saw him again was when he appeared as a witness in the fraud case. To give him his due, he was clearly reluctant to say anything that told against me, but his airy evasions just managed to suggest there was a helluva lot of stuff to hide, and the fact that he kept glancing across at me with a look of rueful bewilderment and saying, 'Sorry, Wolf', didn't help much either.

Just when you think things can't get worse, they do. Six months after I'd started my sentence, Ed Trapp came to see me. I could tell it was bad news. Typically he didn't muck about.

'Your dad's dead,' he said. 'Sorry.'

I never got to see Fred. I just assumed that soon as he was fit to travel he'd come down to see me. News had begun to sound a bit more promising. Progress continued, very slow but steady. And then he'd had another stroke, so massive that despite being where he was, they could do nothing.

I didn't bother to apply to be allowed to go to the funeral. What was the point? He'd be laid to rest in St Swithin's up at Mireton. Everyone would be there. He was well liked. All that my presence would do would be to attract the media swarm, all pointing their cameras to see how I would react as they lowered into the ground the father that I'd killed.

That's how I felt, Elf, that's how I feel. I don't need the papers to say it. One way or another, I killed Fred, I acknowledge it.

And that's not all. Fill your boots, this is payday for you.

After I heard about Fred, I sat down and wrote a letter to Ginny. I'd written to her several times in the period leading up to the trial. No reply, either because she didn't want to, or maybe she never got my letters. After I was sentenced, I wrote again, and again nothing came back. I didn't blame her. It's a lot for a young kid to get her head around, being told her father's a pervert and a fraudster. Give her time, I thought, let her grow up. Christmas cards, birthday cards, let her know I was still alive. But she'd been close to her granddad, and I wanted her to know . . . I don't know what I wanted her to know, except that I loved her. When I finished the letter I read it through, once, twice, three times. Then I tore it up, because in my mind's eye that's what I could see her doing.

Another mistake. I should have had the courage to send it. I should have moved heaven and earth to make contact with her. Maybe if I'd been able to talk to her, maybe I could have persuaded her I was innocent, maybe she wouldn't have let them pack her off out of the country like they did . . .

Maybe she would still be alive.

But now I look back on her childhood I see how rarely I'd been there for her. I'd always thought of myself as a loving dad, but thinking about her after my sentence, I realized the last time I'd seen her before everything blew up was early in that last summer vacation when she asked me to help her with her Wordsworth assignment. Shortly afterwards I'd shot off on a business trip and by the time I returned she'd gone back to school. In fact that had been the pattern of our contact for the past few years: me away a lot of the time, only getting to see her if my presence in England co-incided with one of her school vacations. OK, I always came back loaded with expensive presents from exotic parts, but what kind of compensation was that for my neglect?

What do you make of that, Elf? Some great dad, eh?

Whatever responsibility others share for putting me in this place and for putting Ginny in the way of harm over there in France, I know the truth of it. She was my responsibility and I failed her. I failed her all along. There's a long trail leading back from that filthy Parisian alleyway she died in, and it starts at my feet.

Is that what you're after, Elf? Is that what you want to hear?

Then you've got it, girl.

Whatever else I may have been framed for, I make a full and frank confession here.

You've got me bang to rights. I let my daughter down and I let my father down.

I killed them both. I killed them both.

Elf

i

This was it. The breakthrough!

She liked to watch sport on television. She got real pleasure out of the grace and athleticism of those involved, and she also learned a lot from observing with clinical detachment the range of human reaction to triumph and failure, to victory and defeat. She had written a paper on the subject for a psychological journal. It was judged to have such popular appeal that a national paper had offered a handsome fee for the right to publish it, but she had refused, mainly because they wanted to make some significant cuts but also because in retrospect her initial delight at the offer felt like taking a step away from a spectating objectivity towards the condition of those in the sporting arena.

But now as she read Hadda's narrative for a second time, she knew at last what it was to feel the impulse to punch the air and let out a scream of *YES!*

This was the crack in the dam that could . . . should . . . might . . . *must* lead to a breach of the huge defensive wall he had thrown up around his actions.

Its form had changed again, this time more subtly. It was back to first-person historical narrative, but it was now addressed directly and specifically to herself. It was a statement that went a good way to being one half of a dialogue.

And its concluding admission that he had failed his daughter and his father beyond any mitigation of circumstance or outside interference was monumental. Even the derisive snarl of *Is that what you want to hear? . . . Then you've got it, girl!* was significant. It showed that he recognized and, albeit with reluctance and distaste, accepted their relationship of patient and therapist.

Of course he was still in denial . . . *whatever else I've been framed for . . .* but the more aggressive he became, the more it demonstrated his inner turmoil as he felt his defences hard pressed.

It wasn't surprising. All the evidence suggested his predilection was for girls in the early pubertal stages. He blamed the Ulphingstones for his daughter's banishment to boarding school, but from his point of view it put her safely out of the way during this dangerous stage of her development for a good two-thirds of the year. And his complaint that business trips frequently took him away from home during her holidays fitted the pattern perfectly. He knew what he was, didn't trust himself round his own young daughter, and protected her and himself by keeping her at a physical distance as much as possible.

It wasn't just guilt at her neglect that he was confessing to; it was the much greater guilt that had caused it!

Now was the time for her to press on – but with very great care. In the long hunt the most dangerous time is when the quarry turns at bay. So she prepared the ground for their next meeting even more meticulously than usual. But in the event she was frustrated.

He refused to see her.

There was nothing she could do.

These sessions were voluntary. No point in trying to work with a prisoner who had to be brought kicking and screaming before you.

The following week it was the same.

She guessed that he was regretting having gone so far to meet her. He felt he had given too much away, put himself in her power.

And perhaps he was fearful of what more might come. This was good. But only if somehow she could gain access to him.

The third week he didn't show either. But Officer Lindale, one of the few she didn't automatically assume would report everything back to Chief Officer Proctor, chose a moment when they were alone to say, 'Hadda asked me to give you this, miss.'

He handed her an exercise book.

She took it and glanced inside.

'Did you read this?' she asked.

'Looked through it, miss. In case it was, you know, offensive.'

And what would you have done if in your judgment it had been? she wondered.

But she knew that Hadda must have chosen Lindale as his messenger because he too trusted him, so all she said was, 'Thank you very much.'

She couldn't wait till she got home. As soon as she slipped into the driving seat of her car, she took out the book and began to read.

Wolf

i

Dear Dr Ozigbo, I won't be seeing you again, not unless they bring me under restraint. At first I thought I'd simply just not turn up any more, but that lets you down too easily, and I've decided to write to you just so you'll know that I know exactly what you've been up to.

You must have been really pleased with yourself when you read what I wrote about Johnny's visit and seen that you'd managed to stir up all kinds of feelings I didn't understand. And when you started in at me about Imogen I guess you didn't have to be Sigmund Freud to spot you'd touched a very sensitive spot. I know you'll say it's your job and everything you're trying to do is for my benefit, and I daresay you half believe it. I was ready to believe it myself to start with, but not any longer. Now I've come to realize you're little more than an interfering busybody poking around in matters you don't understand on the basis of gross misinformation and all you've managed to do is disturb whatever equilibrium I've achieved to see me safe through my sentence.

This writing business, for instance – you said the point of it was to get me to externalize my memories and feelings about what happened so that I could stand back and take it all in and come to terms with it – OK, you'd probably wrap it up in some trick cyclist's mumbo-jumbo but that's what it amounts to – right? Clarity. It's meant to give me clarity, but all it's done is create utter confusion.

When I started, I thought I'd get you off my back by giving you a blow-by-blow account of what happened to me and my take on the reasons why it happened. Instead I've ended up doubting my own memories. Is that your job – to leave your patients more fucked up than when you found them?

Take sleeping, for instance. I used to sleep OK. I used to sleep sound. But ever since I started seeing you I've started having broken nights, bad dreams, the cold sweats, and it's got steadily worse. Recently my dreams have been getting really terrible, I do some really bad stuff in them, I won't tell you what because I know you'd just seize on it to support whatever it is you imagine you're doing with me. But I know what you're really doing. I've been reading about it in the library; false memory syndrome, they call it, which is when some trick cyclist is so obsessed with the notion that their patient has been abused in childhood that they keep on and on at the poor sod till he or she starts agreeing with them, and then the psych says *Hooray! This is a repressed memory brought to the surface through my clever therapy* when all it is is a disgusting idea that he or she has actually planted there!

I think this is what you've been doing to me, drip drip drip, going on at me about the paedophilia stuff, till you've got inside my head and put these false memory nightmares there. Look, I'll give you the benefit of the doubt and accept that this probably wasn't your intention. You read the trial transcripts and decided I was guilty and never once did you let it enter your head that maybe the stuff I was writing was the truth and you'd got it all wrong. No, from the start you reckoned I was in denial, isn't that what you people say? That my accounts were just my effort to hide from the knowledge of my own perverted crimes.

Well, congratulations, Dr Ozigbo. I'd never looked at images of kids being sexually abused till Medler showed me those that had been planted on my computer. I thought I'd cleansed them out of my memory. But now, thanks to you, I'm seeing them all the time. They're in my mind, in my dreams, in my nightmares, exactly where you've put them!

That's what you've done to me. I was in control, eating my porridge, ticking down the minutes and hours and days till I got out of here.

Now I'm in hell.

Thanks a bunch.

And goodbye for ever.

Elf

i

As soon as she'd read Hadda's letter, Alva Ozigbo asked to see the Director.

During her time at Parkleigh she had come to admire Simon Homewood. He was by no means the bleeding-heart liberal the right-wing papers liked to caricature him as. There was a strength in him that even George Proctor had to respect, though the Chief Officer made no secret of his belief that all this syrupy-therapy stuff, as he called it, was a waste of time that could more usefully have been spent picking oakum. But after some preliminary tussles, Proctor had come to realize that unless the prison was run the way the Director wanted it run, he might as well start looking for a new post.

Homewood asserted that his primary duty was one of care for the prisoners in his charge. Get that right and all the other penal issues of punishment, rehabilitation and public safety could be resolved. So now when Alva spoke to him about Hadda, she simply stated that in her judgment the prisoner had reached a stage in his journey to self-awareness where the burden of recognition might be stressful enough to provoke self-harm.

The Director had never made any attempt to pressurize her for confidential details of exchanges between herself and Hadda or any other prisoner, and nor did he now.

He asked, 'Do you think he needs to be hospitalized?'

'No,' said Alva firmly. 'It's best if what's going on inside him works itself out inside. If he becomes aware he is an object of concern, this will allow him to externalize his fears and doubts once more. As it is, I'm the sole external target for his redirection of blame. At the moment he is asserting vehemently that he never wants to see me again. Eventually his turmoil will come to a climax which he can only resolve by demanding to see me. But it is not an outcome that he will admit willingly, and it may be that, as he approaches it, he'll look for a way of avoiding it.'

'Suicide, you mean?'

'I think he might see it as an attempt to re-enter the comatose state he existed in for nine months,' said Alva slowly. 'When he came out of it, the medical concentration was, quite naturally, on his physical condition. I wish there'd been more attention paid to what was actually going on in his mind, both before and after recovery. As far as I can make out from the records, the head trauma itself wasn't serious enough to explain such a long period of unconsciousness.'

'You think he might have somehow been seeking it out for himself?'

'Perhaps. He certainly talked of feeling a kind of nostalgia for the coma period in the months after his recovery.'

'If it was such a desirable state, why did he ever wake up?' enquired Homewood.

'Because there probably came a point where whatever element of choice was left to him had to opt between living and dying,' said Alva.

159

'And now you fear the decision might be reversed,' said Homewood, frowning. 'OK, I'll put Hadda on suicide watch.'

'With maximum discretion,' said Alva. 'It's best if he isn't aware he's giving concern to anyone except me.'

As the Director picked up his phone and summoned George Proctor to make the arrangements, she glanced over her notes. When she looked up, she caught Homewood watching her. As their eyes met, he gave her a faintly embarrassed smile and looked away.

This was the only flaw in their otherwise excellent working relationship. At first she'd been slightly amused when she detected that she aroused him sexually. In her experience a dash of unreciprocated sexual attraction, openly acknowledged, could lead to a fruitful relationship like that between herself and Giles Nevinson. Now and then he would try to pounce, of course, and when rejected accuse her of being a common-or-garden prick teaser. 'Are you saying you don't like your prick teased?' she'd respond. And they'd laugh and fall back into their easy friendship till next time.

There wasn't going to be any of that with Homewood. His arousal was clearly a deep trouble to him. He was, she gathered, a highly moral man, happily married with a deep-rooted Christian faith. She guessed he probably rationalized these pangs of lust by treating them as a strengthening test of his beliefs.

It was clear he believed he'd successfully concealed all signs of their effect, and Alva in her turn was eternally vigilant not to let him see that she was aware of his feelings. The only person she'd mentioned it to was John Childs, whom she still met from time to time. *Their* relationship was completely asexual; indeed she found it hard to categorize it as friendship; yet she rarely refused his invitations to have lunch or occasionally go to a concert.

Their meetings all took place on such neutral territory until one evening after a concert she invited him back to her flat for coffee, she wasn't sure why except that perhaps after more than a year she felt completely safe with him. The following Sunday, as if he felt the need for balance (or perhaps, she joked with herself, he now felt completely safe with *her*!), he invited her to his 'little place' for tea. This 'little place' turned out to be a three-storeyed house overlooking Regent's Park. She found out later he'd inherited it from his grandmother. He seemed to live in it alone. She did not feel their relationship permitted her to ask any direct questions about his private life, but she did ask if she could take a look around while he was seeing to the tea. In his study on the top floor looking out on the park, one wall was lined with framed photographs. One showed a man in tropical kit glaring at the camera as if he did not care to be photographed. He had a look of Childs, as did the boy in the next one who stood smiling shyly alongside a dark-skinned youth in Arab dress who had a much wider smile on his face and his arm draped familiarly over the boy's shoulders.

The other pictures were all of young men, one of whom she recognized as Simon Homewood. She presumed that these were the fortunate recipients of Childs's friendship that Giles Nevinson had told her about. A gap in the line suggested that things did not always work out well. The last and newest, an unsmiling young man with a great mop of black hair blowing across and half obscuring his face, she guessed was his godson, Harry, the tyro psychiatrist who provided the topic for a great deal of their conversation. His ambitions, her expertise, these she'd decided explained Childs's evident desire to keep their relationship going. Giles, however, insisted it was a strong masculine streak in her character, the one enabling her to resist his own advances, that formed the attraction.

'I thought we might have our tea in here,' said Childs,

coming in with a tray. 'For London, it's a fine view.'

He set the tray down on the desk, nudging over a thick stack of manuscript sheets to make room.

'You're not writing a novel, are you?' she said, smiling.

He looked at her blankly and for a moment she thought she might have gone a familiarity too far, then as her smile faded, his arrived and he said, 'Oh, this stuff, you mean? No, just a little thing I'm trying to put together on the Phoenicians.'

'Not so little, from the look of it,' she said. 'Why the Phoenicians?'

'Perhaps because they were not unlike the British. Great traders, fine ship-builders, hugely ingenious in matters of practical technology. Same stubbornness too. When their principal city, Tyre, was taken by Alexander, none of the men under arms took advantage of Alexander's offer of mercy to any who sought sanctuary in the temples. Rather they chose to die defending their own homes.'

'And you think that's what would happen here?'

'Perhaps,' he said, smiling. 'But it does us good to seek help and refuge in the deep past sometimes, don't you think?'

'I think you're right,' she said. Then, encouraged by his easy reception of her inquisitiveness, she went on, 'I was looking at your photos. Is the boy you?'

'Yes,' he said. 'And that's Father.'

'I can see the likeness,' she said. 'I notice Simon's here, too. Looking very attractive. Still does, of course. Though I could wish that he wasn't attracted to me.'

She wasn't quite sure why she said it. Perhaps she was looking for advice. Or perhaps she simply wanted to test the continuing strength of the psychological links between the man and his protégés.

Childs did not respond straight away but regarded her seriously for a moment with those mild blue eyes.

He should have been a saint, thought Alva, beginning to

162

feel a little guilty. Or a priest, maybe. Not one of your hell-fire brigade, but one of those who sought to lead his flock to heaven through love, not drive them there by fear. Which was a strange judgment coming from a devout atheist who earned her crust digging for the roots of human evil!

Then he smiled and said, 'Frankly, my dear, I don't see a problem. Nice to know that Simon's human. His one fault perhaps is that he can be a bit of a boy scout. But as Baden Powell was not unaware, even boy scouts can fall into temptation. BP's remedy was cold showers, but I'm sure with your professional skills we won't need to turn on the water! Now, let's have tea.'

Alva didn't feel this was the greatest compliment she'd ever received, but it did confirm her feeling that, unfair as it might seem, though the problem wasn't hers, the solution had to be.

She made sure that her relationship with Homewood never became too informal; not always easy, as she liked him a lot. It was in some ways easier for her to deal with George Proctor, who now came into the office and performed his customary semi-military halt before the Director's desk.

He then accepted an invitation to sit down, which he did, disapprovingly, perching himself right on the edge of his chair. For the next minute or so he listened carefully to Homewood's detailed and comprehensively glossed instructions, at the end of which he nodded and said, 'So, suicide watch but we don't let him know we're watching, right?'

Homewood, long used to Proctor's reductionism, smiled and said, 'I think that just about sums it up, George. Anything to add, Dr Ozigbo?'

'Only that if ever Hadda asks to see me, please try to get in touch immediately, no matter what time of day.'

'You think that time could be of the essence here?' said Homewood.

'The disturbed mind is constantly opening and closing windows. It's important not to miss the opportunity when the right opening comes,' she said.

'I understand. You got that, George?'

'Yes, sir. Buzz Dr Ozigbo's pager any time of day or night. Best make sure you keep it switched on then, miss.'

'Oh, I will, George. I will.'

Proctor got up to go and Alva rose too. Homewood hardly seemed to notice she was leaving, busying himself with some papers on his desk. A gentleman in the old-fashioned sense, he normally would have risen and escorted her to the door. But in the presence of Proctor or any of his officers, he had taken to making a conscious effort to show that he classified her simply as a staff member like any other.

As they walked together down the corridor, Proctor said, 'Fancy a cuppa, miss?'

This was a first. She knew Proctor had a little office of his own next to the warders' common room, but she'd never been inside it.

Intrigued by the motives for this sudden attack of sociability, she said, 'That would be nice.'

The room was small and functional. Its furnishings consisted of a desk, two hard chairs and a filing cabinet on top of which stood a portable radio.

Proctor said, 'Have a seat, miss, while I pop next door. Milk and sugar?'

'Just milk,' she said.

'Right. Won't be a sec. Like some music while I'm gone?'

Without waiting for an answer he turned the radio on. It was tuned to a non-stop music station that seemed to specialize in hard rock. The music bounced off the walls at a level just short of painful but she didn't want to risk marring this moment of rapprochement by turning it down.

Proctor returned from the common room carrying two

mugs of tea. He placed one in front of her and took his seat at the other side of the table.

'Cheers,' he said.

'Cheers.'

They both drank. The tea was extremely strong. Alva was glad she'd asked for milk.

'You and Mr Homewood seem to get on well,' said Proctor.

Alva had to lean across the table to catch his words above the noise of the radio but long usage had presumably inured the Chief Officer to the din.

'Yes, I'd say we have a good working relationship,' said Alva carefully. She sensed that Proctor was not just making casual conversation, so care seemed a good policy till she knew where he was leading. Her first guess was that he'd detected Homewood's feelings for her and for some reason felt it incumbent on him to warn her not to lead him on. Which, if the case, was a bloody cheek!

'Funny places, prisons,' he resumed. 'Ups and downs, lots of atmosphere, easy to get funny ideas.'

Was he perhaps a nonconformist preacher in his spare time, lumbering towards a stern moral reproof?

She said, 'Yes, I suppose it is, George. You should know that better than anyone. Because of your long service, I mean.'

'Very true,' he said. 'Bound to be the odd disagreement, though. Between you and the Director, I mean.'

'Not really,' she said firmly. 'I think we're very much on the same wavelength.'

'That's good. Mind you, Dr Ruskin and the Director were like that too, until they fell out.'

There had of course been various references made to her predecessor during Alva's time in the post, but this was the first mention of a dispute.

'I didn't know they'd fallen out,' she said.

'Oh yes. I mean, that's why the job came vacant.'

This was even more of a surprise.

'No, surely it was because of the car accident?' she said.

'Yeah, well, him dying like that meant they didn't have to say he'd resigned. Best to keep quiet about that, Mr Homewood said.'

'Why did he need to say that to you, George?' said Alva.

'Because I was waiting outside his office with my daily report when they had the row. Couldn't help noticing, there was a deal of shouting, Dr Ruskin mainly. Then he came through the door yelling, "You'll have my resignation in writing by the end of the day." I gave it five minutes before I went in, but the Director knew I was there. That's why two days later, when Dr Ruskin had his accident, he brought it up with me. Said best to keep quiet about Dr Ruskin wanting to resign. That way it would make things straightforward with Dr Ruskin's widow for the pension and such.'

Alva digested this, then said, 'So why aren't you keeping quiet about this now, George?'

'Oh, you don't count, miss. You're one of the family. No secrets in a family, or it just leads to bother, eh? How's your tea, miss? Like a top-up?'

'No thanks, George. I'll have to be on my way now,' said Alva, recognizing that the significant part of the conversation was at an end.

But what did it signify? she asked herself as she walked away.

She felt she'd received a warning, but Proctor's motive in offering it was obscure. Could be kindness, so her sense of being on the same wavelength as Homewood wouldn't lead her into dangerous areas of over-presumption. Or maybe it was just a malicious need to insert a small wedge in what he saw as a wrongheaded liberal alliance.

Time would probably reveal all. It usually did. She focused

her attention instead on the delicate stage she had reached in her treatment of Wolf Hadda. She had a feeling that something was going to happen in the next couple of weeks. At least it seemed likely that George Proctor's new friendliness meant he would live up to his promise of giving her a buzz as soon as it happened.

ii

The buzz came sooner than she expected.

Three days later at half past four in the morning, to be precise. She picked up her bedside phone and dialled. Proctor answered instantly.

'Tried to slit his wrist, miss,' he said. 'And as they took him off to the hospital wing, he kept saying your name.'

'I'm on my way.'

She walked through the shower to wake herself up. As she towelled dry, she glimpsed herself in the full-length wall mirror. There was, she thought, a great deal more to her than her prison outfit promised. If Homewood could see her like this, the poor man would probably burst out of his trousers!

She excised the narcissistic thought, pinned up her hair and pulled on her prison kit.

She arrived at the prison at the same time as Homewood. He'd been told first about the suicide attempt, of course, but he had slightly further to come. She'd heard he had wanted to live close to his place of work but his wife had insisted that, in choosing a home for herself and her three children, other considerations came first. Alva sympathized. Homewood's devotion to his job probably meant he took it home with him. That must be bad enough without having the looming gothic reality of the place just around the corner.

He said, 'You were right.'

It sounded as much an accusation as a compliment.

Proctor was waiting for them.

As they walked with him towards the hospital block, he told them what had happened.

'He got into bed at lights out, settled down, seemed to go to sleep, but some time in the night he slashed his right wrist with a razor blade. Normally he's a very restless sleeper, and he's been a lot worse lately, tossing and turning all night, sometimes just lying there with his eyes wide open like he didn't want to go back to sleep. Fortunately Lindale was on duty. He's got a good nose for anything different and it struck him that Hadda was lying unusually still, so he took a closer look.'

'How the hell did he get a razor blade into bed with him?' demanded Homewood.

Proctor said woodenly, 'Looking into that, sir.'

Alva guessed he was thinking, If we ran this prison on my lines, not yours, there'd have been a lot less chance of this happening.

On admittance to the hospital block, they found the doctor waiting for them. His name was Martens. According to his own account, he'd been a star student and he couldn't disguise his sense that fate had played him a dirty trick by leaving him high and dry as a prison doctor in early middle age. He was certainly no great fan of forensic psychiatry, but her first glimpse of him this morning was reassuring. He had the weary, irritated look of a man eager to get back to his bed rather than the sad resigned expression of someone who's just lost a patient.

'Oh good. You're here at last, *Doctor*,' he said in the faintly sneering tone with which he always used her title.

Homewood frowned and asked brusquely, 'How's Hadda?'

'Hadda is fine,' said Martens. 'In fact, he might well have been fine even if he hadn't been found till breakfast. Despite what one may glean from sensational literature, wrist-slitting is a pretty inefficient way of committing suicide. Most people slash, as Hadda did, across the wrist, and few go deep enough to get to the artery. If your blood is normal, the body's pretty efficient at sealing up a severed vein. Opening it up longitudinally rather than laterally gives you a much better chance of success . . .'

'But he's going to live?' interrupted Homewood impatiently.

'Oh yes,' said the doctor. 'Still, I suppose it's the thought that counts.'

'Is he conscious?' asked Alva.

'Indeed he is. He became quite agitated when I tried to sedate him. He's mentioned your name several times, *Dr* Ozigbo. Not always in the most complimentary of terms.'

He said this not without satisfaction. Clearly, in his eyes, for a psychiatrist's patient to attempt suicide was prima facie evidence of failure.

And in mine . . .? she asked herself.

She moved forward into the ward. Homewood was going to follow her but she put her hand on his chest.

'Just me,' she said.

Hadda was watching her as she approached his bed. He looked pale so far as it was possible to tell on that scar-crossed face. His right wrist was heavily bandaged but it was the ungloved hand that drew her eyes. It was the first time she'd seen it plain. She understood now why he usually wore the black protective glove. The absence of two fingers was a disfigurement more startling than the facial scars or even that suggested by the eye-patch.

He said, 'Come to gloat?'

'I'm sorry?'

'Don't play not understanding,' he said. 'Everyone's entitled to an I-told-you-so, even psychiatrists.'

'You need to spell it out, Wolf,' she said. 'What is it you think I told you so?'

His gaze drifted away from hers and his expression froze as though his facial muscles were resisting his brain's command. Then, with a perceptible effort of will he brought his eye back to focus on her face.

He said, softly at first but with growing strength, 'Everything they said about me at the trial, the paedophile trial, I mean, was true. And a lot more besides. I know the dreadful things I did. I know the dreadful person I was, the dreadful person I still am. I'll spell it out to you, chapter and verse, if that's what you want. I know it, I admit it, I acknowledge it.'

Now she saw his eyes filling with the tears that she'd been hoping to see from the start of her involvement in his case, but the sight filled her with pity not pleasure.

Whether it was her pity or his pain that made things unbearable she could not know, but now he broke eye contact with her and turned his head away and buried his face in the pillow. But he was still talking and she lowered her head close to his to catch what he was saying.

Distant, muffled, half sobbed, half spoken, she made out the words.

'Help me . . . help me . . . help me . . .'

BOOK TWO

the beautiful trees

Ich habe die friedlichste Gesinnung. Meine Wünsche sind: eine bescheidene Hütte, ein Strohdach, aber ein gutes Bett, gutes Essen, Milch und Butter, sehr frisch, vor dem Fenster Blumen, vor der Tür einige schöne Bäume, und wenn der liebe Gott mich ganz glücklich machen will, lässt er mich die Freude erleben, dass an diesen Bäumen etwa sechs bis sieben meiner Feinde aufgehängt werden.

Mit gerürhrtem Herzen werde ich ihnen vor ihrem Tode alle Unbill verzeihen – die sie mir im Leben zugefügt – ja, man muss seinen Feinden verzeihen, aber nicht früher, als bis sie gehenkt werden.[†]

Heinrich Heine: *Gedanken und Einfälle*

[†] I am the most easygoing of men. All I ask from life is a humble thatched cottage, so long as there's a good bed in it, and good victuals, fresh milk and butter, flowers outside my window, and a few beautiful trees at my doorway; and if the dear Lord cares to make my happiness complete, he

might grant me the pleasure of seeing six or seven of my enemies hanging from these trees.

From the bottom of my compassionate heart, before they die I will forgive then all the wrongs they have visited on me in my lifetime – yes, a man ought to forgive his enemies, but not until he sees them hanging.

1

The ruts on the lonning up to Birkstane Farm were frozen hard.

Even at low speed, the old Nissan Micra advanced like a small boat in a rough sea and Luke Hollins, its driver, winced at each plunge into a new trough. His only consolation was that if the track hadn't been frozen, he'd have been walking through ankle-deep mud for a quarter mile. On the other hand it might have been wiser to walk. As a country vicar with four parishes to cover, he couldn't afford serious damage to his suspension. Not in any sense. Four parishes, one stipend. The Church of England in the Year of Our Lord 2017 did not require its priests to take a vow of poverty. No need when it was a built-in condition of the job!

In sight of the house his way was barred by a rickety old gate. He got out, forced it open a few feet and decided to walk the rest of the way. As he approached he could see signs of the attack that had brought him here. Smashed windows roughly patched with squares of cardboard, scorch marks up the barn door, and across the wall of the main house in red paint the words *Fuck off peedofile!*

Was there anything he could have done to stop this? He

doubted it, but he still felt guilty that he'd found reasons to put off visiting his new and controversial parishioner ever since news had run round the area two weeks earlier that, seven years after Fred had died, there was a Hadda back in Birkstane.

No one had gone out to tie yellow ribbon round the old oak tree.

Jimmy Frith, landlord of the Black Dog and the kind of conservative who made Torquemada look like an equal-opportunities counsellor, spoke longingly of the rack and the stake. Many of the local women whipped themselves into a frenzy of indignation. Even Hollins' wife, a determinedly counter-traditional vicar's spouse, made it clear that in this case she was at one with the Mothers' Union. Hollins himself had acted disappointment, but beneath his plea for compassionate understanding he couldn't suppress an instinctive sympathy with the scripturally endorsed view that the best treatment for paedophilia involved millstones.

Then the previous evening at a parish council meeting he'd learned that twenty-four hours earlier a gang of young hotheads had mounted an attack against Birkstane with a view to letting Wolf Hadda know he wasn't wanted.

'Would have burnt the barn down, and not much bothered if he were in it,' said Len Brodie, his churchwarden, father of three daughters. 'Only that sudden hail shower put the fire out and sent them scuttling back to the Dog. Daresay you'd call that divine intervention, Vicar.'

He wouldn't, but he'd certainly felt it as a firm reminder that the cure of souls did not contain any opt-out clauses.

So now he approached the vandalized house with the reluctant determination of Roland coming to the Dark Tower.

Tentatively he tapped on the solid oak of the front door.

There was no sound from within and he'd raised his fist to deal a firmer blow when behind him he heard a deep-throated growl.

He spun round and found himself confronting a big man with a deeply scarred face not improved by an empty socket where his right eye should have been. His right hand was missing two fingers and his left leg looked as if it had been removed by force and stuck back on with plastic filler.

He noticed the ruined hand because the man's remaining fingers were wrapped around the handle of a tree-feller's axe, and the ruined leg because the man was stark naked. Alongside the damaged leg, and presumably the source of the growl, was what looked like a wolf badly disguised as a Border Collie.

Stepping back so quickly he collided with the door, the vicar exclaimed, 'Jesus Christ!'

'Wolf Hadda,' said the man. 'Glad to meet you, Mr Christ. Thought for a moment you might be one of them yobs, come back for more.'

'No, I'm sorry, my name isn't . . . I mean . . . I was just a bit surprised . . .'

He caught a gleam of amusement in the man's one eye, which was a relief. Mockery was fine. It came with the job. Axes were something else.

Recovering he said, 'I'm Luke Hollins, your vicar. I thought I'd drop by to see how you were settling in. I'm sorry about this . . . it's youngsters who can't hold their drink . . .'

He gestured towards the graffiti and the broken windows.

'Just letting off a bit of steam then?' said Hadda. 'With Jimmy Frith stoking the boiler, I'd guess. It's still Jimmy running the Dog, is it? How he's survived as his own best customer for forty years, God knows. It was always a high price to pay for a pint, listening to him putting the world to right. Do they still call him Jimmy Froth?'

'Not to his face,' said Hollins. 'Can we go inside, Mr Hadda? You're looking a bit cold. Do you always walk around naked?'

'No. I was just taking my morning shower. I get my water

175

piped from the beck behind the house, but it comes in such a slow trickle it's quicker to step outside and wash at source. There's a little fall I can sit under. I heard your car and after the other night . . .'

He turned away round the side of the house, swinging the axe and burying its head in a chopping block as he passed. He did this one-handed with an ease that made Hollins glad he hadn't done anything to provoke attack. If ever that did happen, best strategy would be to run, he decided. The man's damaged left leg seemed to be locked at the knee, producing a laboured rolling gait. That, combined with the facial disfigurement, should have produced a totally ogreish effect but, walking behind him, Hollins found himself enjoying the play of muscles in that broad scarred back. He dropped his gaze to the tight smooth buttocks, then quickly raised it to the sky.

Careful, boy! he admonished himself. You're a happily married C of E parson!

Inside, the house wasn't much warmer than out. There was a log fire laid in the open fireplace in the kitchen.

Hadda said, 'Stick a match in that, will you? Sneck, lie by.'

The dog settled down across the hearth, producing the deep growl once more as Hollins gingerly reached over him to light the fire. It caught quickly and he sat down at the old table and took in his surroundings.

The room didn't look as if it had changed much in the last couple of hundred years. There were ham hooks in the black ceiling beam, the small window panes had swirls and gnarls in them, and the woodwork had that bleached, weathered look you only get from long use or large expense. The rough plaster on the walls followed the swells and hollows of the granite stones from which they were constructed. Almost at ceiling height an ancient bracket clock hung from a six-inch nail driven into the crack where two stones met.

Below it a shorter nail driven into the same crack supported a lettered sampler rendered illegible by an accretion of cobwebs. The room's furniture consisted of a square oak table that looked as old as the house, a trio of kitchen chairs perhaps a couple of centuries younger, and a bum-polished rocker by the fire. The twentieth century was represented by an ancient electric oven and the twenty-first by a stream-lined jug kettle standing by the sink.

A surreal note was struck by the presence in one corner of a small deflated rubber dinghy and a foot pump.

Hollins stared down at this for a moment then turned his attention to the sampler. Unwilling to brush aside the cobwebs, he had to peer close to make out beneath their silvery threads the Gothic lettering painstakingly sewn by some human hand.

It was the Lord's Prayer.

'Don't get your hopes up, Padre,' said Hadda drily from the inner door. 'I think it hides a patch of damp.'

He moves very quietly for a big lame man, thought Hollins, noting with some relief that his host was now wearing a heavy polo-neck sweater, old cords, and boots. He'd also covered his empty eye socket with a black patch and pulled on a black leather right-hand glove.

'Is it fear of damp that's making you prepare an ark?' said Hollins, glancing at the dinghy.

'What? Oh that. I used to trawl the local tarns when I was a boy. I came across it stored away with a lot of other childish stuff, thought it might be worth getting it seaworthy again in case I need to go foraging for my own victuals. Talking of which, you'd like a coffee?'

'Yes, please.'

Hadda ran some water into the kettle, switched it on, put several spoonfuls of ground coffee into a pot jug, then sat down and studied his guest.

Luke Hollins had grown used to being studied, usually with disbelief.

He had a close-shaved head and an unshaved chin. He wore a bright red fleece with a full-length zip, khaki trousers that could be turned into shorts by zipping off the bottom half of the legs, and Nike trainers. His only sartorial concession to his calling was the reversed collar visible under the fleece, and even that had acquired a greenish tinge.

'Lady Kira must love you,' said Hadda.

'Sorry?'

'The castle's in your parish, isn't it? I'm sure Sir Leon still does his Lord of the Manor thing and invites the parson up to lunch after morning service from time to time.'

'Once to date,' said Hollins. 'I'm not holding my breath for the next invite.'

'It'll come. The Old Guard deals with tradition breakers by kettling them inside the tradition,' said Hadda. 'How long have you been here?'

'Six months,' said Hollins, thinking, How come I'm not asking the questions?

'As long as that? They must be desperate.'

'The only other candidate was a woman,' Hollins heard himself explaining.

'Must have been a close call. So, what can you do for me, Padre?'

'Sorry?'

'You know, if you listen to the words that are spoken to you and ascribe to them their conventional meaning, then maybe you'll find it unnecessary to say "Sorry?" all the time. You've come knocking at my door. I presume you don't want to borrow a pound of sugar or ask for a donation to the Church Missionary Society. So, likely you've come to offer your services. Not literally, I hope. I don't do prayer. So what can you do for me?'

178

'I can offer a sympathetic ear . . .' began Hollins.

'Really? You a pervert then?'

'Sorry . . . I mean . . . sorry?'

The kettle boiled. Hadda switched it off, waited till the water had stopped bubbling, then poured it into the jug, stirring vigorously.

'That's what I am, isn't it? Therefore a sympathetic ear implies . . . sympathy. But that's your problem. Listen, I don't want you sneaking up on my soul from behind, so let's get down to it and ask the big question. Do you get Tesco deliveries?'

He poured coffee into two heavy pot mugs and passed one across. No milk or sugar.

Biting back another 'sorry?', Hollins said, 'Yes, I mean . . . yes, we do.'

'Good. They won't deliver here, say the lonning's too rough. And even if I do a bit of fishing and so on, I'm still going to need stuff. So if I give you a list from time to time, you can add it to your order, right? Then ferry it out to Birkstane.'

'Well, yes, I suppose so . . .' said Hollins, thinking of his wife's probable reaction.

'Come on! Don't worry, I'll pay my whack. Anyway, I thought feeding the poor came under your job description.'

'Of course. It will be a pleasure.'

'A pleasure, is it? Maybe I shouldn't pay you. Right, jot your phone number down and I'll be in touch.'

He glanced up at the bracket clock on the wall, then rose to his feet.

'Got to leave you now,' he said. 'Appointment with my probation officer in Carlisle. That and reporting my movements regularly to the local fuzz in Whitehaven are the highlights of my social life. You stay and finish your coffee. Oh, and next Sunday when you get up in your pulpit you can tell those moronic parishioners of yours two things. The first

179

is, I'm no threat to their kids, I've taken the cure, swallowed the medicine both literally and metaphorically, I'm fit to retake my place in society – and if they don't believe you, they can ask Dr Ozigbo.'

'Ozigbo? That sounds . . . unusual.'

'Foreign, you mean?' Hadda grinned. 'I forgot, they still think folk from Westmorland are foreign round here. Nigerian stock, I believe, but she's British born and bred. And educated too, better than thee and me, I daresay. Yes. Dr Ozigbo's my psychiatric saviour. And I'm one of her great successes. Wouldn't surprise me if she'd put me in a book by now. So tell the dickheads that. Now I'm off. If I'm late I may get detention. I'll be in touch. Sneck!'

Leaning heavily on a stout walking stick he limped slowly out of the door. The dog, with a promissory growl at the vicar, rose and followed.

After a moment Hollins tipped his coffee into the sink – he was a two sugars and a dollop of cream man – and rinsed the mug in a trickle of peaty brown water. It occurred to him that this might be a good opportunity to have a poke around, but not even radical C of E priests did that.

He went outside. The scorched barn door was open and the sound of an engine clanking to life emerged, followed shortly by an ancient Defender. As it drew up alongside him he saw that Sneck occupied the passenger seat.

'That your Dinky toy?' said Hadda through the open window, nodding towards the bright blue Micra by the gate.

'Yes.'

'Next time, leave it at the top of the lonning. You were lucky to get as close as you did. And if you want to last the winter, I'd trade it in for one of these beauties.'

As the Defender's engine growled as if in appreciation of the compliment, Hollins shouted, 'You said there were two things I should tell my congregation?'

'Nice to see you were paying attention,' Hadda shouted back. 'The second is, I may be no threat to their kids, but next time Jimmy Froth sends any of his hotheads from the Dog up here, they'll find my axe will be a threat to them. End of lesson. A-fucking-men!'

2

Davy McLucky had bought a *Glasgow Herald* to read on the train. Automatically he opened it at the classifieds to check his ad was there.

> *Got a problem?*
> *GET McLUCKY!*
> *Confidential enquiries*
> *Security*
> *Debt Collection*

In fact he rarely did any debt collection, it required a level of hardness he didn't aspire to, but Glaswegians hiring a PI liked to think they were getting someone hard. It was a front he'd learned to adopt from an early age. *Your blether's aye been tae near your eyeballs*, his father had said when he came home with a tear-stained face after a hard day in the school playground. *You need to stand up for yersel'*.

I don't want you teaching wee Davy to be hard, his mother had protested.

I'm no teaching him tae be hard, said his father. *I'm teaching him tae act* hard!

He'd learned the lesson and it had helped him survive childhood and adolescence in parts of Glasgow that somehow didn't quite make it into the European City of Culture. And it had helped him when he moved South and joined the Met. Conditioned by the telly, his new London acquaintance, both colleagues and crooks, were ready to be impressed by a hard-talking Glaswegian. But in that unrelenting atmosphere where every day brought new tests of what you really were, his basic soft-centredness did not go undetected, and in the end it was made clear to him that detective constable was his limit. In his mid-thirties, divorced and disillusioned, he'd decided that he'd had enough of both the Met and the metropolis and resigned from the service. Back in Glasgow, living with his mother, he had got a job with a private security firm. Then his mother had died suddenly and he found himself the owner of the small family house on the edge of Bishopbriggs. Amazed to discover how much it was worth, he sold up and used the money to start his own PI business.

GET McLUCKY! Not a bad slogan, he thought complacently. After a sticky start, his reputation for reliable service and reasonable prices had started bringing in a steady stream of work, enough in a good season to give him scope to be a bit picky, turning down jobs he didn't like the look of, beginning with debt collection.

So why was he travelling down to Carlisle to meet a notorious ex-con?

This was the question that had made him raise his eyes from the ads section of the *Herald* and sit staring out at the frost-bound Border landscape as he headed back towards England for the first time since he'd handed in his badge.

Hadda's phone call had taken him by surprise.

'You the McLucky used to work in the Met?'

'That's me.'

'This is Wolf Hadda. Remember me?'

'Aye.'

'I'd like to hire you.'

'To do what?'

'We'll talk about it when we meet. Thursday next, two o'clock, the Old Station Hotel, Carlisle. I'll pay you for your journey time and fare before we start talking, OK?'

'Now hang about, I'd like a bit more . . .'

'When we meet. Goodbye, Mr McLucky.'

And that had been it. He'd thought about it a lot before opting to make the trip. And he was still thinking about it as he sat with his unread newspaper on his lap, staring out at the passing landscape, oblivious to its lunar beauty under the winter sun.

He had almost two hours to spare when he arrived in Carlisle. After locating the Old Station Hotel, he went for a walk around the town to see the sights.

A mini cathedral and a low squat castle, both in red sandstone, seemed to do the job. He felt no great impulse to enter either and there was a razor-edged wind following him round the quiet streets so he headed back to the hotel and was sitting in the bar, nursing a Scotch, when Hadda limped slowly in, looking warm in a long field jacket and leaning heavily on his stick.

He came straight to the table, cleared a space to stretch out his left leg, and sat down.

'You're early,' he said.

'You too.'

'Yes. My probation officer decided I'd been a good boy and didn't keep me long. First things first. What do I owe you for your train ticket and associated expenses?'

He pulled out a wallet as he spoke. McLucky noted it looked well filled.

He said, 'That'll keep. If I don't take your job, I'll not take your money.'

'Why's that?'

'Because if I don't take your job, it will likely be because it's something I don't want to be associated with, so I'll not be seen to have taken any money from you either.'

'I like your thinking,' said Hadda. 'Why'd you leave the Met?'

'Because it had nothing more to give me. And maybe I had nothing more to give it. How did you get on to me?'

'I made enquiries. I was told you'd retired and gone back home to Glasgow. I asked myself, what do old detectives do? And I got McLucky.'

'Fine. That's the how. Let's move on to the why.'

'Hold on. My turn to ask a question, I think. You were still a DC when you left, right? Did that have anything to do with your decision?'

'Yes and no,' said the Scot. 'If you're asking whether I felt being a detective constable in some way demeaned me, the answer's no. It was a decent enough job. If you mean, did I get pissed off seeing little gobshites with worse records and no more brains heading up the slippery pole, the answer's yes.'

'DI Medler, was he one of the aforementioned little gobshites?'

'Could be,' said McLucky, finishing his drink. 'There's a train back I could catch in half an hour. So maybe we could move things along?'

A waitress had brought some sandwiches for a couple on a nearby table. Hadda summoned her with a wave of his stick.

'Another drink? And a sandwich? You can pay for your own if I ask you to smuggle me out to Thailand.'

McLucky didn't reply and Hadda ordered anyway.

'Taxpayers picking up the tab for this?' wondered McLucky.

'What makes you think I haven't got a job?'

The PI ran his dispassionate gaze over Hadda and said, 'Well, I canna see you doing much in the world of international finance, so what else are you qualified for?'

Hadda gave a grin that matched his sobriquet.

'Back to basics, maybe. You don't forget what you learned at your father's knee.'

'So what does that make you?'

'A woodcutter,' said Wolf Hadda. 'Something you can help me with. Did Medler ever come to see me in hospital?'

The Scot nodded.

'Aye. Not long after you woke up. Just the once.'

'I'm glad about that,' said Hadda. 'I was never quite sure whether I was in or out of my mind back then. My recollection is he looked lightly grilled and he was wearing a Hawaiian shirt that looked like it had been made for some other life form.'

'Aye. He'd gone to live in Spain after he retired, so maybe that accounts for it.'

'I daresay. So when he retired, what was the word?'

'Eh?'

'Come on. I'm sure your squad was as gossipy as an all-girls marching band. What were people saying?'

McLucky thought for a moment before replying, 'They were saying that a guy who knew all the moves must have had good reason for moving out.'

'And what reason did he give?'

'Health problems, stress-related.'

'Staying in would have got him where?'

The Scot shrugged.

'Up to commander, maybe. But walking the high wire, it only takes a fart to blow you off.'

'You saying he was bent?' said Hadda.

'If I'd thought that and done nothing about it, then I'd have been bent myself. He wasn't my best buddy, guys like him don't have best buddies. Maybe he was a bit self-centred and cut a few corners, but that doesn't make him a bent cop. Look, where's all this leading?'

'I'm not sure,' said Hadda. 'He can't have been all that self-centred, though. He did come back to check me out even though he was long gone from the case. That has to mean something. What do you think, Mr McLucky?'

'Well, he could have been driven by compassion for a fellow human being in trouble.'

His expression was deadpan, his tone neutral.

Hadda said, 'Maybe. And he must have been really concerned about me to ask one of his old colleagues to keep him posted about any change in my condition.'

'Could have read about it in the papers.'

Now Hadda shook his head.

'No. The info wasn't released to the public until two weeks after I woke up. I checked.'

The sandwiches and drinks arrived. A scotch was put in front of McLucky.

Hadda, he noticed, was on orange juice.

He said, 'I can still catch that train if I move quick, so say something to make me stay.'

'All right. It's bothered you, hasn't it, something about my case?'

'Why do you say that?'

'Because in the hospital all those years ago, you started by doing your job conscientiously, but you ended doing it compassionately. Nothing dramatic, but by the time I got transferred to the Remand Centre, you were treating me like a human being.'

'You look after a scabby rat long enough, you can become fond of it,' said McLucky.

'Maybe. But there's something else.'

'What?'

'You're here. How many ex-detectives do you know would travel a hundred miles just for the pleasure of having a drink with a recently released fraudster and paedophile?'

'You saying I've fallen in love with you, Sir Wilfred?' said the Scot mockingly.

'Mr Hadda, please. Don't you recall, once I was convicted, they looked to see if there was anything else they could take away from me after my family, my fortune, my friends and my future, and someone said, he's still got his title, I expect Her Majesty would like that back. So they took it. No, unless your tastes are even more perverted than mine are reputed to be, you have no special feeling for me. I, on the other hand, do have a special feeling for you.'

'You do? Mind if I have the smoked salmon sandwich? It's likely from the Highlands and I'm starting to feel homesick.'

'By all means. Yes, my special feeling is based on you being a member of a very exclusive club. You see, Mr McLucky, I think that despite the fact that you only knew me for a few short weeks, and unlike my friends and colleagues who'd known me forever, or my psychiatrist who knew me in depth probably better than anyone else, or for that matter the Great British Public who knew bugger all about me – as I say, despite that and unlike them, you found it hard to be absolutely one hundred per cent sure that I was guilty as charged. Yes, that qualifies you for a very exclusive club indeed.'

McLucky swallowed the mouthful of salmon he was chewing, washed it down with whisky, and said, 'Tell me what you want, Mr Hadda, or I'm out of here soon as I finish this sandwich.'

'Thank God for the Scottish hatred of waste, eh? All right, I tried to contact you via the Met in the hope you could be persuaded to answer a few questions about DI Medler. Then

I found you'd retired into the private sector, and it occurred to me that maybe we could put our relationship on a proper business footing.'

'A job, you mean? Doing what exactly?' asked McLucky, placing the last piece of the sandwich in his mouth.

Hadda said, 'To start with I'd like some basic information about the people on this list: where they are, what they're doing.'

He handed over a folded sheet of paper.

The Scot glanced down it and whistled.

'What are you after, Mr Hadda?' he asked.

'I told you. Information. To start with.'

'Aye? And to finish with?'

'A little practical assistance, maybe. Always within the bounds of legality, after making allowances for the necessary deceptions of your profession.'

McLucky gave him a hard stare then said, 'Talking of legality, last I heard, you were bankrupt. This kind of stuff could pile up the hours, not to mention the expenses. You'd need to be doing a lot of woodcutting to afford my bills.'

For answer Hadda reached inside his field jacket. This time it wasn't a wallet he produced but a bulging A5 envelope.

'There's a thousand in there,' he said, laying it on the table. 'Also my mobile number. Keep a running total and when the thousand looks like running out, give me a ring.'

'And you'll do what?' asked McLucky. 'Go into the forest and chop some more trees?'

'Like I say, you never forget what you learn as a kid,' said Hadda.

McLucky picked some crumbs from his plate and asked, 'What's the time?'

Hadda glanced at his watch. When he looked up, the envelope had vanished.

'I think you've missed that train,' he said.

'No problem. There's another in an hour. Any time scale on this?'

Hadda shook his head.

'I want it done well. Take as long as it needs. All winter, if necessary.'

'All winter,' echoed the Scot. 'And what will you be doing all winter, Mr Hadda?'

'Sharpening my axe,' said Wolf Hadda.

3

Imogen Estover awoke and lay still, trying to identify what had woken her.

Old buildings have their own language as meaningful to the initiate as the singing of whales and the howling of wolves. Imogen could interpret just about every sigh and creak of her Holland Park house. She'd had plenty of time to learn in the two decades since she and Wolf Hadda had first moved in here.

Toby Estover had wanted to sell. It was strange, she'd said to him, that a man who had no scruples about taking possession of his friend's wife should balk at taking possession of his friend's property. She loved the house. She saw no reason to leave it.

So they had stayed. There had been changes. Wolf had known what he liked and seen no reason why his home should not reflect his tastes as well as his wife's. All traces of his rough masculinity had long since vanished and as Toby had shown no interest in leaving his own scent marks on the house, it was now redolent of Imogen alone.

Toby shifted heavily beside her and threw an arm across her chest.

He was getting fat, she thought. She knew that Wolf had changed physically. She had seen him during the trial. His face, his hand, his leg. And the years of imprisonment had doubtless wrought other changes. But she was certain he would never let himself become fat.

Would she still find him as magnetically attractive as she had way back? He had tried to describe to her the effect she'd had on him when he first saw her dancing on the castle lawn. She'd made no attempt to let him know the effect he'd had on her, either then or later. Attraction exerted was power. Attraction felt was weakness. Life was a struggle if you left yourself at the mercy of feelings. She had learnt that from her mother.

By now she had isolated what had woken her. It was a distant sound, very regular, part thud, part crack. It hovered on the edge of familiarity without spilling over into recognition.

She moved her husband's arm and slipped out of bed.

Toby grunted, 'What?'

She didn't reply but went to the door. The sound was too faint to have come from the front of the house which their bedroom overlooked. Out on the landing she could hear it much more distinctly. She looked towards the tall arched window that stretched from the first floor to the half-landing. It overlooked the garden and she was sure the sound was coming from out there. To get close to the window she had to descend to the half-landing. As she moved forward, she felt the cold air caress her naked body. If Toby had his way, the central heating would have stayed full on all over the house throughout the winter. She'd told him to wear bed-socks and a thicker nightshirt.

She reached the half-landing and looked out into the garden.

It was a murky night. The air was full of dank vapours

dense enough in patches to negate even the perpetual half-light of the sleeping metropolis. Slowly her eyes adjusted to the outer darkness and began to etch shape, trace movement.

A big shape – the old rowan tree.

A smaller shape – a figure standing beside it.

And now a movement.

Over the figure's head something caught what little light drifted between the vapours. Bright, metallic, swift.

And then the sound again. Now it was unmistakable. How many times had she heard it in the estate forest surrounding Ulphingstone Castle?

The sound of sharp steel biting deep into wood.

She recalled the rowan standing proud among the dreary conifers of Ulphingstone forest, much smaller than these foreign invaders but large for its kind and brighter far. It had been one of their favourite trysting spots in that first crazy year when they had roamed the countryside together, making love on fellside and in forest whenever the urge took them. And often the urge had been so strong that they had not moved from beneath the rowan's shade before their first coupling.

When Wolf had learned from his father that this section of forest was scheduled for harvesting and realized that almost inevitably the rowan would be flattened along with its tall neighbours, he'd said, 'No way!' and at vast expense arranged for it to be dug up, roots and all, and transported three hundred miles to begin a new life in their London garden.

In defiance of Fred Hadda's assurance that it was an insane waste of money and the tree would be dead in a fortnight, the rowan had flourished and blossomed and fruited. Imogen recalled how her daughter, Ginny, had been tempted to feast on the bright red berries. Refusing to be put off by the bitter taste she had persevered till she'd been sick. Granddad Fred had laughed when the girl told him the story and assured her that at Christmas they'd reckoned nowt to a roast goose unless accompanied by a dollop of his Aunt Carrie's rowanberry jelly. After that Ginny hadn't rested till a recipe was found, by which time the birds had eaten all the berries. But the following autumn she'd remembered and, under Mrs Roper's supervision, she'd boiled up the berries with slices of apple and cloves and grated cinnamon and triumphantly burst in upon her mother a couple of hours later flourishing a small jar of what turned out to be a surprisingly tasty relish.

Thereafter it became an annual event, with the jelly saved for Christmas Day. When this was celebrated up in Cumbria, Sir Leon declared it was the finest rowan jelly he'd ever tasted and even Lady Kira compared it favourably with the crab-apple relish served by her family with the festive roast suckling pig. Everyone had smiled at the little girl trying in vain to look modest in face of such praise, and for a few moments they had felt like a real united family.

All because of a crop of blood-red berries from this same rowan tree that someone was now chopping down.

She drew in her breath.

As if hearing the sound, the figure paused and turned to look towards the house. The air was far too opaque for her to make out features. She had the impression he was looking straight at her, but if she could only see him dimly, he would not be able to see her at all.

Slowly he raised his right arm, stretched it out, placed the palm of his hand against the trunk of the tree, and pushed.

In the same moment Toby's voice grumbled, 'Jesus, it's like an ice-box out here. Imo, what are you doing?'

And the landing light came on, wiping the garden from her sight.

She knew to the man in the garden she would be framed naked in the window, but she did not move.

There was noise outside once more, different, no single sound this time but a drawn-out creaking, tearing noise accompanied by a confusion of groans and cracks all climaxing in a single thud.

Then silence.

'Toby,' she said calmly, 'put the light out.'

'What? Oh, all right. What the hell's going on?'

The light went out.

It took a few moments for her night sight to return, but in her mind she already knew what she was going to see.

The figure was gone. And after all those long years of growth, first in Cumbria where it had come to maturity in her father's forest, then here in London where it had put on new strength in this milder clime, the rowan tree lay overturned across the ravaged lawn.

She found she was weeping.

For what, she wasn't sure.

4

A week after his first meeting with Hadda, Luke Hollins had found a message on his mobile dictating a grocery list. He turned up at Birkstane with the supplies a couple of days later.

It occurred to him that if Hadda had to drive to Carlisle from time to time to see his probation officer, there was nothing to stop the man picking up his groceries at one of the big supermarkets. Perhaps he didn't care to stump around the aisles, leaning on his trolley like a Zimmer frame. Or perhaps, despite his declaration of unsociability, he needed some human contact locally, some line of communication with what was going on around him, how people were feeling about him.

Hadda gave no evidence of such curiosity. His grunted greeting made even Sneck's rumbling growl sound more welcoming. Hollins had parked the Micra at the head of the lonning, not wanting to risk his suspension again. There were too many boxes to carry on one trip so he had to go back for the second instalment. Hadda did not offer to accompany him and the vicar tried charitably to put it down to his disability, but it was hard to keep resentment out.

On his return, very much out of puff and slightly out of temper, he found Hadda transferring the contents of the first load to his kitchen cupboards. On the table he'd placed a bag of sugar, a carton of cream, and a packet of dog chews.

'What's them?' he said. 'Not on my order.'

'Not on your bill either,' said Hollins. 'A gift.'

'Oh aye? You'll not get round Sneck that easy.'

Or me, was the implication.

Hollins opened the chews and tossed one to the dog, who caught it, nibbled it cautiously, then swallowed it whole.

'How did you find him?' he asked.

'Didn't. He found me. Takes a one to know a one.'

Meaning outcast, the vicar assumed.

'Why Sneck?'

''Cos with a dog like him you don't need one. If that hail storm hadn't started when it did, I'd have turned him loose on those idiots who came up from the village the other night.'

A sneck, Hollins had discovered in his time here, was Cumbrian for a door- or gate-latch.

He tossed the dog another chew. A sop for Cerberus.

Hadda, who'd resumed putting the shopping away, said, 'Make yourself useful then. Brew us a coffee.'

Hollins obeyed, careful to follow his host's procedure on his previous visit as closely as possible.

When he'd filled the same two mugs as before and sat down at the table, Hadda pushed the sugar and cream towards him.

'Care to try your gift?' he said sardonically.

He drank his own black and unsweetened.

'Not bad,' he said. 'A teaspoon short, I'd say.'

'You're very precise.'

'One thing I missed inside. I think they used gravy browning. The other cons were mostly trying to get smack smuggled into the jail. With me it was coffee.'

'Did you have a hard time? I've heard that people with your kind of conviction . . .'

'At first, yeah. Fortunately, at least it seems that way now, I wasn't registering all that much to start with, so it mostly bounced off me. When I began to take notice, I hit back. Didn't matter who it was. Got me a lot of trouble, but eventually the message got round. They could have their fun but they'd always have to pay for it.'

'Sounds a bit Old Testament,' said Hollins.

'You reckon? Well, that's where all the best bits are, isn't it? Including rules for survival in a primitive society.'

'And you survived.'

'I suppose so. Time helped. Good old Time. Either makes or breaks, even in prison. You stay inside long enough, you start getting treated for the way you are, not the reason you ended up there.'

Over the next few weeks, Hollins saw something of the same process taking place locally. The initial outrage faded and there were no more vigilante attacks. Perhaps the news that Sneck had adopted him helped. It turned out the dog was well known locally as an unapproachable renegade, more elusive than a fox, and as vicious a killer. He would have been shot long since if any of the local farmers had been able to get him in their sights. Hadda's own comment of *takes a one to know a one* was often repeated.

It also helped that no one could complain that the returned and unforgiving prodigal was provocative. Hadda steered well clear of the village, though occasional reports of sightings of his solitary figure trudging round the countryside came in. No one cared to approach him. Even had they wanted to, Sneck and the fact that he often carried a lumber axe were considerable disincentives. Occasionally the noise of an axe at work in some remote piece of woodland cracked through the chill air.

'Sounds more like a man attacking something he hates than just cutting down a tree,' opined Joe Strudd, his nearest neighbour.

'Does it not bother you, having him living so close to thy farm, Joe?' enquired Len Brodie, the churchwarden.

Strudd, a pillar of the chapel who reckoned that Anglicans were papists in mufti, said, 'God looks after his own, Len Brodie. Now if you were the bastard's neighbour, then I'd be worried!'

If ever a note of sympathy did enter a reported sighting, contrasting the energetic athletic young man Hadda had once been with the shambling, stooped, scarred and limping figure he had become, it was quickly countered with the stern asseveration that this was no more than just payment for his foul sins.

'Fifty years from now, mothers will be frightening their naughty kids with a bogeyman called The Hadda,' forecast Hollins.

'Let's hope he doesn't start frightening them a lot sooner than that,' said his wife, Willa, sourly.

It was odd, thought the vicar. Willa, childless and, in the eyes of many of his flock, outrageously liberal in her views, was the most determinedly unrelenting in her attitude to Hadda. He sometimes got the disturbing impression that she'd almost welcome an attack on a young girl to prove how right she'd been.

Hollins's grocery deliveries were of course common knowledge almost as soon as he started them. He soon realized that the price he was paying for the message of tolerance and understanding he preached was that he'd been elected Hadda's keeper.

'How's he doing then, Vicar?' he'd be asked – very few people actually spoke the name.

'Going on steady,' was the reassuring reply they wanted. 'Very quiet, that's the way he wants things.'

Only at the castle did he find this kind of bromidic response inadequate.

He could not believe it a coincidence that after he started his regular visits to Birkstane, lunch invitations to the castle became almost regular as well.

The first time he was summoned, Lady Kira ignored him till he was looking down at his plateful of steamed duff and custard. Lady Kira never touched it herself, but as a keen traditionalist, once she'd established this was as essential a part of the Sabbath to Sir Leon as Communion wine and wafers, she'd made it a permanent feature of the castle menu.

Hollins was aware that her attention had turned to him even though he wasn't looking at her. She had that kind of presence. The years that had turned Sir Leon into a white-haired patriarch had been much kinder to her, and now the twenty-two-year gap between looked as if it might be twice as much. At sixty she was still a very attractive woman, if you liked your women lean and predatory. Occasionally Hollins had felt that penetrating gaze running up and down him as he ascended into the pulpit to deliver his Sunday sermon. His wife had laughed and said, 'Wishful thinking' when he told her that now he understood what women meant when they talked of some men stripping them with their eyes. But he knew what he meant.

Waiting till he was raising the first spoonful of duff to his mouth, she said, 'So how is our resident monster, Mr Collins?'

Her determined Anglophilia had made her a keen fan of Jane Austen (Dickens, except on Christmas, being far too radical) and on the few occasions she addressed the vicar direct, she always called him Mr Collins. Sir Leon did this too, but in his case, it seemed possible it was a genuine mistake. Not in Lady Kira's.

For a moment he thought of exacting a mild revenge by

pretending not to know who she was talking about, but it hardly seemed worth it.

Lowering his spoon, he said in a measured tone, 'While I wouldn't call Mr Hadda a fit man, he seems determined to be independent. Apart from the loss of an eye and a few fingers, his upper body seems in good working order, and he certainly gets plenty of shoulder-muscle exercise by wielding an axe. But I regret to say that it appears as if his damaged leg still gives him considerable pain. Perhaps the cold weather doesn't help.'

'Considerable pain?' echoed Lady Kira, visibly savouring the words. 'Well, that's something. And his state of mind, how do you judge his state of mind, Mr Collins?'

'He seems to bear his lot with some equanimity, Lady Kira.'

'Indeed. Well, that's more than I've enjoyed since they permitted him to camp on our doorstep.'

'The chap's entitled to live in his own house, my dear,' protested her husband.

'There wouldn't have been a house if you'd bulldozed it down while he was enjoying his incredibly short holiday in prison,' spat Lady Kira. 'And how is it that he has a house anyway when all his other properties had to be sold off to pay for his fraudulent transactions, virtually putting our daughter on the streets!'

'Bit of an exaggeration there, I think, my dear,' said Sir Leon, glancing apologetically at Hollins. 'Point is, as I've explained before, by the time Fred died, the Woodcutter finances had all been sorted out so no one had a claim on Birkstane when Wolf inherited it. All above board and by the law.'

'The law!' exclaimed his wife. 'I thought the law banned these perverts from taking up residence anywhere near children. What about the village school?'

This was the first time she'd ever shown the slightest

interest in the village school, despite Hollins's efforts to get the castle involved in opposing the council's education 'rationalization' policy which proposed closing Mireton Primary and bussing the couple of dozen local kids fifteen miles to a larger school.

He said, 'Birkstane is seven miles from the village, Lady Kira. In any case, unless we can persuade the council to change their minds, the school will be closing next summer.'

Sir Leon shifted uneasily in his chair. Poor devil feels guilty he hasn't done enough to support the campaign, guessed Hollins. But nobody in the county had any doubts who called the shots at the castle.

'Lot of fuss about nothing, eh, Vicar? They'd hardly have let Wolf out before his time was up if he hadn't been cured.'

'Cured?' cried Lady Kira. 'You mean they took a pair of gelding shears to him?'

Hollins had a flashback to his first sighting of Hadda and restrained a smile as he said, 'I don't think any actual surgery was involved, Lady Kira, but I gather he was and probably still is under psychiatric care and supervision. I'm sure Sir Leon's right, he wouldn't have been released on licence unless he'd satisfied experts that he was no longer a menace.'

'While he's still a man, he's a menace,' said Lady Kira. 'Where do these experts live, eh? Not round here, that's for sure. Take that axe of his and cut it off, that's the only way to guarantee we are safe.'

With that, she seemed to lose interest in both the topic and her guest, and with evident relief Sir Leon said, 'Thought I might take a gun out in the Long Spinney this afternoon. Do you shoot, Collins?'

And Hollins, who'd been asked this question several times already, replied again, 'No, Sir Leon,' but he no longer added the word *sorry*.

5

Even nature seems occasionally nostalgic, and this year just when the English had become resigned to a future of dank wet winters, the season went retro with day after day and week after week of old-fashioned dazzling sunshine following nights of biting frost.

Not just in England either. This bracing weather stretched across the Channel and down the Bay of Biscay, till even the heliotropic ex-pats along the Spanish *costas* found they were given unwelcome reminders of what they thought they'd left behind. Tiled floors, so deliciously cool in summer, now felt icy beneath bare feet and stored luggage was ransacked in search of carpet slippers.

Arnie Medler drove carefully down from his mountain villa into Marbella. At least at this time of year, and in these conditions, there was no problem parking right outside the Hotel Gaviota, which for his money provided the most authentic Full English Breakfast to be had the length and breadth of the Costa del Sol. In the summer he was happy enough with cereal and fruit juice, but from time to time during the dark months he felt the need for cholesterol shock, and Tina, his wife, had made it clear that she hadn't come to Spain to slave over a hot frying pan.

This winter had turned him into a regular customer and he was greeted by name as he entered the restaurant. He took his usual seat at a corner table by a window overlooking the hotel pool, deserted now. The restaurant was only half full. The hotel ticked over during the off-season by offering reduced rates, mainly taken up by UK pensioners keen to escape the latest flu bug. Medler amused himself by listening to their often surprisingly intimate conversations. Many things had changed in this twenty-first-century world, but the English still headed into Europe like eighteenth-century aristos, treating Johnny Foreigner as a kind of moving wallpaper, and after a decade here the sun had burnt his skin brown enough and his Spanish had become good enough for him to pass as a native to anyone who wasn't a native.

This morning those nearest to him were couples who seemed to have said all they had to say to each other half a lifetime ago and he let his gaze wander round the room. A man was being shown to a table at the far end.

With a mild shock, more of surprise than alarm, Medler registered that his face looked familiar.

Better safe than sorry. Changing politics and economics meant that the costas were no longer the refuge of choice for British crooks, but there were still enough of them about to make a retired cop proceed with caution.

He raised his napkin to his lips and held it there till the man had been seated with his back towards him.

When he'd finished his meal, he left the restaurant by the kitchen entrance. The head waiter was in there and he looked at him in surprise.

'Señor Medler,' he said, 'is there something wrong?'

He was proud of his English and Medler knew he would

smile sympathetically and wrinkle his brow if he tried to reply in Spanish.

He said, 'José, could you help me? There's a gentleman by himself, over there . . .'

He pointed through the circular window of the kitchen door.

'. . . I think I may know him. Could you find out who he is?'

He was known as a generous tipper and José had no problem in cooperating.

A couple of minutes later, by the reception desk, Medler learnt that the solitary man was his former colleague, David McLucky, that he was booked into a double room but he'd turned up alone, and that he was here for another five nights.

So, not a crook who might feel like banging him on the nose for old time's sake.

But the question remained: of all the gin joints in all the towns in all the world, was it just coincidence he'd booked into this one, and alone?

'Thanks,' said Medler, peeling off a twenty-euro note.

'Is he your friend, señor?'

'We'll see. No need to mention my interest, eh?'

Another note.

'Of course not, Señor Medler. I hope we see you again soon.'

'Perhaps.'

In fact it was the following morning that the head waiter saw Medler return to the restaurant. McLucky was already at his table, talking into a mobile phone with what looked like increasing exasperation.

Medler strode confidently towards his own table, glanced towards McLucky as he passed, did a double take, then diverted.

'Davy McLucky, is that you?' he said.

The Scot looked up and said, 'Who's asking?'

'Come on, Davy. Should auld acquaintance and all that!'

'Fuck me, is it Medler?' said McLucky without any noticeable enthusiasm.

'It most certainly is! What the hell are you doing here?'

'Trying to get out and not having much luck.'

There was a tinny voice coming out of the phone.

McLucky barked, 'Sod off!' into the mouthpiece and switched it off.

'Problems?'

'I'm trying to get a flight out and not getting any joy, not without coughing up a small fortune.'

'Perhaps I can help, if it's a language thing,' said Medler, pulling out a chair. 'Mind if I sit down?'

'You never used to be so polite.'

'Never needed to be, when I could pull rank,' laughed Medler. 'So how are you, Davy? Still with the Met?'

'No. Asked for my cards years back.'

'Followed my good example, eh?'

'Not exactly. They said you were sick. Me, I was just sick of the fucking job.'

'You always were a bit of a loner, Davy. So what are you up to now?'

'Security,' said McLucky shortly.

'Oh Christ. What's that mean then? Nightwatchman at a building site?'

The slightly jeering tone seemed to provoke the Scot.

'No! I run my own enquiry firm in Glasgow.'

'Oh yes? And are you here on business?'

'I wish,' said McLucky. 'It would be nice to think some other poor bastard was paying me to be in this dump.'

'Oh dear. Is the wife with you? What's her name . . . Jenny, right?'

'Jeanette. No, took off with her hairdresser couple of years

206

before I left the Met. Helped me make up my mind. You can imagine the jokes.'

'I'm sorry,' said Medler. 'So you're here by yourself?'

McLucky stared at him aggressively for a moment, then shrugged and said, 'Aye, that's right, I'm a real sad bastard, eh? Not the plan, but that's how it turned out. Me and a friend – a former friend! – we thought we'd take a break away from the blizzards back in Scotland. Picked this cheap last-minute deal on the Internet. Then I got a call at the airport: she couldn't make it, family emergency. Bitch! Got a better offer, I reckon. I thought I might as well come anyway, it was a no-refund deal. But I wish to hell I hadn't bothered. It's almost as bad here as back in Glasgow! That's what I was trying to do, get an early flight back home. There must be any amount of spare space on the charters, but no, it's scheduled or nothing, the bastards tell me.'

He looked at Medler calculatingly and said, 'You really think you could help? I'd appreciate it.'

He offered his phone.

'Maybe,' said Medler, smiling. 'But tell you what. Why don't we have some breakfast first, chew the fat about old times? Then we'll see.'

6

As the days shortened and winter bit deeper and deeper into the earth as though determined to give global warming a good run for its money, the Reverend Luke Hollins's thoughts turned to Christmas. While naturally his main focus was on the spiritual dimension and he lost no opportunity to decry the unrelenting commercialization of the festival, there was a part of his mind preoccupied with more mundane questions, such as which was more likely to get a result? – a plea to the bishop for a new heating boiler in the vicarage or a letter to Father Christmas at the North Pole?

Most of his parishioners, including Hadda, seemed impervious to the cold. Cumbrians, he decided, had a strong proportion of ice water in their veins. Only at Ulphingstone Castle did he find someone who longed for heat as much as he did and as that person was Lady Kira, this coincidence of feeling brought little mutual warmth.

The lunches, and Lady Kira's questions about Hadda (now punctuated by strident and abusive commands to servants, her husband and occasionally the vicar himself to pile more logs on the fire) continued throughout the winter.

There was, however, no reciprocal curiosity at Birkstane.

If there had been, Hollins would probably have been as discreet in his replies to Hadda as he was in those he offered Kira. But the man's apparent indifference to news from the outside world in general and the castle in particular was somehow provocative. So some time in mid-December, the vicar heard himself saying as he placed the last grocery box on the kitchen floor, 'Sir Leon was telling me his daughter's coming up for Christmas.'

Hadda, who was pouring hot water into the coffee jug, paused and said slowly, 'Now why should you imagine that bit of information holds the slightest interest for me?'

'Well, she did used to be your wife, didn't she? And I thought I'd mention it just to give you a forewarning against a potentially distressing and embarrassing chance encounter . . .'

He was waffling, he realized, and he brought himself to a halt.

Hadda stirred the coffee vigorously.

Then he smiled.

'That shows Christian foresight, Padre. Lead me not into temptation, eh? Talking of which, is that a bottle of Shiraz I see sticking out of that box? I don't recollect putting that on my list.'

'Sorry . . . I mean it's a gift, it was on offer and I thought you might like it.'

The addition of a packet of chews to the order had come to be accepted, and though Hollins would not have cared to put his relationship with Sneck to the test, the dog's growl when he arrived was now anticipatory rather than minatory.

For a moment the scowl on Hadda's face made him fear the wine was going to be a gift too far.

Then his features cleared and he said, 'Thank you kindly. Much appreciated. But I really must ask you not to repeat the generosity. On the pittance the State allows me, I can't afford to develop expensive habits.'

'Come on, it only cost four quid,' protested Hollins.

'Nevertheless . . .'

He poured the coffee and they drank in silence for a while.

'So what are you doing for Christmas?' asked Hollins.

Hadda let out a snort of laughter.

'Ask me again after I've had time to sort through all my many invitations. But, like I say, definitely no more gifts, eh? I'll save the Shiraz for Christmas Day. As for a Christmas tree, well, I've got several thousand of those just over the wall in the estate.'

The vicar looked at him in alarm and he said, 'Relax. Only joking. Now look at the time. Got to dash off to see my PO, it's have-you-been-a-good-boy? time again. Stick the rest of this stuff in the cupboard, will you?'

He was on his feet and limping towards the door as he spoke. His parting request was tossed almost casually over his shoulder and suddenly Hollins felt himself greatly irritated. What he wanted to say was, 'I'm not your bloody valet!' but what he heard himself asking somewhat aggressively was, 'Is that really how you feel about these sessions with your probation officer?'

Hadda paused and looked back at him in surprise.

'To coin a phrase . . . sorry?'

'You always seem to refer to your meetings frivolously, as though they were nothing more than a necessary chore.'

'Didn't realize I did. Though, come to think about it, what else should they be?'

'I don't know. A time for self-assessment, perhaps. A time to quantify progress.'

'Progress? From what? To what?'

Hollins hesitated before replying. He hadn't planned to go down this road at this stage in their relationship, but now he'd started, it would be cowardly to turn back.

He said slowly, 'From what and to what isn't for me to say.

210

But I do know what I'd call the actual journey. Repentance.'

'Re-pen-tance,' said Hadda, as though trying to commit to memory a new word in a foreign language he was learning.

'Yes. I'm sure your prison psychiatrist, Dr whatsername . . .'

'Ozigbo.'

'. . . Ozigbo would have other terms for it, but that's what the Church calls it. I should have thought it was an essential element in whatever process you went through to get here – outside, I mean, back in the community. To be honest, there are a lot of things I've seen in you during our short acquaintance. Fortitude, self-control, temperance, resolution. But I can't say I've detected much evidence of repentance.'

'So how would it show itself then?' asked Hadda. 'Hair shirts? Self-flagellation? Prayer and fasting? I think I could put my hand up for the fasting. Some nights I can't be bothered to make myself anything more than a mug of coffee and a hunk of cheese. Does that count, Holy Father?'

'You see, there you go,' said Hollins wearily. 'Putting up a front's fine, but do it too much and the front becomes a fixture that no one, not even yourself, can look behind.'

'Let me guess, that must be New Testament,' said Hadda. 'Nothing like that in the OT among all the smiting and begatting. I'm a bit disappointed, Padre. I was almost beginning to think you were a real post-modern priest – you know, to hell with old-fashioned preaching, let's treat people like people. But if you're going to revert to type, then you can sod off out of here and take your cut-price Shiraz with you! Think about it while you're stacking my shelves.'

He left the kitchen. Sneck, with what seemed almost like an apologetic glance back, followed him. A few minutes later, Hollins heard the Defender start up.

After its clatter had faded down the lonning, he began to put the groceries away. Eventually only the wine bottle remained. If he left it, Hadda would think he'd caved in. But

211

if he took it, then that could be the end of their regular contact. He half regretted his outburst, but only half. He'd found himself coming to like the man but he felt the danger in that, especially when the relationship was developing very much on Hadda's terms. He recalled a seminar on the paedophile threat to the Church given by an elderly priest during his training course.

'Never forget,' the tutor had said, 'paedophiles are among the most cunning creatures on God's earth.'

The man had spoken with the voice of experience. Currently he was serving two years for indecent assault on an altar boy.

So he'd been right to confront Hadda, even if it was only to draw a line in the sand.

But every particle of reason and judgment in him said that the man was OK, that his past was a closed book that would never be opened again. In fact, come to think of it, those medieval manifestations of repentance that Hadda had mockingly cited, weren't they all around him? Living in this cold damp cheerless house, bathing each morning in the icy beck, surviving on the pathetic groceries that Hollins brought every couple of weeks, and which Hadda always paid for in full out of his social security pittance, weren't these the modern forms of hair shirt and self-flagellation?

Somewhere a mobile rang.

His own was in his pocket. This had to be in the house. Upstairs, he worked out. Hadda must have forgotten it. Would be furious if it turned out to be his probation officer, cancelling their meeting.

He started up the stairs to answer it but the ringing stopped before he was halfway up. It seemed as easy to continue as turn on the narrow staircase and he carried on up to the landing. Through a half-open door he saw the mobile lying on an unmade bed.

212

After a moment's hesitation, he went into the room and picked it up. The display said *1 message.*

He pressed the call button without thinking. Or without letting himself think.

Listen to message?

If it was his PO cancelling, he thought, maybe I can think of a way to intercept the Defender.

He didn't give himself time to deconstruct this piece of irrationality, but pressed again.

The voice that spoke had a strong Scots accent.

Hi. I'm at the villa! Dinner invite turned to 'Stay as long as you like'. Christ. He's done well for himself. All mod cons, swimming pool, jacuzzi. Very security conscious, big gate, high fence with what looks like razor wire on the top. All windows and doors fitted with metal security shutters that come down sharp when he presses the button. Could do with them to keep his wife at bay! She's a nice little package of simmering hormones. After the second bottle of Rioja, she started eyeing me up like she was contemplating inviting me to share her paella. Wish I'd got one of them shutters on my bedroom door! I'm out of here soon as I can! I'll stop off in London, see if there are any developments on the home front. It'll be good to get back somewhere with a bit of life. You can keep the Costa Geriatica for me. I'm glad you're paying for it. I'll be in touch. Maybe I'll even beard the Wolf in his lair on my way home. Cheers!

What was that all about? wondered Hollins.

He switched the phone off and laid it on the bed.

Then he looked around the room.

Not much furniture but maybe that was all there'd ever been. A bedside table, an ancient Lloyd Loom chair, a picture of what looked like a lumberjack on the wall, a wardrobe that looked as old as the rough-plastered wall it stood against.

The door was ajar.

Peering inside without opening it any further wasn't poking around, was it?

You should have been a Jesuit! he told himself pulling the door wide.

Couple of rough shirts and two pairs of heavy trousers. And on the floor a cardboard wine box.

He checked its contents.

Half a dozen of Gevrey-Chambertin plus a couple of bottles of fifteen-year-old Glen Morangie.

He thought of his four-quid bottle of Shiraz on the kitchen table. The cheeky sod had said he'd save it for Christmas! So where had this lot come from? Perhaps with the economy soaring to record levels once more, social security were being unusually generous with the Christmas bonuses.

He looked round the room for other signs of unexplained affluence.

Nothing obvious, but the blankets draped over the bed had been caught by something pushed underneath.

He knelt down and pulled out an old metal chest, rusting at the corners, painted in flaking black enamel, with the initials W.H. stencilled on the lid in white.

It felt quite heavy.

There was a key in the lock.

So, nothing to hide there, not with the key left in the lock . . .

Why am I still looking for excuses? he asked himself.

Surely that wine box is justification enough?

He was still debating the point mentally as he turned the key and opened the box.

It was full of money. Bundles of fifty-pound notes, neatly laid out four times six, and at least five layers of them, with a couple of bundles missing from the top layer.

Oh hell! thought Luke Hollins, sitting heavily on the bed.

Now at last he had something to take his mind off the vicarage boiler.

7

Wolf Hadda realized he'd forgotten his phone when he was halfway to Carlisle.

Old age, he thought. Not that it mattered. The call he wanted to make was perhaps better made from the anonymous security of a landline rather as part of the babbling traffic of the air.

Public boxes were thin on the ground these days and he was on the edge of the city before he spotted one. It occurred to him that in the years since he'd rung this number, it might well have changed. In fact it was answered almost immediately.

'Chapel Domestic Agency, how can I help you?' said a bright young voice.

He said, 'I'm looking for a woodcutter.'

'Hold on.'

There was a long silence then a man's voice said, 'Good day.'

'And a good day to you too, JC.'

'How nice to hear your voice. What can I do for you?'

'I need something.'

'Really? And what makes you imagine I may be in a giving mood?'

'The fact that I've not been pestered by hordes of journalists lurking in the undergrowth. Only reason I can think of for that is editors have had their arms twisted. Only one old twister with that kind of strength I can think of.'

'I'm almost flattered. But if I have already done so much for you, why do you think I should want to do more?'

'Because having done so much suggests there's a bit of guilt there, JC. How much, I'm not sure. Eventually I'll find out, but till then you might feel the need to establish a bit more goodwill.'

'Have you never heard of simple altruism?'

Hadda replied with a silence more telling than laughter.

'All right. What do you want?'

'A couple of kilos of coke.'

'I see. Any chance of giving a reason?'

'Call it necessity.'

'In that case, give me a moment.'

'I'm in Cumbria, on the western outskirts of Carlisle, if you're running a trace.'

'Of course you are,' said the man. 'Which may in fact be pertinent. So, let me see . . . Ah, yes. Here we are. Now I think a couple of kilos might be difficult.'

'A kilo might do, at a pinch.'

'No, the problem is in the other direction. If you could make do with a hundred kilos, I might be able to help. In fact, geographically speaking, you are particularly well placed. Interested? If so, ring off and I'll get back to you in a few minutes.'

Hadda rang off and went to sit in the Defender. Three minutes later the phone rang.

He answered it, listened, made a note, and said, 'Thanks.'

216

'Be careful. These are professional people. And you are not as young as you were.'

'I'm not as anything as I was,' said Hadda harshly and rang off.

He got back into the Land Rover and drove away.

As he negotiated the increasing traffic into the heart of the ancient city, he said to himself, 'Now that was very easy. Just how guilty do you feel, JC?'

8

With her parentage, Alva Ozigbo felt she ought to be able
to switch seasonally from a stoic indifference to the chills of
winter to a sensuous enjoyment of summer heat.

The truth was her slim Scandinavian mother hated to be
cold and enjoyed nothing more than luxuriating in the
scorching rays of a southern sun, while her bulky Nigerian
father strode around in sub-zero temperatures wearing a
short-sleeved shirt and at the first sign of milder weather
started mopping his perspiring brow and turning up the air
conditioning.

Alva felt she'd got the worst of both worlds. She was no
sun-worshipper and she hated the pervasive chill of the
wintry city.

This evening as she returned home from work, the east
wind that had been pursuing her like a determined stalker
ever since she got out of her car managed to squeeze enough
of its presence into the entrance hall of her apartment block
to keep her shivering as she paused to check her mail box.
It contained only one letter and as she saw the postmark,
she shivered again.

Cumbria.

218

As far as she knew, she had only one connection with Cumbria.

But she didn't recognize this handwriting.

Quickly she ran up the stairs to her second-floor flat. The central heating had already switched itself on and she turned her electric fire up high to give herself the thermal boost she needed.

Then she sat down and opened the envelope.

St Swithin's Vicarage
Mireton
Cumbria
Dear Dr Ozigbo
I am sorry to trouble you but I need advice and, so far as I can judge at the moment, you are the best person to give it to me. I am vicar of St Swithin's here in West Cumbria and since last November Wilfred Hadda has been one of my parishioners. Let me say at once I know that as he is a former, perhaps indeed a current, patient of yours, the usual strict rules of medical confidentiality will apply and I'm not about to ask you to do anything that may break them. All I can do is provide you with some information and ask for your expert guidance on what, if anything, I should do about it.

I visit Mr Hadda every couple of weeks or so. While I can't say his return was welcomed locally, after some initial violent reaction things have settled down considerably, helped by both the relative remoteness of Birkstane, his house, and also by Mr Hadda's own self-prescribed remoteness. So far as I know, he has made no attempt to communicate with anyone in the parish. My own conversations with him have, on the whole, been at a fairly social

219

level, but I haven't evaded the subject of his offence and its consequences. While I've got the impression of a pretty calm and well-ordered personality (and to my surprise a rather engaging one, too), I am very aware that the baggage he carries must at times weigh heavy. One thing I didn't spot, however, was any overt sign of remorse or repentance. When I put this to him he more or less told me to mind my own business.

Now, in a very real sense, this is my business, and I cannot let my generally good impression of Mr Hadda and my respect for his rights come before my responsibilities to the rest of my parishioners. I want to be able to assure them with no reservation that I've found nothing in Mr Hadda's attitude or behaviour to suggest he could ever be a threat to their families. I suppose it could be argued that the fact that he doesn't wear remorse on his sleeve is a good sign. I mean, a paedophile still seeking the opportunity to offend would be at pains to advertise his change of heart, wouldn't he? I'd be interested to hear what you have to say about that. But the reason I'm writing to you is that, whatever the state of his libido, I've come across something that suggests in his other sphere of crime, financial fraud, he may still be adept at concealment.

Mr Hadda claims to be surviving on state benefit alone. But by chance when I was alone in his house yesterday I came across a crate of expensive wine and a box full of money. A lot of money. I didn't count it, but it must have amounted to several hundred thousand pounds, in bundles of forty £50 notes, two of which seemed to be missing (= £4,000).

I've thought about this and a possible explanation seems to be that when he was in business, knowing the risks he was running, he put aside an emergency fund, and hid it so well that the Fraud Squad investigation didn't manage to turn it up. This implies a level of foreplanning and powers of deception that trouble me. I don't know what to do. To talk to the authorities opens up the possibility that this has been a breach of his probation conditions, which would mean an instant return to jail. I don't want that on my conscience. But if it is symptomatic of a naturally deceitful character, and if at some stage it turned out he was also concealing his old urges, and these burst out and resulted in damage to any of my parishioners, I could not easily forgive myself.

I could of course confront him and demand to know where the money came from, and what he has spent £4,000 on since his release. But this would certainly shatter our delicate relationship and I doubt if I have the skills to sort the wheat from the chaff in any explanation he cares to offer.

So in my dilemma, I'm turning to you, Dr Ozigbo. Mr Hadda has mentioned your name and your job, lightly but affectionately I felt, and I've tracked down your address via the Internet. No such thing as privacy these days! And what I want to ask you is this. As the psychiatric expert who supervised his progress through the regeneration course (sorry, don't know what you call it, but that's how I think of it!) how convinced are you that he is no longer a menace to the community?

Obviously you must have been very convinced last autumn or you wouldn't have recommended his

release on licence. But in the light of what I've just
told you, how convinced are you now?
    We are both employed in the cure of souls, Dr
Ozigbo, though not in the same sense of the term.
Your concern is individual; you try to repair
damaged psyches. Mine is pastoral; I try to look
after the welfare of my flock. If you do not feel able
to reply to this letter, or if in your reply you are not
able to offer total reassurance, then my duty will be
clear and I'll have to report what I know to the
authorities even though I fear that the consequences
for Mr Hadda might be severe.
    I look forward to hearing from you.
Yours sincerely
Luke Hollins

After she'd read the letter, Alva went into the kitchen, took
a prepared chicken salad out of the fridge, poured herself a
glass of white wine, carried food and drink into the living
room and sat down by the fire. Before she started eating,
she switched her radio on to catch the six o'clock news.

Its burden was familiar. The world was in a mess. Not
quite the same mess it had been in when Wilfred Hadda
started his sentence – the worry now was that the economy
was overheating again rather than bumping along the bottom
– but the same wars were being fought, the same groups
were blowing people up in the name of the same gods, the
ice-mass was a little lower, the sea levels were a little higher,
a couple more species had been declared extinct – no, on
the whole Hadda would probably not have noticed any significant change on his release.

She brought to mind their last meeting, some three months
earlier. She had met him as he came out of the prison. The
only other person there was a small bespectacled man in a

222

battered Toyota. She recognized him as Mr Trapp, the solicitor. They hadn't met, but she had glimpsed him when he was acting for Hadda as his probation hearing approached. He wasn't the most impressive representative of the legal profession she'd met, but he seemed to know his business.

It occurred to her it must have been a pretty big favour he owed Hadda to still be paying it off after all this time. Or maybe it was Hadda's capacity to inspire personal loyalty that she saw working here. She'd felt it herself and there were suggestions in Luke Hollins's letter that he'd come under the influence.

It was a dangerous quality in a man with his sexual predilections.

There was no such thing as a cure, of course, not unless you went a lot further down the chemical road than she was able to contemplate. All you could do was try and restore that barrier between impulse and action that keeps most of us within the bounds of socially acceptable behaviour. First of all you had to strip away all the excuses and evasions, the explanations and deceptions, and once you had got the patient to see what he was, then you could start building up a positive image of what he might be.

It was a tortuous road that you trod with great care, for at the end of it lay the question, Is it safe to let this man out into the world again?

She had of course discussed progress with Simon Homewood at regular intervals. He had been consistently helpful and supportive. And always he had talked about the final recommendation for parole as being their joint decision. Technically this was true, but nothing Homewood said could blur Alva's awareness that ultimately the responsibility for Hadda's release would be hers.

She'd also spoken of the case in general terms with John Childs. Curiously she derived much more comfort from her non-specific chats with him than she did from her much more detailed discussions with the Director. Perhaps this was because his response was tinged with a gentle cynicism against which she was forced to test her own conclusions and intuitions.

'Is it inevitable,' he asked, 'that recognition of the evil of one's actions is accompanied by regret for performing them?'

'Not in certain extreme cases of sociopathic behaviour,' she replied. 'But I do not categorize my client as a sociopath.'

'Then what?'

'A man with a compulsion he deplores so much he could only deal with it by denying it completely. Like some alcoholics.'

'Isn't that a rather easy judgment? I mean, alcoholics don't hurt other people. Except their families. And they have the AA to help them. And I doubt the public would tolerate a support organization called Paedophiles Pseudonymous.'

'The Law makes judgments,' said Alva. 'My job is to assess and, where possible, adjust.'

'And ultimately to advise,' said Childs. 'It's a huge responsibility.'

'And you think I should duck it by leaving my client banged up for ever?'

'Good Lord, no. I'm sure you wouldn't dream of letting him loose if you had the slightest fear he'd still be a danger to young girls. Whether, of course, he might be a danger to anyone else hardly falls within the brief of your terms of employment.'

He smiled as he spoke, so she decided he was making what in the Home Office passed for a joke and smiled back, and the conversation then moved on to young Harry's imminent enrolment at university.

By the time of Hadda's parole hearing, she entertained no doubts about his fitness to return to society, and her certainty carried the day with the panel. Nor did she feel any pang of unease as she saw him emerge from the jail and stand for a moment, looking up at the sky.

She got out of her Fiesta and advanced to meet him. Trapp had remained in his car.

'Elf,' said Hadda, 'it's good of you to come. Good to see you exist outside.'

'That's the point,' she said. 'You've got to know that my concern for you doesn't stop at the prison gate. It never did.'

'I appreciate that. And I know I thanked you inside, but now I want to thank you outside for all you've done for me. Without you . . . well, I don't know what I'd be. I certainly know where I'd be! Thank you. And I'm sorry for all that crap I fed you.'

She shook her head and said, 'You were in denial. Anyway, it was full of truths; not always the truths you imagined, but without them, I'd never have known how to move forward.'

This amused him enough for the transforming smile to flicker briefly across his lips, and he said, 'So a diet of crap can do you good? Must remember that whenever I hear myself moaning about prison food. Now I'd best be on my way. I'm due at the hostel at ten. Don't want to start my new life by being late.'

She knew he was booked into a halfway house, knew also that when he moved out of there after a couple of weeks, he planned to return to his family home in Cumbria.

She'd said, 'Good luck. The probation service will keep me updated on how things are going, but if you ever feel the need to get in touch direct, don't hesitate.'

He had smiled and for a moment she'd thought he was going to lean forward and kiss her goodbye. But in the event he only gave the kind of head bob men give to royalty, then went across to the old Toyota, got in and was driven away without glancing back.

225

A job well done, she'd thought. Not necessarily a job finished. When you're dealing with the human mind, you can never say the job's finished. But so far, so good.

And now there was this letter.

She made herself finish her meal and wine before she picked it up again.

Luke Hollins was worried and so was she. Even though the syndrome Hadda had presented with predicated great powers of deception, this firm evidence of their continuance was disturbing.

Even more than the source of the money, she shared Hollins's concern about the missing four thousand.

A man with Hadda's record spending that kind of money in a few months . . . her heart sank.

She knew what she ought to do and that was drop this lock, stock and barrel into the lap of the probation service. And she knew that the almost inevitable result would be a revocation of Hadda's licence and a return to custody, at least until his case was reviewed.

These things she knew.

At the same time she realized that, without spending long hours in soul-searching and mental debate, she knew exactly what she was going to do.

9

Drigg Beach on the Cumbrian coast is a heavenly spot on a fine summer day. A couple of miles of level sand, skylarks above the dunes, oyster-catchers at the water's edge, the Irish Sea sparkling all the way to the Isle of Man, to the south the bulk of Black Combe looming benevolently over the land, to the north St Bees Head staring thoughtfully out to sea, all combine to provide a setting in which even the prospect of Sellafield Nuclear Power Station slouching in the sunshine can attain something of a festive air.

But in the darkness of a cold December night with scorpion tails of sleet riding on the back of a strong nor'wester that drives the white-maned waves up the shore like ramping hosts of warrior horse, it can feel as remote and perilous as the edge of the Barents Sea.

Tonight, however, there was human presence here, on the shore and on the water.

A motor-powered rubber dinghy came riding up the beach till it grounded on the sand. Two men in wet suits jumped out carrying between them a large leather grip. At the same time two more men climbed out of a Toyota Land Cruiser parked on the shore and ran down to the water's edge where the first pair deposited the grip. As they returned to the dinghy, the men from the Land Cruiser carried the grip to the car. They were ill matched in build, one large and lumbering, the other much slighter though with an athletic rhythm of movement that gave promise of strength. He certainly seemed to take his share of the load as they hoisted their burden into the Toyota's load space.

Meanwhile the dinghy men had unloaded a second grip on to the sand. They then climbed into the dinghy, the helmsman put the engine into reverse for a few metres then swung round and accelerated out to sea.

By the time the shore men had carried the second grip to the Toyota, the dinghy had vanished into the darkness.

Once more the two men bent their backs to swing their burden up into the load space.

'I shouldn't bother,' said a voice.

From the landward side of the vehicle stepped a figure. He was tall, broad-shouldered; his features were hard to make out but they could see that over one eye he wore a piratical patch; and in his hands he carried a long-handled axe.

The smaller man reacted first, releasing his hold on the grip handle, and reaching into his jacket. The shaft of the axe swung and caught him under the jaw and he collapsed to the ground without a sound.

The taller man had been unbalanced by having to take the full weight of the grip and by the time he let go and straightened up, he found the blade of the axe was six inches from his neck. It stayed steady even when the axeman took his gloved right hand off the shaft and reached down to pluck a gun from the unconscious man's jacket.

'Makarov,' he said dismissively. 'Just an old sentimentalist then.'

He tossed it behind him, then nodded down at the grip.

'Open it,' he said.

The big man obeyed.

The grip was full of transparent packs of white powder.

'Lay them along the sand,' said the axeman. 'In a straight row.'

When that was done he pointed to the grip already loaded.

'Again,' he said.

The man repeated the process except that this time when there were only a couple of the packs left, the axeman said, 'That'll do. Now walk slowly along the row.'

The man started to walk. Suddenly he cried out in terror as the axe-blade whistled past his ear. Then it buried itself in the first of the packs, splitting it open so that the powder spilt out across his shoes.

The process was repeated till all the packs had been burst. By the time they returned to the car, the tide was already running up over the line.

'The fish will be happy tonight,' said the axeman. 'See if you can revive your mate.'

He laid his axe on the sand, took an empty rucksack off his back and placed the remaining two white powder packs in it. The big man knelt by his companion.

'Hey, Pudo, Pudo, you OK?'

There was no response, so the big man tried slapping his face. Perhaps he meant to be gentle, but he wasn't built for refinement. With a scream of pain, the recumbent man tried to roll away from his companion.

'I'd say if poor old Pudo's jaw wasn't broken before, it certainly is now,' said the axeman. 'See if you can get him on his feet without breaking anything else.'

He shrugged the rucksack on to his broad shoulders, retrieved his axe, raised it high and brought the broad back of the head down on the pistol barrel. He then picked up the weapon and chucked it into the back of the Land Cruiser.

'I wouldn't recommend trying to use it,' he said. 'But what I would recommend is for you to get your mate into your car and drive away as fast as you can. If you're tempted to hang around this neck of the woods, just remember that, next time we meet, I may not be in such a generous mood. Tell whoever sent you that he should find himself another landing spot. This coast is out of bounds. You got that?'

The big man nodded. His injured companion was now upright. He still looked as if his knees would buckle without the support of the other's arms, but the gaze that he fixed on the axeman was lively enough. His eyes were black and glittered with hatred. He tried to speak but the damage to his jaw made this impossible.

'No need for thanks, Pudo,' said the axeman. 'Get him aboard.'

The big man half carried, half dragged the other to the passenger door and pushed him on to the seat. Then he walked round to the driver's side. Here he paused by the door, looking round, as if expecting further instruction.

But the axeman had vanished just as completely as the white powder scattered along the beach had disappeared beneath the onward surging waves.

10

Imogen Estover arrived at Ulphingstone Castle four days before Christmas. She parked her sky-blue Mercedes E-Class coupé, sounded the horn, and strode through the main entrance confident that her mother's well-trained staff would take care of her luggage without need of any further instruction.

'Darling, you're early. How nice,' said Lady Kira, offering the double air kiss that was the nearest she permitted to physical contact when her make-up was on.

'London's hideous. You can smell the fug in Oxford Street three miles away,' said Imogen. 'I thought of the fells in the sunshine and had to escape. I can't wait to get out.'

Lady Kira wrinkled her nose. Though occasionally she might affect nostalgia for the great swathes of Caucasian wilderness her family had allegedly once owned, or even join a shooting party on the estate – usually proving herself a better shot than most of the men – she was no lover of the Great Outdoors. Fell walking was, in her vocabulary, a euphemism for trespass, and all that could be said for rock climbing was that from time to time it killed one of the idiots who indulged in it.

Her daughter's enjoyment of these pursuits she treated as a sort of venereal infection resulting from her marriage to the woodcutter's son. But if the years of motherhood had taught her anything it was that Imogen had a will as strong as her own, so she passed no comment but said, 'Where's Toby?'

'Probably clearing his desk so he can roger his fat secretary on it,' said Imogen. 'He'll be up tomorrow on the train.'

Kira screwed up her mouth and for a surprised moment Imogen thought the reference to Toby's infidelities had disconcerted her, but she was quickly reassured.

'On the train?' said Kira in disbelief. 'Pasha's driving up tomorrow, or rather being driven up in that lovely Bentley of his. I'm sure he'd be delighted to give Toby a lift.'

'I think Toby would prefer the train.'

Her mother frowned.

'Prefer travelling with hoi polloi rather than with someone who is his very important client, my relative, and everyone's friend?' she said. 'Why would he prefer that?'

Imogen said, 'I really can't imagine, Mummy. Can you?'

Her father appeared.

He said, 'There you are, my dear. Saw the car,' and gave her a hug.

'Hello, Daddy,' she said. 'You're looking well.'

'Am I?' said Sir Leon doubtfully. 'Nice of you to say so. Staying long?'

'Well, till after Christmas anyway.'

'Ah, Christmas. Toby with you?'

'He's coming tomorrow. And I gather we're having the pleasure of cousin Pasha's company too.'

'What? Oh yes. Nicotine,' said Sir Leon with no sign of enthusiasm.

'*Nik-EE-tin,*' said his wife in an exasperated tone.

Imogen smiled at her father and patted his arm gently.

'I'll go and get unpacked,' she said.

Her parents watched her leave the room then Sir Leon said, 'She know that Wolf's back at Birkstane?'

'I expect so,' said his wife.

'But you didn't mention it?'

'If she knows, why would I remind her?' asked Lady Kira. 'And if she doesn't, why would I tell her?'

They stood and looked at each other, she with indifference and he with the blank incomprehension that had quickly replaced that now almost mythic sense of pride he had felt when, aged forty, he had turned to see his beautiful eighteen-year-old bride processing up the aisle towards him.

Upstairs, their daughter stood in the wide bay of her dressing room and looked out over the lawn to the forest. Frost still sparkled on those shaded areas of grass that the sun couldn't reach. The air was so clear she could pick out the individual branches and trunk markings of the first line of trees and in the distance she could make out some of the great Lakeland fell tops whose names were as familiar to her as those of most of her friends.

She knew her Cumbrian weather. Meaning she knew there was no way of knowing what was going to greet her when she woke the following morning. When you see what you want, don't hesitate, had long been her philosophy. Ignoring her unopened cases, she went downstairs to the drying room where she'd dumped her gear last time she was here. Boots, cleaned and waxed, stood neatly on low shelves, jackets and waterproofs hung from their pegs. Who was responsible for the cleaning and tidying she'd no idea, except that it was unlikely to be her mother. She slipped on a pair of light-weight boots, grabbed a jacket at random and went out of a side door.

She met her father at the corner of the terrace.

'Hullo,' he said. 'Off for a stroll?'

'Shame to waste this weather,' she said, not pausing in her easy, deceptively fast stride.

He watched her go. She had matured into an elegant, shapely woman, but as she walked away from him now, she didn't look all that different from the young teenager who'd run wild around the estate a quarter of a century ago. The thought took him somewhere he didn't care to go. Suddenly it was his granddaughter he was seeing ... Ginny ... lovely lost Ginny. At her christening he'd sworn to himself that he'd do everything in his power to protect her, and he'd failed. As usual, the women in his life had had their way and she'd been whisked out of his sight to France ... and finally out of his sight for ever ...

He shook the pain from his head and refocused on his daughter. From the direction she was taking across the garden he guessed where she was headed. Nothing to be done about it, he thought as she vanished into the wood.

Nothing that ever could be done about it.

Half an hour later, Imogen was standing on the far edge of the forest looking out at the back of Birkstane Farm. The boundary wall was tumbledown here and she stepped easily over the moss-wigged stones. Through the kitchen window she glimpsed movement. She was not a woman who hesitated action and she went straight up to the back door and pushed it open without knocking.

Her face rarely registered surprise, but it did now.

It wasn't Wolf Hadda she found sitting at the kitchen table but a slim black woman with high cheek bones and fine shoulder-length hair of a curious ochrous shade that didn't look artificial.

Imogen said, 'Hello.'

The woman replied, 'Hello.'

Imogen's gaze moved round the room. Unwashed dishes

in the sink, one cup, one bowl, one plate. Wolf, alone, never washed up after a meal, always before the next one. So breakfast for one.

She said, 'Wolf not home then?'

The black woman said, 'Evidently not.'

'You're waiting for him?'

'For a while.'

Imogen liked the non-aggressive way she refused to initiate an exchange of information. At the moment, in the unspoken contest to establish who had the greater right to be in Wolf's kitchen, honours were pretty even.

In the fireplace paper and kindling had been laid and several dry logs were stacked ready on the hearth.

She said, 'Too nice a day to waste indoors, but if you're going to sit here long, I'd put a match to the fire.'

Then she turned and left, not bothering to close the door behind her.

11

You should have closed the door, thought Alva Ozigbo.

She'd known this was Hadda's former wife as soon as the woman stepped into the kitchen, and not merely because her files on the man contained photographs. In fact, to identify her from the photos wouldn't have been easy. They all showed her in urban mode, elegant, composed. The figure that stepped through the door in her boots and ancient jacket, her face flushed from walking fast in the cold air, and with bits of twig and bark in her hair from ducking under low branches, was very different. But Alva had recognized her at once. Perhaps it was the composure. That was still very much there.

But she hadn't closed the door behind her. Probably because she did not want to risk even the suggestion of a slam.

They must have made a magnificent couple, thought Alva. Both tall, strong-featured, blue-eyed, blond-haired, with the poise that comes from physical athleticism and psychological certainty. Both qualities vanished in Hadda's case, but from this one brief glimpse, as present as ever in his ex-wife.

She glanced up at the old bracket clock hanging on the wall.

Half past three. She'd wait another half hour, she decided. Luke Hollins had said that if Hadda was out and the Defender was in the barn, that meant there was a good chance he'd be back before dusk, which began to fall about four o'clock this time of year.

She looked up and he was there, standing in the open doorway.

'You should have lit the fire,' he said.

'That's what your ex-wife said.'

He showed no surprise but moved across the kitchen with that slow limping gait she remembered so well, stooped over the hearth, struck a match and set it to the paper. Behind him a dog paused in the doorway to study her, then, growling softly in its throat and never shifting its gaze, padded across to the fireplace and lay down.

'You knew she'd been here?' she said.

'I saw her leaving.'

'But you didn't speak?'

'No,' he said indifferently. 'For the time being, I've nothing to say to her. Anyway, I can't manage a conversation with two women at the same time and I wanted to talk to you first.'

'How did you know I was here?'

'I saw your car at the end of the lonning.'

'You saw a car. How did you know it was mine?'

'I saw you in it outside of the prison, remember? Grey Fiesta, very anonymous, a real psychiatrist's car. Hollins tell you not to try to bring it all the way up?'

'Yes. He said there were ruts you could lose a sledge team down.'

237

Hadda smiled.

'Nice turn of phrase for a parson. I keep telling him he ought to dump that Dinky he drives, but he says he can't afford a four by four.'

'Perhaps you could loan him the money. I gather you're quite flush at the moment.'

She saw no reason to dance around the reason she was there. If he'd worked out that Hollins must have been responsible in some way for her visit, then he must also suspect – or have deduced from some trace the vicar had left of his search – that the money box had been discovered.

'Perhaps I could. I feel guilty that the poor devil has got to carry my groceries the last quarter mile. So what did you and Imogen find to talk about?'

If this was evasion, he disguised it very well as indifference.

'Absolutely nothing. We didn't even introduce ourselves.'

'No need,' said Hadda. 'Clearly you recognized her. And she'll be able to find out everything she needs to know about you.'

'How?' asked Alva, puzzled.

'Striking black woman arrives at vicarage then drives out to Birkstane. Every detail will have been noted and analysed by the locals. Hollins and his wife will be quizzed. No need to tell you how much can be given away by even the most noncommittal of answers. Add to this your car. Even anonymous psychiatrists' cars have numbers. When Imogen left she headed out up the lonning so she'll have had a good peer around it too. Did you lock it?'

'I'm not sure. No, I didn't. Somehow, leaving it out here . . .'

'. . . in the middle of nowhere, it didn't seem necessary,' he finished her sentence. 'You'll learn. Leave anything lying around in there?'

Alva said, 'My case is in the boot.'

Hadda whistled.

'Hope you didn't pack it with confidential files. So you're not staying at the vicarage?'

Very quick, she thought. Perhaps his emotional turmoil during most of their later sessions in the prison had obscured just how sharp his mind was.

'Mr Hollins did ask, but I'd booked a room at the village inn. Only, when I got there, it turned out there'd been a mix-up. The landlord said he was sorry, it must have been the girl who took my order, but they were full.'

'That would be Jimmy Frith, better known as Froth,' said Hadda. 'Big fat man, in his sixties, sharp intake of breath when he saw you, smiled a lot as he told you to sod off?'

'Are you suggesting he lied because I'm black?' said Alva. She'd suspected it herself, but couldn't be bothered to make a fuss.

'Hard to prove,' said Hadda. 'For a start, it's against the law, and you need to get up very early in the morning to catch our Jimmy breaking the law.'

'Then perhaps someone ought to get up early in the morning,' she said, irritated at what seemed a rural complacency in the face of prejudice.

'Maybe somebody will,' he said, smiling. 'So you didn't head back to the vicarage to take up the padre's offer?'

'No, I thought if I came straight out here, maybe I could take a good step south this evening.'

He said, 'You can stay here if you like.'

The offer took her by surprise.

She said, 'Thanks, but I don't think . . .'

'It's all right, you don't have to brush up your transference theory, I haven't taken a sudden strange fancy to you,' he said. 'It will be getting dark soon, the mist will be rising, the frost falling, and you don't want to be driving round our narrow roads in those conditions.'

'It's not dark yet,' she said.

'No, but it will be by the time you interrogate me about the money,' he said.

I was right, she thought. He knows exactly why Hollins contacted me. This is not a good start!

He went on, 'Also you'd be doing me a favour.'

'How so?'

'Imo won't come back if she thinks you're still around and, to be honest, I don't think I'm ready yet to meet her face to face.'

This was indeed honest. One thing you learned to distrust in patients like Hadda was a show of honesty.

Delaying her decision, Alva said, 'But having me here one night wouldn't be much help. Surely she'll be staying at the castle for the entire holiday?'

He said, 'Someone more suspicious than me might think you were fishing for an invite to spend all of Christmas at Birkstane.'

'Someone couldn't be more wrong,' she said. 'My parents are expecting me.'

'And you want to spend Christmas with them?' He sounded genuinely curious.

She said, 'Certainly I do.'

'Touching,' he said, regarding her expectantly.

Why am I delaying this decision? she asked herself. She knew it ought to be *No*. But she also knew it was going to be *Yes*.

She said, 'Thank you, I will stay here tonight.'

'Great. Off you go and get your case. I'd offer myself but you'll be twice as quick. And lock the car this time. Oh, hang on a sec.'

He went out of the kitchen and returned with a couple of heavy blankets.

'Here,' he said. 'Take these.'

For a moment she thought he was inviting her to make herself a bed on the kitchen floor, or out in the barn. Her uncertainty must have shown for he grinned and said, 'Drape them over the bonnet of your car. It's going to be a bloody cold night and we don't want your radiator to freeze up, do we?'

She took the blankets and left the house. When she returned, she saw he'd been busy. Logs had been piled on to the kitchen fire, the washed dishes were draining by the sink, and an electric kettle came to the boil and switched itself off as she entered the room.

He must have heard her come in. From somewhere above, his voice called, 'Up here.'

She left the kitchen and went up a steep flight of worn stone stairs.

Sound and an open door led her into a bedroom where she found Hadda shaking a fresh white sheet out over a bed.

'Tuck that side in, will you?' he said.

She obeyed. As she helped him with the second sheet, she noticed a pile of bedding on the floor by the door.

'This is your bedroom,' she said.

'That's right.'

'But I can't move you out of your own bed,' she protested.

'No problem. There are two other rooms with perfectly good beds in them,' he said, swiftly and efficiently piling blankets on top of the sheets. 'But they'll need a bit of airing.'

'I'd be perfectly happy . . .'

'I wouldn't,' he interrupted. 'I can guarantee your virtue is safe under my roof, but I can't do the same for your respiratory system if you don't use this room.'

'But what about you?'

'You forget where I've spent most of the last decade,' he said. 'Her Majesty's hospitality either wrecks you or leaves you with the constitution of a polar bear. The speed I move,

241

I've had to develop highly efficient heat-conservation circuits. There, if you need more blankets, you'll find them in that chest. I've laid a fire in the grate to take the chill off the air. There should be plenty of space in the wardrobe unless that bag of yours holds a lot more than it looks to.'

He stooped to set a match to the fire as Alva put her bag on the bed and unzipped it. Then she went to the wardrobe to check if Hadda's notion of plenty of room matched hers.

It did, though the wine box on the wardrobe floor might impede the hang of the one long dress she'd packed – not in any expectation of needing it but because her actress mother had taught her what she claimed as an old touring adage, *When packing, try to anticipate the extremes which are, sleeping on your dressing-room floor or dining with a duke.*

'Yes,' said Hadda behind her. 'That's the secret booze hoard I'm sure Hollins has told you he chanced upon. And seeing as you know about it, we might as well spare ourselves Tesco's cut-price Shiraz.'

He stooped down and drew out a bottle.

'He told me he chanced upon your money chest too,' said Alva.

'Is that how he put it?' said Hadda. 'Well, if like a timid old maid, you check under the bed before you get into it, you'll work out that he must also have chanced to get down on his knees, pull it out, turn the key and raise the lid.'

'I might have done the same, out of curiosity,' she said.

'So you might. But you are my guest and this is your room, and therefore you have certain rights of access.'

Then he laughed and said, 'But don't worry, I'll practise what I presume Hollins preaches and forgive him. Now, have you got everything?'

'I think so. Let me see . . .' She looked around. A stack of books on the deep sill of the small window caught her eye.

'. . . Yes, even bedtime reading. Hello, I thought I recognized that lurid green jacket . . .'

She went to the window and picked up a copy of *Curing Souls*.

'Now this is very flattering,' she said lightly. 'What happened? You got a psychic message that I might be coming, so thought you would try to impress me?'

'Something like that,' he said, smiling as he took the book from her hand.

'At least let me sign it.'

'Later perhaps,' he said firmly. 'Oh, one thing I forgot. Bathroom is first left. Water pressure is pathetic, hot water is in short supply, but don't be put off by the faintly brown tinge, it makes a lovely cup of tea which will be awaiting you when you're ready to come down.'

He left her.

She thought of only unpacking what she'd need for tonight to make a statement. But it would only be a statement if at some point he came into the room to notice.

She unpacked everything. As she hung her clothes up, her thoughts kept turning to the box. Should she open it or not? He'd more or less given her permission. More or less. In any case, no need to admit to opening it. Unless there was some way he could tell if it had been touched, some little trick he'd picked up in prison, a hair across the lid, for instance . . .

This is silly, she told herself. Open it, and if he asks, admit to it.

She knelt on the floor by the bed, reached under and drew the tin chest out.

It scraped along the bare floorboards.

She had a picture of Hadda standing directly underneath, looking up at the ceiling, and smiling.

She turned the key, lifted the lid.

The bundles of banknotes were there as Hollins had described. But there was also a scrap of paper lying on top of them.

On it was written *Your tea's getting cold*.

So it's games time, she thought.

That was fine. He might think he was good at game-playing, but she had degrees in it.

She shut the box and went downstairs.

12

At two thirty that afternoon Toby Estover had not been rogering his secretary on his cleared desk as his wife had theorized.

He'd completed that task mid-morning, shortly after his arrival in the office. In the years since his marriage he had started to put on weight and now his elegant suits were cut to disguise his middle-age spread rather than show off his youthful figure. Also he'd been diagnosed with a slight heart problem, which meant he ended up post-coitally slightly more breathless than his doctor would have cared to see, even though the secretary, Morag Gray, an obliging Scottish girl built on the same generous lines as all her predecessors, made sure he had little to do other than lie back and think of England (who, incidentally, were also feeling slightly breathless as they received yet another comprehensive thrashing in their final one-day game in distant Mumbai).

After a lengthy recovery period, hindered rather than helped by several cups of strong coffee which did nothing for his blood pressure, he had asked Morag if there'd been anything in the morning mail that required his attention before he began his extended festive break.

She replied, 'Not really. A few Christmas cards.'

She scattered them on his desk. He made a dismissive movement and she began to gather them together again. Then he reached forward, eased one of them out of the pack with his forefinger, and impatiently waved the rest of them away.

She observed him curiously as he studied the card at length.

In her eyes, it wasn't at all Christmassy. It showed a tall figure wearing a floppy hat and some form of overall. His right hand rested on the haft of a long lumberjack's axe, and he was standing on a ridge looking out over a mountainous landscape. The sky was filled with dark lowering clouds. It was a composition in blues and browns. The only touch of brightness lay in an edging of red along the blade of the axe.

Now Estover picked up the card and opened it. There was an inscription printed in a bold red font.

> *May your Christmas be merry*
> *and New Year bring you all that you deserve.*

There was no signature.

He said, 'Where's the envelope?'

'Shredded,' she said. 'Why?'

'No reason. See if you can get Mr Nutbrown on the phone . . . no, on second thoughts, forget that. Some things are better face to face.'

'Aye, I know what you mean,' she said huskily.

He looked at her blankly. Please yourself, thought Morag. Her employer didn't do sexy small-talk. She knew this, but she was basically a sweet girl and kept on trying.

He stood up and headed for the door, slipping the card into his inside pocket.

There was something there already and he pulled it out.

He paused, turned, said, 'Nearly forgot. Merry Christmas, Morag. See you next year.'

After he'd left, Morag checked the plain buff office envelope he'd handed to her. No writing on it. She opened it. Bank notes, used, not in sequence. Generous, but no accompanying message. It would have been ironic if this year Estover had made some more personal gesture, but now into her third year in his employ, like the absence of intimate chit-chat, this was what she'd come to expect. This was the measure of his trust.

She picked up her phone and dialled.

'Hi, Mr Murray,' she said. 'It's Morag. He saw the card and he's away out. I think he's going to see Mr Nutbrown.'

'Guid girl,' said a man's voice.

Their shared nationality had certainly made it easier to accept this man's proposal, though she assured herself she would never have betrayed her boss if there'd been the slightest hint of any emotional connection in their sex. But not once in the two and a half years she'd worked for Estover had he given her anything but money, which made her . . . well, she didn't care to think what it made her, but it didn't make her loyal, that was for sure.

She slipped the envelope into her bag and put Toby Estover out of her mind. Christmas and Oxford Street were just around the corner. What with her bonus and her new Scottish friend's contribution, she could do full justice to both.

13

Toby Estover was not much given to flights of fancy, and he had long since forgotten all of his classical education save some scraps about Roman Law, but as he eased his Lexus out of the gloomy underground car park up into the bright winter sunshine it occurred to him that this must have been how it felt to emerge from Hades.

Except of course that London's traffic as the modern Saturnalia raged to its climax was just another form of hell. As he progressed slowly northwards, he was tempted to abandon his plan and use the car phone to contact Johnny. But he'd tried that several times recently, he reminded himself. He had an uneasy feeling that, despite all his urgings that whatever they did, they must do it in unison, Pippa Nutbrown was plotting some independent action. He needed to see for himself.

Finally with huge relief he joined the M11, still very busy but at least he was able to spend more time with his foot on the accelerator than the brake for forty miles till he turned off towards Saffron Walden.

His destination, Poynters, Johnny Nutbrown's country retreat, wasn't easy to find even for a frequent visitor, and now Estover drove slowly by choice to make sure he didn't miss the unclassified road that eventually led him to the old stone gateway marking the entrance to the grounds.

'Well, well, well,' he murmured, bringing the car to a halt. There was a *For Sale* sign by the gate.

He sat and studied it. The agent was Skinners of Mayfair. He knew them. They specialized in top-of-the-market country estates. Claimed to get the highest prices. Which was just as well, as they charged the highest commission.

Approached up the drive, the house sold itself. Warm red brick below, black timbers against dazzling white mortar above, not one of your great rambling Tudor mansions, relatively small but perfectly formed, all bathed in the brightness of winter sunshine that either reveals flaws pitilessly or, as in this case, emphasizes every perfect detail of line and contour. It looked like most Englishmen's unachievable dream of a place in the country.

Johnny had achieved it, and Estover knew how much he loved it. Which made it all the more worrying that he was trying to sell it.

He parked the car and tugged at the old bell-pull at the side of the almost square front door.

After a few moments it opened and a woman looked out at him with little sign of enthusiasm.

'Pippa,' said Estover, smiling. 'The house looks so well that, if I had bucolic longings, I might be tempted to buy it myself.'

Pippa Nutbrown in her youth had always had a faint look of dissatisfaction even at moments of great pleasure, as though the peach she was eating could be juicier, or the music she was hearing could be better played, or the sex she was enjoying could be more ecstatic. But youthful beauty, good skin tone and a lively manner had obscured the expression, or else merely inspired the men in her life to attempt to do better next time.

Now, however, time, which had made this house look more beautiful, had in her case merely eroded everything else and left her looking permanently and unmistakably dissatisfied.

'Toby,' she said coldly. 'I hope you're not expecting lunch.'

'Why should a man need lunch who has your beauty to feast upon?' he asked.

'If I want a combination of meaningless noise and crap, I'll take a walk through the rookery,' she said.

She turned away and he followed her into the house.

Her arse, he remarked with the eye of a connoisseur, was the only feature that age had improved. Once a tad angular for his taste, it had broadened into a saddle fit for a champion jump jockey. Perhaps this was the best angle of approach. He had sampled Pippa face on in their shared youth, but had not been tempted to repeat the experiment. He liked to see his own rapture mirrored in the eyes of the women he screwed, not a pair of scoring discs reading five point two.

But she had other attractions, one of them being an almost complete lack of any moral sense, and another an almost complete control over her husband. She would have needed that to persuade him to put Poynters on the market.

She pushed open the door of a small sitting room and said, 'Johnny, here's Toby.'

Johnny Nutbrown was relaxing on a huge Chesterfield that must have cost half a herd of cattle their skin. He was eating a piece of pie, presumably the end of the lunch Estover had been told not to expect.

'Toby!' he said. 'Marvellous. Just the man. Good to see you.'

His enthusiasm did not impress. Estover had known him long enough to suspect that if Adolf Hitler himself had goose-stepped into the room, Nutbrown's greeting would probably have been unchanged.

250

'And you,' he said. 'You're a hard man to get hold of these days. In fact, you both seem pretty inaccessible.'

The Nutbrowns exchanged glances, his interrogative, hers monitory.

'Busy busy,' said Johnny. 'Sit down, try this claret. Pippa, bring the man a glass. And one for yourself.'

Pippa obeyed. Her husband took the wine bottle from the table by his elbow and poured.

'Here's health,' he said.

They drank, Nutbrown deep, Estover a sip, Pippa a moistening of her lips.

'I didn't realize you were thinking of moving,' said Estover.

Pippa didn't reply but turned a gaze like a remote control on her husband.

'You know how it is,' said Johnny. 'Old bones, English winters, as easy to move on lock stock and barrel as pack up all the gear needed for a couple of months in the sun.'

He spoke the words like a schoolboy repeating a rote-learned formula.

'You're going abroad then?'

Pippa said, 'California. We like it there.'

'Very nice.' He set down his glass. 'And the Americans are so fussy about who they let in, aren't they? One strike and you're shut out.'

'That's right,' said Pippa. 'You got a problem with that, Toby?'

'No, indeed. Oh, by the by, I received an interesting Christmas card at the office. Wondered whether you got one too?'

He produced the card.

Pippa scarcely glanced at it before saying, 'Yes, we did.'

Johnny said, 'Did we? Don't recall. Nice picture, though. I'm sure I've seen it somewhere before.'

Estover looked at Pippa and raised his eyebrows.

The doorbell rang.

251

She didn't move. Her husband didn't even look as if he'd heard it.

There was another ring, more protracted this time.

Now without a word she rose and left the room.

As the door closed behind her, Estover said, 'So tell me, Johnny, has Wolf tried to contact you?'

'No. Why should he?'

'Because you are, you were, his very dear friend.'

'You too, Toby.'

'I married his ex-wife, remember?' said Estover grimly. 'That puts me a little further beyond the pale, I think. And you might say that chopping down our rowan tree was a form of contact.'

'Yes. You ever do anything about that?'

'No. I wanted to get the police, Imo said no. No way to prove it was Hadda, but some cop would certainly make a bob or two by tipping off the press and we'd have those bastards crawling all over us.'

'Probably right. Imo usually is,' said Nutbrown. 'Wish you hadn't mentioned it to Pippa though. Last straw for her, I think. She'd been fussed ever since we heard Wolf was getting out early. Funny how you got that wrong, Toby. What was your forecast? Good for the whole stretch, you said! You really must tell me what you fancy for the George on Boxing Day.'

He smiled as he spoke but Estover was reminded that, though Pippa might pull the strings, Johnny Nutbrown's limbs could still kick independently.

'Give it a rest, will you?' he said wearily. 'I assume this move's mainly down to Pippa, right? How about you, Johnny? Not worried Wolf might come calling?'

'Not likely, is it? I mean, we've really lost touch. OK, I know there was a good reason for that, but it happens even if you don't go to jail. Look at you and me, sometimes months go by without us meeting up.'

'It's certainly been hard to contact you recently,' said Estover. 'I've tried several times. I'm particularly surprised I didn't hear from you professionally when you decided to put your house on the market. Unless you're doing your own conveyancing?'

'Pippa's handling all that,' said Nutbrown. 'Not your sort of thing, conveyancing, is it, Toby? You're far too important for that. No, it made sense to go local.'

'So you were just going to pack up and leave all this behind you without so much as a word?'

Nutbrown's gaze went slowly round the room as if for the first time the reality of leaving all this behind him had struck.

Estover pressed on.

'Johnny, isn't this a bit of an over-reaction? OK, we need to take stock, but as long as we stick together, what do we have to worry about?'

'That's what I said to Pippa,' said Nutbrown. 'Wolf's out, so what? In fact, I was jolly glad to hear the news. Being banged up all that time, it makes me shudder just to think about it. Which is why I try not to. Incidentally, any idea how he managed to get out so early?'

'I put out some feelers. Discreetly, of course. Seems he put his hand up for everything, took the cure,' said Estover.

'Good lord, why would he do that?'

'To get out, of course,' said Estover irritably. 'Was a time when a prison sentence meant what it said. Now they employ people to help the bastards work the system! They've got some black bitch trick cyclist at Parkleigh, evidently. Pity she didn't stay in the woodpile.'

Nutbrown grimaced and said, 'Pippa says he's gone back up to Cumbria. Is that right?'

'Pippa's always right. Yes, he's up there, and I'm keeping a close check on him, believe me.'

'Let me guess: the ineluctable Lady Kira?'

'Yes. And from what I hear, he's leading a hermitic existence, he's a physical wreck, he exists on his social security hand-outs and, as for his state of mind, well, perhaps religion really has reared its ugly head as the only person he talks to is the local vicar.'

'There you are then,' said Johnny. 'What's to worry about? How's Imo? You two heading off to Frog-land for Christmas?'

The Estovers had a farmhouse in Gascony.

'No. Imo's been rather off France since Ginny died. She doesn't show it, but she took it really hard. So we're going up to the castle. Imo's there already. I'm joining her tomorrow.'

'Wow,' said Nutbrown, impressed. 'Bearding Wolf in his lair, eh? Sounds more Imo's style than yours, Toby.'

'It is not, I assure you, my intent to do any bearding,' said Estover. 'You know Kira. She so loves an old-fashioned English house-party.'

'Sounds grisly. Anyone I know?'

'Nikitin's going to be there, I believe.'

'Pasha? He can be fun.'

'Depends how you define fun.'

'Still sniffing around Imo, is he?' said Nutbrown sympathetically. 'Still, the fees he pays you, I daresay he feels he has a big share in what's yours. Only joking, old boy. And he is family, after all.'

'He's a cousin so often removed that Kira wouldn't have paid the slightest heed to him if he hadn't turned up in England trailing a few billion roubles,' said Toby sourly. 'Now I catch her watching me all the time, and I can almost hear her thinking: If only I'd trodden water a little longer, rather than encouraging Imo to marry this nobody, I could have had the fabulously rich Pavel Nikitin for my son-in-law. I'm sometimes tempted to tell her how he makes his money!'

'You think it would make a difference?' said Johnny. 'At

least she helped you get him as a client, so not all bad. Anyway, my love to all. And if you do bump into old Wolf, give him my best.'

Estover shook his head in bafflement. Talking to Johnny was like swimming in a goldfish bowl: you never ended up very far from where you'd begun. Except when you moved from words to figures. Ask Nutbrown how much they were worth and where it all was, and suddenly you were out in the open sea, only too glad to have this instinctive navigator leading you to Treasure Island. But on most other matters, to change the metaphor, it was like going down the rabbit hole.

As he rose to leave he said, 'So how's the sale going? Any interest?'

'Nothing close to the asking price,' declared Johnny, not bothering to hide his pleasure. 'And you know Pippa, she likes her pound of flesh.'

'Yes, I remember,' said Estover, smiling reminiscently.

'I daresay you do,' said Nutbrown, returning the smile. 'Though, from what I hear, in your case a pound might be stretching things a bit.'

Yes, when Johnny's limbs moved independently, he could manage a fair old kick, thought Estover as he left the room.

In the hall he heard voices and tracked them to the kitchen where he found Pippa drinking coffee with a long thin man with a slightly lugubrious face. She was smiling and looked very like her young self till she became aware he'd entered the room.

'Toby, you off then?' she said brusquely.

'Yes. If I could have a quick word . . .'

He glanced at the man, who stood up and offered his hand.

'Donald Murray,' he said in a Scots accent. 'Not here to look at the house, I hope?'

255

'No, just a friend.'

'Good! This is my second viewing and it's looking even better than on the first! No appointment this time, but Mrs Nutbrown's such a welcoming kind of body, I thought as I was in the area . . .'

'No problem, Mr Murray,' said Pippa, smiling again. 'Look, why don't you wander around by yourself while I talk to my . . . friend. I won't be long.'

The Scot nodded at Estover and left the room.

'High hopes there, then?' murmured the solicitor.

'Hopes,' said Pippa. 'So what can I do for you, Toby?'

'Nothing, it seems. I just wanted to wish you a Merry Christmas.'

'What? No wise words? No little lecture?'

'No. You've clearly made a decision.'

'Yes, I have. If I had any doubts, that card removed them.'

'You think it's from Wolf?'

She laughed and said, 'You know it is. It's that bloody picture he was so fond of he had a copy in his office at work and another in his study at home. *The Woodcutter*, it's called. But you know that, don't you, Toby?'

'Perhaps. But so what? Perhaps these are some cards that survived from the old days. Perhaps the poor chap can't afford to buy new Christmas cards.'

She shook her head and said, 'Do people really pay you thousands to talk such bollocks, Toby? What's the problem? You can't drop everything and leave the country and you'd rather we didn't either? Safety in numbers, that what you think?'

'Safety from what? It's a Christmas card, not a threat.'

Pippa said, 'Take another look, Toby. I checked it out on the Internet just to be sure. In the original painting, the blade of the axe doesn't have any red on it.'

Estover examined the card, frowning, and said, 'Just a

256

poor reproduction, perhaps. I noticed you don't seem to have shared any of your concerns with Johnny.'

She shook her head impatiently and said, 'Of course I haven't. You know Johnny. He can't take too much reality. You haven't been upsetting him, I hope?'

'Upset Johnny?' Estover laughed. 'You're joking, of course. You know what he said to me as I left? *If you run into Wolf in Cumbria, give him my best!*'

She said, 'And that didn't convince you we were wise to be getting away?'

'On the contrary. If Wolf did have any notion of coming after us, Johnny in the witness box would be worth at least six jury votes.'

She said incredulously, 'You think Wolf would be using the law? Jesus!'

'What else would he do?'

Pippa shook her head and said, 'You may be a great lawyer, Toby, but it's real life out here, not just words. Didn't having your tree chopped down teach you anything? I doubt if Wolf Hadda is looking to get himself a good brief. He's a dangerous man.'

'You think so?' said Estover. 'Well, I have some dangerous friends too. But it bothers me to see you reacting like this, Pippa. I've always regarded you as a rock. Why would you think Wolf might be truly dangerous? I understand he's pretty well a broken reed after all those years inside.'

'I just don't care to be around if and when he puts himself together again,' she said. 'You can rely on your dangerous friends for protection, Toby. From my memories of Wolf, I prefer distance.'

Estover observed her thoughtfully for a moment, then began to smile.

'Now what memories would they be? Let me guess. I often wondered why you were such a non-fan of Wolf's. I'm guessing that, back in the golden days when we were all such dear friends together, you tried your charms on him and he turned you down. He must have given you a real scare for you to be still feeling the aftermath!'

She didn't react to his gibe but said quietly, 'Right as always, Toby. He said, "I'll screw you if you really want it, Pippa. But I'm sure that, even while you were hitting the high notes, you'd be thinking of half a dozen good moral imperatives for confessing to Imo. So I'd probably have to kill you soon as we finished. So what do you say? Still up for it?"'

'And you actually believed him?' said Toby.

'I'm selling the house, aren't I? And I'd better get on with it. By the way, you got your card at your office, did you?'

'That's right. Why?'

'Interesting he didn't send it to your house. Perhaps he's got some other form of greeting in mind for Imo. Have yourself a merry little Christmas, Toby.'

She walked out of the kitchen. When Estover followed, she was halfway up the stairs.

She didn't look back.

14

A noise woke Alva Ozigbo in the middle of the night and for a second she experienced that heart-stopping feeling of not knowing where the hell she was.

Then she remembered, and in her confused mind *where?* was pushed aside by *how?* and *why?*

Professionally, there was nothing wrong in a psychiatrist accepting overnight hospitality from a patient. As long as they didn't share a bed, of course, and she had minimized any danger of this by wedging a chair against the door. Not that anything in Hadda's manner had suggested he regarded her as desirable. Indeed, as her analysis had probed deeper and deeper after that first impassioned cry for help, he had revealed that his sexual urges seemed to have gone into hibernation during his prison sentence.

'I don't even wake up with an erection now,' he told her. 'But of course you'll probably have to take my word for that.'

And this, apart from the time he had tested her assurance that the sound channels of the CCTV system were turned off, was the only time he had come close to suggestiveness.

But hibernation was not a permanent state, and better

safe than sorry, so in lieu of a lock, the chair had been jammed up against the door handle, though she couldn't avoid a sense that her motives for such a melodramatic gesture were at best muddied.

She set that aside for later consideration and concentrated on examining how she'd come to be staying at Birkstane.

Her practical reasons were those urged by her host. Dusk had been fast approaching, the first swirls of mist were already rising, and she needed more time to talk to him about the money. Pretty feeble. The mist had proved little more than a frost haze, she would have had no difficulty in driving slowly back to the village, and even with the pub a no-go area, the vicar would hardly have turned her away.

In the event, the fact that she stayed had turned into a reason for denying her the object of her staying.

Their simple dinner had been accompanied by a far from simple bottle of excellent burgundy. She'd examined the label and felt this was a good cue to bring up the subject of the money chest. As soon as she started, Hadda had put one of the two fingers on his right hand to his lips and said, 'Football and finance are banned topics at civilized dinner tables.'

'I thought it was religion and politics,' she said.

'Not in Cumbria,' he said.

Afterwards, mellowed by the wine plus a shot of whisky in her coffee, she had not resisted when in reply to her attempt to return to the subject he said, 'Let's leave the dénouement till tomorrow, like in the *Arabian Nights*, OK?'

It was only as she was on the point of slipping into sleep that it occurred to her that in the *Arabian Nights* it was Scheherazade who kept on postponing the conclusion of her tale because she knew that, when it was finished, she would be put to death.

Now, waking, it struck her that the bedroom was remark-

260

ably light. Her last impression just before she closed the curtains had been of complete and utter darkness, the kind of dark that anyone used to the permanent half-light of the modern city never sees. So the square of brightness marking the small window made her wonder if some intruder had triggered a security light, though somehow the ideas of Birkstane and modern technology didn't sit well together.

She slipped out of bed and drew back the curtains.

Not modern technology; more like ancient mythology.

The evening mist had vanished and the moon had risen. Its pearly light suffused the sky and the countryside, exploding to brilliance, like gunpowder scattered over embers, wherever it touched the hard hoar frost clinging to twigs and branches and blades of grass and the ribs and furrows of ancient stone walls.

It wasn't a human landscape she looked out upon, it was the land of faerie, a land where human *why's* and *how's* didn't apply. It was magic that bound her here. Her only safety lay in flight from the enchanter, but her books of knowledge held no elfish charms to see her safe through these fields of light.

Her gaze drifted down to the farmyard below her window. There were marks on the whitened cobbles as if something had moved across them since the frost fell. She remembered that a noise had awoken her but she couldn't remember what it was.

She went back to bed, and must have slipped back into sleep immediately for it seemed only a few seconds till she was woken again, this time by a fist banging on the bedroom door and Hadda's voice calling, 'Breakfast in fifteen minutes. After that it's DIY!'

She rose. Perhaps the remnants of the fire in the grate had still been warming the air when she got up in the night as she hadn't noticed the cold then, but now it was freezing.

261

She dragged on her clothes. Through the window the countryside still looked magical, but only in a glitzy Christmas card kind of way. She removed the chair from the door and headed out to the bathroom. There was a trickle of warm water. Getting enough to fill the ancient tub would have taken half an hour, by which time she would probably have contracted pneumonia, so she settled for a perfunctory splash in the cracked basin. Then after dragging a comb through her hair, she descended to the kitchen.

Here there was warmth from the crackling fire and the smell of frying bacon. Hadda greeted her with, 'Perfect timing, Elf. Sleep all right?'

This was the first time since her arrival that he'd used the nickname. Last night he'd called her . . . in fact, he hadn't called her anything, and she realized now that this sense of a barrier raised had distressed her.

'Yes, thanks. Anything I can do?'

'Make the coffee, if you like.'

His face had a healthy ruddy glow that made the scars on it stand out like ribs of quartz in a granite boulder. His hair, she noticed, was damp and looked as if it had been roughly ordered by drawing his fingers through it.

As she made the coffee she said, faintly accusing, 'You look as if you've had a shower.'

He said, 'What?'

Then he put his hand to his head and smiled and said, 'Of course. Didn't I mention the shower facilities?'

'No, you didn't,' she said.

'Well, no time now, but after breakfast if you still want one, just go out of the door, head towards the estate boundary wall, you'll meet a beck. Turn left and follow it upstream about twenty yards and beneath a little waterfall you'll see a pool, just room enough for one. I'll get you a towel.'

It took a moment to realize he wasn't joking. She thought

of that frost-bound world out there and shuddered.

He took some plates out of the oven where they'd been warming, put the bacon on them, quickly scrambled some eggs in the remaining fat, spooned them alongside the rashers and said, 'Grub up.'

The plate looked to hold more calories than she usually consumed in a day, but she cleared it without any noticeable difficulty.

He sliced a loaf thickly, impaled one slice on a toasting fork, another on the bread knife and said, 'Now it really is do-it-yourself time.'

They sat before the fire, toasting bread, spreading it thick with butter and marmalade, then washing it down with coffee.

'Enough,' she said after three slices.

'Eat,' he commanded. 'Lunch is a moveable feast at Birkstane.'

She remarked, but didn't remark upon, the assumption that she'd be staying for lunch.

Their breakfast conversation was desultory in an easy domestic sort of way, touching on how old the house was (500 years, give or take); who had embroidered the Lord's Prayer sampler hanging on the wall (Great Aunt Carrie); why toast done on an open fire was so much better than under a grill or in a toaster (how could it not be?); but finally she felt it was time to say, 'So, Wolf, this matter of the money...'

'Not before the dishes are washed,' he said firmly.

'This another old Cumbrian custom?'

'Oh yes. We always washed up before going out to kill the Scots or the Irish. Whichever happened to be invading at the time.'

You can't have been in a Celticidal mood yesterday, she thought, recalling the sinkful of dirty dishes.

She stood up and went to the sink.

'Let's get to it,' she said. 'Washing-up liquid?'

'I seem to be out,' he said, coming to stand beside her. 'Look, it's a bit crowded by this little sink. Why don't you wander off and check that your car's survived the night. Sneck, you go with Elf.'

In other circumstances she might have replied that she didn't mind a bit of crowding. Instead, obediently she slipped on her jacket and set out gingerly across the yard which the frost had turned into a frozen sea.

Sneck, equally obedient, followed her. Whether his function was to watch over or simply watch her, she didn't know, and she didn't care to test it by diverting from the direct route along the lonning to her car.

The blankets were still in place, stiff in their folds. She sat in the car and turned the key. The engine started first time and she let it run while she opened the boot. She took out her walking boots. Had it been some kind of vanity that prevented her from changing from her smart trainers when she arrived yesterday? She did a quick self-analysis. A psychiatrist was as susceptible to mixed motives as anyone else, but needed to be a lot clearer about them! No, she decided. Yesterday afternoon the frost had thawed enough for the surface of the lonning to be tacky rather than polished. This morning, however, a bit of substantial ankle support was very much in order. An immobilizing sprain was the last thing she wanted.

Could it be that Hadda had considered the possibility when he suggested she went out to the car?

Now she was really being paranoid!

She was roused from her reverie by Sneck letting out a bark.

After a while she heard what he'd already heard, an approaching car, and a moment later a blue Micra that she'd last seen outside the vicarage came into view.

To her surprise, Sneck advanced to meet it, wagging his tail.

Luke Hollins got out and reached out his open hand to the dog with something on the palm that Sneck removed with surprising gentleness.

'That's a pretty convincing demonstration of the power of faith,' said Alva.

'Just the power of food, I'm afraid,' replied Hollins. 'I always bring a packet of treats with the groceries. No groceries today, but fortunately I remembered to fill my pocket with Sugar Puffs. How about you? What have you done to tame the beast?'

Sneck had returned to Alva's side and was lying down on the icy ground with his shoulder warm against her leg.

'Nothing, really. I used to have a dog, when I was a child. Not as wolfish as this one, but pretty crazy. Spot, I called him, but my father said I should have called him Sufficient.'

Hollins looked puzzled and Alva laughed and said, 'Don't you do the Bible any more in the modern church? *Sufficient is the evil!* Spot used to terrorize the neighbourhood, dig up the garden and chew the furniture if he was left in the house by himself.'

'So you're used to dealing with wild things,' he said.

He glanced toward the house as he spoke.

She frowned then said lightly, 'So, if no groceries, what brings you here?'

'I just wanted to check that everything was OK. I called in at the Dog first thing. They were in a bit of a tizz. Jimmy Frith, that's the landlord, always likes a glass of ale with his breakfast but when he drew it, it came out foaming.'

'Isn't that what ale is meant to do?'

'No, I mean really foaming. It was the same in all the pumps and when he checked he found someone had got down in the cellar and put washing-up liquid in all the casks.'

Instantly she thought of the noise that had woken her, the spoor on the frost whitened yard, the lack of washing-up liquid in the cottage. Could Hadda have gone down to the village in the night to exact revenge on the pub land-lord for his racist rudeness? It didn't seem likely. Getting into the cellar and doctoring the beer would have required a dexterity quite beyond a man who walked like a wounded bear. But somehow the idea made her feel warm.

Hollins was offering his own much more reasonable explanation:

'Serves Jimmy right for letting the kids who come in drink more than they should. His nickname's Jimmy Froth, so as practical jokes go, it was pretty apt!'

He grinned as he spoke, then, as if realizing that the discomfiture of one of his parishioners was not a proper subject for mirth, he overcompensated into a tone of deep concern as he said, 'Anyway, when I found you hadn't stayed there, I got really worried and thought I'd better head out here straight away.'

'Thinking Wolf might have murdered me?' she said. 'Well, as you can see, he didn't.'

'But you did spend the night here at Birkstane?' He said it with a casualness more significant than reproach.

'Yes. His wife . . . his ex-wife showed up while I was waiting for Wolf. We chatted briefly then she went. Wolf seemed to think my presence would deter her from coming back.'

It rang pretty unconvincingly in her own ears but the vicar seemed ready to accept it was reasonable.

He said, 'So what was his explanation of the money?'

'He hasn't offered one yet,' said Alva. 'But he has worked out where I got my information from. I was just on my way back to the house for a heart to heart. Why don't you join us?'

Hollins looked doubtful.

'Don't know if that would be a good idea. If he knows it was me who . . .'

But the issue was resolved by a cry of, 'Is that you, Padre? Didn't they teach you at your seminary not to keep a lady standing in the cold? Come along to the house, for God's sake!'

Hadda had appeared at the bottom of the lonning.

He whistled and turned away. Sneck, with an appreciative glance at Hollins, raced after him and was alongside the slow-moving figure in an instant.

'There you are,' said Alva. 'All is forgiven.'

As they walked together down the lonning, Hollins said, 'So how did you find him?'

Alva said, 'As my host or as my patient? Not that it matters. Good manners prevent me from commenting on him in the first capacity, and professional ethics in the second. I'm sorry, but as you said in your letter, our concerns here are rather different. I'm very glad however to have you present to hear his explanation about the money. In this case I think that four ears may definitely be better than two.'

Hadda was brewing more coffee when they entered the kitchen. She saw his gaze take in her change of footwear and foolishly felt glad that her boots had the well-worn, well-cared-for look that showed they belonged to a serious walker.

'Car all right?' he said.

'Yes, thanks. I'm glad you suggested the blankets, though. They're frozen solid.'

'It was a hard night. I had to break some icicles off the fall this morning else I might have been speared as I showered. How about you, Padre? That vicarage still an ice-box?'

'The boiler heats the cellar perfectly adequately but then seems to deny the basic law of physics that says heat rises,' said Hollins.

'It's the Church of England's subtle technique for keeping its priests moral,' said Hadda. 'Here we are. Coffee. Sorry, no cream, Padre. My guest polished off the last of your little store last night. By the way, I suggest you keep on feeding my dog whatever it is you've got him hooked on, else you're going to lose your jacket.'

Hollins fed another handful of Sugar Puffs to Sneck, who was sitting alongside him with his nose pressed close to the provender-bearing pocket.

'Right,' said Hadda. 'Now I think it's time we dealt with the main item on both your agendas, which I take to be, am I complying with the letter and the spirit of my licence, or should I be manacled and fettered and cast back into the deepest oubliette the state can provide? So, if you are sitting comfortably, then I'll begin.'

15

It was, thought Alva, either a consummate performance or a consummate act.

In her vocabulary the term *performance* was neutral. It did not imply dissimulation or dishonesty. Long jail sentences turn most of those who suffer them into performers in some degree or other. Ultimately, survival in jail can depend on working out what disparate groups of people want and giving it to them. The face a man presents to his fellow prisoners will probably differ from the face he presents to the warders, or his visitors, or the governor, or the parole board.

Or the prison psychiatrist.

But performing is not the same as acting a part. Or it need not be. It can simply mean emphasizing one aspect of personality over others. A performer can be the sum of his performances while an actor is rarely the sum of his parts.

So, performance or act?

It occurred to her that she probably knew more about Wolf Hadda than anyone else in the world. But she also knew that in the mental as in the physical sciences, conventional knowledge could only take you so far; after that you were into quantum theory where none of your carefully tabulated laws applied.

Yet she'd been confident enough of her judgment that he was no longer a threat to recommend his release on licence as powerfully as she'd ever made any recommendation.

Which of course was why she was here now. A question had been raised. If she turned out to have been wrong, the damage to her reputation would be large but survivable. But if some young girl were harmed . . .

So, performance or act? He had certainly started by establishing himself as an almost theatrical presence, taking a position in front of the fireplace, resting most of his weight on his good leg, and looming over them like a soloist on a concert platform. Even Sneck turned from his absorption with the vicar's pocket to look up attentively as his master started to speak. Alva established her own parameters by interrupting him to take her notebook out of her purse and poising her pencil over it.

Then she smiled at him and nodded permission to continue.

'I'll come straight to the point,' he said. 'Out of the goodness of my heart, and not because I feel any compulsion to do so, moral or legal, let me give you an account of how I come to have a chestful of banknotes in my bedroom. Or would either of you like to hazard a guess?'

He paused expectantly.

The vicar looked uncomfortable, Alva's pencil scrawled shorthand hieroglyphics across her notepad. What she wrote was, *How rarely people who say they are coming straight to the point do! Now he'll answer his own question.*

'Come on! Don't be shy,' said Hadda. 'I bet the proceeds of some old fraud was top of your list. Some account I'd cleverly concealed from the Fraud Squad. Or a pay-off from some of my confederates for keeping my mouth shut. Or maybe I robbed a bank. The police are looking for a man with a badly scarred face, a marked limp, and a vicious-looking dog. There are no suspects.'

Another pause. Another silence. Alva made a note.

'Oh, all right,' he said, affecting disappointment. 'I'll put you out of your misery. I inherited the money. There! You look surprised, Padre. Or should I rather say incredulous? And you, Alva, have that look of concerned neutrality, if that's not a contradiction, that I know so well. OK. Here are the facts. Way back in the dark ages when I returned from my quest for self-improvement and claimed my bride, I told my father that I wanted him to have a share in my new and ever-increasing affluence. Fred, in any circumstances, would have found it hard to feel beholden, even to his own flesh and blood. In the circumstance that he was seriously pissed off with me about my choice of bride, he said he wanted no part of my money. He told me I should keep it, and where, in a very precise anatomical way.'

His lips faked a smile but it didn't get beyond his mouth as he turned to the stone mantel shelf where he'd placed his coffee mug. He raised the mug, but Alva could tell he wasn't drinking.

Then he turned back to them and continued briskly, 'Yes, he was a cussed old sod. Some folk reckon I take after him, though I can't see it myself. But I do admit I can be a bit cussed too on occasion, so I simply arranged for a thousand quid a month to be paid into his bank account. It was his to do with what he wanted. I was very willing to make it a lot more if necessary and I kept an eye on him, but he never showed any sign of being strapped for cash, and I knew that to mention money would just get us into a row, so for all the years of my prosperity, Fred was getting his monthly thousand. And what was he doing with it, do you think?'

Luke Hollins spoke, almost with relief.

271

'He was drawing it out as fast as it was paid in, and storing it in that tin chest.'

'Spot on, Padre. I reckon he didn't want it in his account, polluting his hard-earned wages. As for letting it lie to gather a bit of very useful interest, perish the thought! No, he drew it out and stored it away, and when he died, his will declared me the sole heir of all his estate. As you probably know, both of you, because he died after all the dust had settled around the ruin of my business, and my creditors had reluctantly agreed that they'd screwed me for every penny they could, then I was able to inherit that estate free of charge, which is how I come to be living in these palatial surroundings.'

'You seem to find them comfortable enough,' said Alva.

'Indeed I do. I'm not complaining. After my years as a guest of Her Majesty, bedding down with Sneck in the barn would have seemed comfortable. Anyway, to cut a long story short, poking around in the attic to rid myself of a couple of rats' nests, I came across Dad's old tin chest. Imagine my surprise when I opened it to see it was full of money. I rapidly worked out what it was. A quick check of Dad's old bank statements confirmed my guess. I took legal advice as to what to do . . .'

'Mr Trapp?' wondered Alva.

'The same. He confirmed there was no obstacle to my hanging on to the money.'

'The Inland Revenue and Social Services might not agree,' said Alva.

'Only if I didn't inform them,' he replied. 'Or perhaps I mean only if I did. Anyway, there you are. Any questions?'

Alva looked at Hollins. The vicar looked at the ground.

'Quite a lot of the money seems to have gone,' she said. 'What have you been spending it on?'

'Good question. This time I won't enquire after possible answers as one of you might say something that would cause us to fall out. I've provided myself with a stock of decent liquor, as you've both observed. My ancient Defender is surprisingly sophisticated under her rustic bonnet. Don't let the noise fool you. I left a few loose bits to create a good rattle, and they're pretty noisy beasts anyway!'

'And that's all? Doesn't add up to a great deal, it seems to me.'

'An accountant as well as a lawyer and a psychiatrist!' he mocked. 'There have been other expenses. For instance, I like to make donations where I think the money might do some good.'

Hollins now raised his eyes and said, 'There was a couple of hundred quid stuffed into the church donations box last month . . .'

'Mea culpa,' said Hadda.

The vicar said, 'Well . . . thank you. I'm very grateful.'

He looked, thought Alva, rather less surprised than he should that somehow this crippled man, this self-defined hermit, this local ogre, had entered the village and visited the church unobserved.

'So, good wine and good works,' she murmured. 'It seems a reasonable balance.'

'Yes, indeed,' said Hollins.

And Sneck let out a low rumbling growl that might have been taken for approval.

'I'm glad you think so,' said Hadda. 'Now, I daresay you'd like to talk among yourselves and, as I have things to do, I'll leave you to it for a while.'

He drained his coffee and headed for the door, Sneck at his heels.

'That went well, I thought,' said the vicar.

'Yes. Thank you for joining me in quizzing him about what he might have been doing with the money,' said Alva tartly.

'I thought he'd take it better from you, being his psychiatrist,' said Hollins apologetically. 'He doesn't care much for me coming the old C of E parson with him, as he puts it. But you have to admit, he did give a perfectly logical explanation.'

'You're not letting yourself be influenced by his donation to church funds, I hope,' said Alva.

'Of course not,' he said indignantly.

'But it didn't seem to surprise you much that a man in his condition had been able to visit the church unobserved?'

'No. The truth is, when I found the money, my first thought was of Mr Hadda,' admitted Hollins. 'That same morning I noticed that someone had planted a couple of rowan sprigs, heavy with berries, in the churchyard. One was on his father's grave, the other in front of the Ulphingstone tomb where his daughter is interred.'

'Why rowan?' wondered Alva, recalling that Hadda had referred to a rowan tree in the garden of his Holland Park house.

'My wife knows about such things,' said Hollins. 'She told me that in folklore the mountain ash is considered a strong defence against evil spirits, and also it can prevent the dead from rising and walking the earth. But I couldn't be certain it was Mr Hadda, until now. So what do you think, Dr Ozigbo? Are you happy with his explanation?'

What Alva was thinking was that if Hadda had planted the rowan in his London garden as a defence against evil, it hadn't been very effective. Also that in her eyes he'd once more become a prime suspect in the case of the foaming beer!

What she said was, 'I think Mr Hadda is maybe even more complex than we'd thought. For instance, I think the real reason he's left us to have a chat by the fireside is that Sneck told him he had another visitor.'

She put her theory to the test by rising and going out into the yard.

She was right. He was standing by the open gate in deep conversation with a tall thin man. The visitor spotted her and said something. Hadda turned, saw Alva watching them, said something to the newcomer, then the two men walked towards her across the yard.

'Elf, we have a traveller in distress,' said Hadda. 'Mr . . . sorry, I don't know your name?'

'Murray,' said the man, in a distinctive Scots accent. 'Donald Murray. Sorry to trouble you. My sat nav's gone on the blink.'

'Never trust technology, eh? Let's get you into the warm and I'll show you the way on a good old-fashioned map. Padre, this will be a busy time for you. I'll not be needing an order till after the festive dust has settled. So, Merry Christmas.'

Hollins, who'd followed Alva into the yard, took his dismissal with Christian fortitude.

'Thank you . . .'

Rather hesitantly he reached into the capacious pocket of his heavy cagoule and produced a rectangular packet wrapped in red-and-green Christmas paper.

'I came across this,' he said. 'Thought you might like it. A Merry Christmas to you, too.'

'A present? Well, thank you, Padre. I'm touched.'

Alva said to Hollins, 'I'll walk you back to your car.'

They walked up the lonning in the kind of silence that gradually magnifies sound. The crunch of the frozen grass beneath their feet, the eerie whistle of a circling buzzard scanning the earth for the corpse of any creature that hadn't made it through the night, the baa-ing of a distant sheep, the rustle as the morning sun thawed the first tiny icicles from the upmost branches of the hedgerow hollies and sent them slithering through the frosted leaves; these and a myriad other small indistinguishable sounds united and increased till Hollins shrank them all back to near nothingness by speaking.

'That man . . .'

'Mr Murray?'

'Yes, him. You recall the reason I chanced upon the money chest was I went upstairs because his mobile rang?'

'But it stopped as you got into the bedroom . . .'

'Yes. But there was a message. I listened to it.'

'Ah. You chanced to listen to it,' said Alva, gently mocking the priest's defensiveness about prying into Hadda's affairs. She smiled to show she didn't blame him. Crimes such as Hadda's meant a forfeiture of trust which in turn could provoke acts that were at least intrusive.

'It was a man speaking. He had a Scots accent. He sounded very like Mr Murray.'

'An accent can be deceptive.'

Hollins said, 'You mean all Scots sound the same? Sounds a touch racist to me, Dr Ozigbo.'

She glanced at him and saw that now he was smiling. Getting his own back. She'd reserved judgment on Hollins, but she found she was quite liking him.

'I take it your fine ear detects distinctions?' she said.

'No, but one of my best mates at college was from Glasgow. So is Mr Murray, and so was the man on the phone.'

'And so are a million other people. You'll need to fine it down a little.'

'Well, it certainly wasn't my mate,' he said. 'Look, all I'm saying is they sounded very much the same.'

And if they're the same, why is Wolf Hadda trying to hide the fact that he knows this man? Alva asked herself. His behaviour in bringing him into the house to show him the way had already struck her as atypical. And he'd only done

276

it when he'd realized it wasn't going to be possible to avoid a meeting with her.

'So what did the message say?' she enquired.

'Something about making contact and going to a villa,' said Hollins. 'I think it was from abroad as he said he'd stop off in London on the way back and check things there. He didn't much like where he was, called it an elephants' grave-yard and said he was glad that Hadda was paying for it.'

Alva, keeping anger but not reproach out of her voice, said, 'And you didn't think this was worth telling me till now? You must have looked at the possible implications.'

'In my business, when you rush to judgment, you end up crucifying people,' said Hollins.

'You were worried enough about the money to contact me,' she said.

'The money was a fact. It needed explaining. Contacting you was, I don't know, more a way of giving myself some extra thinking time. I thought at best you might write, or email, or even phone. I didn't expect you to turn up person-ally. When you did, I thought I'd wait and see what transpired – about the money, I mean.'

'And you found his explanation satisfactory enough to still your doubts, even though you knew for sure he was lying?'

'What do you mean?'

'You'd heard the message. You knew that whatever the man on the phone, that man back there possibly, is doing, Hadda is paying him to do it. So there's something more than good wine and good works going on here. The fact that he slipped a couple of hundred pounds into your poor box doesn't make him a saint, Mr Hollins. Suppose rather than making a charitable gesture it was more like purchasing an indulgence? Was that what you gave him just now? A papal indulgence?'

They had reached her car. Parked behind it was the vicar's Micra, and behind that a black BMW.

'Got the wrong church there, I think, Dr Ozigbo,' Hollins said. 'Look, there may be a perfectly reasonable explanation for that phone message. And you've only got my not-too-reliable memory to suggest that it was whatsisname? Donald Murray, who left it.'

'We've got Sneck. He doesn't accept strangers without his master's say so, and he looked pretty comfortable with Mr Murray out there.'

As she spoke, Alva peered into the BMW. Recalling her readiness to leave her car unlocked in such a remote area she tried the door. Mr Murray wasn't so trusting. On the back seat she saw a document case, embossed in faded gilt with the initials D.M.

Donald Murray. Right initials, but was that really his name? Something in the way he'd said it when prompted by Hadda had rung a false note. Of course it might be that too many hours spent straining to detect false notes had over-sensitized her. Sometimes she wondered if she would ever again hear someone say something she could take at face value.

'What will you do?' asked the vicar.

'What will *you* do?' she retorted.

He said, 'Sorry, I wasn't trying to offload responsibility. I'll pray, and then I'll decide. I meant, what will you do now? If you want to stay another night but not here at Birkstane, you're very welcome to a bed at the vicarage. And we have a real shower.'

She felt reproved. She should be able to tell the difference between a man trying to marshal all known facts before making a decision and a man trying to duck responsibility.

She said, 'That's kind, but if I do decide to stay another night, I'll be all right here. The shower apart, that is. I'll ring you before I leave.'

'I'd appreciate that.'

They shook hands and she watched as he did a three-point turn.

As he drove away, her phone started ringing.

Her mother said, 'Alva, you are not to worry . . .' and instantly she started worrying.

Hadda and Murray looked up in surprise as she burst into the kitchen and Sneck was on his feet in a flash, crouched low, teeth bared.

She said, 'I've got to go. My father's ill. Heart attack. Fortunately it happened at work.'

'Fortunately?' said Hadda.

'He's a surgeon in Manchester. I'll just grab my things and be on my way.'

When she came down a couple of minutes later, Hadda wasn't in the kitchen.

Murray said, 'He's outside. I hope your dad's OK.'

No false note there. He sounded genuinely concerned.

She said, 'Thanks,' and left. Hadda was sitting in the Defender.

'Don't want you cracking your ankle running up the lonning,' he said.

She scrambled in beside him. As he drove he said, 'Leave me your mobile number. I'd like to be able to check on you.'

Something wrong with that picture, she thought as she scribbled it on the cover of a road map. When they got to her car, he reached into the back seat and handed her a flask.

'Coffee,' he said. 'Drive for an hour and a half, stop and drink it, then drive on.'

The precision of the instruction was oddly comforting.

She got into her car. The engine again started first time. He took the blankets off the bonnet and tossed them into the Land Rover.

She turned the car, looked up at him through the open window and said, 'Thanks.'

'You're welcome,' he said. 'Good luck, Elf.'

He stooped to the window and his lips brushed her cheek.

It was, she realized, the first physical contact they'd ever had. What did she feel about it? Was it significant? If so, how?

There might be a time to consider these questions but it certainly wasn't now.

Now all she could think about was her father, that huge bear of a man whose sloe-black skin seemed to pulsate with energy, lying helpless on a bed in his own hospital.

She put her lights full on and sent the car hurtling along the narrow country road.

BOOK THREE

unions and reunions

Christmas was close at hand, in all his bluff and hearty honesty; it was the season of hospitality, merriment, and open-heartedness . . . How many families, whose members have been dispersed and scattered far and wide, in the restless struggles of life, are then reunited, and meet once again in that happy state of companionship and mutual goodwill, which is a source of such pure and unalloyed delight . . . How many old recollections, and how many dormant sympathies, does Christmas time awaken! . . . Happy, happy Christmas, that can win us back to the delusions of our childish days . . .

Charles Dickens: *The Pickwick Papers*

1

Like most men, ex-DI Medler imagined that he'd once enjoyed Christmas.

In his case the enjoyment must have been brief and infantile, for that miasma of disillusion, disappointment, cynicism and scepticism which men call maturity descended early on the boy, Arnie.

Indeed he was only six when he decided that a year of fulltime education was more than enough for the cultural, spiritual and intellectual needs of a growing boy and resolved to hand in his resignation from Wapping C of E First School with immediate effect.

He first shared this resolution with his gran, Queenie Medler, who appeared to Arnie as a benevolent old lady full of wisdom and insight, and to her many admirers across the bar of the China Clipper on Wapping Wall as a right little cracker, game for anything.

Queenie advised him to sleep on it. He flew into a childish tantrum, the burden of which was that he found the prospect of another ten years of education unbearable and wished passionately that he could be grown up and rich enough to lie in bed as long as he fucking well liked, answerable to no man.

Queenie had chuckled at the same time as she lightly clipped his ear and told him to watch his language and be careful what he wished for as the gods who like a laugh might just make it come true.

Well, they had, and now, forty years on, he thought gloomily that the bastards must really be laughing.

Early retirement to a sunny clime with a pension pot sufficiently deep to keep him in comfort till the end of his days. That was all he'd wanted. That was his adult version of his childhood wish. And that was what he'd got.

He'd also got boredom. And he'd got a wife who saw no reason why not being married to a football star should stop her spending like a WAG. And he found that in ex-pat social circles, the crooks treated him as a cop and the straights treated him as a crook.

He'd never been a man who made friends easily, or indeed thought he needed them, but he'd come to realize the truth of what some cynical Frog philosopher probably said, that it wasn't enough to get what you wished for, there had to be someone around who envied you for it.

Tina's friends and relatives didn't count – they were, on the whole, a bunch of wankers. As to his own acquaintance from the old days, in the beginning one or two, lured by the thought of a freebie in the sun, came to stay and confirmed that he'd got it made, which was good, but rarely came a second time, which was puzzling.

His encounter with Davy McLucky had turned into a real ego-titillating treat, all the better because it had started so unpromisingly, with the ex-DC naturally showing little enthusiasm at running across an ex-boss who'd never done him any favours. But after reluctantly accepting an invite to come out to the villa, McLucky had not been able to conceal his growing envy as he was taken on the grand tour. Even Tina had played a part. Roused from her customary domestic lethargy by the sight of a new man, she'd led the way, waggling her bum and shaking her tits in a manner that certainly caught McLucky's attention.

His tongue loosened by a couple of bottles of Rioja, McLucky had bemoaned the contrast between his fate after retirement – *gloomy fuckin' Glasgae 'n' squalid fuckin' divorce cases!* – and Medler's – *sunshine 'n' tottie 'n' fuck all tae do but booze 'n' fornicate yer fuckin' life awa'!* Medler had rubbed it in by assuring him that this life could be his too, presenting a balance sheet of property values and living expenses as if they were dirt cheap, knowing full well that they were a million miles outside of McLucky's range.

Maybe he'd overdone it. Maybe he always overdid it. Certainly the next day his guest had shown no enthusiasm when pressed to stay longer, not even when the pressure had been applied by Tina's melonic breasts.

Arnie hardly knew the guy, he'd only invited him to the villa to parade his comparative wealth, yet when McLucky said he was going home, he'd felt utterly bereft.

That had been more than a week ago. He was used to troughs of depression but usually he managed to drag himself back to the surface in a couple of days. This time, however, he felt himself sinking in darkness deeper and deeper, beyond all hope of day.

Now it was Christmas Eve, the season for friends and family and universal jollity, and here he was, sitting on the terrace overlooking his pool, with a fag in one hand and a glass of cognac in the other, wondering how the hell he was going to spend the rest of his life.

Tina wasn't here. Far from a devout Christian, she nevertheless adhered to the superstitious patterns of her upbringing by attending services at the English Church on Easter morning and at midnight on Christmas Eve. Afterwards no doubt she would be inveigled into having a festive drink with some of her friends. People liked Tina, and they liked her all the more he guessed, when he wasn't around.

Well, that didn't bother him. He didn't know how far she strayed, but he knew she wasn't going to risk straying so far she couldn't find her way back to the source of all comforts. There were plenty of guys out there who'd like to give her one, but not many who'd want her to stay on in the morning to give her another. Perhaps it might be a good thing if she did find an alternative bankroll. Perhaps that would give him the incentive to change his life around.

He almost wished it would happen, that something, *anything* would happen, to jerk him out of this state of enervating depression.

Be careful what you wish . . .

'Hello, Mr Medler. And a happy Christmas to you.'

On to the terrace stepped a figure of nightmare. Literally in that he saw it occasionally in his nightmares. The scarred face, the eye-patch, the gloved right hand . . .

Only the gloved left hand differed significantly from his guilty imaginings.

There it was sometimes pointed at him accusingly.

Here it carried a small and shining axe.

Two hours later, Tina Medler's taxi drew up at the main gate of the villa. She'd had to pay a small fortune to get the guy to come all the way out here, and he'd insisted on having the fare upfront. The least the bastard could do was get out from behind the wheel and open the door for her.

On the other hand, if he did that he might notice that she'd been comprehensively sick all over the rear seat. Fortunately the racket of his clapped-out engine had covered her discomfiture. She pushed open the door, pulled her already short skirt up even higher and managed a not too undignified debouchment. The driver was clocking her lacy briefs.

'Not for you, *compadre*,' she said. 'I've left you a tip in the back. *¡Felices Pascuas!*'

She slammed the door so hard the glass shook. The driver made a rude gesture then sent the cab rattling away into the dark.

Seeing a light on in the villa, she pressed the bell-push and waited for the gates to be unlocked. Nothing happened. Arnie must have got himself pissed again and passed out. Stupid sod. At least she never reached that state. Always knew what she was doing, though sometimes she didn't know why she was doing it.

She dug through the junk in her purse till she found the remote, pointed and pressed, and the gates swung open. Would have been a bugger if she'd forgotten it. Arnie was big on security and even with her skirt round her bum she wouldn't have fancied trying to scale the garden walls with their coronet of razor wire. Best she could have hoped for was to trigger the alarm system and hope that the din roused the useless piss-artist.

She closed the gates behind her, slipped off her designer sling-backs, which were giving her gip, and walked up the smoothly paved driveway in her bare feet. Cup of coffee, fall into bed, wake up around midday tomorrow, couple of corpse-revivers, and then it would be prezzie time! Arnie tended to be a bit mean on the present front, but never mind, she'd made a couple of purchases on his behalf, and he could hardly complain so long as she showed her gratitude in the usual way, always supposing he wasn't still too pissed to get it up.

As she approached the villa she realized the light she'd spotted was the light on the pool terrace, so that's where she headed. She noticed to her surprise that all the metal security shutters were down. As she rounded the corner she saw the empty lounger, the low table on which stood an almost empty bottle of cognac, and shards from a shattered glass all over the tiles. One of her best crystal set, from the look of it. Useless bastard! Christmas or not she'd tear him limb from limb when she laid hands on him.

But first she had to lure him out of hiding.

She called, 'Honey, I'm home!'

Nothing.

The bastard must really have tied one on tonight. Suddenly, fearful that he might have been stupid enough to go for a drunken swim, she peered into the pool.

Just a lilo on the surface and nothing underneath.

She felt a pang of relief. Arnie wasn't much, but he wasn't so little she could be indifferent to his death. The relief was already morphing back to irritation as she turned to face the villa.

Something caught her eye, lying on the tiles at the foot of the heavy security shutter that protected the patio door. Some things.

She went forward.

There were two of them.

Gloves, she thought. Odd. These December nights got chilly, even here on the Costa del fucking Sol, but surely it wasn't so cold that Arnie, with enough alcohol in him to fuel a rocketship, would need to wear gloves? She herself, fearing to damage her long, beautifully manicured and lacquered fingernails wouldn't dream of wearing them; she didn't even know Arnie owned a pair of gloves . . .

And why had he placed them so neatly, almost flush up against the metal shutter . . . ?

Finally her mind gave up the effort to conceal beneath this tangle of irrelevant thought the truth of what her eyes were telling her.

Not gloves.

Hands.

Severed from their arms, which were presumably on the far side of the patio shutter.

She recognized the signet ring on one of the fingers, and went down on her knees, not to look more closely but because her legs refused to support her.

She'd thought she had left all that there was to bring up on the back seat of the taxi, but now she found she was wrong.

And when she stopped retching, she raised her head to the Christmas stars and started to scream.

2

After matins on Christmas Day, most members of St Swithin's congregation were eager to head off home to their secular celebrations. There was a good smell of roast fowl rising over Mireton, and Luke Hollins was looking forward as much as anyone to closing his front door and stretching his legs under his own well-laden table.

This was his first Christmas in the parish and by chance it was also going to be the first that he and Willa had spent alone. Usually her parents joined them, and sometimes his sister and her family. But a new baby in the latter case, and reluctance to make the long journey from Devon in the former, had left them with no one to please but themselves. And of course any members of his parochial flock who cared to put their needs before the vicar's relaxation.

As he exchanged greetings by the door with the last of the worshippers, he saw that the castle party was still in the churchyard, over by the Ulphingstone family tomb. This was by far the most prominent sepultural monument, resembling in Hollins's democratic eyes one of those blockhouses still visible on parts of the UK's sea coast out of which the aged eyes of Dad's Army peered in fearful expectation of seeing cohorts of Nazi storm-troopers goose-stepping out of the waves.

The tomb was marked off from its populist neighbours by a metal fence, its uprights shaped like Zulu assegais, its interstices filled by curlicues of cast iron in a Celtic knot-pattern, all enamelled black except for the spear blades, which were picked out in gold. Whether its function was to keep the living out or the dead in, Hollins didn't know. But he did know he found it as offensive to good taste as it was to democratic principle.

The most recent entrant to the tomb had been, according to the lapidary inscription, Virginia, beloved daughter of Imogen, and granddaughter of Sir Leon and Lady Kira Ulphingstone.

Hollins thought of how Wolf Hadda must have felt when he came down here in the dark of night to lay his bough of rowan before the tomb and saw that his name didn't get a mention.

The girl's death had predated Hollins's own arrival in Mireton. He had referred to it once at the lunch table, but had been blanked out by Kira, while Leon's face had twisted into such a mask of grief that Hollins had found himself babbling about the church-tower restoration fund in an attempt at distraction.

The castle party were being lectured by Lady Kira, who took her family responsibilities very seriously and expected her guests to do the same. There were half a dozen of them beside the elder Ulphingstones. Quite a small house-party by Kira's standards if this were all, which presumably it was, as you didn't stay at the castle without processing down to the church for morning service. In fact he'd discovered soon after arrival that the verger didn't start ringing the calling bell until he had the castle party in his sights even if this meant delaying the start of things by four or five minutes.

Lady Kira was equally imperious at the other end of the service. Today, in her haste to illustrate the antiquity of the Ulphingstones by close reference to the tomb, she had ushered her party straight by him without a glance as he stood at the door to wish his home-going congregants Merry Christmas.

Well, good luck to them! he thought as he turned to go back into the church, looking forward to getting out of his canonicals and home to his turkey. Then Sir Leon's voice came drifting through the clear air.

'Vicar, hold on a tick.'

If he hadn't had one foot across the threshold of God's house, he might have muttered, 'Oh fuck!' but he nipped the profanity in the bud and turned with a smile.

'Yes, Sir Leon?'

'Don't think you've met my daughter,' called the old man.

Chance would have been a fine thing, he thought as he advanced towards the tomb.

The woman he'd already identified from the pulpit as being Wolf Hadda's ex-wife turned towards him at a touch from her father's hand. Almost of an age with her ex-husband, she seemed to have marked time while time was marking him. She was serenely beautiful with a lovely fair complexion, blue eyes, golden hair – a very English kind of beauty, he thought, that must have come from Sir Leon's side of the family as it had little to do with the high-cheek-boned dark-eyed good looks of her mother.

'Imogen, this is, er, Mark . . .'

'Luke.'

'That's the fellow, knew it was something religious. Luke Collins, been with us six months. Settling in well. Considering.'

'Hollins,' said the vicar. 'Glad to meet you.'

She took his proffered hand and shook it firmly. He looked at her with a mixture of curiosity and compassion. The compassion came from his knowledge of the crap life had chucked at her. Young woman with everything – lovely home, wealth, comfort, a beautiful daughter – discovers that her apparently devoted and hugely successful husband is in fact a pervert and a fraud. He goes to jail, she remarries, tries to rebuild her life, and her daughter dies in tragic, sordid circumstances.

As for the curiosity, well, a measure of how well he was settling into his new job – *considering!* – was the degree to which many of his parishioners were now dropping their guard. They no longer stopped conversations short at his approach. He might be an odd bugger but he was *their* odd bugger. Now when they went all feudal and closed ranks to protect the Ulphingstones from the intrusive gaze of nosey off-comers, he found himself included in the closed ranks. And he soon found out that feudal loyalty earned you the ancient feudal right of close observation and closer analysis of *them up at the castle.*

According to local lore, *that lass Imogen* from the castle had a mind of her own. From an early age she'd led Fred Hadda's lad, Wilf, by the balls. Tossed him aside like a shit-sac from a spring nest when her dad found out, but sat up and took notice when he turned up five years on with a walletful of money and his manners mended.

Then comes the trouble and she divorces him while he's still on trial and marries his lawyer! And when the daughter she's dumped on the Continent in the care of a bunch of foreigners goes to the dogs and dies, she brings her body back to be laid to rest at St Swithin's, then doesn't show up more than once a year to pay her respects!

In other words, though there was next to no sympathy for Hadda himself, there was a lot less for his former wife than might have been expected.

She was still holding his hand after the conventional shaking period had elapsed.

She said in a loud clear voice, with that indifference to being overheard no matter how personal the topic that marks the ruling class, 'Mr Hollins, I understand you're the main point of contact locally with my ex-husband.'

He noted she gave him his correct name with sufficient aspiration to let him know that she was aware she was doing so.

He said cautiously, 'I do see Mr Hadda from time to time, yes.'

'Then I wonder if you know where he is just now?'

He said, 'To the best of my knowledge, he's up at Birkstane.'

She let go his hand and frowned.

'Then the best of your knowledge isn't worth much, Mr Hollins. I called there last week and all I found was a black woman who, I gather, is his psychiatrist. When I called again yesterday, there was still no sign of him, and his vehicle wasn't in the barn.'

'He is not, so far as I know, constrained to stay within the house,' he said.

The rest of the party were still peering at the tomb, apparently taking no interest in the conversation, though Hollins suspected Kira was recording it verbatim. A small, thin-faced dark-complexioned man, wearing only an exquisitely cut lightweight suit despite the cold, came to stand alongside Imogen. The second husband? guessed Hollins. He had noticed him sitting close to her and sharing a hymn book in the castle pew.

'In my country he would be constrained to stay in a prison cell,' he said.

While Hollins was wondering why an English solicitor should talk like a foreigner, Sir Leon said punctiliously, 'Don't think you've met. Paddle Nicotine, cousin of my wife's, Mark Collins, our vicar.'

Hollins for once didn't mind Sir Leon's cavalier way with his name when he saw the small man wince and heard him say, 'Pavel Nik-EET-in.'

Now another member of the castle party, a slightly florid man beginning to run to fat, got in on the act and declared somewhat officiously, 'If you do know where he is, Vicar, and it turns out he's breaking the terms of his licence, you realize you too would be guilty in the eyes of the law?'

Imogen frowned at the interrupter then said apologetically to Hollins, 'My husband. He's a solicitor, therefore sees everything in legal black and white. Toby, be civilized. Mr Hollins is our vicar, not a hostile witness.'

'Sorry,' said the man, offering his hand. 'Toby Estover. It's just that it's a bit worrying, Hadda wandering round loose. Of course we may find it's all been cut and dried with his probation officer. You don't happen to know who that is, do you?'

'I'm afraid not,' said Hollins.

'No?' said Estover dubiously. 'Thought you might have set up some kind of liaison with him, in the circumstances.'

'The circumstances being?'

'A man on the sex offenders' list living on your doorstep, a man who must presumably still be the cause of some concern to our probation service if his prison psychiatrist is making home visits; doesn't that concern you, pastorally if not personally?'

'It's the Law that let him out, Mr Estover, not the Church,' said Hollins. 'Maybe you should be talking to somebody else. Sorry I can't be more helpful, Mrs Estover. Now if you'll excuse me, I think I can smell my turkey burning.'

He moved back towards the church.

'Beat you on penalties, I reckon,' said Imogen to her husband.

Nikitin laughed and Estover said sharply, 'I think he's more worried than he's letting on, which suggests he may have more to worry about than he's letting on.'

Lady Kira, accepting that the tomb was played out as a focal topic, now joined in.

'I've been telling Leon to get rid of him ever since I first saw him,' she declared.

'Keep telling you, the living's not in the castle's gift, not for a century and a half,' said Leon. 'As for Wolf, why all the fuss? You complain when he's on your doorstep and you complain when he's not. Can't see why you'd want to see him anyway, Imo.'

'Can't you, Daddy?' said Imogen. 'Let's go home. I wonder what's for lunch?'

She moved away. Pavel Nikitin hurried to catch up with her.

'Imo OK, is she?' Sir Leon said to his son-in-law.

'As far as it is possible for anyone ever to say,' said Estover. He turned his head slowly, taking in the landscape beyond the church and the scatter of village houses. The fells lay sharp as wolf fangs against the cold blue sky, their edges gleaming white, their craggy lower slopes like diseased gums smudged with black where the frost had lost its grip. He longed to be back in London.

'Could be the bloody Caucasus,' he said with a shudder.

Lady Kira shrieked an unexpected laugh.

'Don't be stupid, Toby,' she said. 'It is nothing like. In the Caucasus, Mr Collins would have been dragged apart by wild horses long since.'

She set off after her daughter and cousin several times removed.

'Reads a lot,' said Sir Leon apologetically. 'Far as I know, she's never been nearer the Caucasus than Monte Carlo.'

The two men shared a rare moment of bonding, then gathered up the rest of their party and set out after Kira.

And finally the few villagers who'd lingered beyond the churchyard wall headed home to their dinners, satisfied that the raree-show was over for this Christmas Day.

296

3

Two days after Boxing Day Wolf Hadda moved slowly through the green channel at Luton Airport, hardly distinguishable from the geriatrics who accompanied him, leaning on their contraband-filled trolleys like Zimmer frames in an effort to win sympathy from any suspicious customs officer.

As he emerged he saw Edgar Trapp standing among the welcomers, most of whom advanced to greet their elderly relatives as if they'd just got back from the Thirty Year War. Before he could reach Trapp, a hatchet-faced woman in a pink jump suit and matching wimple with enough cigarettes on her trolley to carcinomate a convent, flung her free arm round his neck and gave him a long sucking kiss.

'Lovely to meet you, Wally,' she said. 'You got my address safe? You be sure to keep in touch, dearie. Go safe with Jesus.'

He disengaged himself with difficulty and a promise of everlasting friendship.

Trapp said, 'Looks like you made an impression there. She really a nun?'

He said, 'If she is, God help us all! I don't know what the NHS is feeding these people, but it ought to be banned. Ed, what were you thinking of?'

'You said you wanted to blend in. Pensioners' package to Fuengirola seemed perfect.'

'I'll ignore that. How's Sneck been?'

'Growled once at Doll, but she spoke firmly to him and he's been good as gold since.'

Hadda nodded understandingly. If Doll Trapp had spoken firmly to him, he too would have been good as gold.

When they got into Trapp's old Toyota, Hadda, who felt his solicitor was a bad enough driver without distraction, did not speak till they were clear of the airport and running down the M1.

'Have a good Christmas?' he asked.

'Usual. You?'

'I think you're being cheeky, Ed.'

'I mean, the other.'

'Oh that. Yes, fine.'

'Bad as you thought then?'

'Bad as I thought.'

'I'm sorry. By the way, there's messages on your mobile from that Scotch geezer. Sounds a bit agitated. Or maybe it's just the accent.'

He'd bought a new PAYG mobile to use in Spain and left his old phone with Trapp. He didn't want any calls made abroad to register on the old one. The new one lay in several pieces in several litter bins in Fuengirola.

Traffic on the M25 was heavy and it was dark by the time they pulled up at Trapp's house in Chingford. It was a substantial pre-war semi, built well enough to have survived with dignity for the best part of a hundred years and now worth more than the whole street had cost back in the 1930s.

When Trapp opened the front door, they were met by Sneck, his back arched, his teeth bared in a long threatening growl. Then, reproof administered for his owner's callous dereliction of duty, he advanced to offer forgiveness by the

298

vigorous application of wet tongue to Hadda's face.

'Dogs and nuns,' said Trapp. 'You got it made.'

Doll Trapp appeared, pushing Sneck aside unceremoniously to give Hadda a hug.

'Wives, too,' he said, giving Trapp a wink over the woman's head. 'Christ, Doll, don't crush me to death.'

Mrs Trapp was large enough to make two of her husband, with a broad face whose naturally stern expression she attempted, unsuccessfully, to soften by her choice of hair colouring. Today it was blush pink.

'You're skin and bones, Wolf,' she declared, releasing him. 'It's all that foreign muck. You must be starved. Come on through. Supper's ready.'

They went through into the dining room. There were things Hadda would rather have been doing, but when Doll spoke, obedience was the best policy.

They ate steak-and-kidney pudding followed by apple pie and custard, all washed down with strong tea. Alcohol wasn't an option in the Trapp household. Trapp had been on the wagon for a couple of decades now and Doll was determined that he would never be led into temptation in his own home.

It was a comfortable meal, the conversation such as it was led by Doll. Anyone seeing and hearing her might have set her down as a confirmed *Hausfrau*, her interests centred on kitchen and family, but Hadda knew better. Trapp's decisions, professional and personal, were all filtered through her. He wouldn't be sitting here at this table if she hadn't given the nod, and it was an endorsement he valued more than his lost title.

At the end of the meal Doll said, 'You with us long, Wolf?'

'Just tonight. I need to get up to Carlisle tomorrow to see my minder, so I'll be off early in the morning to beat the traffic. No need for you to get up.'

'Don't be daft. I'll want to say goodbye to old Sneckie, won't I? I'll really miss him.'

299

Hadda glanced down at the dog lying alongside his chair and got a return look which, if he'd been anthropomorphically inclined, he might have interpreted as, 'And what's so odd about that?'

Trapp said, 'I've put your phone in your room. And my update.'

He said, 'Thanks,' and excused himself.

On the bed lay the phone and a file.

First he checked his messages. There were a couple from Luke Hollins, hoping all was well and asking him to get in touch. And three from Davy McLucky, starting the previous day, growing increasingly imperative, the last left only a couple of hours earlier.

'Hadda, last fucking chance, whatever you're doing, give me a ring. We need to talk. Now!'

He pressed the return call key.

'McLucky.'

'Hadda. You left a message.'

'Where've you been?'

'Nowhere. Sorry not to get back to you sooner. Let my battery run down and I've just recharged it. So what's so urgent?'

A silence. The silence of disbelief? Maybe. But why should the Scot react to a very believable lie with such scepticism?

Now he spoke.

'The old mate from my Met days that I got Medler's address from gave me a bell. Said if I hadn't made contact yet, not to bother. The good life's over for Arnie. He's dead.'

'*What?*'

'You didn't know then?'

'No, I didn't. Has it been on the news?'

'No, and probably won't be. Yard's been notified because he was one of their own, but seems there's been a note to keep it under wraps as much as possible. Must have been a pretty heavy note as there's nothing the press likes more than

300

a nice grisly human interest story over the festive season.'

'Grisly? What the hell happened?'

'Wife found him Christmas morning. He was in their lounge. His hands were on the patio. The security shutter had come down and chopped them off. He bled to death.'

'Jesus! Your mate tell you anything else?'

'That he had more booze in him than a cross-Channel ferry, and the local cops reckon he was so pissed that either by accident or design he pressed the shutter control then fell forward with his arms outstretched across the patio door.'

'That's terrible,' said Wolf.

'That's what I said. Then my mate asked me, dead casual, if it had been anything important I wanted to get in touch with Arnie about.'

'And what did you tell him, Davy?'

'Well,' said McLucky slowly, 'I know what I should have told him, being ex-job, not to mention a PI with his licence to worry about. I should have told him, I've been working for this guy, got form, been paying me good money to find out where Medler lived, his habits, the layout of his villa, all sorts of stuff. You might want to give him a pull, check how he spent Christmas . . .'

Now it was Hadda's turn to be silent.

He said, 'I think we should meet.'

'You don't expect me to go wandering round that fucking wilderness you live in again, do you?'

'I'll be in Carlisle tomorrow, could you manage that again? It's not like leaving the kingdom; it was once the capital of Scotland, they tell me.'

McLucky wasn't in the mood for lightness.

'Same time, same place. I'll be there.'

The phone went dead.

Hadda switched off and sat in thought for a few moments. Then he picked up the file and opened it. It only took ten

301

minutes to read. Trapp was not a man to waste words.

He finished, opened his grip, put the file inside and took out a large bottle of expensive perfume, a handsome gold-plated watch and a compact digital recorder. He was at the door when he remembered something and went to the wardrobe. From one of the shelves he took a package. It was Luke Hollins's Christmas gift that some atavistic superstition had prevented him from opening before Christmas.

Trapp and his wife were sitting before a glowing fire in a living room that could have been a tribute to the seventies.

Hadda said, 'I've got a little recording I'd like you both to listen to. Then I've got a sad and rather troubling story I need to tell you. But first things first. Christmas prezzie time! Sorry yours aren't wrapped.'

He handed Doll the watch and Ed the perfume, then said, 'Whoops, I was in prison a long time,' and swapped them round.

They both smiled and said thanks, then watched as Hadda unwrapped his parcel.

It was a postcard-size picture stuck in a gilt frame. It showed a bearded man with a halo. He carried what looked like a small tree in one hand and an axe in the other. There was a post-it note attached to the frame.

It read: *This is St Gomer or Gummarus. The double name may come in useful if you're ever asked to name three famous Belgians. He is the patron of woodcutters and unhappy husbands. Hope he might come in useful. LH*

Hadda began to smile and finally he laughed out loud.

'What?' said Doll.

'Nothing. Just my friendly local vicar. I told him I didn't care to be preached at, so I think he's decided, if you can't convert them with sermons, next best thing is to have a laugh with them!'

He looked at the picture again, then nodded, and added, 'You know, he could be right!'

302

4

The nearest Alva Ozigbo got to the pleasures of a traditional Christmas was the rather grisly festive atmosphere that hung over the hospital wards.

The balloons and decorations stopped short of Intensive Care but nowhere was beyond the reach of the sucrose notes of old Christmas hits seeping out of the in-house radio system. When she arrived, she'd found her father scheduled for angioplasty the following day and her mother in a state of near collapse. Alva was prepared for this, being aware since childhood that Elvira's way of dealing with bad situations was to anticipate the worst, as if by embracing it, she could avert it. Her gloomy prognostications were uttered in a tone which her husband and daughter had often theorized would surely have won her a part in that Bergmann movie if only she could have produced it at the audition.

The operation went well, and by Boxing Day patient and wife were both making a good recovery. Indeed, Ike Ozigbo already seemed bent on proving the truth of the old adage that doctors make the worst patients, and his surgeon, Ike's registrar, told Alva that her father should be ready to move back home by the New Year, adding 'and that's by popular appeal!'

Elvira's superstitious gloom having achieved its goal, she reverted to her usual brisk efficient self. Her husband's health naturally still preoccupied her mind, but other concerns were now allowed to surface, principle among them being a probing inquisitiveness about the state of her daughter's sex life.

Even in her time of deepest Scandinavian depression, she had registered that Alva was taking phone calls from a man. This was Wolf Hadda, who rang twice, once on the evening of her departure from Cumbria to check she'd reached Manchester safely, the second time a couple of days later. Moving out of range of her mother's hearing but not her speculation, Alva found herself going into what seemed later to be unnecessary detail about Elvira's behaviour. Hadda said, 'I'm with your ma here. Hope for the best, prepare for the worst, that's sound sense. Inside, we're all hoping for the best. So feed the hope and put up with the rest. But I'm teaching my granny to suck eggs.'

Alva said, 'None of my grannies was English. Do English grannies suck a lot of eggs?'

He said, 'It's a condition of service. Listen, I just wanted to say . . .'

What he just wanted to say was drowned in a burst of noise.

She said, 'Say again. I didn't get that.'

He said, 'Sorry, radio on. Look, I've got to dash. You take care.'

Then he was gone, leaving her looking at her phone and wondering whether she should check the radio schedules to see if there was anything on that might be broadcasting a noise like a loudspeaker announcement on a railway platform or in an airport.

Of course she didn't. Her life was too busy for luxuries like reading the *Radio Times*.

But she felt disappointed when he didn't ring again and found it difficult to analyse why.

Two days after Boxing Day, things (meaning Elvira) had settled down enough for Alva to think of accessing her London apartment phone to check on messages. She'd made sure everyone likely to want to contact her had known she'd be away, so there weren't many, and only one that held her attention. It had been left the previous day.

'Dr Ozigbo, this is Imogen Estover. I thought it might be useful for us to talk. I'm up here at the castle for a few more days, then I'll be back in London.'

She left her mobile number and the message ended. Her voice had been cool, almost expressionless, but Alva would have recognized it even if she hadn't given her name.

Useful. To whom, she wondered as she saved the mobile number.

She thought of ringing back that same evening, but decided to sleep on it.

Next morning as she helped Elvira with the breakfast dishes, her phone rang.

The display showed a Cumbrian number. Either Hadda or his ex-wife, she guessed as she put it to her ear. But she was wrong. It was Luke Hollins.

She went out of the kitchen into the garden. It was chilly, but here she could keep an eye on her mother through the window with no risk of being overheard.

'Dr Ozigbo, hi, I've been meaning to ring to see how your father is, but it's been a busy time for me. So how are things?'

She'd rung him before Christmas to explain why she hadn't contacted him as promised before leaving Cumbria.

After she'd brought him up to date on Ike, he said, 'That's good to hear. You'll be staying on there for a while?'

'I was always planning to stay till the New Year,' she said, not adding her mental rider, unless my mother has driven me to flight with her catechism about my private life!

'Good. That's good.'

He wants to tell me something but is reluctant to pile more stuff on me during a family crisis, she thought. There was only one possible topic.

She said, 'How are things at Birkstane?'

That turned on the tap. He told her about his encounter with the Ulphingstones on Christmas Day.

'I got worried, so I called at the house on Boxing Day. Not a sign. I tried again yesterday. Still nothing. The Defender wasn't in the barn. Of course no reason why he couldn't have been out all day. So I was up there at the crack this morning. Nothing. There's no escaping it, he's not here, probably hasn't been here since before Christmas.'

'That doesn't mean anything,' said Alva. 'The terms of his licence don't preclude movement within the country.'

'Yes, I realize that, but he'd need to keep his probation officer informed, I should have thought? And definitely the police?'

'So have you checked?'

'Well, no,' said Hollins hesitantly. 'To tell the truth, I didn't want to stir things up unnecessarily. I thought maybe you . . .'

'I see,' said Alva.

What she saw was how yet again the priest's personal liking for Wolf was at odds with his pastoral concerns. She should have been irritated by his efforts to share the problem with her, but she realized she wasn't.

She could see Elvira behind the kitchen window, still at the sink, watching her as she dried and re-dried the same cup.

She's dying to know if there's a man in my life! thought Alva. How would she react if I told her there were two men, one a convicted pederast, the other a married vicar!

She waved at the watching woman and raised her face

to catch the morning sun still low on the south-eastern horizon. It wasn't nine o'clock yet. The day stretched before her, full of hospital smells and Elvira's subtle questioning. The sky was cloudless. She took a deep breath of the sharp air and it seemed to scour her mind.

The motorway wouldn't be back to its normal overcrowded state yet. She could be back in Cumbria in a couple of hours. To do what?

Hollins said, 'Hello? Dr Ozigbo, are you still there?'

She said, 'Yes, sorry. Look, are you going to be around later this morning? I could come up . . .'

He said, 'Great. That would be helpful.'

She wanted to ask him, *How exactly?* but it didn't seem apt.

She said, 'Till later then,' switched off and went back into the kitchen.

'Mum,' she said, 'would you mind if I ducked out of the visits today?'

'Of course not, dear. You deserve a break. Is it something special you want to do?'

'I thought I might take a little drive and maybe look up an old friend.'

'Anyone I know?' said Elvira, very casual.

'I think you know all my old friends, Mum,' she said.

Her mother smiled but didn't press.

She's spotted that there's more going on than I'm saying, thought Alva, but naturally her interpretation's romantic. A date, an assignation, even an affair!

She gave her mother a hug and said, 'Great. Give my love to Daddy. I'll be home this evening some time. Don't wait supper for me.'

As she drove away from the house, she felt a pang of guilt at her own sense of release. It had come as a disappointment to her as a student to realize that understanding the often irrational origins of common emotions didn't stop you feeling them. When she told her father this, he'd boomed his great laugh and said, 'Even dentists get toothache!'

And even cardiologists have heart attacks, she told herself.

She set the guilt aside and concentrated on her driving as she swept down the slip road on to the motorway.

She soon realized she'd been wrong about the traffic, or perhaps everyone had made the same miscalculation. Her two-hour estimate rapidly stretched to three, giving her both the incentive and the time to ask herself precisely why she was doing this.

Striving for that complete honesty she looked for in her therapies, she systematically listed all her motivational springs.

First the professional: concern for a patient; concern for a community; Luke Hollins's request for help; Imogen Estover's desire to speak with her.

Then the personal: her fear that she might have got things wrong; her irritation at the feeling that Hadda was mucking her about; her frustration in the presence of mysteries she'd not yet been able to disentangle; her simple need to have a break from her mother's company and hospital visits!

There it was. Can't get any honester than that, she told herself.

Except that, as her college tutor had loved to iterate, complete honesty is like clearing a cellar. When you've got all the clutter neatly laid out in the back yard, don't waste time congratulating yourself on a job well done. Head down those steps again and start digging up the concrete floor.

She dug. She knew already there was something to find. Something so deeply repressed that she couldn't be sure it wasn't a figment of her imagination, the crocodile under the sofa that had made her sit with her legs tucked up beneath her as a child, the trolls in Elvira's Swedish fairy tales who

308

lived beneath the rockery in the garden. Unreal things, but her fear was real till she discovered that the simple way to dispose of them was to expose them to daylight and watch them shrivel away.

This was what she tried now. It didn't take long to find it, not because it wasn't buried deep but because she knew where to start digging. And there it was, hidden beneath all that stuff about his face-transforming smile, that dangerous charm which she had complimented herself on being so alert to.

She spoke it out loud so that there could be no fudging.

'Deeply repressed reason for driving north to Birkstane: I am sexually attracted to Wolf Hadda.'

Now she could submit it to the test of exposure to the clear light of day.

But it wasn't shrivelling.

Damn! But no need to panic. Such things happened. Usually the other way round, of course. And it seemed peculiarly perverse in every sense that her urges should have focused on a man who was physically scarred, psychologically damaged, and morally repugnant. But if human beings weren't perverse, she'd be out of a job.

She would deal with it, just as Simon Homewood dealt with his feelings for her.

Her self-examination had taken care of the time nicely. She saw a sign telling her that she was now in Cumbria.

She wasn't altogether sure what had started here all those years ago, but one way or another all journeys are circular. We never arrive anywhere that we haven't been before.

Where was Hadda now? she asked herself.

And where did he think he was heading?

She switched on her left indicator and prepared to turn off the motorway.

5

McLucky was late.

'Fucking trains,' he said. 'They couldn't run a raffle.'

'That's all right,' said Hadda. 'I'm just here myself. My probation officer was very keen to exchange notes on how we'd enjoyed our respective Christmases.'

'Me too,' said McLucky, sitting down heavily.

The lounge door opened and a young, pretty waitress backed in carrying a heavily laden tray.

'I ordered you a scotch,' said Hadda. 'And some smoked salmon sandwiches.'

'And I told you before, I'm choosy who I eat with.'

'If you don't stop snarling, the waitress will be thinking we're having a lovers' tiff.'

'Would it put her mind at rest if I gave you a thump?'

'She looks the happy-ending type to me, so she'd probably prefer if you gave me a kiss.'

That didn't make McLucky smile but his face relaxed a little and when the waitress reached their table and set down the plates and glasses, he picked up his glass.

'I'm not so choosy who I drink with,' he said. 'Cheers. Now, answers.'

'Yes, I've been to Spain,' said Hadda. 'Yes, I saw Medler. No, I didn't kill him.'

McLucky said, 'Jesus.'

'You did ask.'

'I didn't actually. I was hoping you were going to turn up with your clerical friend and he was going to swear on the Bible you'd not been out of the county all Christmas. How the hell did you manage it? I thought there were travel restrictions.'

'There are. I would have needed permission. If I'd asked.'

'But your passport . . . you'll be on record . . .'

'Mr Wally Hammond, widower, of Gloucestershire, is on record as having enjoyed a festive break with sixty other geriatrics at the Hotel Flamenco. I have a friend who knows how to arrange such things. He is, as you'll probably have gathered, a cricket fan.'

McLucky looked at him blankly, then said, 'Why are you telling me this?'

'Because I think the only way to persuade you I'm telling you everything is to do just that. I went to see Medler late on Christmas Eve, having seen his wife head off to the midnight service at the English Church. We had a long conversation. I left him a sadder and I hope a wiser man about twelve thirty. He was alive and well. Except for being pretty drunk. And he must have got drunker from the sound of what happened. Happy now?'

'Happy? You must be joking.'

'You've still got doubts? I thought that tape you brought me of Estover and the Nutbrowns chatting at Poynters would have cleared your mind.'

'It was suggestive, but a long way from conclusive,' said McLucky. 'Anyway, it just says something about what you maybe were. It's what you might have become that bothers me.'

311

'Fine.' Hadda sipped his orange juice. 'In your shoes, maybe I'd be cautious too. Why don't you see how suggestive you find this? Me, I'll just check that Sneck's all right in the van. Give me a ring when you've had time to listen to it.'

He pushed across the table a digital recorder with an earpiece attached.

McLucky studied it suspiciously for a moment then fixed the device in his ear and pressed the start button. Hadda rose and, leaning heavily on his stick, made his way out of the lounge, smiling his gratitude at the young waitress who rushed forward to open the door for him.

In the car park he opened the Defender's tailgate.

'Out,' he said to Sneck.

The dog woke up, yawned as if thinking about it, then jumped down. Hadda locked the car, walked to the edge of the car park and sat down on a low wall bordering a patch of municipal greenery. Sneck jumped over the wall, sniffed around, cocked his leg against a tired-looking tree, then returned to lie across his master's feet and went back to sleep.

Hadda, leaning forward with both hands resting on his stick and his chin resting on his hands, closed his eyes too and let his mind go back to his encounter with Arnie Medler on Christmas Eve.

6

It had taken a minute or more for Medler to recover from his initial shock. Hadda saw no reason to make things easier. He settled in a chair opposite the man and stared at him fixedly as if able to read the confusion of emotion running across the ex-policeman's mind. Finally he reached forward with the axe and nudged the cognac bottle towards the ex-cop.

'You look like you need a drink,' he said.

'Bloody right, I do,' croaked Medler. 'Seeing you there waving that fucking hatchet around, wonder I didn't have a heart attack.'

'Can't have that,' said Hadda. 'Not before we talk.'

Medler topped up his glass, emptied it, filled it again then looked at Hadda.

'You?'

'No thanks. I'm driving.'

The conventional response plus the drink seemed to help Medler's recovery and his voice was stronger as he said, 'So how'd you find me? McLucky, was it?'

'Might have been.'

'I knew there was something. First lesson in CID. Never trust a coincidence.'

'So why did you go along with him?'

'Don't know. Could have snuck off home soon as I clocked him, pulled down the shutters. I suppose I was just glad to see a face I recognized from the old days. Any face. Someone to talk to who knew me when I was . . . someone.'

'A good honest cop,' said Hadda with savage irony.

'That's right! That's what I was. All right, I cut a few corners, took a couple of drinks, but only to help me get where I wanted to be.'

'You mean, like *here*?'

'*No!* I mean get a result. Saw no harm in letting a few sprats swim loose if they helped me catch a fucking great shark. And if I picked up a few backhanders on the way, that just increased my credibility, right? Come on, Sir Wilf, you were a financial whiz. All right, you may have taken the rap for stuff you didn't know about, but you can't have made all the money you did without dipping your fingers in places they shouldn't have been.'

'You trying to say I got what I deserved?' said Hadda incredulously.

Medler shook his head.

'No. Of course not.' He tried a laugh, but it didn't come out right. Nevertheless he pressed on: 'I'll tell you something funny, though. In one way it *was* your own fucking fault you got what you did. Ironic that. Like in Greek tragedy. That surprises you, eh? I'm not just a dumb plod, I got O-levels.'

Hadda leaned forward and said harshly, 'I'm not here for literary fucking criticism, Medler. Just tell me what happened. And quick. I don't want to be still here when the lovely Tina returns from her devotions.'

'Don't worry, one way or another I reckon she'll be on her knees for a couple of hours yet. But all right, here goes . . .'

314

He emptied his glass again. Refilled it. He was beginning to feel he had some control over the situation. Hadda didn't mind. It was a delusion easily remedied.

'Sure you won't? OK. Well, it started with a tip, an anonymous email, said we might like to take a close look at Sir Wilfred Hadda, mentioned a website, InArcadia. We knew about InArcadia. Clever buggers, they were. Everything heavily encrypted, more layers to get through than you'd find on an Eskimo whore, ducking and weaving all the time so that just when you thought you'd got a handle on them, they'd be over the hills and far away. It was only a matter of time, though, and we'd just had a big breakthrough when we got this tip about you. While we hadn't laid hands on the people running it – not surprising, they could be anywhere in the world – we'd got about twenty thousand client credit-card records.'

'Twenty thousand!'

'Tip of the fucking iceberg. There's a lot of weirdoes about. Anyway, among all these credit-card records we found a couple that we traced back to your company. That with the email allegations was enough to get a warrant to take a closer look. Maximum discretion. You were an important man.'

'Maximum discretion!' exclaimed Hadda. 'The media turned up mob-handed! You couldn't resist it, could you, Medler? A big hit, you wanted all the world to see you making it, right?'

The ex-cop was shaking his head vigorously.

'You're wrong, Hadda. Man like you with fancy-dan lawyers, we tread careful till we're sure. I played it by the book, need-to-know op, me the lowest rank needing to know. Nearly shit myself when I arrived and saw it was looking like a muck-rakers' convention.'

No reason for the man to lie, thought Hadda. Meant someone else wanted the world to be in on the act from the start . . .

'But I bet you enjoyed it, all the same.'

'Why not? Everyone likes taking a swipe at a tall poppy. Build 'em up, knock 'em down, that's what makes celebrity culture go round. And when I clocked that stuff on your computer, I thought, Hello! This case isn't going to do me any harm whatsoever.'

'Made your mind up straight away, did you?' said Hadda. 'Innocent till proved guilty doesn't apply, not when you've got yourself a big one.'

Medler laughed again and shook his head.

'That's where you're wrong again, Sir Wilf . . . sorry, Mr Hadda. That's the irony I was telling you about. If you hadn't reacted the way you did, punching me in the mouth, twice, and doing a runner and getting yourself hospitalized, you know what you'd probably be doing now? You'd be relaxing in your Caribbean mansion, having a drink, looking forward to eating your Christmas turkey on the beach!'

'What the fuck are you talking about?'

'I'm talking about me being a good cop,' said Medler, suddenly animated. 'I'm talking about me doing the job I was paid for. We do a real job on sifting through evidence, and not just because we know rich bastards like you will be spending more than the department's annual budget on putting together a defence. We do it for rich and poor alike, because it's the right fucking thing to do!'

Hadda had come prepared for many things, but not moral indignation.

He's talking like he's still in the job! he thought.

But even as he looked he saw the indignation fade and awareness of the truth of his situation return to Medler's eyes.

He rubbed his hand over his face and said wearily, 'Yeah, that's right, Mr Hadda. If you'd just sat on your hands, protesting your innocence, and let us get on with the job of investigating the case, I reckon that a week or so later, I'd have been making a statement to the media saying Sir Wilfred's been the victim of a scurrilous attempt to smear his good name and, as far as the Met's concerned, he's being released without a stain on his character.'

He filled his glass again and regarded his visitor with a malicious glint in his eyes.

'But you couldn't sit still, could you? Not the great Wolf Hadda, the City's own action man. You had to hit out and make a run for it, and suddenly everything changed. You were lying on your back with lots of bits missing and enough machinery attached to you to run a small factory, and it was impossible to find a bookie who'd give odds on you lasting the week out. So, like you, the case was put on ice. We had plenty of living perverts to pursue without wasting too much time on the moribund. In fact, at the time, following up all these payment trails from InArcadia, things got really hectic.'

Wolf Hadda suddenly reached forward and seized the brandy bottle. He raised it to his lips and took a long swig. Finished, it took all his will power not to hurl the bottle against the villa wall. Instead he lowered it gently to the table and said, 'So when did you realize I was innocent, Mr Medler?'

'Month or so on. Most of the media boys had lost interest, they like their meat to be still on the hoof, so I was surprised when my boss asked for an update on your case. We went back a long way, him and me, so I told him I'd better things to do than investigate a living corpse, and he told me it wasn't his idea but there was "an interest". Now that's code for politics or security or both. Somebody somewhere wanted to know whether you'd been sticking it to little girls or not. You got any idea who, Mr Hadda?'

He was starting to sound far too like his old cocky self.

And his old cocky self would be sifting through truths, weighing alternatives, looking for opportunities.

Wolf brought the hatchet blade down on the arm of the recliner just an inch from Medler's wrist, causing him to jerk away so violently his glass flew out of his hand and smashed on the tiled patio.

'Jesus Christ! What you do that for? You could have had my hand off!'

'Your hands are the least of your worries if you start jerking me around, Medler. We're not having a conversation. Just tell me what happened!'

'All right, all right, keep your hair on!'

He reached for the cognac and took a long pull straight from the bottle.

'What I did then was go away and do what I'd have done if you hadn't been such an action hero. I took a long hard look at the case notes and the evidence file. On the surface it all looked pretty sound, but once I started digging, it didn't take long to smell a rat.'

'Meaning, you started to suspect that I'd been fitted up? Why?'

'There were patterns I looked for. You got to understand, this wasn't the first time this kind of thing happened. You get everyone from redundant employees to betrayed wives or even pissed-off kids thinking, Wouldn't it be neat to download some mucky images on to the old bastard's computer and give the pigs an anonymous tip? Often it sticks out like a sore thumb. Yours was a rather more sophisticated job. Whoever did it knew what they were doing. Took me the best part of a week, on and off, but in the end I got there.'

'Well, congratulations,' sneered Hadda. 'So why didn't you go to your superiors, tell them what you thought, get my name cleared publicly?'

Medler smiled bitterly, 'Oh, I was going to, believe me.

But first – this'll make you laugh – I thought, wouldn't it be nice to get a line on the bastards who'd been shafting you? All right, you'd split my lip, twice, but that didn't mean you deserved this.'

'I'm very touched. So what did you do?'

'I went along to see Toby fucking Estover. He was still your solicitor then, of course. This was before he went public about banging your missus. Sorry. All I intended was to have a chat, see if he could give me any line on who was most likely to be responsible. But you know what? I hadn't been in his office two minutes when I realized I need look no further. Whatever was going on, whoever had initiated it, Mr Toby Estover was in it right up to his lily-white upper-class neck!'

Now as he regarded Hadda, his expression was no longer malicious but pitying.

'Come on, Hadda,' he said. 'You've had years to think about this. You must have suspected.'

'I suspected . . . lots of people,' said Hadda. Then he took a deep breath and demanded, 'So your super-sensitive copper's nose put Estover in the frame. What did you do about it?'

'Without evidence, what could I do except sit back and let him go on thinking that I'd come to talk to him because I was on to his little game? At this point all I was interested in was letting him incriminate himself so that I could bang him up! Estover, Mast and Turbery, in the Met they're high on most people's hate list! I'd be flavour of the month if I could throw a spanner in their well-oiled works. And when he began hinting a pay-off, I began rubbing my hands at the prospect of getting him on a bribery count as well.'

'But in the end he offered enough to make you change your mind,' said Hadda.

'Not exactly. Or at least, not straight away. After half an

hour of me looking like I knew everything while really I knew fuck all and him giving off enough legal smog to contravene the Clean Air Act, we agreed to meet again the following day. I naturally took the chance to get myself wired. When the bribe was clearly offered, I wanted it on tape.'

'Still thinking like an honest cop,' mocked Hadda.

'Yeah, surprisingly, I was. But someone had been keeping tabs on me. I was sitting at my desk, writing up my report when my boss ushered this geezer into my office and said, "This is Mr Wesley. He'd like to talk to you about the Hadda case. He has full clearance." Then he left me with Mr sodding Wesley.'

'Wesley?' Hadda frowned. 'What did he look like?'

'Nothing special. Hard to say if he was fifty or seventy. Hair thinning, a bit wispy, sort of brown turning grey. Five foot ten, slim build, blue eyes, not much chin, nice smile, except it didn't always go with the things he was saying. Expensive suit, MCC tie. Softly spoken, posh but not grating, slight hint of East Anglia in there, maybe.'

'For someone nothing special, he seems to have made an impression,' said Wolf.

Medler shrugged and said, 'When I heard what he had to say, I made sure I'd know him again. What about you? Sounds familiar, does he?'

He hadn't lost his super-sensitive copper's nose, thought Hadda.

'Maybe. What did this Mr Wesley say?'

'I told him what was going off, what I suspected about Estover. He asked me who else knew what I was doing. I said my boss a bit, but not much. And nobody else. He said keep it that way. If Estover did offer me a bribe, push him to see how far he'd go. But don't take any action till I'd talked to him again. And nothing in writing or in my computer. I said, "How do I get in touch?" and he smiled and said, "Don't worry about it."'

'And you didn't argue or talk this over with your boss?'

Medler shrugged and said, 'Not the kind of guy you want to argue with. But if he's a friend of yours, you'll know that. Anyway, I met Estover again. I could tell straight off he was easing towards a deal. He started by talking about you, showed me the latest medical report. Just one step back from a death certificate, he said. "And you can't harm the dead," he told me, "so why harm the living?" Trying to soften me up, I suppose. But he still didn't say anything like, Here's ten k, it's yours if you keep your mouth shut.'

'Ten k? You didn't get this place with ten k,' said Hadda.

'No. I played it like Mr nothing special Wesley told me and gave him a push.'

He smiled as if relishing the memory.

'Suddenly I stood up and said, all pompous like, "I hope you're not offering me an inducement, Mr Estover. Because if you are, I think you ought to know, I'm not the kind of cop who'd put his reputation on the line for a handful of silver." "How about a handful of gold?" he said, laughing to show it was just a joke. And I said, "What would I do with gold? No, I'm a man of simple needs. All I'm looking to do is to get enough years in to retire early to somewhere sunny like Spain." Then I said we'd need to talk again, I'd give him a ring. And I left.'

'And not long after you left a car drew up and Mr Wesley invited you to take a ride with him,' said Hadda.

'Where were you? Hiding in the boot? Sorry. Yes, he took charge of the tape. Didn't bother to listen to it, but he seemed to know what had gone off. He asked me if there really was somewhere in Spain I had in mind. I said there were a couple of places. I'd always kept an eye on the Spanish house market. Most of the stuff I fancied was way out of my league normally, but I knew that with the banking crisis getting worse every day, a lot of overstretched ex-pats were going to be looking to sell cheap. I'd just got the details of this place. It was still only a pipe-dream. Even with a fifty per cent discount, I'd never be able to afford it. But now Wesley said, "Show it to Estover. Ask his advice."'

'Which you did when you met again?'

'Yeah. Next day. Not in his office this time. I chose the rendezvous, outside, down by the river. He was as cautious as me. The way we patted each other to make sure neither of us was wired, anyone watching must have thought we were a couple of poofs! Then I showed him the details of the villa, asked what he thought. He said it looked a good investment, how much of the cost would I be looking for? And I said, "Well, all of it. Plus I'd need a bit of a lump sum to cover maintenance and so on."'

He paused for effect. He was beginning to enjoy his narration again.

Hadda flourished the hatchet and snarled, 'For fuck's sake, get on with it!'

'Sorry, sorry,' said Medler, taking another swig of brandy. 'I expected him to start to haggle, but he didn't even blink. He said, leave it to him. He'd do the negotiating. And he'd get it all registered in my name. Plus a nice maintenance account.'

'And that was it?' said Hadda. 'Sounds like you were getting a helluva lot for not very much.'

'There was something else,' said Medler uneasily. 'Estover said, "We need guarantees. No come back. Whatever happens. Never."'

'So what did you have to do?' said Hadda softly, breathing on the hatchet blade and polishing it on his sleeve.

'He told me that, for both our sakes, I'd need to make sure that if ever anyone looked at the details of the charges again, they'd find a truly watertight case.'

'And then?'

'We shook hands and left. I met Wesley later. He told me to sit tight for a couple of days, mention nothing of this to no one. Later in the week he turned up in my office. Said it had been decided I should go along with Estover the whole way. I said, "What's that mean?" He said, cool as you like, "I mean let him buy the villa and make it over to you. Then you do what he asked and make sure that the case against Hadda is tighter than a duck's arsehole." I said, "What about the fraud case?"'

'Why'd you say that? You weren't anything to do with the Fraud Squad.'

Medler grinned and said, 'Everything's about sex or money, and this clearly wasn't about sex. Fitting you up on the porn charges had just been a way of making sure your name stank before the Fraud boys got their teeth into you. Stands to reason.'

'You reckon? And what did Mr Wesley say?'

'Told me to stick to my business and live happily ever after.'

'He said that? Interesting choice of phrase. And you said, all right, I'm yours body and soul for a place in the sun and a bottle of sangria.'

'No, I bloody well didn't! Listen, you got to believe me, Hadda, I didn't like where all this was going, and I said so.'

'So what precisely did you say, Arnie?' asked Hadda quietly.

'I said, the fraud stuff was one thing – way it looked to everyone back then, all you lot in high finance were on the fiddle and deserved every bit of shit that could be thrown at you – but the other stuff, to shovel that on to an innocent man, that just wasn't on.'

'Nice of you to be so concerned,' said Hadda. 'And your Mr Wesley replied . . .?'

'He said you were to all intents a dead man and dead men didn't mind whether you shovelled earth or shit over them.

As for Estover, he would be more useful on the end of their string than relaxing in comfort at Her Majesty's expense. I said, "You mean this has all been for nothing?" And he laughed and said, "Hardly nothing. You've got yourself a nice retirement villa out of it, haven't you? Of course you might turn out to be the gabby type. In which case I don't think retirement would be an option." So what could I do?'

He looked at Hadda pleadingly. The bastard wants me to feel sorry for him in his sad predicament! he thought.

'You could have told him to get stuffed! But instead, you accepted a large bribe from Estover and his associates to conceal the fact that they'd framed me. And in addition, before you left, you made sure their botched-up job was completely watertight, right?'

For a second, Medler looked ready to argue, then he shrugged and said, 'Yeah, more or less. Once I was happy with the way your case file looked, I went sick, made sure I got the maximum severance payments – why not? I'd worked all those years in a really shitty job, I reckon I'd earned it!'

Now he was looking defiant. As if this were a point really worth arguing.

Hadda said, 'So we've got Estover right in the middle of the frame. What about the others? You're a nosey little fox, I'll give you that. I bet you had a chat with your mates in Fraud. What were they saying?'

Medler said, 'They were pretty sure your finance guy, Nutbrown, had to be involved. Where'd you find him? Fell out of the moon, I'd guess! The Fraud boys said trying to get a line on him was like trying to get water out of a pond with your finger and thumb. In the end they were happy to have him on board as a fully cooperating witness! I'd say Estover was pulling his strings. And Nutbrown's wife too. I only met her the once, that was enough!'

'Anyone else?'

Now the man looked at him shrewdly and said, 'You're thinking about your ex-missus, aren't you?'

'Just answer my questions, Medler,' growled Hadda.

'Right, right, keep your hair on. Listen, she struck me as a very together lady, never showed no signs of falling apart despite everything. At the time I thought it was just that upper-class stiff-upper-lip thing, but when I heard later that she dumped you and married Estover, well, it speaks for itself, don't it? Come on, Hadda, you know her a lot better than me. Was she so thick that greasy bastard could take her in? I don't think so!'

He gave a knowing sneer, reminding Hadda of his manner on their first meeting.

It was a provocation too much.

He leaned forward, shoved the hatchet against Medler's crotch and snarled, 'So why'd you come to see me, fuck-face? Brought some poisoned grapes, did you?'

It was even more effective than he'd hoped. The man went pale, or at least his tan went sallow, and he shrank back as far as he could get in his chair.

'An old mate rang and told me you'd woke up,' he gabbled. 'I couldn't believe it. I mean, no one expected it, not after all those months . . .'

'And you were so relieved you had to come straight to my bedside?'

'I wasn't thinking straight,' admitted Medler. 'I had to see for myself. I mean, for all I knew you were a drooling idiot, right? At the hospital I talked my way past the guy on duty . . . come to think of it, it was McLucky, wasn't it? Yeah, it was. Jesus, how could I have forgotten that? After that I talked to Estover . . .'

'Did he contact you or did you contact him?'

'I don't know. It was him contacted me, I think . . . yeah,

325

that's right . . . all he wanted to know was, had I really tidied things up? I said yes, I was sure. Then I said, did he understand, the way I'd left things, you could go down for a really long stretch? He said, "Too late to worry about that now." But I did worry, Hadda, you've got to believe me. I mean, I was just covering myself . . . I never thought . . . I believed you'd be dead!'

'Oh, I can tell you were really bothered,' said Hadda. 'That's why you went straight round to the Yard and told them everything.'

'I couldn't do that, I'd have ended up worse off than you!' he cried. 'I got a card wishing me a happy retirement. It was signed Wesley. Even if I'd given an anonymous tip-off, no way that smiling bastard wouldn't have traced it back to me. I'm sorry, I'm really sorry, there hasn't been a day since when I haven't thought about what was happening to you, how people must be thinking about you . . .'

'Wish I'd known,' said Hadda, standing up. 'It would have been such a comfort.'

'What are you going to do?' asked Medler, looking up at him fearfully.

'I'm going to go away and consider my options,' said Hadda. 'The two top ones are, I could come back here and chop your balls off with my axe and stick them in a highball glass and make you drink them down. Or I could take this along to the Yard and play it to your old colleagues and see what they have to say.'

He flourished a digital recorder in the air.

'Either way, Arnie, I reckon you're fucked. Merry Christmas!'

7

'Get a job!'

Wolf Hadda sat upright. A middle-aged woman with a laden shopping bag was scowling down at him. On the ground between Sneck's paws someone had dropped a handful of change. Not her, he assumed.

His mobile rang.

The woman went puce with righteous indignation.

'My stockbroker,' said Hadda.

When he returned to the bar a few moments later, he saw that McLucky had finished his drink. But the sandwiches were still untouched.

'So?' he said, sitting down. 'Happy *now*?'

'You could have switched off, then dealt with Medler. You had an axe, for God's sake!'

'Little hatchet. It was Medler's, actually. Picked it up from a storage shed in the villa garden. Anyway his hands got chopped off by the security shutter, wasn't that what your informant said?'

'You could have made it look that way.'

'Clever me,' said Hadda. 'So you're still not sure about me. Then why aren't you ringing the cops?'

'Maybe because the little gobshite was definitely in line for a good kicking after what he did to you. You'd be OK over there. These Latinos understand revenge. Provocation, you didn't mean him to die, manslaughter.'

'And how long do these sympathetic Latinos bang you up for that?'

'I don't know. You'd need to consult a lawyer.'

'I have done,' said Hadda, smiling. 'He reckons three, four years, maybe, if I got lucky. Then back here to serve the rest of my current sentence.'

'With this,' said McLucky, holding up the recorder, 'they'd surely quash that.'

'Without hard evidence?' said Hadda. 'Parole breaker. Responsible for the death of an ex-cop. Over here they don't make allowances for revenge. One way or another, I'd be back inside. Look, I could have gone to the Yard with this, but not now Medler's dead.'

McLucky regarded the other man speculatively.

'Don't know if you're fooling yourself, Hadda, but you don't fool me. I think I knew from the first time we talked. All this stuff you've been paying me for, you're not interested in proving your innocence, are you? You want to sort it out yourself.'

'You doing an extension course in psychology?'

'Maybe I should. Like I say, I'm not so easy to fool as that nice black lass that helped get you out of jail. Or is she in on this?'

Hadda shook his head.

'Absolutely not.'

'Very positive. Meaning you've either got a conscience about her or you're lying.'

'Lying? When have I ever lied to you?'

'How about every time I see you shuffling across a room like you couldn't raise a sprint if a randy gorilla was chasing you across the veldt with its cock at the ready?'

'Think your natural history might be a little rusty.'

'That's because I'm spending all my time on the psychology.'

'So where do we go from here?' said Hadda.

McLucky said, 'I don't know about you, but me, I can go any which way I fucking well like. I can still back away from all this shite with none of it sticking to me. What have I done? Gone to Spain, chatted to an old colleague. OK, I've pretended to be interested in buying your old mate's house, but I've not got any financial advantage out of that, so no crime.'

'Well, you did plant a couple of bugs so we could know what they're saying,' corrected Wolf. 'But of course I'd not expect you to break the law seriously. Not for the money I'm paying.'

He smiled as he spoke.

'Sounds like the start of a negotiation to me,' said McLucky. 'Listen, before I decide anything, I want to know what all this stuff about "an interest" means. What are we talking here? Whitehall? Spooks?'

Hadda shrugged.

'God knows. Probably DTI, worried about how my trial might affect British commercial interests. I was quite important, remember?'

McLucky bared his teeth and snarled, 'Don't bullshit me. This guy Wesley's no civil fucking servant. I listened to the tape, remember? The way you repeated *Wesley*, that sounded like it meant something to you. And Medler certainly thought so.'

'Just reminded me of someone I used to know,' said Hadda lightly.

'Aye? Old friend or old enemy? Mind you, with old friends like you've got, I dread to think what your old enemies must be like!'

'I do still have a few real friends,' said Wolf.

'You mean like this solicitor of yours and his guidwife? Aye, they sound like real chums to cover for you like they're doing. Or do you just know where they buried the bodies?'

'No, Ed and Doll are the real deal. Good people, too. I'd like you to meet them. Maybe I'll fix that up when you go back down to London. In fact, they could put you up. Be a damn sight cheaper than these fancy hotels you keep piling on your expense sheet.'

'Hold it there! You want someone to stay in fleapits, you should have sent that dog of yours. And who says I'm going back to London? I've got other clients to think of.'

'Name three,' said Wolf. 'While you're thinking, why don't you try a sandwich?'

McLucky studied his face for a moment, then selected a sandwich, opened it, sniffed the smoked salmon and took a bite.

'That's agreed then,' said Hadda. 'Now it's just a question of haggling over your fee and sorting out when you head back to the Smoke. That right, Davy?'

'Davy? You thinking of paying me enough to call me Davy?'

Hadda shook his head.

'I always call my friends by their first names, and I'd like to think that anyone I'm employing to do what I'm asking you to do was my friend.'

McLucky finished his sandwich, picked up another.

'I'm getting used to the smoked salmon, Wolf,' he said.

8

Mireton looked deserted but Alva felt herself observed as she drove through the village past the church to the vicarage.

Hollins came out the front door as she got out of the car.

Eager to greet her, or trying to pre-empt an encounter with his unfriendly wife?

He said, 'Dr Ozigbo, I'm so sorry. You've had a wasted journey.'

'You mean, he's back?'

'On his way. Like I said, I've left several messages on his phone. I thought I'd try him one more time just a few minutes ago, and he answered!'

'And where is he?' asked Alva.

'He's in Carlisle. Visiting his probation officer.'

'That's what he told you?' she said, trying to keep the doubt out of her voice.

'No. That's what his probation officer told me. Mr Hadda put him on. It seems he spent Christmas in London, staying with his solicitor and his wife.'

For a second Alva thought crazily he was referring to the Estovers.

Then she said, 'Mr Trapp, would that be?'

331

'That's it!' Hollins looked delighted that she knew the name, as if this confirmed all was well. 'And the arrangement had been made in advance, and Mr Cowper, that's the probation officer, had checked it out, and Hadda was sorry not to have replied to my calls but his battery had gone flat and he hadn't noticed till he tried to use the phone himself last night.'

It was a good story, and one so easily checked it had to be watertight, thought Alva.

So why didn't she feel as relieved as she ought to?

Maybe because part of her was resenting the knowledge that when Hadda had gone through the motions of pressing her to stay at Birkstane over Christmas, he had already made his other arrangements!

She really needed to get these distracting emotions sorted out. Head back to London, throw herself into her work at Parkleigh, remind herself that Hadda still legally belonged there, and of the reasons why. That should sort it.

'He sends his regards, by the way,' added Hollins.

'You told him I was coming?'

'Yes. Sorry, shouldn't I have done? I just wanted to make it clear that going off like that without a word had caused a lot of worry. He said he was really sorry, asked after your father, and said that if you wanted a bed for the night, Birkstane was at your disposal.'

'Big of him, but I don't think so,' said Alva drily, trying to conceal, not least from herself, how attractive the offer was.

'No, of course, you'll want to get back to your mother. I'm sorry you've had a wasted journey,' said Hollins. 'Look, why don't you come inside and have a spot of lunch before you set off back? Willa would love to see you again.'

Was this faith at work, or just a simple clerical lie? wondered Alva.

332

'Thanks, but no,' she said. 'But you can tell me how I get to Ulphingstone Castle.'

'You're going to the castle?' he said in surprise.

'Yes. It's all right. I'm expected, sort of. Mrs Estover said she wants to talk to me. I can only imagine it's something to do with her former husband, so naturally I'm curious. I hope she's still there.'

She wasn't certain why she was being so forthcoming with Luke Hollins. Except of course that she liked him, and liked particularly the way he had responded to the arrival of Hadda on his parochial doorstep. Vicars generally she regarded as either inadequates compensating for poor human relationship skills by claiming a special relationship with God, or social workers in drag. Hollins fitted neither of these categories. He was a nice young guy who hadn't yet made his mind up where he wanted to be.

Perhaps his strong-willed wife would be able to steer him right.

Wasn't that what wives were for?

She doubted if Wolf Hadda would agree with her.

He said, 'Yes, she's there. I rang this morning when I heard from Mr Hadda. His disappearance over Christmas seems to have got them in a bit of a flap. For all the wrong reasons, of course. So I was pleased to be able to assure them that it had all been quite legal and above board.'

She was too kind to remind him it was his own 'flap' about the possible wrong reasons for Hadda's absence that had got her driving all the way here this morning. Instead she said, 'And how did she take the news?'

'I didn't actually speak to Mrs Estover. One of the house guests, Mr Nikitin, answered the phone. He said that the others had all gone down to the stables to see a new foal. He himself does not care for horses, I gather. But he promised to tell Mrs Estover when she got back. That was a couple of hours ago, so she should be back by now. How long does it take to look at a foal?'

'Depends whether you're buying or selling, I suppose,' said Alva. 'This Mr Nikitin, is that a Russian name?'

'I believe so. Some distant relative of Lady Kira, I understand.' He hesitated, then went on, 'I got the impression that he might be a bit stuck on Mrs Estover.'

Alva smiled at the old-fashioned phrase, which she suspected had been chosen for fear of offending her with something more modern like *got the hots for.*

'And Mrs Estover . . .?'

'Hard to tell what she is thinking. But I only met her briefly. Now, let me give you directions . . .'

His directions were brief, as indeed was the journey, and five minutes later she was turning through the rather grandiose gateway. The drive up to the castle along an avenue of old oaks was also quite impressive, as was the line of cars she parked alongside. A Bentley Continental in burgundy, a sky-blue Mercedes and a black Range Rover – maybe there was somewhere round the back for grey Fiestas! But the building itself might have been a disappointment if Hadda's description hadn't prepared her for it. A substantial mansion in dark granite, with not a battlement, moat or portcullis in sight, it didn't get anywhere close to being a castle.

For all that when she got out of her car and looked up at the forbidding three-storeyed front, she felt herself repulsed.

The main door opened as she approached and a man came out. Late seventies, early eighties, with a mane of grey hair swept back from his patrician head, he had the kind of looks a director of Roman epics would have given his script-writer's right hand for.

Had to be Sir Leon, she thought. Unless the baronetcy went in for look-alike butlers.

'Hello,' she said. 'My name's Alva Ozigbo. Mrs Estover left me a message inviting me to have a chat.'

Her clever wording looked to be a wasted subtlety. The man regarded her so blankly she began to wonder if she'd misunderstood the vicar's directions. Maybe half a mile further on there was a real castle with moat and portcullis.

She said, 'It is Sir Leon, isn't it?'

His name seemed to trigger awareness.

He said, 'Ozigbo? You the psycho thingy?'

'That's right. Is your daughter at home?'

'Glad to meet you,' he said, shaking her hand. 'Very glad. Imo? Think she's around, though you never know with that girl. Was the same when she was young. Came and went at her own sweet will. Moves like a ghost.'

'Ms Ozigbo, you got my message then. I really didn't expect the pleasure of seeing you in person. A phone call would have done.'

Imogen, as if to prove the accuracy of her father's simile, had materialized in the doorway. Last time Alva had seen her, she'd been wrapped up in winter walking gear. Even that hadn't been able to disguise how attractive she was. Now in a flowered skirt and a sleeveless top, she looked ready for a glossy photo-shoot.

'I thought it would be good to meet face to face. If you're not too busy, that is?'

'Not at all. Come in. Thank you, Daddy.'

Dismissing Sir Leon almost as if he *were* a look-alike butler!

Alva followed the woman into a hall that had a definite touch of the baronial about it, and up a staircase that might not have been sweeping enough for a coach and horses but could certainly have accommodated a couple of armoured knights side by side.

'In here,' said Imogen, opening a door.

Baronial stopped. They entered into a room that could

335

have illustrated an article in a modern style and design magazine. Carpeted in pale ivory, with everything else in subtly varied shades of the same colour, it was a room for someone who moved like a ghost. The only strident note was sounded by the one painting, an abstract, an undulating line of bright green over a flat plane of glowing orange above another broader plane of fiery red underscored by a jagged band of pure black. Rothko, maybe? guessed Alva. What did having a Rothko on your wall indicate? Apart, of course, from a desire to say, Look at this, you peasants, and acknowledge we're stinking rich! From what she'd gathered about Lady Kira, this might well be her style.

She said, 'Lovely room. Is that a Rothko?'

Imogen said, 'Don't be silly. It's something I did years back to go with my room.'

Now that was much more interesting. Nothing to do with Lady Kira. Imogen's own painting in Imogen's own private room. No; more than that. Through a half-opened door, Alva glimpsed a bed. Her own private suite! Most children became very possessive about their own bedrooms. Not many had the ego – or the space – to demand and get their own private sitting room too. Or perhaps it was termed a dressing room?

She said, 'Is Mr Estover still here?'

'No. Toby had to go back to town yesterday. Business. All the Western world is closed down for a fortnight, but Toby still has business. Do sit down.'

The only seating available was a chaise longue with a chair set at its head.

Imogen indicated neither. There was a faint smile on her lips. She's waiting to see if I take the therapist's or the patient's option, thought Alva.

She moved the chair so that it was facing the chaise and sat down.

She expected Imogen to recline along the chaise but instead she perched on its edge, like a child nervously awaiting an interview with her head teacher.

'I hope you didn't have to come too far,' she said. 'Did you spend Christmas in Cumbria?'

It occurred to Alva that perhaps the woman had suspected her absence and Wolf's were connected.

'No. In Manchester.'

'That's far enough. But you wouldn't have come all this way just on the chance I'd be at home?'

'Hardly. I really just felt like a day away from home. My father's been ill and things have been quite fraught.'

'I'm sorry. Nothing too serious, I hope?'

'Heart. But he's doing well.'

'I'm glad. At least he's in the right job.'

She's been checking up on me, thought Alva. And she doesn't mind letting me know.

'Yes. Why did you want to talk to me, Mrs Estover?'

And now she's got me to open the bowling!

'Of course. Let me come straight to the point,' said Imogen, somehow making Alva feel it was her fault they hadn't come to the point a lot earlier. 'As you know, I tried to see Wolf. I didn't succeed. I called again twice, once in the evening, once early morning. He wasn't there.'

She paused as if inviting an intervention. She doesn't sound as if she's got Luke Hollins's message, thought Alva. Perhaps Mr Nikitin's English isn't so good.

Imogen nodded as if the intervention had been made, and went on, 'My reasons for wanting to see him are varied, if not to say confused. But I expect that, in your line of work, you are used to that.'

'I'm not used to people admitting it so readily,' said Alva.

'Perhaps that's because I'm not talking to you as a patient,' said Imogen with a faint smile.

No? In what capacity do you see yourself talking to me? wondered Alva.

Again the woman gave a little nod as if her guest had spoken.

'One of the reasons I wanted to see Wolf was to check if he were a threat to me or my family,' she said. 'It struck me that, in his absence, perhaps I could get the answer from you.'

The opening exchange was over, thought Alva. Now things should liven up.

'Why should you think he might be a threat?' she enquired.

'He was always a very ruthless man. You of all people should be able to tell me if and how prison has changed him.'

'By ruthless, are you implying he was violent?'

Imogen considered.

'Not to me, certainly. But in his drive to get what he wanted, I don't believe he ever excluded the option of violence. And his temper had a short fuse.'

'So, he'd lash out violently if provoked? And if he had time to think about something, and violence seemed the most productive way of proceeding, that's the way he'd go? Sounds like a pretty definitive description of a violent man to me, Mrs Estover.'

'Perhaps my fear is making me over-emphatic.'

Somehow fear and this woman didn't seem to go together. For the time being, though, it was best to go with her flow.

'You still haven't said why you feel afraid. He's confronted what he did. He's accepted he is solely responsible for the crimes that got him into prison. He's taken control of his life. What do you imagine he might blame you for?'

Imogen ran her hand down the side of her face, down her slender neck, down till it rested on her right breast. She had been sitting so still, the movement was almost a shock.

She said, 'Come now, Ms Ozigbo. Are you telling me he doesn't blame me for not standing by him? For marrying Toby? For my daughter's death?'

My daughter, Alva noted.

Alva said, 'If you really fear he might be a threat to you, going to see him unaccompanied in a lonely farmhouse doesn't strike me as the wisest move.'

Imogen said, 'When Wolf and I used to go climbing together, he taught me, when you're working at a line of ascent, look for the most hazardous route, the closer to impossible the better. Then resist the temptation to try it if you can.'

'I'm sorry. I don't get that.'

Imogen smiled as if unsurprised.

She said, 'Wolf used to say that rock climbing wasn't about getting to the top, it was about falling.'

'Conquering the fear of falling, you mean?'

Imogen shook her head impatiently.

'Conquering the desire to fall,' she said.

Alva ran this through her mind. Was she saying that meeting her ex alone was the most attractive option because she knew it was the most dangerous?

The psychology of rock climbing was interesting. But then so was the psychology of morris dancing.

Hoping by silence to draw the woman into further speech, she let her gaze run round the room. Strangely, despite the obvious differences of size, comfort and decoration, it put her in mind of Hadda's cell at Parkleigh. Apart from the painting, it contained nothing personal. No photographs, no books. Had it looked different before the tragedies of first her husband's downfall and then their daughter's death?

Her gaze returned to Imogen. The woman gave no sign of wanting to say anything further. Whatever her reason for wanting this conversation, presumably it had been satisfied.

Alva looked at her watch and said, 'I ought to be going. Mrs Estover, all I can say in answer to your question is that if ever I feel Mr Hadda is a danger to anyone, I shall of course convey my feelings to the appropriate authority.'

She stood up.

Imogen said, 'Does he blame me for Ginny's death?'

Well, that had certainly done the trick. The question sounded as if it had burst out of her in contrast to the control that had marked the rest of her speech.

'Not as much, I gauge, as he blames himself,' said Alva.

'I see.' She fixed her eyes on her visitor as though in some doubt whether to proceed or not. But suddenly Alva knew there wasn't really any doubt. What the woman wanted to say to her was going to be said now.

Imogen said, almost casually, 'Then in your judgment would it make things better or worse if I told Wolf he wasn't Ginny's father?'

Jesus! What's she trying to do – use me as a messenger?

Before she could marshal her thoughts and come up with a response, the door opened. If there'd been a tap, it was too perfunctory to be noticed.

A woman came in, coldly beautiful with the kind of skin and bone structure that is hard to age, tall, supple, dressed in very English heather-mix tweed that didn't hinder her from exuding a sense of something dangerously exotic.

She said, 'Imogen, I did not know you had company,' not much bothering to make it sound unlike a lie.

'Mother,' said Imogen, unfazed, 'this is Ms Ozigbo, Wolf's therapist.'

'Not a job for a woman, I shouldn't have thought,' said Lady Kira coldly. 'And I suppose it's public money that pays your fees?'

Alva may have been fazed by Imogen's assertion about her child's parentage, but patrician rudeness she took in her stride.

'Nice to meet you,' she said, rising. 'Please don't apologize for disturbing us, I was just leaving.'

Lady Kira looked inclined to deny even the thought of apology, but Alva had turned back to Imogen.

'Goodbye, Mrs Estover,' she said. 'It's Dr Ozigbo, by the way. Do ring me if you'd like to talk again?'

Imogen said, 'I think we're done, doctor.'

She too rose and moved to face her red-and-orange painting.

From the doorway, Alva said, 'Your ex-husband seems to be fond of a painting by Winslow Homer. *The Woodcutter*, I think it's called. Is there any particular reason he's so fond of it?'

'Perhaps because it shows a man faced with simple problems that can be overcome by his own strength and resources,' said the woman, not turning round.

'That's an interesting idea,' said Alva. 'Your picture, by the way, what do you call it?'

'*Falling*,' said Imogen.

9

Alva closed the door behind her. It might be interesting to hear what mother and daughter had to say to each other, but the door was too heavy to make eavesdropping possible without pressing her ear to the keyhole.

At the foot of the staircase she found Sir Leon waiting.

'Got a moment, my dear?' he said.

Before she could reply, a door behind him opened and a smallish man, in his late thirties, handsome in a high-cheek-boned, slightly toothy Slavic sort of way, came out.

His eyes ran up and down Alva's body with an almost insolent slowness.

He said, 'What a surprising county this Cumbria of yours is, Leon. I had not expected such rarities. Will you not introduce me?'

'What? Oh yes. Ms Ozigbo, friend of Imogen's. And this is Mr Nicotine who's staying with us.'

'Nik-EE-tin,' said the man. 'Pavel Nikitin. My friends call me Pasha. I'm pleased to meet you.'

He looked the type who might be inclined to take her hand and suck on her fingers, so Alva, who did not care to be called a rarity like some kind of ornithological specimen, put her arms behind her and nodded. One question had been answered. Whatever reason Nikitin had for not passing on Luke's message, there was no problem with language.

'If you'll excuse us,' said Sir Leon. 'Something I need to show Ms Ozigbo.'

He didn't wait for a response but took her elbow and urged her into a small alcove and through a door into what appeared to be a Hollywood producer's impression of an English gentleman's study.

'Foreigner,' he said, as if that were both apology and explanation. 'Wife's cousin or some such thing. *Pasha!* Do you think he gets called that because of the Nicotine connection? Sorry, probably far too young – you, I mean. Used to be a peculiarly foul cigarette my ma smoked during the war when she couldn't get anything else.'

Alva smiled at him. She could understand why Wolf was so fond of the old boy. He might live in a Wodehousian world of his own, but in his forays into the real world he seemed entirely without malice which was why she felt no inclination to remind *him* that she was *Dr* Ozigbo.

Now she took in the room. You could tell a lot from rooms.

A huge mahogany desk dominated, bedecked with silver photo frames, a pewter inkstand, and a black Bakelite dial telephone. One wall was almost filled by a huge bookcase in which Alva glimpsed bound copies of *Punch* and various shooting magazines as well as the transactions of the Cumbrian Archaeological Society dating back to a period itself worthy of research. The opposing wall held a locked gun case flanked by the head of a twelve-point stag and, most weird of all, that of a wolf.

'Last wolf shot in Cumberland,' said Sir Leon, following her gaze. 'Least, that's what the fellow she bought it from told Kira. Load of nonsense. Anyone can see it's a Canadian

343

timber wolf, and pretty decrepit at that. Probably died of old age in some zoo.'

'Your wife has a taste for history?' ventured Alva.

'If that's what you call it,' said Sir Leon. 'Did this room up herself. Used to be a perfectly decent hideaway in the old man's day. Now look at it. I can hardly bear to come inside.'

'In that case . . .?' said Alva.

'What? Oh yes. Not likely to be interrupted. I wanted to ask you, how is Wolf?'

Her thoughts still on the mangy creature on the wall, Alva was thrown for a moment.

'Mr Hadda, you mean?'

'Yes, Wolf,' he said impatiently. 'I've thought of calling round at Birkstane, but it would just cause bother. Don't need security cameras out here in the sticks. Kira would hear about it before I got home! So how is he?'

'He was well when I saw him before Christmas,' said Alva slowly. 'Of course by comparison with the way you'll remember him, he moves rather slowly. And his face is scarred . . .'

Sir Leon was shaking his head.

'Poor boy, poor boy,' he said. 'But in himself, his state of mind, I mean, how are things there? He was always so full of life and high spirits.'

'I think, all things considered, that it's fair to say he's doing pretty well,' said Alva.

She was puzzled. This was not a kind of conversation that she could have imagined having with the father of a girl whose marriage to an undesirable had turned out even more badly than forecast.

'Good, good, I'm glad to hear it. Funny thing, life, what it does to you. But you'd know all about that in your job, my dear. All those years locked up. Don't think I could bear it myself.'

344

He turned away to the window as if to hide his emotion. Alva moved forward to stand by his side.

'Sir Leon, is there any message you'd like me to give to Wolf?'

'Just say I was asking after him.'

'I will. But if you don't mind me saying, I'm a little puzzled why you should be. I mean, so far as I know, you were absolutely opposed to the marriage, weren't you? You did everything you could to stop it.'

'I thought I did. But it wasn't enough. I should have tried harder.'

'And circumstances proved you right, and things worked out even worse for your daughter than you could have imagined, so why –'

'No, no,' he interrupted her. 'You're barking up the wrong tree. I didn't want to stop the marriage for Imo's sake. She's always been perfectly capable of looking after herself. It was poor Wolf I was concerned for!'

This was truly bewildering.

'But why . . .?'

'Because the apple doesn't fall far from the tree. I love my daughter, Ms Ozigbo, but a father's love isn't blind. Fred Hadda was a decent man, a loyal worker and a good friend. I'd seen what it did to him when the boy vanished for all those years. That was down to what Wolf felt about Imogen. When he came back and I saw it was all going to start up again, I couldn't stand by and let Fred's boy destroy himself, could I? But in the end . . . Well, what's done's done. Better get you out of here before we get noticed.'

He feels spied upon in his own house, thought Alva. She still wasn't altogether clear what lay at the bottom of the old man's attitude. There was neither the time nor was he a suitable subject for subtle psychological questioning, so she took the direct route.

She said, 'Sir Leon, I'm still not sure what you're saying. Did you feel that this was a mismatch for social reasons? That Wolf would feel out of his depth by being transplanted from one class to another?'

She had learned that, even in twenty-first century England, class still mattered. *Cherchez la femme* might apply in France, in England it was usually *cherchez la classe!*

'What? No, of course not,' he replied, a touch indignantly. 'Used to be the case if you didn't go to the right school, you were always playing catch-up. Maybe there's still a bit of that around, but a chap like Wolf, he'd catch most of them up and be whizzing by in no time at all. In fact, that's what he did, wasn't it? No, this was personal. Imogen wasn't right for him. He was always going to get hurt.'

'And Imogen?'

'Imo? I love my daughter, Ms Ozigbo. Funny thing, though. In forty years I've never seen her cry. Not even as a baby. Funny.'

If true, this was pretty amazing. Though it might just be a physiological oddity.

She asked, 'And did you say anything about this to Wolf directly?'

'No point. He wasn't going to take any notice, was he? When the blood's bubbling along a boy's veins, first thing that goes is his hearing, eh?'

He turned her away from the window and for the first time she saw the photos in the silver frames. Lady Kira featured prominently. She obviously believed that family photos on the desk were as intrinsic a part of the traditional gent's study as hunting trophies on the wall.

In one of the photos she stood looking down possessively at a pretty girl leaning forward to blow out the candles on a birthday cake. The girl had such a look of Imogen, it had to be her daughter, thought Alva.

She picked up the photo and said gently, 'It must have been a terrible shock to you, losing your granddaughter.'

Immediately she wished she hadn't spoken. The old man's face, indeed his whole body, seemed to shrivel up as if in a desperate attempt to contain an emotion that might rip him apart if he let it out. Here was a man born into wealth and privilege, with all the attendant comforts and opportunities tossed into his cradle. Yet Alva felt she was looking at the kind of pain and despair you usually glimpsed on your TV screen after some momentous life-shattering natural disaster.

'I'm sorry, I'm sorry,' she said wretchedly. 'It's just that she looks so lovely in the photo.'

'What photo?' said Leon, taking refuge from his grief in irritation. 'Got no photo of Ginny here. Couldn't bear it.'

'But this one here,' said Alva, holding up the frame. 'Isn't that her?'

'Don't be silly. Of course not. That's Imo.'

'Imogen? Your daughter?' said Alva incredulously, trying to count the candles.

'That's right. Fourteenth birthday. Fourteen going on forty, isn't that what they say about young girls today, eh?'

Fourteen! Imo's age when she and Hadda first met.

There was only one thing wrong. She'd discounted the possibility that this might be Imo because this girl bore no resemblance whatsoever to her mental image of the skinny pre-pubertal creature who'd allegedly offered herself to Hadda on Pillar Rock. This was a healthy young teenager whose scoop-neck top revealed as she bent forward to blow out the candles a pair of very well-developed breasts.

There are times when even a psychiatrist can receive too much information.

Despite Sir Leon's obviously growing eagerness to get her out of the study and off the premises, she stood transfixed, staring at the photo.

She needed to talk further with the old man, she needed to talk again to Imogen, above all she needed to confront Hadda.

But in what order and in what manner she ought to do these things wasn't clear.

Then her phone rang. Sir Leon grimaced at the sound. She took it out and glanced at the display. It was Elvira.

Checking up on my putative date, she guessed. Well, she can leave a message!

Sir Leon now took a firm grip on the situation and her elbow, and a minute later she was outside the house with the door closing in her face.

She still hadn't got her thoughts in order. Not to ask Imogen more questions while she was here seemed a missed opportunity. Perhaps she should go back into the house and press for answers. But when she glanced back at the house to its general air of unwelcomingness were added the sight of Lady Kira's face peering down from an upper window and Mr Nikitin's from a lower.

She got into her car and let what she had learned scroll across her mind, trying to assess its significance and turn it into usable data.

The main items were:

One: Imogen said Ginny wasn't Hadda's child. True or false?

Two: Leon said he had objected to the marriage for Hadda's sake, not for his daughter's, and class had nothing to do with it. Almost certainly true, she judged.

Three: at fourteen, Imogen was a mature girl with a well-developed bosom. Definitely true!

So what to do?

She could drive back to Manchester and ponder. She could get out of the car and bang on the door and demand readmittance. She could head round to Birkstane and lie in wait for Hadda. She could . . .

348

She shook her head impatiently. Choice is a largely delusional concept, her tutor used to say. Whether in politics, morals or shopping, we have far less than we imagine. In the end what we have to do often doesn't even figure on our list of pseudo-options.

She took out her phone and played her mother's message and was yet again reminded how right her tutor was.

'Alva! Where are you? You've got to get back here as soon as you can. Your father's much worse. They think he's going to die!'

10

Wolf Hadda liked to believe he had his feelings under tight control. You didn't survive a long stretch in jail by letting your imagination roam free. Deal with the minute and let the hour look after itself. A man can dig his way out with a teaspoon, but only if he takes it one scrape at a time. But if you let yourself relax too much, sometimes feelings and imagination can sneak up and take you by surprise.

He had spent a good part of the afternoon talking with Davy McLucky, then he had diverted on the way home to a supermarket. It was a couple of weeks now since he'd given Luke Hollins a Tesco order and fresh supplies would be running low. On the way back he stopped on a high fell road to give Sneck a bit of a run and it was getting on for eight o'clock as he approached Birkstane.

Perhaps it was the pleasure of heading back to the only place in the world he thought of as home that relaxed him, but he realized that somehow over the last few miles his mind had been playing such a lively picture of reaching the turn into the Birkstane lonning and finding Alva Ozigbo's grey Fiesta parked there that he felt a totally illogical shock of disappointment at its absence.

'Just thee and me then, Sneck,' he said to the dog as he brought the Defender to a halt in front of the closed barn door.

The dog jumped out and started quartering the yard, muzzle low, sniffing the cobbles and growling softly in its throat.

Wolf watched him for a moment, before climbing down stiffly. With his supermarket bag swinging from one hand and leaning heavily on his stick with the other, he limped slowly towards the house.

The kitchen felt cold and unwelcoming. He realized his fantasy had expanded insidiously to finding Alva had got the fire going and was brewing a pot of coffee. But now his earlier disappointment had turned to relief. As he closed the door, he saw a sheet of paper that must have been pushed beneath it.

He smoothed it out on the kitchen table and read the words scribbled across it.

I'm at the castle till the New Year. We ought to talk.

No signature. None needed.

He used it to help start the fire and while it got going he put the kettle on the hob, switched on the radio, turning it up loud. All this he did with a slow and laboured movement that would have caused Ed and Doll Trapp serious concern. When the kettle boiled he made himself a cup of coffee and sat at the table with his back to the small window. After a while he rose, shivering, and went to the window to draw the curtains, as if to keep out the draught.

But when he turned away he didn't sit down. Moving now with decisive swiftness, pausing only to pluck his long-handled axe from the wall, he headed out of the kitchen and up the stairs to the bedroom on the far side of the house from the yard. This was north facing and its window was small even by Cumbrian farmhouse standards but he went

351

through it on his back, head first, reaching up to take a grip in a crack between two of the rough granite blocks, and hauling himself out till he stood on the sill. Then he dropped down till his arms rested on the sill, reached in and retrieved his axe.

Sneck stood alert, watching him.

He said, 'Guard!'

It was a stronger command than *Stay!* In Sneck's mind *Stay!* had a time-limitation clause. After ten minutes max, he'd reckon it had expired and start thinking independently. With *Guard!* he'd stay all night and attack anyone who came near.

Now, hanging one-handed, Hadda lowered his body full length then dropped the remaining five feet to the ground.

Picking himself up, he made for the old forest wall, climbed over it with silent ease and went a couple of yards into the trees. Here he turned south and moved parallel to the wall till he was opposite the side of the barn.

Now he emerged from the forest and climbed back over the wall and waited.

A man emerged from the barn and flitted silently across the yard. He was dressed in black and in his right hand he carried a gun.

Slowly he turned the handle of the kitchen door then flung it open and stepped inside.

A moment later he reappeared and made a signal. A second man came out of the barn as the first went back into the house.

So, two of them. The first had expected to surprise him in the kitchen. That having failed, he was now going to search the house, and he'd called up the second to watch his back.

Could there be a third? Doubtful. If so, a pair of them would probably have made the initial sortie.

He didn't waste time debating the point, reaching his conclusion and the second man crouched by the kitchen door almost simultaneously.

The man must have heard something, for he turned – which was unfortunate for him. Instead of the stunning blow to the base of the neck that was intended, he took the full force of the axe's shaft across his Adam's apple. There was usually only one result of such a blow, but Hadda was in too much of a hurry to check it out.

The kitchen was empty, the living room too. The second man had gone up the stairs. If he opened the door of the bedroom which Sneck was guarding, the dog would attack. And a bullet moves quicker than even the fastest dog.

Hadda went up the stairs not bothering to try for silence. The man was pushing open the bedroom door. He glanced round as he heard Hadda's approach. Then Sneck hit him with such force he was driven back across the narrow landing. He'd instinctively raised his left arm to ward off the attack and he screamed as Sneck's fangs tore through the fabric of his tight-fitting top and dug into the flesh beneath. But his right arm was still free and he raised his weapon to put the muzzle to the dog's head at the same time as the axe blade drove down through his skull.

The gun went off.

The man slid to the ground, blood and brains trickling down his face. Sneck lay on top of him, his teeth still fixed in his arm. Hadda dropped the axe and knelt down beside the dog. There was a smell of scorched hair coming from a burn line between his ears, as though someone had laid a hot poker there. But the eyes that looked up at Hadda were as bright as ever.

'OK, you can let go now,' he said, and turned his attention to the man.

'Damn,' he said. Then he looked closer. Death, especially

when caused by a blow from an axe, changes features somewhat, but there was something familiar about the face.

He stood up and went back down stairs. When he checked
out the second man in the yard, he said, 'Damn,' again.

It seemed a long long time ago that he'd driven down the
lonning, buoyed with a foolish hope that he'd find Alva
Ozigbo waiting to welcome him.

Instead he had two dead men on his hands. He wasn't
sure yet how he felt about that. Disappointed didn't seem
to do it.

'Good job you're not here, Elf,' he said to the dark sky.
'I don't have time for psycho-analysis right now!'

He set to work. The living first.

He checked Sneck's burn mark. It didn't look too bad. He
smeared some antiseptic cream along the line of the bullet,
then commanded the dog to lie down in the kitchen.

Then the dead.

He went through their pockets and found nothing, but in
the barn he found a small back-pack containing two mobile
phones, a Toyota key, and the OS sheet for the area. The
key he pocketed, the phones he set aside for later examination, the map he opened. There was a cross on the unclassified road about half a mile north of where the Birkstane
lonning turned off. He brought the place to his mind. There
was an old track there, no longer used, leading to one of
the sad heaps of stones that marked where a thriving hill
farm had once stood. Some scrubby woodland offered good
temporary shelter for a vehicle. Then they would have walked
back along the road and down the lonning and, realizing he
wasn't home, settled to wait.

But that implied they knew he was coming home.

He put that problem aside with the phones.

There were lots of old plastic sheets in the barn, remnants
of better days.

354

He set about parcelling up the bodies, placing large rocks alongside them before securing the plastic with baler twine and wire. He then loaded the grisly packages into the Defender and returned to the house to clean up the mess on the landing. The blade of his axe he washed beneath the running tap in the kitchen.

The bullet that had burned Sneck was buried in the bedroom wall. He would dig it out later.

He went back to the barn and opened the lid of an ancient but still solid metal feed box. It was in here that he'd found on his return, neatly packaged and labelled, all the stuff that had been his as a boy. At some point during his runaway years, his father must have collected all his gear together and set out to make sure it would still be to hand and serviceable on his return. It had made him weep to see the care with which the task had been carried out, and to imagine Fred's state of mind as he went about the job.

Of course when he came back he'd been, in his own eyes at least, a man and far beyond childish things. Looking back now, he found it unforgivable that his fixation on Imogen, and his euphoria at winning her, had deadened him completely to any real appreciation of what he'd put his father through. It wasn't till he himself experienced the gut-searing pain of loss all those years later that he came, too late, to understand.

Now he lifted out of the box the inflatable dinghy that had been in the kitchen on the occasion of Luke Hollins's first visit. It had required very little work to render it serviceable. Look after your gear and your gear will look after you, was a lesson Fred had drummed into him, and he practised what he preached. The rubber had been heavily oiled and the inflation nozzle coated in a thick layer of protective grease. How many times had his father renewed it over the years – as if by preserving it he also preserved the hope that somehow the young boy who had left him would return unchanged?

He put the dinghy and the foot pump in the back of the Defender. Then he went into the kitchen, stoked up the fire and set the kettle to boil again.

He didn't have much of an appetite, but he knew he had a long night ahead and his body needed fuel. So he opened a can of stew, heated it up and ate it straight out of the pan, wiping the sides clean with a hunk of bread. Sitting drinking tea and chewing on a muesli bar, he checked out the mobile phones. No messages. He brought up their phone books. None of the numbers was familiar. Next he checked their photo stores. One specialized in close-ups of female genitalia. Maybe it was some kind of trophy thing. They did nothing for Hadda. The other had shots of a family picnic, a handsome woman with an Eastern European look and a couple of young kids, sitting on a sunny hillside overlooking the sea. This did something for him. It made him feel bad.

He looked at his watch. It was eleven o'clock. Three hours had passed since he came home. But it was still too early. He fed Sneck, who seemed none the worse for his close encounter with the intruder's gun, then he settled in the wooden rocker by the fire and closed his eyes.

In Parkleigh he had learned to sleep almost at will and to wake at whatever hour he ordained, but sleep came hard now. When he finally nodded off he went straight into a dream in which he was being pursued through a dark forest by two men whom he couldn't shake off no matter how he twisted and turned. Then in the space of a single stride he was no longer the pursued but the pursuer, his quarry not two men but a single woman whose skin as she ran naked through the moon's shadows gleamed first white as pearl then dark as ebony.

He awoke to find he was sexually aroused.

356

'What the hell was that all about?' he asked the dog who lay at his feet, watching him.

It was one o'clock. He stood up, made another pot of tea and drank a burning mugful. The rest he poured into a thermos flask which he put into his backpack with a couple of bars of chocolate. He changed into his warmest mountain gear and pulled on his walking boots.

'Right, Sneck, how are you feeling?' he asked.

The dog rose instantly.

'OK, if you're sure. But we could face a long walk.'

The Defender, as ready it seemed as the dog, burst into life at first time of asking and he set it bumping back up the frozen lonning.

He found the intruder's car exactly where he'd estimated. It was a Toyota Land Cruiser. Now he knew where he'd seen the first dead man before. But he was pretty sure the other body wasn't that of the other man on Drigg Beach, the one called Pudo. Probably still recovering from a broken jaw.

The Land Cruiser had a capacious boot so there was plenty of room to transfer his grisly cargo and the rest of his gear. As an afterthought, he took the jerry can of petrol he always carried in the Defender and tossed it into the back of the Toyota.

'OK, Sneck, here we go,' he said.

The narrow winding road he followed ran up the remote western valley of Wasdale. It ended at the valley head, so unless there was anyone heading late for the tiny hamlet situated there, or the old inn, he was unlikely to have company at this hour of a freezing winter night. It wasn't just the remoteness that attracted him. It was Wastwater, the darkest and deepest of all Cumbria's lakes, lying between the road and the Screes, the awful precipitous slopes plunging down from the long ridge between Ill Gill and Whin Rigg.

He parked as close to the edge of the lake as possible and

set about inflating the dinghy. As far as he could make out in the near pitch darkness, his father had done an excellent job of storage and the rubber expanded and tautened and held its shape when he finally stopped pumping.

He lifted the topmost body out of the car and laid it in the dinghy. As expected, there was only room for one of the bundles. Indeed, there was scarcely room for himself and he had to kneel with his knees resting against the dead man as he began to paddle the vessel out from the bank. An unimaginable distance above him the sky was crowded with stars but the light that had set out earthward so many millennia ago seemed to fail and lose heart as it was sucked into the terrestrial black hole of Wasdale's lake.

Ahead was darkness, behind was darkness, all around was darkness. He struck with the paddle and struck again. The temptation to push the body over the side then turn to regain the shore was strong, but he knew he had to go much closer to the furthermost side. At its deepest the lake measured more than two hundred and fifty feet, well below the safety limit for the district's recreational divers. But it was the Screes ahead that plunged to this forbidding depth and to deposit his burden too soon might mean it would come to rest on the much shallower northern shelf.

Now it seemed to him at last that the view ahead was mottled with different intensities of blackness and a couple of strokes later he began to make out the detail of the precipitous slopes soaring two thousand feet above his head.

He laid the paddle in the dinghy and tried to ease the body over the side. Lifting it in and out of the car had been hard enough. Moving it all in the unstable confines of this small craft was back-breaking and perilous. For a moment one side dipped down beneath the surface and water came slopping in. He had no illusions. Weighed down with boots and clothing as he was, he would find it hard to survive long enough in water at this temperature even to struggle to the visible shore. Then he'd have to walk all the way along the boulder strewn track to one end of the lake or the other and back along the road to the car.

It would take the best part of a couple of hours, he would be wet, cold, and exhausted, and he'd still have the second body to deal with.

The thought steadied him. Human beings are better at avoidance than achievement. When things are bad, don't look for a good to struggle to, look for something worse to struggle from!

He wondered how this downbeat view of the human psyche would appeal to Alva. All that mattered now was that it worked for him. At last he got more of the plastic-wrapped package out of the dinghy than was in it and suddenly, as though it too had made a choice and opted for a peaceful rest in the dark deeps, it slid easily over the side and was gone.

Without that dead weight, it now seemed to him that the dinghy moved like an elfin pinnace (where did that phrase come from?) under his strong even strokes and what had felt like an immeasurable distance on the way out was behind him in no time and Sneck was welcoming him back on dry land with a wild oscillation of the tail.

But now it was all to do again.

He didn't take a rest because he feared that if he did his heart might fail him.

They say that having performed a difficult task once gives you confidence and makes the second time easier.

As usual, the bastards lie!

The lake seemed wider, the night seemed darker, the dinghy rode even lower in the water, and at one point he felt so totally disorientated he could not with any confidence say in what direction he was paddling.

Then he got guidance, but in a form that was more frightening than the situation it rescued him from.

A car's headlights came splitting the darkness along the road, heading up the valley.

It seemed to slow momentarily as it approached the point where he'd left the Toyota. And then, perhaps theorizing that the most likely reason for a car to be parked so late at night in such a remote situation was that the inmates were engaged in a very private activity, the driver speeded up again and soon the light faded as he wound his way to the distant inn.

This brief interlude of illumination deepened the resurgent blackness to impenetrability, but Hadda had once again got his bearings. A few more strokes, then, careless of the water he was shipping, he rolled the second body over the side and began to paddle back to the shore.

No elfin pinnace now, the dinghy felt heavy and wallowed through rather than cut across the water. But finally he made it. He was tempted to puncture the inflatable and let it sink, but that would be stupid. It wouldn't go to the bottom, it would easily be spotted, people would get worried, the car driver might recall the parked vehicle, and even if his belief that the bodies were sunk too deep for retrieval turned out to be true, the incident might be picked up by someone anxious to know what had happened to the two men he had sent out on a murderous mission . . .

He deflated the dinghy, jumping up and down on it to remove the last bit of air, and flung it into the back of the Land Cruiser.

'Right, Sneck,' he said. 'Let's go!'

He drove through the hills, past dark farms sleeping under ancient stars, meeting no traffic till he reached a main road. Even here at this hour there was only the very occasional car. Eventually he turned off again and was soon back on the single-track fell road where he'd paused on his way home to let Sneck have a run before the light faded completely from the sky. At its highest point he bumped off the tarmac on to the frozen grass, keeping going till the engine finally stalled. Now he got out of the car with the dog at his heel. From the load space he retrieved his rucksack and the jerry can.

The dinghy he left lying there.

He unscrewed the jerry can and soaked the vehicle's interior with petrol. His thinking was simple. Leave an empty car in the Lake District and eventually someone would report it, mountain rescue might be called out to do a search of the nearby hills while the police concentrated on tracing the owner of the vehicle.

What was relatively commonplace, however, was for a gang of local tearaways to help themselves to a car after a night on the beer, enjoy a bit of wild joy-riding on the quiet country roads, and finish up by torching the vehicle in some remote spot before heading off home.

So a burnt-out wreck would draw far less attention because it carried with it its own built-in explanation.

He laid a trail of petrol across the ground for some twenty feet or so from the car, then returned to hurl the jerry can into the back. Picking up his sack, he shrugged it on to his shoulder and made his way back to the end of the petrol trail.

Now he took out a box of matches, struck one and tossed it on to the ground.

'Heel,' he said to Sneck, and set off at a steady pace that would have surprised those who only ever saw him limping slowly across the ground.

Behind him he heard a whoomph! as the line of fire reached the car.

He didn't look back until a few minutes later he heard the explosion that told him the car's tank had gone up.

Now he stopped and turned.

He'd already covered a quarter-mile and climbed a couple of hundred feet.

Below him he could see the flames from the burning car licking the darkness out of the air. Two thousand years ago people would have taken it for a funeral pyre. In a way, it was. He thought of the two men anchored for ever (he hoped) to the bed of the cold lake. He knew from experience how long it took for the human mind to come to terms with responsibility for a human death. Eventually factors in mitigation would loom larger – they had, after all, been out to kill him – but for the moment their innocence or guilt did not signify. They were just two lives that he had brought to a sudden end. The man with the mucky pictures on his mobile and the man with the loving family were equally dead.

It would take a long time for him to deal with it, but seven years in prison had taught him how to compartmentalize his thoughts.

He turned his back on the accusing flames. It was five o'clock in the morning and he had a long walk ahead of him.

To start with his way lay east and already, though dawn was still hours away, he thought he could see the line of the dark hills before him beginning to be outlined against a paler sky.

There was always a growing light to walk towards as well as a dying light to leave behind.

And the ground he walked on was holy. His great mistake had been ever to leave it.

'Come on, Sneck,' he said. 'Let's go home.'

BOOK FOUR

the noise of wolves

Meanwhile abroad
Incessant rain was falling, or the frost
Raged bitterly, with keen and silent tooth;
And, interrupting oft that eager game,
From under Esthwaite's splitting fields of ice
The pent-up air, struggling to free itself,
Gave out to meadow grounds and hills a loud
Protracted yelling, like the noise of wolves
Howling in troops along the Bothnic Main.

William Wordsworth:
The Prelude (Book 1)

1

Johnny Nutbrown was truly a man of the moment, indifferent alike to future fears or past regrets. To him, each day was a box that closed at bedtime. During the night it was taken away, marked *not wanted on voyage*, and stored in some deep dark hold. Thus he never woke to a new day without feeling happy to greet it, and on the odd occasion when returning consciousness brought with it the awareness of some threat serious enough to ripple even his equanimity, the disturbance rarely survived a hearty breakfast.

One that did sometimes stay with him through lunch was the proposed sale of Poynters and the move to California. Toby Estover's visit had rattled his cage more than he cared to admit, but as the Christmas holiday dragged its grossly inflated length towards New Year it was easy to fall back into his usual insouciance.

Every year the Nutbrowns gave a much-anticipated Hogmanay party and as usual Johnny was the perfect host. Booze, food, entertainment were the best money could buy, while the scag and coke he supplied for the delectation of his most trusted guests was of such a quality that many of them pestered him to learn the source of his supply. But the vagueness that had stood Johnny in such good stead throughout all his life was certainly not going to fail him in this instance. He knew there was a link that led from his supplier to Toby Estover's client Pavel Nikitin, and that was not a man he cared to irritate.

'Oh, just a chap I met at some club,' he said. 'Harold, I think his name was. Or George. Gosh, look at the time! Everyone into the Great Hall!'

And a few minutes later he was standing on a chair, leading the raucous midnight countdown as though he truly longed to ring out the old and ring in the new, though to tell the truth he'd never seen much reason to distinguish between the last day of December and the first of January.

So when a neighbour sighed, 'Another great party, Johnny. Hard to believe it will be the last,' he just looked at the woman blankly till she added, 'Sorry, I thought Pippa said you'd found a buyer, or at least someone so interested he was paying for a survey.'

'Ah, that,' he said without much enthusiasm. 'Yes, there was some Scottish fellow Pippa thought might be good for the asking price.'

'That would be very good news,' said the woman, too tipsy to recognize how this contradicted her recent expression of regret at the possibility of losing her neighbours.

In fact there were mixed feelings but there was no insincerity here. It was the local consensus that the Nutbrowns would have to come down a couple of hundred k at least to make a sale this side of summer. On the other hand, while no one likes to be proved wrong, if by some miracle they did get what they were asking, the implication for all neighbourhood values would more than compensate for the loss of *Schadenfreude*.

In the early hours, after speeding the last of their departing guests with affectionate farewells and promises of eternal friendship, the Nutbrowns surveyed the melancholy relics of their passing.

'Can't say I'm sorry I shan't be seeing any of that ghastly crew again,' said Pippa.

It was part of Pippa's capacity for disappointment that all social gatherings, including her own, left her with feelings of deep antipathy towards the guests.

'Let's go to bed,' said her husband, ignoring this oblique reference to their possible departure. 'Hope Mrs P and her crew don't make too much row.'

This was Mrs Parkin, their cleaner, who traditionally came mob-handed on New Year's Day to restore order.

'Can't lie in too long,' said Pippa. 'Need to be up to see Parkin doesn't skimp. I want the house to be looking its best when Mr Murray comes on the third.'

'Who?'

'Murray who's interested in buying the house. So interested he's bringing his own surveyor to look the place over this time. I did tell you.'

She hadn't, but she knew her husband wouldn't argue the point.

'Good God,' he said in some agitation. 'I thought these Scots spent the first week after Hogmanay in a drunken stupor.'

'Don't be racist. And come to bed.'

It was quickly apparent that despite the lateness of the hour Pippa wasn't ready for sleep. Parties always left her with a residue of nervous energy which would keep her awake all night if she didn't dissipate it. She stepped out of her clothes, helped her husband out of his, then fell back on the bed, pulling him on top of her.

Johnny's great virtue as a sexual partner was that he was rarely importunate but when called upon was always ready and able to do exactly what was wanted in the proportions and for the length of time that Pippa wanted it. Five minutes did the trick tonight. After she came, she pushed him off, rolled over and went to sleep. Johnny lay awake a little longer, staring into the darkness, not exactly thinking but aware that there were thoughts in the room that might keep him awake were he foolish enough to think them. Finally he too fell asleep.

The day of Donald Murray's visit was a perfect selling day. New Year had blown in on a sleet-filled easterly straight from the Steppes, but after two days this had died away to leave clear skies and bright sunshine that touched the property with the delicate skill of a Hollywood lighting engineer, every shadow and every highlight making the director's point, which was in this case *love me! buy me!*

Johnny had opted to head for the golf course. Ignoring the fact that you were selling up was hard when you had a surveyor clunking around the property. He looked up in alarm when the doorbell rang just as they were finishing breakfast.

'Good God, is that them already?' he said.

'They're not due till ten,' said Pippa. 'Probably the post.'

She returned a few moments later bearing the morning mail, which included two identical parcels, about twelve by six by three, addressed one to him and one to her.

They removed the outer brown paper with a synchronicity that would have got them into an Olympic synchronized paper-removing team, only to find themselves confronted by a substantial layer of clear plastic wrapping. This too they removed. Now each of them had something like a shoebox.

Each removed a lid.

'Now why would anyone want to send me two Gideon Bibles?' wondered Johnny. 'What have you got, old girl?'

'The same,' said Pippa.

'Seriously weird. What do you think it means?'

'God and presumably Gideon knows, and I don't intend wasting time trying to puzzle it out,' said his wife.

She gathered together all the wrapping and the books, took them out of the kitchen into the utility room where their variously coloured recycling boxes stood, and returned saying, 'Rubbish to rubbish.'

'Good girl. I'll be off then,' said Nutbrown.

His wife was glad to see him go. Bargaining, she preferred to do alone, and even though she and Donald Murray had agreed a price, she had a feeling there was still a bit of negotiating to be done.

Dead on the stroke of ten, the doorbell rang again and she opened it to see the long spare figure of Mr Murray standing there, smiling down at her. Some way behind him, looking up at the façade of Poynters with the expression of traveller who has stumbled upon the House of Usher moments before its fall, lurked a second man who was summoned forward to be introduced as Duff, the surveyor. Whether this were forename or surname wasn't clear, but either way, Pippa guessed he too was a Scot.

Her guess was confirmed when in response to her bright, 'Well, you've brought the good weather with you,' he sniffed the air vigorously as though already scenting damp and dry rot, and said something in an accent so thick it might as well have been the Gaelic.

She glanced at Murray and he interpreted, 'Is it OK for Duff to have a poke around?'

'Of course,' she said. 'Go anywhere you like.'

They watched as he shuffled off, bent under the weight of a haversack that presumably held the tools of his trade.

'You brought him all the way down from Scotland, did you?' she asked wonderingly.

'Aye. When I'm paying for a service I like to know I've got someone I can trust.'

'It's your money,' she said. 'Now, while he's doing his job, is there anything you'd like to take a closer look at, Mr Murray?'

He gave her a quizzical smile and she feared for a moment he might lurch into a pass. Not that she had any objection in principle to being the object of a pass – accepted or rejected, it usually established a relationship with her on top. But mixing pleasure with business in Mr Murray's case would not, she intuited, be a good idea.

Happily she was wrong, or he decided against it.

'Aye,' he said. 'A wee trip round the policies again would be nice, to see if it's all as grand as I remember.'

They did the tour, outside and then in, seeing nothing of Duff but hearing creaks and clanks that suggested he was hard at his task.

They ended up in the kitchen, where she offered to make coffee. He said yes and she asked if he'd like to go through into the living room, but he said no, the kitchen suited him just fine, he always felt it was the centre of a house.

'Mr Nutbrown no' around?' he asked.

'No. Business, I'm afraid,' she lied.

'So you're left to deal with the sale, eh? Lucky man, to have such a capable wife,' he said.

He sounded as if he meant it.

She said, 'Would Mr Duff like a cup, do you think?'

'Duff's not a coffee man,' he said. 'Irn-Bru, with a whisky chaser. But never on the job. He's a man who likes to focus. He'd really hate it if he missed anything that came up later.'

'I hope he's not going to find much that need come up at all,' she said, a touch acidly.

He gave her that quizzical look again, then said, 'You needn't fear I'm setting up to stiff you, Mrs Nutbrown. Me, I'd rather be buying a house the way we do it in Scotland: I make an offer, you accept it, we shake hands and the thing's done. On the other hand, a wee reduction would be nice.

Still, we've all got to live, even estate agents, eh? How much are Skinners charging you? Five per cent?'

'Six,' she said.

He whistled.

'They live up to their name. Six per cent's a mighty chunk of money once you get into the six-figure bracket.'

Here it comes, she thought. This was the kind of pass she'd been ready for ever since she met Murray.

She said, 'Would you like a slice of cake?'

He looked at the lemon drizzle sponge she'd set on the table.

'In a minute maybe,' he said. 'Talking of Skinners, what kind of agreement do you have with them anyway?'

'The kind I can easily terminate,' she said. 'I made sure of that when they told me their charges. They in return made sure they drew my attention to the fact that the terms of the agreement would hold even after termination if ultimately I sold the house to anyone they'd introduced.'

'Aye, that's normal practice,' he said. 'Else why would anyone ever pay the sharks, eh? On the other hand, suspecting and proving are very different things, as the minister said when he got caught coming out of the massage parlour.'

'Meaning?'

'Meaning, like the minister, I may have been a bit vague with my details when I made the appointment. And I did it on the phone, so I never actually met anyone from Skinners face to face. Also, for tax purposes, if we did reach an accord, Mrs Nutbrown, I'd probably do it through a wee holding company I use from time to time.'

He looked at her expectantly.

She said, 'Are you ready for that slice of cake now, Mr Murray?'

'Oh, I am,' he said. 'I am.'

2

It was the second week of January before Alva Ozigbo got back to London.

Her father's relapse had been serious but he had survived.

'The good thing,' his second-in-command had told her, 'is that perhaps now Ike will stop thinking he knows best and trying to treat himself.'

'I shouldn't bet on it,' said Alva.

By the time the New Year came, the prognosis was once again optimistic, but this time Elvira put no faith in it and Alva had realized there was no way she could leave her mother till she too had recovered from the shock. Early in the New Year Ike was pronounced fit enough to return home, but only if he had full-time nursing care. When he reacted angrily to this, Alva spoke to him severely.

'Stop being such a diva and think of Mum for a change,' she commanded. Then she softened her tone as she added, 'Anyway, give it a few days, and it will probably be Elvira who bumps the nurse.'

Which was more or less what happened, with Elvira assuring the nurse, a laid-back Oldham lass called Maggie

Marley, that she was more than capable of managing her husband's health regime.

'Fair enough,' said Nurse Marley. 'But I'll still call round every other day just to check up, OK?'

Ike regarded this as a major victory.

'Who's a clever little psychiatrist then?' he said. 'So what now, Miss Motivator?'

'I leave you two to it,' said Alva. 'And God help you both!'

She'd been doing what she could by phone and Internet to reorganize her own work, but of course all her patient contact had to be either postponed or reallocated, both of which options were far from satisfactory. Her interest in Wolf Hadda's case was shelved completely. During this period leaving her mother to make another Cumbrian visit hadn't been an option, even if she'd wanted to. She'd phoned Luke Hollins to explain her situation, told him that it was her unofficial opinion that Hadda was no danger to anyone, but of course if the vicar had any further cause for concern, he must take whatever steps he thought appropriate, and implied without spelling it out that her own involvement in the case was over unless it were officially revived.

As for her visit to the castle and what had transpired there, she examined each seemingly significant element clinically.

Imo's assertion about the paternity of her daughter, true or not, meant nothing. Wolf's grief at her death was not likely to be diminished, while his pain at his wife's betrayal could hardly be intensified.

Sir Leon's claim that when he resisted the marriage it had been Wolf's well being he was concerned about rather than Imogen's was surprising till you considered what the poor old sod's life must have been like with a domineering wife and a wilful daughter. Also he'd been on the spot to see what the disappearance of Wolf had done to Fred Hadda, his loyal and loved head forester. The prospect of more pain being heaped on the poor devil's head by his son's insistence on what Fred saw as a foolish and potentially disastrous marriage must have affected him deeply. No wonder that he'd thrown all his feeble weight against the proposed union.

Finally the photo. Maybe the old man had got the birthday wrong. Maybe Wolf's memory had been at fault. Maybe in view of his subsequent sexual predilections, he had unconsciously been trying to stress that pubescent girls could be active temptresses.

Conclusion. Individually each of these 'significant' elements was explicable and disregardable. She had merely overreacted to their coincidence.

There was however another coincidence that surprisingly proved more resistant to clinical analysis.

Twice she had got herself involved in something that was no longer her business, twice she had found herself acting more like a private detective than a clinical psychiatrist.

Both times she had been interrupted by news that her father was dangerously ill.

She was not superstitious, but she knew superstition was the name people often gave to feelings and intuitions that conveyed useful warnings outside the sphere of rationality.

While not persuaded that Hadda was, in any sense that should alarm her professionally, dangerous, she had started to believe that there was danger in his proximity. So when she finally got back to London, in her mind she consciously, perhaps even a touch self-consciously, drew a line under the Hadda case.

As for those little stirrings of desire she felt when she thought of him, she assured herself they were no more troublesome than the small pangs of indigestion she got after eating blue cheese.

And just as easily treatable by giving it up.

She threw herself into her work. After her extended break

there was a lot of it to throw herself into. At Parkleigh, Simon Homewood welcomed her enthusiastically.

'God, I've missed you,' he said.

His fervour sounded more than professional. He didn't look well and when she asked him how his Christmas had been, he said, 'Traditional,' and changed the subject.

A few days later she dropped into his office at the end of the day to give her customary updating on her work. During this she would pass on any particular concerns she had about individual prisoners, but she was scrupulous about not sharing any detail of her work with them that she would have classed as confidential had they been free agents.

When she had finished, to her surprise he opened a drawer in his desk and brought out a bottle of sherry and two glasses.

'You shot off so quickly before Christmas I never had time to offer you a festive drink,' he said.

Her reason for leaving so precipitately had been her decision to visit Hadda in Cumbria. She hadn't mentioned it then and saw no reason to do so now.

He poured and passed her a glass.

'Happy New Year,' he said. 'We both deserve it, I think, to make up for what sounds like a couple of rotten Christmases.'

He knew about her father, of course, but why his should be termed rotten she did not know.

'So what made your Christmas so bad?' she asked.

'Oh, domestic matters,' he said vaguely. Then he took a drink and said, 'Why am I being so coy? It will get out soon enough. Sally and I are splitting up.'

Selfishly her first thought was, *Oh shit!* This changed everything. With luck he might postpone making any move on her till he got his domestic problems in some kind of order, but after that . . .!

No doubt he'd try to take her rejection like an old-fashioned gent, but things were bound to change. She couldn't see him settling for the kind of open, friendly if occasionally prick-teasing relationship she had with Giles.

She said, 'I'm sorry to hear it.'

'Thank you,' he said, regarding her speculatively. She was suddenly fearful he might be about to jump the gun. Seeking a diversion, she heard herself saying brightly, 'By the way, I ran into Hadda over the holiday.'

He didn't look surprised.

'Ah yes. Hadda. And how is he getting on up there in his mountain fastness?'

Why the hell had she got into this? she asked herself.

'He seemed fine,' she said. 'Very domesticated. Quite a good cook, actually.'

'You had a meal with him?'

She said, 'More a snack, really.'

'Just the two of you?'

'Well, the local vicar was there for part of the time.'

As she said this, she was asking herself, Why am I feeling guilty? And what right does he have to question me like he was a Victorian father worried in case his daughter had compromised herself?

Or am I overreacting and is he just questioning me like a prison director discussing a parolee with his prison psychiatrist?

Homewood said, 'Hadda's the responsibility of the probation service now, Alva. Best to leave it to them, eh? You did marvels with him while he was here, and with your annual review due shortly, we don't want anything muddying the waters, do we?'

He said this with an emphasis she didn't care for. She was halfway through her four-year contract and she'd assumed the pattern for the built-in annual review had been set last year when it had taken the form of a casual chat followed by an assurance that the Director would be ticking all the right boxes. The unpleasant thought slid into her mind that maybe Homewood had brought the subject up to remind her that it was in her interests to stay on friendly terms with him!

No! She wouldn't believe that. But that didn't mean she had to sit down under his implied criticism.

She said defiantly, 'Just because a client leaves Parkleigh doesn't stop him being a client in my book. If I feel a patient needs help, that's what he gets from me.'

'And you felt that Hadda needed help? On what grounds, may I ask?'

She thought of telling him about Luke Hollins's letter, but that could lead to an unravelling of the whole visit to Birkstane and that was something she preferred to avoid.

She said, 'No particular reason. Just checking up that all was well.'

'Very conscientious of you,' he said. 'Though why this should involve a meal and an overnight stay, I don't quite see. Look, Alva, this isn't me talking as your boss, it's me talking as your friend. You ought to be more careful. It's all right meeting these people in controlled conditions, but they can be unpredictable. Hadda might have been playing games when he was in prison, but that doesn't mean he hasn't been indulging in real sexual fantasies about you, and I doubt if they just involve your foot!'

Prat! she thought. If this was how you tried to control your wife, no wonder she dumped you.

She emptied her glass and stood up.

'I have to dash,' she said. 'Thanks for the drink. Good night.'

She left not quite at a run but fast enough not to give him time to protest.

As she approached the main gate, she saw another visitor being let out. She hurried to save the duty officer the bother of shutting and opening the gate again, but Chief Officer Proctor stepped out of the gatehouse and fell into step beside her. At the gate he nodded to the duty man and said, 'I'll see Dr Ozigbo out.'

He watched till the man vanished into the gatehouse, then said, 'Sorry to hear about your father, miss. Hope he's OK.'

She'd seen him distantly a couple of times since her return, but this was the first chance for conversation they'd had.

She said, 'Thank you, George. He's doing fine.'

'Good. And how are you doing, miss?'

'I'm fine too, George.'

'That's good. Mr Homewood missed you.'

'Did he? I hope you missed me too, George.'

She spoke rather sharply, her mind going back to that earlier occasion when she'd felt Proctor was trespassing on private ground. What was his motive? Perhaps he'd heard of Homewood's marital problems and was now trying to act as his pandar! No, that didn't really make sense . . .

'Did, as a matter of fact, miss. Know we don't always see eye to eye, but you're straight. Straight and discreet. Mr Ruskin, he was straight too. Maybe not quite so discreet. Anyway, like I say, we're all glad you're back. The Director especially. Lonely job, that. Needs to know everything, if he's to do it properly, that's why he takes such an interest. Mustn't hold you back, miss. I think we're in for a bit of rain. Goodnight now.'

What the hell was that all about? she asked herself as she walked the short distance to the visitors' car park. Standing by the entrance she saw the man who'd left the jail ahead of her. This time she recognized him. It was Wolf Hadda's solicitor, Mr Trapp.

They had never met formally but she had glimpsed him at the time of the probation hearings and when he'd picked up Hadda on his release.

A flurry of rain gave her an excuse to put her head down and hurry past without glancing his way. They only had one connection and her brief exchange with Homewood had made her realize how dangerously alive in her mind Wolf Hadda still was.

She got into her car. The rain was setting in now and she switched on the wipers. Each sweep of the running wind-screen brought Trapp into view. Why on earth was he just standing there, hatless, umbrella-less, protected only by a thin raincoat that already looked as if it had reached saturation point?

Now she saw him, now she didn't. It was as if the wipers were offering her a choice. Or rather, as if a choice was being made for her. Like plucking petals off a flower . . . he loves me . . . he loves me not . . . She could just drive out of the exit. She didn't even have to go past him.

But the car was moving towards him. My choice, she told herself firmly. A humanitarian act, nothing more.

She wound down the window and said, 'Mr Trapp, isn't it?'

'Yes,' he said.

She said, 'You're getting wet.'

He said, 'Yes.'

Losing patience with herself more than him, she said, 'Well, get in, man!'

He hesitated then walked round the car and slid damply into the passenger seat.

He really was an unprepossessing-looking little man; not quite scruffy, but close to down-at-heel. She'd seen photos of Toby Estover. From that smooth, sophisticated, immaculately tailored figure to Mr Trapp was an uncomputable distance. Put them side by side and you had a measure of Hadda's fall. Yet from what she read of the trial records, Trapp had done his job well. And hadn't Hadda, in one of

379

his biographical pieces, said something that implied a previous acquaintance? Something about a favour, and something more than merely professional, she guessed, if Wolf had been a house guest of the Trapps at Christmas . . .

Careful, you're being a PI again, she warned herself.

She said, 'Alva Ozigbo.'

'Yes, I know,' he said. Then, as if feeling a need to offer explanation, he added, 'My wife's picking me up. She shouldn't be long. I finished earlier than expected.'

'Well, let's see if we can get you dry for her,' she said, turning the heater up full blast. 'It would be unjust if you caught a cold just because you were super efficient.'

He smiled, a gentle, not quite melancholy smile that lit up his face.

'Hardly that,' he said. 'When I told my client that in my judgment appealing against his sentence was a waste of time, money and energy, he indicated to me that sending him a bill for my services would enjoy much the same status, and if I cared to argue the toss, his brother would offer a few clinching arguments with a baseball bat.'

'He sounds a well-educated man.'

'That was the gist,' he said primly. 'His choice of words was more idiomatic.'

She laughed. There was clearly more to Mr Trapp than met the eye. Or rather, met her eye. Presumably not Hadda's.

As if merely thinking the name forced her to utter it, she heard herself asking, 'Did you know Mr Hadda before you acted as his solicitor at the time of his trial?'

I'm just making conversation, she assured herself. Till his wife arrives.

He took his time replying. Finally he said, 'We'd met.'

'Professionally?'

He smiled again and said, 'Yes. Our first meeting was professional.'

Our first meeting. She tried to imagine a situation in which Wolf Hadda, newly wed to his princess and striding forth to conquer the business world, would have needed a solicitor like Trapp. Not completely impossible, but very unlikely.

So this contact probably dated back to the five years between young Wolf running away from home and his return with his three impossible tasks accomplished.

The mystery years, the years of emerald mines, piracy, buried treasure . . .

A car turned into the car park, a muddy and dented Toyota. Trapp leaned across and pressed the horn, catching the Toyota driver's attention, and it drew up alongside.

Alva wound down her window and found herself looking at a broad-faced woman with rose-pink hair and a disconcertingly direct unblinking gaze.

Trapp said, 'Doll, this is Dr Ozigbo. She kindly offered me shelter till you came. Dr Ozigbo, my wife, Doll.'

'I'm pleased to meet you,' said Alva.

'Likewise,' said the woman. 'Hope he's not messed up your car.'

'Thanks a lot,' said Trapp, scurrying round to climb in alongside his wife.

In a moment we'll go our separate ways, thought Alva. Fate does much, but you've got to take a few steps to meet it.

She called, 'Mr Trapp, I meant to ask, how is Mr Hadda? A lot of people are concerned to learn how he's doing. I'd like to be sure everything's going well . . .'

'Fine, so far as I know. I'll tell him you were asking after him, shall I?' said Trapp.

'Thank you,' she said. She felt there was something else she ought to say but couldn't imagine what it might be.

The woman, who'd been staring fixedly at her during this exchange with her husband, now stuck her head out of the window as if to take an even closer look. Alva had to force herself not to flinch before that fierce, assessing gaze.

Doll said, 'That colour, how do you get it?'

It took a second to register the reference was to her hair not her skin, though in both cases the answer was the same.

'Actually, it's natural.'

'Oh. Pity. Wouldn't have minded giving it a try. Nice to meet you, dearie. You're ever in Chingford, give us a call.'

She handed Alva a card. Then the window wound up and the Toyota pulled away.

So what's happened here? wondered Alva. The card suggested that Doll Trapp anticipated meeting her again, and probably not to discuss the colour of her hair.

The one subject they had in common was Wolf Hadda.

If Homewood hadn't offered her a drink, she would have been in her car and on her way home before Trapp left the prison. She might even have escaped George Proctor's interception. So she'd have been home by now enjoying a pleasant evening in front of the telly instead of driving along, her thoughts moving in time with the screen wipers between Hadda and Proctor and Simon Homewood.

One thing her encounter with the Trapps had made her recognize was that the line she had drawn under Hadda had been for emphasis not closure.

By the time she drew up in front of her flat, a screech from her wipers as they swept drily over the screen told her the rain had stopped. It also did something else, bringing together the three men who'd been dividing her thoughts during the drive.

Proctor had said Homewood needed to know everything to do his job properly.

But now she'd had time to examine their encounter with the emotional temperature turned down, there were certain aspects of the Director's knowledge that puzzled her.

For a start, when she said she'd run into Hadda he'd instantly assumed it was in Cumbria rather than in Manchester, where he knew she had been staying with her parents.

OK, that might not be all that significant. But later he'd referred to her spending the night at Birkstane even though she'd deliberately avoided mentioning it.

A lucky guess, perhaps.

But the final thing couldn't be put down to guesswork. He'd mentioned her foot.

So how the hell did he know about the sexual charade Hadda had played with her to find out if the surveillance audio really was switched off?

3

Toby Estover was wondering whether it were time for a change of secretary.

It wasn't that Morag wasn't as efficient as ever in her professional duties and as obliging as ever in her personal services. The trouble was that in the first couple of weeks after his return to the office in the New Year she had shown signs of looking for something more from their relationship than a regular desktop bang.

To start with she had tried to engage him in an exchange of idle chit-chat about the Christmas holiday, giving him more details of her family celebrations than he needed to hear, then leaving a gap that he was clearly expected to fill with more details of his festive break than he cared to give.

Also after kneeling astride him and bringing him to climax, she no longer immediately rose with a friendly smile and retired to the washroom, emerging a few minutes later, perfectly composed and ready to take dictation. She had taken to sinking forward against him, offering her lips to be kissed and murmuring inanities like, 'Was that good for you, lover?'

When by his responses he made it clear that he wasn't in

the market for either idle gossip or post-coital *tendresse*, she desisted, but the experience had not been pleasant. So, time for a change, perhaps. Not in terms of size, of course; he liked his office furniture well upholstered; but colouring was another matter. Morag was fair and freckled, her generous breasts milky pale and small nippled. He found himself fantasizing about a brown-skinned girl with nipples like thumbs set in a boss of plum-dark crushed velvet . . .

The thought made him languid and he looked with displeasure on Morag as she entered his office after a barely perfunctory knock and said, 'You're no' forgettin' you're lunching wi' Kitty Locksley?'

Was his hearing faulty or had her Scots accent grown more intrusive in the past few days? She really would have to go. He'd have a word with Miss Jenner, the office personnel manager. She would arrange for a transfer to general duties downstairs. No drop in pay, but they usually got the message and left of their own accord after a week or so.

He said irritably, 'Of course I haven't forgotten. Though why I'm lunching with the bitch, I've no idea. Still, always best to keep the press on board.'

Kitty Locksley was the news editor of one of the slightly more literate tabloids, the kind that people he knew sometimes admitted to reading.

He stood up and waited. Morag usually went into the cloakroom to fetch his overcoat and help him into it. Today she didn't move. That did it. She definitely had to go. He got the coat himself and as he struggled into it he said, 'I should be back by three. Ask Miss Jenner to come and see me then, will you?'

Morag waited till she heard the lift door close, then took out her mobile and dialled.

'Hi, Mr Murray,' she said. 'He's on his way.'

'Good girl. Got to go. Talk later.'

She put the phone down and strolled round Estover's expansive desk and settled into his very comfortable leather swivel chair. She prided herself on always trying to see things from other people's viewpoint and things certainly looked very different from here. Not that she was complaining. She'd come into the job with her eyes wide open. She'd have had to be very naïve indeed not to recognize what was on Toby Estover's mind as his eyes ran up and down her body at the interview. Well, that was fine, he seemed a nice enough guy, and she was a thoroughly modern girl with no hang-ups about enjoying sex for its own sake, plus there were all kinds of perks as well as the Christmas bonus. So it had merely amused her when some of the other girls felt it their bounden duty to tell her that on average Estover's secretaries lasted three years. There would come a time when Miss Jenner, the office manager, would approach her, shoot some shit about moving staff around to give them a variety of experience, then invite her to leave her comfortable ante-room outside Estover's lofty office and dive into the common pool below.

'That'll be nice,' she'd replied with a smile. 'I really look forward to seeing more of you guys.'

On her return to work after the Christmas break, she'd been almost immediately approached by her Scottish friend. He had a new proposition that took her aback. Keeping Murray apprised of Estover's movements was no more than a bit of harmless disloyalty. But, however you wrapped it up, accessing, copying and selling Estover's confidential records was unambiguously criminal.

The money Murray offered had been good. And she liked the guy. So she hadn't refused him out of hand. Next time they met, he brought up the proposition again, upping his offer from good to generous. Also he assured her he was working for the good guys and that nothing would happen to Estover as a result of her actions that he didn't deserve. Which, from her own knowledge of Toby's working practices, suggested the poor bastard was in for a very bad time indeed!

Still she hesitated. As well as being a thoroughly modern girl, Morag was also an old-fashioned sentimentalist. She didn't expect declarations of eternal love from Estover, still less did she have any hope or indeed desire that he should make an honest woman out of her. But she did feel that after what they'd been to each other for the past couple of years, there must be some affection there.

Since then she'd given Estover every chance to show his regard for her, to demonstrate he regarded her as something more than just a high-class wanking machine.

He hadn't taken the chance. So a few days earlier she'd taken the plunge. Next time she saw Murray she'd passed over the tiny flash drive he had given her.

'Everything's on there,' she said. 'A lot of it's encrypted.'

'No problem,' he said. 'I'm grateful.'

Then he'd leaned forward and looked into her eyes and she'd thought, here it comes – he's going to hit on me!

But instead all he said was, 'If you ever fancy a job back in Glasgow, I might be able to fix you up.'

She was surprised to realize how disappointed she was his proposition was commercial rather than personal!

'I'll think on it,' she said coolly.

'Good,' he said, sitting back. 'Now some time soon, a journalist called Kitty Locksley is probably going to want to fix up a meeting with your boss. Over lunch, I'd guess. I need to know where and when.'

Back to business, she thought. They're all the same! One way or another, they'll squeeze every last drop of use out of you, then it's *On your bike, girl!*

He was muttering something else that her irritation made her miss.

'Eh?' she said.

'I was just wondering,' he said rather awkwardly. 'Maybe you and me could meet for a drink some time, you know, just to meet.'

'Like a date, you mean?' she said, hiding her pleasure.

'Aye.'

'I'll think about it.'

Well, now she'd thought about it. A date seemed good. And as she had no intention of letting the bitches downstairs get in their cracks about her being rolled off Estover's desk a year earlier than the average, what Murray had said about working in Glasgow sounded good too. She'd had enough of the fucking Sassenachs – in every sense.

She picked up the desk phone and punched in Miss Jenner's number.

Estover, meanwhile, was finding his welcome at the restaurant more to his taste than his departure from the office. As the pretty blonde on reception helped him off with his coat, she said, 'Nice to see you again, Mr Estover. Miss Locksley's already at your table.'

'Thank you,' he said, giving her a warm smile. Pity she was so willowy. And fair-skinned too, so probably no crushed velvet there.

'Miss Locksley?' said a man's voice. 'That Miss Kitty Locksley?'

He turned to see a man in the courier's outfit of crash helmet and leather jacket standing behind him. He was lanky, what was visible of his face had an impatient expression on it, and he had a Scottish accent which at the moment Estover felt was a strong strike against him.

'Who are you?' he said in his most patrician fashion.

'Courier. Got a package for her. Here, chum, could you take it? The bike's on the pavement, probably being clamped by now!'

He thrust a small package into Estover's hand then turned and left.

Bloody cheek! thought Estover. The Celtic fringe seemed to be in a conspiracy to irritate him today.

'Shall I take that, sir?' said the receptionist.

'No, that's all right.'

At the table Kitty Locksley smiled up at him as he approached. He stooped to give her a perfunctory kiss. Small, fine-boned, with not enough flesh on her to feed a hungry bluebottle, she definitely wasn't his type.

As he sat down he said, 'This is for you.'

'A late Christmas present, Toby?' she mocked.

'No! Courier was leaving it as I came in.'

She slipped it into her bag down at her feet and said, 'You'd think they'd let me enjoy my lunch in peace!'

'But this is a working lunch, surely?' said Estover. 'You haven't just asked me out because you've taken a sudden fancy to me, have you, Kitty?'

'Definitely not,' said the woman, rather too emphatically for Estover's liking. Even where he did not desire, he liked to be found desirable.

A waiter interrupted them to ask if they'd like a drink and they chatted in a desultory fashion till her gin and tonic and his large scotch came. When he was talking to journalists, Estover liked to have a prop to hand, in every sense.

'So, Kitty, what's this all about?' he said. 'My secretary said you were quite mysterious.'

'I certainly didn't mean to be,' she said. 'It was just a rather odd thing. Does the name Arnie Medler mean anything to you?'

Now Estover was glad of his prop. He took a long pull at the scotch and said cautiously, 'It does ring a bell.'

'DI in the Met, till he retired to live in Spain.'

'Yes, of course. That's how I know the name. The fuzz.

In my line one has to make contact from time to time.'

He was sounding a little too jolly, perhaps. He resisted the temptation to take another drink and said, 'So?'

'I'm glad he's not a friend,' she said. 'Because he's dead.'

'Good Lord!'

'Yes. He died in a rather macabre accident some time over Christmas. You didn't know?'

'No, why should I? Was it in the papers?'

'No. Not a trace. Mind you, so many good stories about rows over Christmas dinner turning into family massacres that an ex-pat's death in sunny Spain was hardly going to stop the presses. So what was your connection with him, Toby?'

By now Estover was fully back in control.

'More to the point, Kitty, as it's you who got me here, what's your interest?' he said.

She shrugged. 'Nothing sinister. Someone rang the desk with the story and said there was a link between you and the dead man that might be worth following up. Also they intimated it was something you'd prefer to discuss face to face, so, as a girl's got to eat, I thought why not get a lunch on the paper with my dear old chum?'

What the caller had actually said was, 'You might like to have Estover where you can watch his reaction, preferably some place he can't have his secretary primed to interrupt him with an urgent call.'

So far the watching had been interesting but a long way from suggestive.

He said, 'Well, as I say, I barely remember the name and I'd need to check back to see what the nature of my acquaintance with the man was.'

She said, 'The caller mentioned something about helping with Medler's purchase of a villa in Spain. Didn't know you went in for that kind of stuff, Toby.'

'Oh well, you know, seven years back, I was still making my way,' he said.

'Really?' she said, noting the clash between the claim of *barely remembering* and the precision of *seven years*. 'Just shows how wrong our records can be. They've got you down as top stud, legally speaking, back then. Didn't realize you were still picking up pennies with a bit of conveyancing.'

He ignored the sarcasm and said, 'So, delightful as it always is to see you, Kitty, I fear your well-known reputation for probity will make it hard for you to claim this lunch on expenses. Retired policeman dies in Spanish accident. London solicitor may have been acquainted with him. Even your ingenious editor would be hard pushed to work that up into a story! By the way, you described the accident as rather macabre. How so?'

He spoke casually. Why was it lawyers always spoke casually when they approached something they really wanted to know? wondered the journalist.

She watched his face carefully as she replied.

'It seems your old friend, sorry, acquaintance, Mr Medler, had taken to hitting the bottle quite hard in his retirement. His wife returned home early on Christmas morning to find he'd drunk himself silly and managed to fall in their villa. As he fell, he must somehow have triggered the mechanism that brought the heavy metal security shutters down over the sliding patio doors. Unfortunately, they were open and he fell with his arms stretched across the threshold. The first thing his wife saw when she got home was his severed hands lying on the patio, looking like they'd been chopped off with an axe.'

Now this was more interesting, thought Kitty Locksley. Either that detail had a special significance for Estover or maybe he just had a very weak stomach. Either way, she didn't think she was going to have to pick up too heavy a bill for his lunch.

And Davy McLucky, now helmetless and sitting in a car parked across the street from the restaurant, was so entertained by Toby Estover's expression that he took another photo to add to the ones he'd already shot of this fascinating encounter.

4

The Sunday after her conversation with the Trapps, Alva Ozigbo ate her frugal breakfast, pressed the mute button on her answer machine, and sat down on the floor of her flat surrounded by all the material she had gathered relating to the Hadda case.

The only thing scheduled for the day ahead was tea at John Childs's house. He'd rung the previous day to say that he'd bought his godson, Harry, a copy of *Curing Souls* for his birthday and hoped she'd be kind enough to sign it. She'd said of course she would and he had then wondered in his diffident manner if she might like to do this while having tea with him the following day.

So she had all morning to trawl through the Hadda files, and seeing them laid out neatly on her floor, it struck her she was going to need all morning!

There was a hell of a lot of material here.

More, she guessed, than normal with the majority of her clients.

But that was explicable, she reassured herself, by the complexity of the case rather than any special interest in Hadda.

She didn't feel all that reassured.

Taking a deep breath, she went back to the beginning.

Three hours later she emerged from her second complete review, poured herself a stiff gin, and in search of a temporary distraction checked her messages.

All were negligible except one from her mother sounding fraught and asking her to ring as soon as she had a moment. Since Ike had come home to convalesce, most messages from Elvira took this form, so she didn't let herself feel too anxious, but she rang straight back. To her relief it was the mixture as before.

'He won't eat what he should, won't rest when he should, says it's all a plot to keep him away from his work and claims I'm up to my neck in the conspiracy!' said Elvira.

As she spoke, Alva heard Ike's rich bass distantly demanding to know who was on the phone. Elvira ignored him, the voice got louder till finally she was cut off in mid syllable and Ike's voice cried, 'Elf! Thank God! Send for the SAS, I'm being held here against my will! Or if you can't do that, restore my sanity by saying something sensible.'

Alva laughed out loud, partly with relief at hearing that voice at its old decibel level, partly because she knew that this was the response her father wanted.

It was strange, she thought, that Elvira, the actress, never seemed to have caught on that her husband's outbursts were usually purely histrionic, and all that was required of his audience was appreciative applause.

Then she recalled her growing suspicion that she'd been played by Hadda and stopped feeling superior.

Her laughing response quickly reduced the performance to a more conventional discussion of Ike's progress. But after they'd been talking a few moments, he said, 'That's enough of me. How about you, Elf? You sound a bit strung out.'

He'd always been very sensitive to her moods.

'I'm fine,' she said. 'I've just realized a patient may have been fooling me, that's all.'

He said, 'Serious? I mean, you've not turned some nut loose who's going around cutting people's throats?'

'No. Nothing like that.'

'Then why so down? Being fooled's an occupational hazard in your business, I should have thought.'

'I know. It's just that I feel like I'd been fêted for translating the Rosetta Stone, only to find out later maybe I'd got it all wrong and the hieroglyphics were nothing but an Egyptian laundry list.'

He boomed a laugh and said, 'Think of it this way. You'd find out a lot more about the Egyptians from a laundry list than the kind of high-falutin' crap folk usually carve on monuments.'

'I suppose,' she said.

'You sound like you're taking it personally,' said Ike. 'Now why should that be? I seem to recall you once telling me that there was a line between professional and personal that your patients were always pressing up against and you had to make sure it was never crossed *either* way.'

God, but he was sharp!

She said lightly, 'Daddy, didn't we agree: you do no analysis and I'll do no surgery?'

'Never agreed to stand by and let my little girl get hurt,' he said.

'And if I want someone beaten up, you're still the first guy I'll call,' she said. 'But I need you back to full fighting fitness for that. So get back into bed and stop being an asshole to Mummy. You know she takes it personally even though it means nothing.'

'Yeah. Maybe that's where you get it from. Bad gene. Don't worry, I promise to be good. You take care, Elf. I love you.'

'Me too.'

She switched the phone off. Was Ike right? Was she taking personally something that meant nothing?

She returned to the notes she'd been making as she went through the Hadda files.

The way in which they differed from her original case notes was the input of new information. Not that this amounted to much.

Imogen Ulphingstone at fourteen hadn't been the skinny, early pubescent girl that Hadda had described having his first sexual encounter with on Pillar Rock. She had been a rapidly maturing young woman with a bosom already giving promise of the perfect breasts Hadda had been distracted by in his first piece of writing.

Sir Leon hadn't objected to the marriage to protect his daughter from Hadda but to protect Hadda from his daughter, and by implication his wife.

So, not much. But it meant she'd needed to take a fresh look at what Wolf had actually written. And she had to admit that her own brief encounter with the two Ulphingstone women had left her with some sympathy for the old man's point of view.

And now the clarity of her original interpretation and analysis had been brought into doubt. The whole thing began to resemble one of those drawings in which a slight change of perception turns a goose into a rabbit. It was all a matter of focus. Her initial perception had been of a paedophile in denial gradually coming to a horrified awareness of what he had done. But change that to an innocent man coming to a realization that his only hope of getting early release was by faking the process, and the whole thing made just as much sense.

She cast her memory back to her developing relationship with Hadda. Her delight when he'd given her the first piece of writing. She had taken his racy description of the events leading up to the accident as clear evidence that he was still in denial. She had never for a second considered the possibility that this might in fact be the plain truth.

And she had almost certainly let her scepticism show.

She recalled the way he'd looked at her before producing his second piece, the description of waking from the coma.

She'd seen this as a definite step forward. And maybe this was exactly the way Hadda wanted her to see it. But only if her reaction to the first piece showed him there was no hope of convincing her he was innocent.

Once he'd taken this path there was no way back. He had played his part perfectly, written and spoken his lines in a way that persuaded her she was guiding him against his will to confront his Brocken spectre. Whereas all the time, he was leading and she was eagerly following . . .

She couldn't believe it, she wouldn't believe it. How could she, the professional, have been fooled by a . . . *woodcutter!* He'd surely have needed expert assistance as to which strings to pull . . .

Then she remembered finding a copy of *Curing Souls* in the bedroom at Birkstane, and the speed with which he'd removed it from her.

Why? A good reason would be that it was heavily annotated.

The bastard had used her own book to get inside her mind, her professional thought processes!

But why the hell was she so pissed off at the thought that this man she felt something for, even if she wasn't yet sure what, might turn out to be innocent of the disgusting crime he'd been sent down for? Wouldn't revelation of his innocence more than make up for the fact that he'd fooled her?

Or maybe of course he was simply even more cunning and manipulative than child molesters usually were.

Alva shook her head angrily.

She needed to put all that personal stuff out of her mind. She was a professional and she had a professional interest here. But even as she made the assertion, she knew she was not going to act professionally. That would mean taking her concerns to the proper authorities – the probation service and/or the police. And of course, if she had serious reason to believe a client was likely to commit a crime, she would have no choice.

But, she reassured herself, you don't! If anything, you're beginning to consider the possibility that a client may have been the object of a crime.

OK, she answered herself, then at least you ought to talk this over with someone whose informed judgment you respect.

Like who?

Her father would normally have been high on her list, but not in his present state. He'd already detected that something was worrying her. If once he got a sniff that what lay at the bottom of her problem was her inappropriate feeling for a convicted pederast . . .

No, Ike was out. Elvira was never in.

And not a colleague.

She knew only too well what another psychiatrist's advice would be. Go to the authorities, get them to initiate a formal investigation. The trouble there was, whatever it produced in the long run, its first fruit would be the return of Hadda to custody. In her mind's eye she saw him drinking his strong black coffee in the kitchen at Birkstane, logs crackling in the hearth across which Sneck lies, gently snoring, while outside the winter wind sends volleys of hail against the panes . . .

Jesus! She was thinking Christmas-card sentimentality now! But she knew she could not be responsible for dragging him away from that without better reason than she had so far.

Not so long ago she might have contemplated an off-the-record chat with Homewood, but having already experienced the irritatingly proprietary attitude probably spawned by his new domestic situation, she had no desire to invite him further down the road of intimacy.

And also there was still the nagging question of how he seemed to know what he couldn't possibly know. She had gone over the exchange again and again and almost persuaded herself that she'd simply misinterpreted something quite insignificant.

Then an inner voice said, Just like all that stuff at Ulphingstone Castle? Right!

So who could she talk to?

One possibility remained and she was seeing him this afternoon!

At four o'clock precisely she rang the bell of Childs's front door. As always, he greeted her with an ego-stroking delight.

'Dr Ozigbo, hello. Come in, come in,' he said. 'It's lovely to see you.'

'And you too, Mr Childs,' she said.

Would their relationship ever move on to a more casual form of address? she wondered. After more than two years, she doubted it, and in fact she didn't mind. There was something pleasantly old fashioned in this friendly formality. It implied the closeness of equality without the dangers of intimacy, though to ask his advice in this instance might bring her perilously close to the borderline between the two.

'Let's go up to my study again,' he said. 'I always think the climb works up the appetite so well.'

On their way up the stairs, he said, 'So how are things going back at work? Settled comfortably into the routine again, are you?'

She said, 'Well, yes and no. Actually there's something I'd really like your advice about, if you don't mind me bringing my problems along to a Sunday tea-party.'

'You interest me strangely,' he said. 'And one good turn deserves another. Now, here we are.'

They had reached the top landing and entered the study. On his desktop lay a pristine copy of *Curing Souls*.

'Perhaps you would like to inscribe it while I get the tea,' he suggested. 'Then we can sit down together and mull over this problem of yours.'

'Of course,' she said. 'What would you like me to write in the book?'

'Oh, something encouraging,' he said vaguely. 'I know he will be so delighted to have your signature and your support.'

She must have looked a little doubtful, for he smiled mischievously and added, 'I daresay he will also be delighted to have my signature on the fat cheque I shall be enclosing with the volume.'

Alva smiled back at him and said, 'I'm relieved to hear it. Universities are full of books, but hard cash is always in short supply.'

She sat down at the desk as he excused himself and headed back down the stairs.

There was a pen in a small jug that acted as a desk tidy. She picked it up and opened the book and tried to think of something witty to write.

She recalled a remark of R. D. Laing's: *Few books today are forgivable.* Yes, that would do, followed by *I hope you will find something to forgive in this one. Good luck and Happy Birthday!*

She picked up the pen and started writing. Or at least tried to. The pen was dry. The only other writing implement in the tidy was a red pencil, which would hardly do.

Without thinking she pulled open the nearest drawer of the desk in search of a more suitable implement.

There were several pens in there. There was also a framed photograph.

She took it out and stared from it to the gap in the line of photos displayed on the wall, then back again.

It was a face she knew, though not like this.

She heard a distant clink of crockery on the stairs.

When the door opened, the desk drawer was shut and Alva was just putting the final flourish to her signature.

'All done?' said Childs, entering with the tea tray.

'Yes, all done,' she said brightly.

Too brightly? She hoped not. But she reckoned she'd done very well to answer him with even a semblance of normalcy while her mind was bubbling with the question: What the hell was John Childs doing with a photograph of the young Wolf Hadda hidden in his desk?

5

Davy McLucky was whistling as he turned into the quiet Chingford street where the Trapps' cosy suburban villa was located. He hadn't been too delighted when it turned out Hadda was serious in his suggestion that on his next trip to London he should stay with the solicitor, but it had turned out fine. The absence of alcohol apart, Ed and Doll were his kind of people, and the hip flask he always carried made up for that single deficiency.

But it wasn't pleasurable anticipation of the warming cup of cocoa and large wedge of chocolate cake awaiting him that put the bounce in his step and the music on his lips, it was the memory of the evening he'd just spent with Morag Gray.

He'd started by coming clean, or at least as clean as he felt he could. She'd shown no surprise when he told her his real name and profession. They'd exchanged biographical details over a couple of drinks, and then they'd gone back to her flat where the exchange became more biological.

Now here he was, striding along the quiet suburban street with a lightness of heart he hadn't experienced since he was a teenager.

402

He reached the Trapps' villa and turned in at the gate.

As he took the key out of his pocket and inserted it in the front door lock, he heard the sound of a footfall behind him. It had nothing of the menacing speed of attack, nevertheless he spun round, his forearms raised defensively.

'Good evening, Mr Murray,' said Alva Ozigbo. 'Why am I not as surprised as I should be to see you here? Or is your sat-nav on the blink again?'

Doll Trapp's reaction when she saw Alva following McLucky into the old-fashioned lounge where she and Ed Trapp were sitting reading the Sunday papers was to smile widely and say, 'Dr Ozigbo! I was hoping you'd show up. Take a seat, dearie. Ed, you make us a cup of tea. Davy, why don't you give Wolf a bell? See what he thinks, OK?'

Alva thought, *Davy*. There'd been a Scottish cop looking after Hadda in hospital. They had seemed to get on well. *Davy McLucky*. That was it: *D.M.*

The Scot followed Ed Trapp from the room.

Doll said, 'I know you said it was natural, but I thought I'd give it a go anyway. What do you think?'

She shook her head to draw attention to her hair, whose pink tinge had been replaced by pale straw.

'It's very nice,' said Alva.

'Yeah, but now I see you again, it's nothing close, is it? Hard to carry colours in your head. You buy a scarf thinking that'll go with my blue jacket and you get home and it clashes like a skullcap in a mosque. Why's it so hard, do you think?'

'Perception's an inexact thing. That's what makes witness evidence so dodgy. Mrs Trapp, is that man David McLucky who used to be a detective constable in the Met?'

'Now how on earth do you know that?' said Doll.

'Wolf wrote about him.'

'Oh yes. And you've put two and two together. He said you were sharp.'

'Not sharp enough, I'm beginning to think. Listen, Mrs Trapp –'

'Doll. Call me Doll. I think we're going to be friends. And leave the questions for a moment, Alva . . . I've got that right, I hope? Such a pretty name. How long does it take a man to make a pot of tea? No wonder it takes for ever to get a plumber. At last!'

The door opened and Ed Trapp entered carrying a tray that bore the tea things and a plateful of biscuits.

'Just look at the way he's arranged those biscuits,' scolded Doll. '"Arranged", did I say? I think he's stood at one end of the kitchen and thrown them at the plate.'

But even as she scolded him, she was smiling affectionately at her husband. This was a very close-knit couple, guessed Alva.

She noted there were only two cups on the tray. As Doll started to pour the tea, Murray/McLucky came into the room.

He said, 'It's OK.'

'Is that all? Come on, he must have said more than that!' protested Doll.

'Aye,' said the Scot. 'What he actually said was, you can either tie her up, gag her and keep her in the attic for a few weeks, or you can tell her anything she wants to know.'

'That Wolf, he's such a joker,' said Doll.

Alva felt she wouldn't have cared to be here if Doll hadn't thought it was a joke.

'Right, you two, off you go and watch some footie or something,' the woman continued. 'Me and Alva have got things to sort out.'

Obediently the two men left.

'Milk? Sugar? Bikky?' said Doll. 'No? No wonder you keep your lovely figure. Too late for me.'

She added a couple of teaspoons of sugar to her tea and helped herself to a biscuit which she dipped into her cup.

'So what made you decide to come round to see us?' she said.

Because I want answers, thought Alva. And because I couldn't think of anyone it's safe to ask except you, and I'm not all that sure about you!

But a good psychiatrist never reveals the depths of her own ignorance. She'd impressed this woman with her identification of McLucky. Build on that.

She said, 'I need to fill in some gaps in my files before I decide whether to go to the authorities or not.'

Doll gave her a wry grin as if she didn't believe a word of it and said, 'Then we have a problem, dearie, as I can't tell you anything without your assurance that nothing you hear here will go any further. Like you were listening to one of your patients.'

Alva said, 'If one of my patients told me he was planning to blow up Parliament, and I believed him, I'd have to tell someone.'

Doll let out a cockatoo screech of laughter and said, 'Me, I'd ask the bugger if he wanted any help! But I take your point. Makes things difficult, though. Up to you, dearie.'

She ate another biscuit, regarding her guest expectantly.

Alva blanked her out and focused on her problem. With everything she did it seemed the gap between the professional and the personal was widening. Her reaction to Luke Hollins's letter had started the rot. Instead of taking it straight to the probation service, she had shot off to Cumbria. All very unprofessional.

On the other hand, until very recently the authorities she was threatening to go to would have included Homewood and Childs, so what was she hesitating for? She'd returned to her flat from tea at Childs's house, her mind sparking with speculation that she knew could lead nowhere except a restless night. She needed more information and the number of people she could approach in search of it was very limited. In fact, the only ones in reach were the Trapps.

Pointless wasting more time on futile thought. She'd dug out Doll's card and headed straight for Chingford, arriving there just in time to see Murray/McLucky walking along the pavement towards the house.

She said, 'If you tell me unequivocally that a crime is about to be committed, then I'll have to speak. Otherwise you'll get maximum discretion.'

Doll screwed up her face and said, 'I suppose that'll do to be going on with. All right, dearie, sitting comfortable? Then I'll begin right at the beginning. Here's how Ed and me first met Wolf. He was just sixteen and me, God help us, I was just turned thirty!'

When Doll fell silent twenty minutes later, Alva said, 'I'd just like to make sure I'm not missing anything. You're saying Ed met Wolf in his capacity as duty solicitor, guessed the boy was under age, believed he was guilty as charged, knew he'd absconded from a Remand Centre and broken into his office . . . And despite this, Ed made no attempt to involve Social Services, got him off the charge, and covered up the absconding and the break-in. Then you took him into your home and found him a job. Have I got it right?'

'Word perfect, ducks,' said Doll. 'Though, I got to admit, hearing you spell it out so precise, it does sound a bit weird.'

'Weird!' said Alva. 'It sounds . . . I'm not sure how it sounds, except I've had patients whose fantasies came over as more down to earth than this.'

'Yes, well, the thing is, you *are* missing something, dearie. Though the fact that you're here at all makes me think maybe you're not really missing it at all, you're just not facing up to it. The thing is, Wolf was . . . is . . . very attractive, I mean, not just in the usual boy–girl way, though that too. But most people just *like* him! Even the cops put in a bit of effort with him. And Ed was full of him when he came back from their first meeting at the nick. I recall saying, "I hope you're not on the turn, Ed!" He just laughed and said, "If you met the lad, you'd see what I mean." Never thought I would meet him, of course. But I did. And I saw. This making any sense to you, dearie?'

It was. Alva thought of what she knew of Wolf's childhood. A loner, yes. But through *his* choice, not other people's exclusion.

In fact (why hadn't she spotted this before?) it was the fact that he was so attractive that had permitted him to go his own way so merrily. The evidence was all there: his teachers cutting him an enormous amount of slack at school; the girls trying to date him; Sir Leon ruffling his hair and talking to him in wolf-language; the mountain rescue men taking him under their wing; Johnny Nutbrown not taking offence when this uncouth yokel punched him on the nose; Imogen pulling her clothes off on the mountain and inviting him to fuck her; and even after his disgrace, a hard-nosed cop like Davy McLucky finding something in this damaged paedophile to like and sympathize with. And Luke Hollins clearly took a more than pastoral interest in his new parishioner.

Then there was herself . . .

Doll, as if following her thoughts, said, 'Yes, and he might have lost an eye, a few fingers and his good looks, but it's still there, isn't it? Don't be ashamed of admitting it, dearie. Impossible not to like him, right? Well, imagine what he was like way back, a young lad adrift and in danger on the streets of wicked old London. Even if I hadn't liked him, it would have been hard to throw him back. But we couldn't keep him living with us for ever. It was before we bought this place. Tight little high-rise flat in Whitechapel. Lots of temptations there for the idle young. He needed a real job.'

'So what was it you found for him to do, Doll?' asked Alva, glad of a diversion from her own feelings for Hadda.

'Thing is,' said Doll, 'to get some idea about Wolf's job, you'll need to know a little about mine. As it was back then, I mean. Now, of course, I work with Ed. But my first connection with the law was I started out as a secretary to a barristers' clerk. Meaning I was mainly an office skivvy. Made a lovely cup of tea, though.'

She smiled reminiscently.

Alva said disbelievingly, 'You're not saying you got Wolf a job in a law office?'

'Not quite the way you mean it,' said Doll. 'Though he'd probably have done better than me eventually. To start with, I had ambitions to become a fully fledged clerk in a top chambers. Lot of money in that game, if you play your cards right. And despite them trying to keep me at the tea urn, I set out to learn the job; after a few years, I reckoned I was good enough to start applying for real clerks' jobs. Some hope! Talk about glass ceilings. This one was bulletproof and electrified at that! After a year of getting nowhere, I was ready to relocate to a cash desk in Tesco's. You ever feel like that, dearie?'

'I've been very lucky,' said Alva. 'But you kept out of Tesco's?'

'Yeah. That was down to Geoff Toplady. He was the one barrister in chambers I really got on with. At first I thought he was just after squeezing my tits. Didn't mind that, so long as he listened to my moans as he squeezed. One day he said if I fancied being more appreciated there was this outfit he knew about who were always looking for talent. I said, I don't fancy lap dancing, and he laughed and said no, this was very respectable, sort of the civil service really. Sorry, dearie, you want to say something?'

'This barrister, Geoff Toplady, he's not a judge now, is he?'

'The very same. Done well for himself, has Geoff. Up in the Appeal Court now. Sky's the limit for Geoff. You know him?'

'Not exactly. Sorry. Do go on.'

'Can't say I fancied being a civil servant, but anything was better than going nowhere, so I attended an interview Geoff set up. I soon realized I wasn't being invited to work in a Whitehall department, I was being recruited into something a lot less high profile. They knew everything about me. I'd filled in a form, told the usual lies, made the usual omissions. They picked them all out one by one, but they didn't seem to care. In fact they asked me if there was anything they'd missed that I'd managed to get past them!

'I was told if I got the job I'd need to sign the Official Secrets Act. They stressed this wasn't just a formality. If I contravened the Act, the consequences would be severe. Very severe. I believed them, and I've never stepped out of line. But I'm stepping across it now, ducks, so I hope your guide's honour is still intact!'

It wasn't Alva's honour that was being troubled, it was her credulity.

'You're telling me you were a spy or something glamorous like that?' said Alva with a scepticism that another woman might have found offensive.

All it got from Doll was another cockatoo screech.

'Glamorous, me? Don't be daft!! Worked in a run-down office in Clerkenwell. Can't tell you exactly where, or I'd have to kill you, but we referred to it as the Chapel, 'cos the building was converted from a disused Methodist chapel.'

'And Wolf worked in the office with you?' asked Alva, wondering what kind of undercover department took sixteen-year-old runaways on as office boys.

'Of course not,' said Doll impatiently. 'Just listen, will you?

409

Like I said, where I sat, the Chapel wasn't at all glamorous. But then, I wasn't out in the big wide world doing an Indiana Jones. I just sat at a computer, putting together bits and pieces of information.'

'What kind of information?' asked Alva.

'Oh, this and that,' said Doll vaguely. 'Pay wasn't all that good, but on the whole I enjoyed the work. We all like knowing things that other people don't. Must be the same in your job, dear. Maybe that's why we understand each other.'

'I wish,' said Alva. 'Did your husband work there too?'

'Ed? No. But it was through the Chapel we got together. After I'd been working for them a year, my boss, JC (not that one, ducks, nothing religious about the Chapel), told me the Chapel needed a solicitor they could use for the occasional job, someone too low profile to be noticed. He wondered if I'd come across anyone who might fit the bill during my time running errands at the chambers. Ed came into my mind, I don't know why. He was very small beer, but even small beer solicitors have clients who need big-time barristers occasionally. Specially the kind of clients Ed specialized in.'

'What kind was that?'

'Bankers *manqués*, Ed calls 'em. People who think other folks' money is better off in their pockets. Anyway, JC had him checked out. Later, when I got interested in Ed personally, I took a peek at the results. God help me, I suppose I knew more about the man I eventually married than any other woman in history!

'But you don't want a blow-by-blow account of our courting. Eventually I told JC we wanted to get married. He said he was fine with that, Ed had signed the Act too, and it was better for me not to have to lie about my job.

'We'd been married a couple of years when Wolf came

410

along. You've heard that story. Upshot was, I told JC all about the boy, said I wanted to find him a job, asked if JC had any advice. He said he'd like to meet Wolf, so one lunch hour we met up in a pub. JC was good at getting people to talk to him. He soon had Wolf eating out of the palm of his hand. And Wolf . . . well, as you know, he didn't have to work at being liked.

'A couple of days later JC told me it was fixed, said he'd arrange for Wolf to be picked up the following morning. And that's what happened. Next morning he packed the few bits and pieces we'd got for him while he was staying with us, thanked us both very much, and left. And that was the last we heard from him for a dozen years or more.'

Doll fell silent. Was it a painful memory? Or was she just trying to work out how much more she could tell?

Alva said casually, 'This JC, your boss. Were those his real initials by any chance?'

Doll gave her that shrewd look again and said, 'Can't tell you that, dearie. I'm already telling you a lot more than I should.'

Casual isn't going to get me anywhere, thought Alva. So let's try direct!

'OK,' she said. 'In order not to trouble your conscience, and in case we're being bugged, let me declare here and now that you have never told me anything to make me think this man JC's full name might be John Childs.'

For the first time, she felt she'd laid a glove on Doll Trapp.

'Well, you really are full of surprises,' she said. 'Interesting theory. I'd be careful who you share it with. Now, where was I?'

That's all the confirmation I'm going to get, thought Alva.

She said, 'You were telling me you got a boy you were concerned about a job with what sounds a very morally ambiguous organization run by a man whose sexual tastes incline to the Greek. Then you managed to lose contact with him for over a decade.'

She didn't try too hard not to sound accusatory.

Doll said defiantly, 'No moral ambiguity about the Chapel, ducks. That's for plonkers who don't care to know what the security services are doing, but are bloody glad to know they're doing it. As for the Greek stuff, no worries there. All in the mind with JC. Sublimation, isn't that what you people call it?'

She spoke with utter certainty. Alva felt she'd need several close consultations with Childs before she shared it. And in view of her growing suspicion just how completely she'd been deceived by Hadda, perhaps even that wouldn't be enough!

She said, 'You must surely have asked how Wolf was getting on?'

'Of course I did. JC would just smile and say, "Fine, fine. He's doing well."'

'And you were happy with that? What about records? They must have kept track of what their employees were up to.'

Doll grinned and said, 'I can see you're as nosey as I am, dear. That's why we get on so well. Yes, I did take the odd peek in some well-hidden corners of my computer.'

'And?'

'I can't be sure, they used codenames at the Chapel – claimed it was good security, but I reckon it was mainly like little boys liking nicknames! After a while I noticed references to someone tagged the Woodcutter. Could that be Wolf? I wondered. I recalled how it had amused my boss when he asked Wolf what else he could do besides climb vertical walls, and he said he could chop down trees.'

'Is that all? You didn't probe deeper?'

'Not wise in the Chapel, going where you didn't oughter,'

said Doll. 'If you really want to know what he did in his Chapel years, you'll have to ask him yourself.'

'I may do that,' said Alva. 'How did you and Wolf make contact again?'

Doll said, 'It was 2001. We'd been really busy in the Chapel since Labour got in and Tony started brown-nosing the Yanks. I worked longer and longer hours without really noticing. And that meant I didn't notice what was happening with Ed.

'His clients were always demanding. I don't know which were worse, the out-and-out villains or the poor bastards that life and circumstance were pushing under. He still got work from the Chapel from time to time, but that wasn't exactly stress-free either.

'To cut a long story short, Ed had a booze problem. I knew he liked a drink. OK, that's a long way from needing a drink, but there's an unbroken thread running between them, and I was too busy to see it being spun out.

'As he got more and more stressed out by his case-load, Ed turned to the booze to help him out. My wake-up call was finding a bottle of vodka hidden in the lavatory cistern. I confronted Ed with it. He denied all knowledge at first, but when that wouldn't wash, he denied it meant anything sinister. But now a whole pattern of behaviour began to make sense. I screamed at him like a fishwife. Not the clever thing to do. Knowing I knew meant he just didn't have to bother to hide the problem any more. After a particularly bad binge, I got him to promise he'd turn himself in to Alcoholics Anonymous. I stood over him while he rang up and arranged to go to a meeting with a counsellor. I'd have taken him there myself, but there was so much on at work. Big mistake. On his way to the meeting, he remembered he was representing a client at the magistrates' court.

'Hardly need tell you the rest. He took a couple of drinks

to steady his nerves. Then several more for no good reason other than he was a helpless piss-artist.

'Unfortunately no one spotted how rat-arsed he was before he got into the court. He made a real idiot of himself. When the magistrate told him to sit down, he became abusive. And when the court bailiff tried to escort him out, he became violent.

'It made all the papers. Looked like the end of his career. He'd be charged, fined, even imprisoned, certainly disbarred. I think he was suicidal. I know I was.

'And then this fifty-thousand-pound car pulls up outside our house and out steps this smart young fellow in a three-thousand-pound suit and when I open the door he takes me in his arms, gives me a big kiss and says, "Hello, Doll. You're looking great."

'It was Wolf. Or as he was now, Sir Wilfred Hadda. He'd read about Ed in the morning papers, cancelled everything and headed straight round to see us.

'I still can't believe what he did, I still don't know how he did it. But in a couple of days it had ceased to be a scandal. Ed was some kind of modern saint who'd broken down under the pressure of too many good works; the magistrate was happy, the Law Society was happy, and best of all Ed was shut away in the country's top addiction clinic, receiving film-star-level treatment for his alcoholism.

'So there you are, my dear,' concluded Doll Trapp. 'If you can't see now why we know Wolf has to be totally inno-cent of all those dreadful things they sent him down for, then maybe you should retrain for another line of work!'

6

John Childs sat in his study working on his book.

At the head of a fresh sheet of paper he wrote *Chapter 97* in the same immaculate hand with which he had inscribed *Chapter 1* nearly forty years ago. Sometimes he looked back a trifle ruefully at his chosen title, *A Brief History of the Phoenician People*, but a delicate sense of irony prevented him from changing it.

A man as meticulous in thought as in script, he calculated that his *Brief History* would take another seventeen years to complete. If he, and the market for books like his, survived till then, he did not anticipate troubling the bestseller lists. In fact it amused him to think that his largest readership might prove to be those colleagues from departments cognate with his own who had been clandestinely checking out the script from time to time just to make sure he wasn't composing a *roman à clef*.

Something scratched against the window pane. He rose to draw back the curtains and open the French window leading on to a small balcony overlooking Regent's Park.

'You could just have rung the bell,' he said.

Wolf Hadda stepped into the room.

'Hello, JC,' he said. 'I needed the exercise.'

The two men looked at each other critically.

'You've aged,' said Hadda.

'And you have . . . well, you look better than you ought to,' said Childs. 'From all accounts you are extremely fit. Does your training regime permit alcohol?'

'In moderation.'

'Then let me get you a moderate scotch. Have a seat.'

Hadda sank into a recliner chair and spun round to take in the whole room. His gaze ran along the photos on the wall – Childs Senior in tropical kit, looking very serious; a boy he knew to be John Childs standing with a young Arab who had his arm round his shoulder; and then the young men, some casual, some formal; and among them a gap.

'*Et tu Brute*,' he said. 'I see I've been banished.'

'What? Ah, yes. A temporary security precaution. Here, let me remedy it.'

He handed Hadda a glass and opened a drawer in his desk. Then he paused, frowning for a moment as if something about the contents had caught his eye. Finally he took out a framed photograph and went to hang it in the space on the wall.

'There,' he said. 'All as it should be.'

'Yes, nothing changed. A few more photos, of course. And the manuscript pile looks a little thicker. The Phoenicians doing well, are they?'

'Steady progress,' said Childs, returning to his seat. 'You always had a good memory, Wolf.'

'Better than ever now, I find.'

'Then you will remember that I have never wished you anything but good.'

Hadda smiled and said, 'If wishes were horses, beggars would ride.'

'Is that one of your old Cumbrian saws?' said Childs. 'I

416

hope so. It seems to imply a recognition that grim necessity takes precedence over all things.'

'A heavy interpretation of one of my Great Aunt Carrie's favourite catchphrases. But, now I come to think of it, I seem to recall you pleaded grim necessity the first time the good you always wished me didn't come through.'

'True. Though in recompense I did help you instead to get your heart's desire.'

'And look how that turned out.'

Childs wrinkled his brow as though contemplating a close philosophical analysis of this proposition, but before he could speak, a mobile trembled in Hadda's pocket.

'Sorry,' he said, taking it out.

He examined the display then said, 'Excuse me,' and stepped back out on the balcony, pulling the window to behind him.

'Hi, Davy,' he said.

He listened for a few moments then smiled.

'She's nobody's fool. I'm sorry I had to make her mine. What to do? Well, you could gag her and lock her in the attic, I suppose. But failing that, I think the best thing is for you and Doll to tell her everything she wants to know. And you won't forget to withdraw your offer for Poynters? Good man. Cheers, Davy.'

He switched off and came back into the room.

'Sorry about that,' he said.

'That's OK. Especially as it seems to have been good news.'

'Still so easy to read, am I? Even with my rearranged face! Ah well.'

He sat down again and took a sip of his drink.

'Now what were we talking about? Oh yes. Grim necessity. Which I presume was your reason for your decision not to intervene, even when you knew for certain I'd been fitted up. In fact, you chose to connive at making the cover up

417

water-tight. Necessity must have been really grim that week.'

'You were in an apparently moribund state. What good would it have done you to set about proving your innocence?'

'And when I came out of my moribund state?'

'Believe me, no one was happier to hear of your recovery than I,' said Childs. 'But once we'd started dabbling, there was no going back, you must see that. All I could do was keep a watchful eye on you. And a caring eye too.'

'You mean you were working behind the scenes for my release?' mocked Hadda.

'Pointless till you wanted to be released. And once you decided on that, you seemed quite capable of making your own ingenious arrangements.'

'You seem very well up on my activities,' said Hadda, frowning.

'Like I say, old acquaintance should not be forgot. And after your release, I was pleased to be able to squeeze a few journalistic scrota to keep the jackals from nipping too closely at your heels.'

'Yes, I did notice. I wondered why you should feel so obligated. Then of course I talked to Medler and found out just how great your obligation really was.'

Childs shrugged and said, 'It would have been easy to prevent your meeting Medler. But I felt you had a right to know everything, and you were more likely to believe what you heard from his lips than mine.'

'I suppose I was. Of course, once he'd talked to me, who knows who he might talk to next? But, happily for you, he had his accident. A form of accident that would put me in a poor light if ever I tried to make public anything poor Arnie might have told me.'

He stared at Childs significantly.

'Yes, there were certainly some at the Chapel who regarded

that as a happy coincidence,' said the other man blandly.

'Not so happy for that poor bastard,' said Wolf. 'And are there perhaps some Chapel-goers who reckon it could be an even happier coincidence if I followed Medler in very short order?'

John Childs sipped his whisky and said slowly, 'You've had trouble? Professional, I mean, not just the local vigilantes?'

'A little.'

'Then I'm glad that you worked out I was unlikely to be directly concerned.'

'Did I? Why do you say that?'

'Because you did not come through my window swinging your axe. What?'

Childs's sharp eyes had detected a reaction.

'Nothing.'

'Let me guess. You had a visitor and you did welcome him with your axe?'

'Visitors,' said Hadda. 'Two of them.'

'That explains it. One you can take alive, two make that less of an option.'

'What makes you think I didn't take them alive?'

'The degree of uncertainty about their origin. While being *almost* sure they weren't Chapel, you still had to ask. If you'd kept one of them alive, I think you'd have known where they came from.'

'Maybe not,' said Hadda irritably. 'I'm not such a cold bastard as you.'

'Yet, despite your inner warmth, they're both dead. How does that work, I wonder? But tell me about them.'

Hadda didn't deny it but explained what had happened.

'One of them was definitely one of the pair I took the drugs from on Drigg Beach,' he concluded. 'OK, so it's understandable that they would want revenge, but how did they get on to me so easily, that's what puzzles me. But I see it doesn't puzzle you, JC.'

Childs smiled and said, 'No, but not for the reason you are clearly suspecting. There was no tip-off from the Chapel. There didn't need to be. Have you ever heard of a man called Pavel Nikitin? I see you have.'

Hadda thought, the old sod still doesn't miss much!

He lied easily, 'Only because when I was talking recently to Luke Hollins, my local padre who takes a strong parochial interest in my affairs, he brought me up to date on matters he thought might interest me. These included a list of people who'd been staying at Ulphingstone Castle over Christmas. And one of them was a man with a name that sounded rather like your chap, Nikitin.'

Childs nodded and said, 'The same. He's a Russian businessman, one of those who rose stinking rich out of the wreckage of the old Soviet Union. Eventually, however, fearing that there were too many ex-comrades back in dear old Moscow who still subscribed to Marxist principles about sharing wealth, about five years ago he opted to settle in the West. He is currently pursuing an application for UK citizenship. With strong political support, I may add. For the very best of reasons, of course.'

'Like, he'd add so much to our cultural diversity? No? Then it must be because once he is accepted as a Brit cit, his wealth too becomes acceptable as political donation.'

'Spot on, as always,' applauded Childs.

'But I don't see how the Ulphingstones fit in here,' said Hadda. 'Leon is the least political person I know, and Kira believes that anyone who relies on a public vote for his power is a dangerous radical. So how come this Nikitin gets invited to stay at the castle?'

'Politically he is very much in sympathy with Lady Kira,' said Childs. 'More importantly, he claims to be distantly related to her. And as he's rich, personable, moves in the top circles, and has important people to stay at his various villas and on his luxury yacht, Lady Kira is happy to acknowledge the relationship. I would guess she sees in him a personification of all the old tsarist values so sadly destroyed in 1917.'

'Sounds just her cup of tea. But if you know so much about him, JC, there has to be more.'

'You know me too well,' murmured Childs. 'The details of the dubious means by which Nikitin made his Russian fortune, I don't know, but I do know the kind of business he has been investing in since coming to the West. Alongside some conventional and legitimate commercial interests, he has a well-balanced criminal portfolio ranging from people-trafficking through drug-dealing to illegal arms sales.'

'Jesus! And Sir Leon lets him into his house!' exclaimed Hadda.

'Now you're being silly. Why should Sir Leon know anything of this? Nikitin can afford the very best lawyers. Any hint of criticism in the media gets sat upon with all the weight of a very well-upholstered legal bum, belonging, as I suspect you know, to our mutual friend, Toby Estover.'

Hadda didn't deny it but said, 'So the drugs I intercepted were Nikitin's?'

'Of course. I suspect that during one of his visits to the castle it occurred to him that parts of the Cumbrian coast-line offered an ideal location for the safe landing of a not-too-bulky illicit cargo. I doubt he'll be using it again.'

'But it doesn't explain how he got on to me so quick. And I still don't understand what he was doing at the castle. OK, I can see Kira falling over herself backwards to get an invite to one of his swell parties. But why the hell would he be willing to accept her invitation to stay at the castle? I used to start yawning as I passed through the door!'

'You're forgetting the Estover connection.'

'You mean Toby introduced him? But that still doesn't explain . . .'

'There's more than one Estover,' said Childs.

It took a moment to sink in.

'*What?*'

'Oh dear. Now I'm really glad you didn't bring your axe. I'm not suggesting that the lovely Imogen was party to the attempt on your life, though why it should bother you so much if she were, I'm not quite sure . . .'

He looked invitingly at Hadda, who brushed aside the implied question and said, 'So what are you saying, JC?'

'Just that it seems Nikitin has taken a very strong fancy to Mrs Estover. Once he realized her mother's background was Russian, he doubtless dug till he discovered, or perhaps he even invented, the family connection. Once he met Kira and saw what she was, he set about making her an ally.'

'And Imogen, does she . . .?'

'I've no idea whether he is her lover or not. But he will know all about you, if not from one or both of the Estovers, certainly from Lady Kira, who is not averse to telling the world that letting you out of jail to settle in such close proximity to Ulphingstone Castle was an outrage to human decency. So Nikitin would have known more than he perhaps cared to know about this large, lame, one-eyed woodcutter who was presented as a threat to the woman he loves. And when his men reported to him that his drugs consignment had been hijacked and destroyed by a large, lame, one-eyed man with an axe . . . well, he knew exactly where to find you, and now he had two reasons, one commercial and one sentimental, for wanting to get rid of you.'

Wolf said, 'So why does the Chapel let this bastard wander around free?'

'Our concern is with national security, not supra-national criminality.'

'You could pass what you know to the police.'

Childs said, 'Who would do what with it? I doubt if it would even come to trial. He is well protected. Objections to his citizenship application have already been dealt with by Mr Estover with his usual silky efficiency, by his friends in high places with their usual winks and nods, and, where persistent, by Nikitin himself with ruthless brutality.'

'You could always fit him up,' said Hadda. 'You're good at that.'

'We'd need to catch him with a body at his feet and blood on his hands,' said Childs. 'Be careful of him, Wolf. He will not be happy that his men have not returned. And the man whose jaw you broke is still alive and he's the worst of the lot. His name is Pudovkin, known to his friends as Pudo. You did well to put him out of commission first, but you would have done better to put him out permanently. He is Nikitin's chief attack dog. You were lucky he was probably still recovering from his experience on Drigg Beach when Nikitin decided to have you taken out.'

Hadda shrugged indifferently and said, 'Maybe he was lucky. It occurs to me, JC, that maybe it's really Estover you're protecting here. That deal you did with him, the deal that put me in Parkleigh for seven years, remember? Access to all his confidential files on all his high-profile clients – how far would you go to protect that?'

'Not perhaps as far as you think,' said Childs. 'In my opinion, Estover is rather *passé* as a source. His loss would leave a very small hole that could easily be filled.'

'So if someone did move to sort him out, you wouldn't be too bothered?'

'Personally, not at all. So long as it was done with discretion.'

'Meaning the Chapel is kept right out of the frame,' laughed Wolf. 'How much do you think Imogen knows about Toby's work?'

'It's hard to say. She is not, so I gather, easy to read. But I need not tell you that. Have you spoken to her yet?'

'Why would I want to talk to her?'

'Wolf, I wish I could tell you how complicit she was in the plot to frame you, but I can't. You must find that out for yourself. To do that, you need perhaps to talk. Or are you afraid of what you might do? Or of what you might not be able to do . . .?'

'Don't try to play your old mind games, JC,' said Hadda.

'No? I thought you were quite partial to playing mind games, Wolf.'

Hadda looked at him sharply, but that bland, amiable face gave nothing away.

'I'll talk to Imogen when I'm ready,' he said.

'Of course you will,' said Childs. 'Now, before you go, is there anything more I can do for you? Don't be afraid to ask.'

Hadda regarded him dubiously then said, 'All right. Any chance of getting me details of the accounts where Nutbrown and Estover have stashed their ill-gotten gains?'

'Ah, the estimable Mrs Trapp is having a problem there, is she? Curious how lawyers protect their own secrets so much more vigorously than they do their clients'! Of course. Anything else?'

'You're being very helpful, JC. You must really be feeling guilty!'

Childs said, 'Perhaps. Though of course I shouldn't. My part in your troubles was late and slight, and based on the happily false intelligence that you were as good as dead. In a sense, we are both victims of accident and grim necessity.'

'Our old friends, eh? I recall what you said when you

introduced them to me way back. Something about love always losing out, I think.'

'I believe I told you that one day you would understand what I meant. I suspect that day is now well behind you.'

'Why do you say that? Nothing's happened to me by accident, except perhaps . . .' he raised his maimed hand to his scarred face and smiled '. . . my accident. As for grim necessity conflicting with love, that happily is a choice I shall never have to make.'

'Really? And how do you propose avoiding it?'

'By avoiding them. By controlling my life from now on in.'

'And you think that's possible? Perhaps it is, but only if you have extremely rare qualities . . . practically unique . . . let me see, I think I can lay my hands on it . . .'

He rose and went to his bookshelf, took down a volume and riffled through it.

'Yes, here it is: *Necessity and Chance approach not me, and what I will is Fate.*'

'That sounds about right,' said Hadda. 'You could have taken the words out of my mouth. Whose mouth did you take them out of?'

'Milton's,' said Childs, holding the volume up so that Hadda could read the title.

'*Paradise Lost*,' said Hadda. 'Never read it. But in my case, it seems pretty appropriate. And whose mouth did Milton put these words in?'

'You should be careful, Wolf,' said Childs. 'It was God's.'

7

There was so much to take in that Alva sat back in her chair and closed her eyes to concentrate on arranging it all into a meaningful pattern. But all she could see was Wolf Hadda laughing when she quoted the *Observer* article that suggested he'd been kidnapped by the fairies, then smiling mockingly as he claimed that, like True Thomas, he too came back unable to tell a lie.

Inside, he must have laughed quite a lot more as he led her along the fallacious road to his rehabilitation.

She opened her eyes. Doll Trapp's face wore an expression of serene confidence. She clearly believed that she had proved Hadda's innocence beyond all doubt. For a second Alva was tempted to point out that being very good in one area didn't preclude being very bad in another. Human beings were much more complex than that.

Instead she said, 'You'd never noticed that Sir Wilfred Hadda, the millionaire businessman, was one and the same as your own Wolf the Woodcutter?'

'No,' said Doll. 'Never paid much attention to the business news, or the gossip columns for that matter.'

Alva wasn't sure if she believed her.

'Fine,' she said. 'Funny though that Wolf didn't get in touch with you himself when he came to live in London.'

Doll laughed and said, 'Not really. I suspect JC had told him it wouldn't do me any good if he tried to renew the connection.'

'Why would he say that?'

'He's a very careful man,' said Doll.

'So why did Wolf renew the connection?' asked Alva.

'That's the kind of guy he is,' said Doll. 'Wolf might have stayed away from paying a social call because he was warned off for my sake, but it would have taken an SAS regiment to keep him away when he heard that Ed was in serious shit.'

'Couldn't your friends at the Chapel have helped sort it out?'

'JC was the first person I turned to,' said Doll grimly. 'He said they already had a watching brief on the situation and, if it got worse, the Chapel might have to protect itself. I got the message. They don't like publicity. Any sniff of Ed's connection with the Chapel, they'd treat like a gas leak: cut it off at the source. No, if it hadn't been for Wolf . . . Anyway when it was all done, I resigned. Didn't go down too well and I didn't get a leaving prezzie unless you count a blunt reminder that the Official Secrets Act was operative till the end of time! I didn't give a toss! I knew that Ed was going to need me close from now on in, so I went back to being a paralegal and kept his business ticking over till he came back to work.'

'And Wolf, how strong were his links with the Chapel at that point, do you think?'

'Don't know, didn't want to know. But, international businessman with contacts everywhere, I'm sure they'd have wanted to use him.'

'So how might they have reacted when his troubles started?'

Doll said, 'Their main concern would have been that something might come out that tracked back to them. Like with Ed, but Wolf was a lot more significant, of course.'

'You sound bitter,' said Alva, who saw no reason not to be as direct with Doll as she was with her.

'Do I? Then I'm being silly. No taste for sentimental mush at the Chapel.'

The kind of mush that made you help a kid in trouble, the kind that brought that same kid riding to the rescue when you and Ed got in trouble, thought Alva.

She said, 'They say in politics that loyalty's a one-way street. So you no longer have any contact with the Chapel?'

'Last time I heard from them was when Ed started acting for Wolf. Phone rang. It was JC. I thought at first he was going to try and warn us off acting for Wolf. Instead, when I told him how bad things were, what with the strong evidence and Wolf's state of mind, he sounded genuinely upset. I made it clear I believed absolutely in Wolf's innocence and he said, "So do I, Doll. So do I. But in this wicked world, innocence is sometimes not enough." And that was that.'

'No offer of assistance then?'

'No way! But at least after talking to him I felt sure it wasn't the Chapel who'd set Wolf up. Not directly, anyway. I know now they got their finger in the pie later.'

Alva made a note of that for future exploration, but she wanted to get the basic picture clear to start with.

'What made you consider the possibility that it was the Chapel setting him up?'

Doll shrugged and said, 'Wolf's a man who likes to make his own choices. Like he did with Ed. If he'd done something that really got their knickers in a twist, the Chapel would have been quite willing and able to put him out of commission. Only it would probably have been less round-the-houses. Car accidents – they were very good at car accidents. So maybe he was lucky.'

'Lucky? You call getting banged up for something you didn't do lucky?' said Alva.

Doll seemed to take this as a reproof.

'We did everything we could for him,' she said angrily. 'Trouble was, back then Wolf just didn't want to know. Imo divorcing him and marrying Estover, his friends deserting him, the accident crippling him. It was all too much. And it didn't stop when he got to jail. First his old dad died, then his daughter. It was like Wolf had died himself.'

'I believe Ginny's death was the trigger that brought him back to life,' said Alva.

'Oh yes? Well, that's your line of country, isn't it? Ed did all he could, and went on trying to find out what was really going on long after Wolf went down. But we're not detectives, and it's hard helping someone who doesn't want to be helped. We thought he was just going to rot inside for the whole length of his sentence. So when he got in touch and asked Ed to help him with the parole hearing, we were really delighted.'

'But weren't you surprised?' asked Alva. 'Ed must have told you that the whole basis of that hearing was his full and frank acknowledgement of his guilt and his willingness to undertake a course of remedial therapy.'

Doll laughed and asked, 'How else was he going to get out, dearie?'

Then she stopped laughing and looked at Alva pityingly.

'I'm sorry. It must have been a real shock to find out how he'd fooled you. But what else could he do when he realized the only way to get out early was getting you to testify that he was no longer a danger to anyone? He had to use you. You must see that.'

Alva nodded, unable to trust herself to speak. Being fooled

was an occupational hazard; every therapy session with a patient was to some extent a contest in manipulation; but to feel personally betrayed was irrational, as if they'd been in some sort of relationship other than therapeutic.

Doll reached over and patted her on the shoulder.

'Don't take it to heart, dearie,' she said. 'He'd have tricked his own mother if that's what had been needed to get him out.'

Alva was back in control now.

She drew away and said, 'What bothers me is that he felt that getting out was worth admitting to the world he was as bad as he'd been painted. He's not interested in proving his innocence, is he? All he wants to do is take revenge on the people he blames for putting him inside.'

Looking uneasy for the first time, Doll said, 'It's not quite like that. What he wants is to find out the exact truth of what happened.'

'And then he'll apply to get his case reviewed, is that what you're telling me?'

Doll shook her head and said, 'No. You've met him, ducks. You know what he's like. And I don't blame him, whatever he does. So long as it's based on the facts.'

She spoke defiantly. She's got reservations too, thought Alva.

She said, 'So how does he intend to get these facts?'

'Oh, he's done that already,' said Doll. 'We're well in to phase two now.'

'Phase two! For God's sake, tell me about phase one before we go there!'

Doll said, 'We're really getting to the edge of girl scout country here, dearie.'

Here it comes! thought Alva. She'd known from the start that sooner or later they were going to leave the ambiguous territory in which she could still persuade herself that keeping silent was a matter of personal choice. Now she was at the border.

She said carefully, 'If Wolf has committed or is planning to commit an act of violence, then I will have no choice but to call in the authorities. But peccadilloes such as breaking the strict terms of his parole licence won't bother me.'

'Great,' said Doll. 'In that case it won't bother you to learn that Wolf went to Spain over Christmas. There was an ex-cop living there, the one who arrested him. He thought he might know something that could help.'

'You mean,' said Alva, 'that while Wolf was supposed to be staying with you over Christmas he was actually out of the country? And you helped him and covered up for him? You realize how much trouble you could be in?'

'Ed's a lawyer,' said Doll indifferently. 'Look, Wolf thought it might help if he talked to this ex-cop, Arnie Medler, who lived in Spain, so that's where Wolf had to go.'

Medler. The name rang a bell. This was the arresting officer that Hadda had assaulted. Twice.

'And did it help?' she asked.

'Oh yes. Wolf told Ed that Medler had been able to confirm a lot of what he suspected. And he got it all recorded. You can listen to the recording, if you like.'

'I will do,' said Alva. 'Me and the authorities too. That should do the trick.'

But Doll was shaking her head.

'Wish it was so simple, ducks. Thing is, not long after Wolf left him, this guy Medler had an accident and died. That's really muddied the water.'

This got worse. Hadda leaves the country illegally to visit an ex-cop he thinks might be withholding information and now the cop is dead. Alva knew how it sounded to her, so she didn't have to take time out to guess how it would sound to the authorities.

'How did Medler die?' she asked.

'His wife found him early on Christmas morning. He'd got so pissed he fell forward unconscious with his arm stretched out across the threshold of his patio door. He must have touched some control panel as he fell. Result, as he lay there some heavy security shutters came down. Chopped his hands right off. He'd bled to death.'

'Oh Jesus,' said Alva aghast. Just when you thought you'd hit rock bottom, the ground opened up again.

'Yeah, I know,' said Doll. 'You're thinking *Woodcutter*. But it's not Wolf's style, ducks. Might have chopped the bastard's head off, if he deserved it, but not his hands!'

She seemed to think this comment should be reassuring. Alva did not find it so.

She said, 'So what do you and Ed do when someone turns up with their head chopped off?'

Doll regarded her quizzically as if wondering whether the first of Wolf Hadda's suggested methods for dealing with her might not have been the better option.

The door opened and Ed Trapp looked in and tapped his watch significantly.

'I think that'll do to be going on with, dear,' said Doll. 'You'll want to get home to listen to that tape and I've got work to do.'

Ed was holding the door open invitingly.

'I'll walk you back to your car,' he said.

They walked to the Fiesta in silence. As she unlocked the door, Trapp said gently, 'Don't worry about Wolf, Dr Ozigbo. He'd never hurt anyone that was innocent.'

'How can you be so sure?'

'There's something in him, connected with something that happened a long time ago, I think. Maybe he did once. He won't do it again.'

'He shouldn't be thinking about hurting anyone, Mr Trapp.

Innocence, guilt, punishment, that's the Law's job. You of all people should know that.'

He smiled at her rather sadly.

'Should I?' he said. 'When the Law kept an innocent man banged up for seven years despite anything I could do? When the only way he could get out was to deceive a woman he likes and respects? Should I? Good night, Dr Ozigbo.'

She got in her car and drove home.

She tried to put everything she had just heard into some sort of order, but every third thought took her back to Mr Trapp's parting words.

A woman he likes and respects.

That had to mean something!

But not, she thought, all that much. Not while the memory of Imogen Ulphingstone was still burnt on his soul like a shadow on a wall left by an atomic explosion.

8

Monday morning dawned bright and very cold, with frost scaling the window panes and highlighting the bare twigs and branches of the trees and shrubbery in the grounds of Poynters.

'Where are you going, Johnny?' demanded Pippa Nutbrown.

'Just for a stroll through the spinney,' said her husband. 'Thought I'd see if I could pick up a rabbit.'

Pippa looked in scorn at the shotgun he carried broken in the crook of his arm.

'As much chance of you coming back with a Siberian tiger,' she said.

'Sorry, old girl, was there something you wanted me to do?'

'Don't be stupid,' she snapped dismissively. 'What the hell would I want you to do that I can't do better myself?'

Nutbrown could think of one thing but he knew better than to say it. Best policy was to make yourself scarce when Pippa was in one of her moods, which she seemed to be most of the time recently. It was a couple of weeks since she'd announced that she'd given Skinners their marching orders and done a private deal with Donald Murray. The news had filled Nutbrown with a dismay that not even his wife's delight could compensate for. But as the days went by and she heard nothing more from Murray, her mood began to darken while her husband's spirits began to rise, though he was careful not to let her see this.

As he walked away from the house, he began to whistle 'Happy Days Are Here Again', though not till he was sure he was out of earshot. He had neither the will nor the guile to resist Pippa's insistence that they should sell Poynters and go to live abroad, but he did have a deep-rooted conviction that this was never going to happen. No logical basis, of course, but nothing new there! His motto had always been, Take the line of least resistance and generally speaking things would work out for the best.

He entered the spinney. The winter sun could hardly penetrate here and the temperature dropped by several degrees. He heard a twig crack and paused. All was silent again. Pity. It would be nice to surprise Pippa and actually come back with something in his game bag. The trouble was, on the odd occasion he'd managed to get something in his sights, he'd rarely been able to bring himself to shoot it. The wild creatures here were also inhabitants of Poynters and deserved as much as he did to pass their lives untroubled.

But not perhaps all of them.

Something growled, a deep threatening rumble, and standing at a bend in the track about fifty feet ahead he saw a dog.

Johnny Nutbrown quite liked dogs. (Pippa didn't, so there were none at Poynters.) But this didn't look like the kind of dog you called *Hey boy!* to and ruffled its ears when it came running up to you, tail wagging. It stood quite still. What light there was under the tree glinted off its yellowing teeth and from its eyes that seemed to have a reddish glow as they focused unblinkingly on the approaching man.

He clicked the shotgun barrel into place.

The beast's ears pricked. It let out one last growl that had something of a promissory note in it, then turned and vanished.

Slowly, still holding the gun at the ready, he advanced round the bend.

And halted.

The dog was there, lying across the feet of a man sitting on the trunk of a fallen tree. If anything, with his scarred face and a patch over his right eye, he looked even more menacing than the dog. Alongside him, resting against the trunk, stood a long-handled axe.

The man spoke.

'When I was a lad, I got taught never to point a gun at anything I wasn't going to use it on.'

Nutbrown took a step closer and said, 'Good God, is that you, Wolf?'

'Who else? Been a long time, Johnny.'

'Too long, Wolf,' said Nutbrown fervently, lowering the gun. 'It's great to see you!'

Wolf Hadda laughed. He hadn't been sure what reaction to expect; certainly not this one, but, now he'd heard it, nothing else seemed possible. He shifted to make room beside him on the trunk. The dog growled as Nutbrown sat down, but ceased at a warning nudge from his master's foot.

'Been here long?' asked Nutbrown, resting his shotgun against the fallen tree. 'Jesus, you must be frozen! You should have come up to the house.'

'I don't think so, Johnny.'

Nutbrown considered then nodded.

'Probably right. Pippa's got a bit of a bee in her bonnet about you, I'm afraid.'

'Really? Now why should that be, do you think?'

'Well, she seems to think there could be some bad blood

between us, after everything that happened, don't you know?'

'Everything that happened,' echoed Hadda. 'That's really what I came to talk to you about, Johnny. Everything that happened. I'd just like to understand it from your point of view, if you've got the time, that is.'

'Of course. Gent of leisure these days. But let's not freeze altogether. Try a nip of this.'

He produced a hip flask, opened it and passed it to Hadda. He took a long pull of the liquor, rolled it round in his mouth, then swallowed.

'Still nothing but the best, Johnny.'

'What else is there? Cheers!'

'Cheers. So, from the beginning, Johnny.'

Nutbrown took another drink as if, despite his apparent ease of manner, he needed a little booster for an imminent ordeal. Or perhaps, thought Hadda, it simply is against the cold.

'Well, it was all that money swilling around,' he began. 'Those were golden days, do you remember, Wolf? And you had the golden touch. It was like taking buckets of water out of a bottomless pond. An endless supply. Impossible to leave a hole!'

'So you helped yourself, is that what you're saying, Johnny?'

'No. Well, yes. But not really. You always saw to it that I had plenty, Wolf. But Toby and Pippa, they felt that you weren't making the most of your opportunities. A wise man fills his boots while he's still got boots to fill, that was how Toby put it. And Pippa agreed. Toby took care of the legal side and Pippa's always been a whiz with computers.'

'And you, Johnny?'

'They needed me to run the figures. Complex business keeping things in balance, you see. My sort of thing. I could hardly say no when Pippa and Toby asked. And they would have brought you in, Wolf, really they would. Only Toby said that, despite you marrying Imo and all, you still had this working-class thing about wealth, and it was best to keep you out for your own sake. Me, I thought it was a load of bollocks, I knew you were one of us from the start, but they insisted that it was best for us to make sure you got your share without you knowing.'

'And you went along with them?'

'All got a bit complicated for me, Wolf. Figures, fine. But forward planning, not my scene. Though, way back in 2006, I did get a feeling things were going pear-shaped.'

'You foresaw the financial crisis as far back as that?' said Hadda. 'Didn't you think it might be worth mentioning it to me?'

'I did, I did,' said Nutbrown indignantly. 'But you were always busy busy, Wolf. And when you did listen, you just laughed and said we were in happy-ever-after land, these were the sunny uplands, no one was ever going to drive us out of here. And I thought, Good old Wolf, it's down to him that I'm so comfortably placed, he always gets things right.'

Hadda regarded him sadly and asked, 'Did I really say that, Johnny? Yes, I believe I did. That's what I thought back then. Maybe you should have kept on at me. Punched me in the nose, maybe. You owed me one.'

Nutbrown laughed, a merry note, and said, 'Yes, I did, didn't I? Still do, I suppose.'

'No, Johnny,' said Hadda gently. 'Not any more. So who else did you try to warn?'

'Pippa, of course. Not a warning as such, just chat over the breakfast table. Ignored me at first. What's new? But once the US housing bubble began to burst, anyone with any sense could see what was coming.'

'Pity you weren't Chancellor,' said Hadda. 'And Pippa started listening?'

'Still told me not to be stupid. But this time she gave Toby a bell and he came round and asked me what it was all about.'

'And what did you tell him, Johnny?'

'I said I thought it might be a good idea to do a bit of forward planning. First thing was to make sure that our little nest eggs were tucked away safe. I made a few suggestions, but he really sat up and took notice when I told him that he ought to have a word with you because, when the markets hit the skids, it was going to be impossible to carry on hiding what we'd been doing. Like I say, a few bucketfuls from a big pond no one notices, but once the pond starts drying up . . .'

'I've got the picture,' said Hadda. 'But Toby didn't take your advice.'

'About placing our money, he did,' said Johnny. 'But as to putting you in the picture, he said he'd need to think about it.'

'I bet. And what was the result of his thinking?'

'No idea,' said Johnny cheerfully. 'I mentioned it to Pippa, but she just said it was in hand. Toby too. When I mentioned you, he said everything was hunky-dory. Finally things began to slowly unravel, just like I'd said. I thought, Good old Wolf will be taking care of things as far as Woodcutter's concerned. Next thing I hear is that they're doing you for looking at mucky pictures on your computer or something.'

'No, Johnny,' said Hadda gently. 'I think the next thing you heard was me on the phone asking you to meet me at The Widow.'

'That's right. Only I was in the office and there was this cop there and he sort of listened in. He asked me where The Widow was and I said, "Everyone knows The Widow!" And he said he didn't, so naturally I told him. Then I got up to leave, but he said I shouldn't bother, it was best for you if one of their chaps went there to meet you. I wasn't all that happy about it, you understand, Wolf. But what could I do?'

Hadda took the flask from Nutbrown's hand and took another long pull. It wasn't against the cold.

'And then?' he said softly.

'Next thing, you're in hospital, on life support, bulletins lousy. Not long after, the banks start going bellyside up, shares drop like a donkey's bollocks, and the Fraud Squad's crawling all over Woodcutter like bluebottles round an open dustbin.'

'And they found . . .?'

For the first time, Nutbrown was looking a little uneasy.

'They found shortfalls, Wolf. I mean, they were bound to. Would have been all right if the good times had continued. We were always well ahead of the game. Would be all right now with everything back to where it was, more or less. But back then there was nowhere to hide.'

'Yet somehow you managed it, Johnny. You hid so well no one even came looking for you. How did you manage that?'

'Just lucky, I suppose.'

He sounded as if he really believed it, thought Hadda. Perhaps he did. And perhaps in his own terms he was lucky. Lucky to exist in an impermeable bubble where thoughts of loyalty, morality, friendship could not penetrate and in which the only reality was his own well being, comfort and survival. He felt no guilt about what had happened, just a touch of regret. While the news of his early release had clearly caused the others considerable disquiet, Johnny's reaction was mild relief that his old friend was free again so no need to worry about that any more!

'But you and Toby must have got your story all neatly prepared,' he said.

Nutbrown nodded emphatically as he replied, 'Oh yes. Toby was marvellous. Had them eating out of his hands. Don't know what I'd have done without him beside me.'

'What a pity I didn't have him beside me as well,' said Hadda. 'When they piled all that shit on top of me, I mean.'

'What? Look, Wolf, I can see how it must look to you. But be fair, by then you were as good as dead, no point in trying to protect your good name, impossible to do that anyway without getting Toby sent down for yonks. Pippa too, maybe. Wouldn't have wanted to see Pippa in jail, would you? No allowances made for women these days!'

This attempt to appeal to his sense of chivalry almost brought a smile to Hadda's lips. He noted also that Nutbrown didn't offer as argument the certainty that he would have been sent down too. Could he really believe he was in some way invulnerable?

He said, 'You didn't say any of this when you came to see me, Johnny. You could see I was alive and breathing then. You had a chance to protect this good name of mine you were so worried about.'

'Not true,' said Nutbrown eagerly. 'Not with that other business hanging over you, and all the papers saying they'd got you bang to rights over that. Besides, everything was signed, sealed and delivered by then. Statements on tape, in writing, even video. And the books had been gone over with a fine-tooth comb, all done and dusted. Too late to turn back the clock, Wolf. Like Toby said, you were a cooked goose. But I did come to see you, didn't I? I really got a bollocking from Pippa when she found out. Toby wasn't best pleased either. But I told them, I owed you a lot, couldn't have lived with myself if I hadn't paid a visit.'

Just when you thought you'd reached the limits of Nutbrown's moral vacuity, you found you were still floating in space!

He said, 'Don't think I'm not grateful, Johnny. So, do you see much of Imo? How's she doing?'

'Oh, fine, fine,' said Johnny, relief at the change of subject manifest on his face. 'Don't see a lot of her, to tell the truth. Pippa and her have a girls' lunch from time to time. She always sends her love.'

'To you, you mean?'

'Well, yes . . . I mean she'd hardly send it to . . . oh, you're having a joke. Ha ha.'

'If you can't take a laugh, you shouldn't have joined, eh, Johnny? As a matter of interest, how much did Imo know about your special financial arrangements at Woodcutter before the tide went out and left all the shit visible on the shore?'

He spoke as casually as he could but a more perceptive man might have noticed the tension in his voice.

'Nothing, not at all, you've nothing to worry about there, Wolf,' said Nutbrown reassuringly. 'No, she wasn't in on any of that. But once we started looking for a way round things, then she had to be told, of course.'

'Why was that?' asked Hadda.

'Look, there was trouble coming, I could see that a long way off. Like I said, I had a hard time convincing Toby and Pippa; they're great at managing things, but when it comes to economics . . .'

He smiled tolerantly. To survive, everyone needs a viewpoint from which they can look down on everyone else, thought Hadda. With some it's intellect, with some it's beauty, with some it's religion.

What is it with me?

Vengeance, came the uncomfortable answer.

'I'm not quite sure I understand,' he said. 'Why Imo had to be told, I mean.'

'If you'd grown up around her like the rest of us did,

you'd know,' said Johnny. 'Any plans we made, if Imo was for them, they worked; if she wasn't interested, they might limp along; but if she was against them, then you were in real shit.'

'So you invited my wife to join in the plot to offload all the blame on to me, right?'

'No, Wolf, it wasn't as simple as that,' said Nutbrown, eager to explain. 'I mean, it wasn't as if you weren't going to be right at the front when the shit hit the fan, was it?'

'I'm sorry?' said Hadda, not believing what he was hearing.

'Well, you were the man in charge, weren't you? Woodcutter was your baby. No way was anyone going to believe you didn't know what was going on. I remember thinking to myself, surely Wolf's got to notice what we're doing!'

There was a note of reproach in his voice. Don't let yourself be provoked! thought Wolf.

Perhaps he even had a point!

'Maybe because I trusted my friends just a little too much,' he said.

'Well, yes, there was that,' said Nutbrown, sounding a little uncomfortable but not too much. 'So look at it from our point of view, Wolf. You were going to get it in the neck anyway, you were the boss man, you were responsible. There didn't seem to be any point in the rest of us catching it too.'

'And Imo agreed with this?'

'Oh yes. After Toby and Pippa explained it to her.'

'You weren't there?'

'No. Didn't seem any point in crowding her.'

'Very considerate,' said Hadda. 'Did you get the impression she took a lot of persuading?'

'Not really. Not once she understood about the money.'

'Which money?'

'The money we'd put aside,' said Johnny patiently, as if

443

explaining to a child. 'The point was, once the dropping markets left us exposed, Woodcutter was dead in the water. You were going to be the Fraud Squad's main man. All your assets would be seized and ultimately disposed of. The only money from the business that would survive were the funds that Toby and me had diverted.'

He said it as if expecting congratulation.

'And if the investigation had you and Toby in their sights, they wouldn't rest till they got a line on that,' said Hadda slowly. 'And even if they couldn't, they'd make sure it was a hell of a long time before you could hope to enjoy it.'

'That's right. So you see, it was a no-brainer for Imo. Whatever happened, you were going down. At least if we stayed out of the frame, she wouldn't be destitute.'

'How much did she ask for?'

'Half. I think Pippa wanted to haggle, but Toby said there was no point.'

He was right, thought Hadda bitterly. They were lucky she left them anything.

And anyway, Toby was probably already mapping out the future. Mastermind the divorce first, then marry her. But if he thought that was going to regain him full access to his ill-gotten gains, he clearly didn't know her as well as he thought!

Unlike himself, who clearly didn't know her at all.

Or perhaps he knew her all too well but had never systematized his knowledge.

She had set him three goals as the price of her hand. A fortune, an education, a social polish. He'd gone away a poor ignorant clod and he'd come back, if not yet a wealthy civilized gent, certainly a piece of malleable clay she could mould into shape.

She'd kept her side of the bargain, more or less. And now she was told that he was reneging on his. Didn't matter that

444

losing his wealth wasn't his fault, obtaining it had been part of the contract.

Was that all their marriage had ever amounted to? It hadn't felt like that. But what had it felt like?

It certainly hadn't felt like she was shagging away behind his back. Yet from the sound of it . . .

He said, 'So things fell out all right for her all round, didn't they? I mean, her and Toby getting together like they did. Things going well there, are they?'

'Seem to be,' said Nutbrown. 'They have their ups and downs, I expect. Don't we all? And you know Toby, he likes his office comforts. Pippa says she'd cut his balls off, but it doesn't seem to bother Imo. Of course, they've known each other a long time.'

'That's true. You were all chums together long before I came on the scene. So how long had they been at it, would you say?'

This time enough of his feelings came through to pierce even the Nutbrown carapace of insensibility.

'Come on, Wolf, no point dwelling on the past, all water under the bridge, eh?'

'Of course it is. Still, just as a point of interest, how long would you say?'

'I don't know. I suppose, off and on for as long as I've known them. Never meant anything, they'd been chums for ever, it was the same for all of us . . .'

All of us! Had they all been at it? Trying each other out, exchanging notes . . .

Don't go down that road. Not now.

'Of course it was. So whenever any two of you met, if you had time on your hands you'd jump over the hedge for a quick one, right? Perfectly understandable behaviour. Among pack rats!'

The snarl in which he uttered the last phrase got Nutbrown

445

to his feet. At the sudden movement, the dog rose too, its teeth bared.

'Easy, Wolf. Don't lose your rag. I remember what you can be like. Don't want another bloody nose, eh?'

Hadda took a deep breath and even managed a smile as he stood up also.

'Don't worry, Johnny,' he said. 'I'm a changed man. We all are, aren't we? *Tempus fugit*. The past's dead, it's the future that matters.'

'You don't know how happy I am to hear you say that, Wolf,' said Nutbrown, looking genuinely relieved. 'Not that I had any doubt. I tried to tell the other two, there's nothing to worry about, let's just be glad Wolf's out of that dreadful place. Look, why don't you come back with me now, see Pippa, let her know that all this business about selling up and leaving the country's just a load of nonsense?'

'Very tempting,' said Hadda. 'But not today. Don't worry, I'll make sure that things are put right between me and Pippa some time very soon, OK? But maybe for the time being it's best not to mention you've met me. Let's pick our moment carefully.'

'If that's what you think best, Wolf,' said Johnny. 'Only, I was hoping it might put the kybosh on this sale thing. It's pretty near being all signed and sealed, you know.'

Wolf smiled and said, 'I shouldn't be too concerned about that, Johnny. I've got a feeling that your sale's going to fall through, and you'll be able to relax and enjoy Poynters and everything that's in it for a little time yet.'

'You think so? That would be great.'

His face lit up with a child's joy at the promise of a treat. The sight of it filled Hadda with a great sadness. He had come to see Nutbrown because the man had come to see him, and he felt he owed him a hearing. McLucky and the Trapps all told him it was pointless, but he'd insisted, even though he knew what he would find: a child in a man's body, a child whose responses were all based on his own immediate needs and appetites.

A child's punishments should be different from a man's. Or maybe a child's punishments always felt different.

'For you, Johnny, it will be like being sent to bed without any supper,' he murmured, half to himself.

'Sorry?'

'Nothing,' said Hadda. 'Here, don't forget your gun.'

He stooped to retrieve the weapon.

'Nice piece of kit. Nothing but the best, eh?'

He raised it to his shoulder, pointed it at Nutbrown, who stepped back in alarm.

Then he saw that Hadda was sighting down the barrel at him with his patched eye.

'Can't see a damn thing!' Wolf laughed. 'Catch!'

He threw the gun to Nutbrown, picked up his axe easily with one hand, slung it across his shoulder, then turned and limped slowly away, not looking back. But the dog who followed at his heels gave many a backward glance.

9

On his way home on Wednesday night, George Proctor knew he was being followed, and he knew who by, and he had a strong suspicion why.

Ahead was a long lay-by, usually packed with lorries there to enjoy the gourmet cuisine offered by The Even Fatter Duck, a mobile catering van that reputedly served the best bacon butties in Essex. But the Duck was long flown on this gloomy winter's evening and the lay-by was empty.

Proctor signalled and pulled in, not stopping till he was almost at the far end. In his mirror he saw the grey Fiesta come to a halt just inside the entrance. He got out of his car and waved imperiously.

After a moment, the Fiesta began to move slowly forward. He made a violent denying motion with his hand, and when the Fiesta stopped again, he jabbed his forefinger towards it two or three times then used the same finger to beckon.

Alva Ozigbo got the message.

She slid out of her car and advanced to meet the Chief Officer.

'What do you want, miss?' asked Proctor.

His breath hung visible in the freezing air. A cartoonist could have written his words upon it.

'I want to talk, George. Privately.'

Her breath balloon rose and merged with his.

'You could have come to my office, miss.'

'Oh, I did, George, remember? Three times I looked in on you this week.'

'And?'

'You wouldn't switch the radio on. In fact, once you switched it off.'

He looked at her frowningly for a moment then his face relaxed into a smile.

'Could tell from the start you was a sharp one, miss. And I tell you, you need to be sharp to survive at Parkleigh.'

'So why didn't you want to have another little confidential chat with me, George?'

'Because I didn't see no point. Anyway, we're talking now, so say what you want to say before we catch pneumonia.'

'We could talk in my car. Or yours.'

'Might be OK. Probably is. But better safe than sorry, eh? So?'

This really shocked her. But even hard-headed men could get bees in their bonnet.

'OK I'll be quick. I get the impression that whatever is said in Parkleigh is overheard.'

'Yeah?'

'And I think you've got that impression too.'

'Maybe.'

'And I think that maybe that was why my predecessor and the Director were having that row you told me about.'

'Could be.'

'For God's sake, George,' Alva said in exasperation. 'Are

449

you going to keep this up till we freeze to death? I'm talking to you because the alternative is to go along and confront Mr Homewood.'

'I shouldn't do that, miss,' said Proctor, alarmed.

'Why not?'

He regarded her dubiously, then shrugged like a man who has counted the alternatives and found none.

'Look,' he said, 'I don't know nothing except that over a long period I started getting this feeling when I was talking with the Director that occasionally he knew stuff before I told him, or sometimes he knew stuff I hadn't told him! I did a couple of little tests and I wasn't happy to find out I was right. It's my guess that when they refurbished Parkleigh, they fitted it up with a wall-to-wall bugging system. Total non-privacy. Everything anyone says anywhere gets heard. So I keep my radio turned up in my office. Or I step outside the main gate when I fancy a bit of privacy.'

This is what Alva had asked for, this is what she'd expected. But this blunt confirmation that her suspicions were shared still came as a shock.

'But why?' she demanded, though she could guess the answer.

'Look at who they've got banged up there. Politicals, terrorists, mega fraudsters, serial killers. Hearing what any of that lot have got to say to their lawyers, their visitors, on the phone, in the yard, anywhere, everywhere – just think how useful that could be. Stick people in Parkleigh, everyone thinks it's like throwing them into an old-fashioned dungeon. But it's really like putting them into the most advanced listening post in the country!'

'You've obviously thought a lot about this, George. But you've never said anything, I take it?'

'Me? No way! I'm not so green as cabbage looking as my old gran used to say.'

'But you talked to me. A bit obliquely, I admit. But you talked. Why was that?'

Proctor slapped his arms around his body to drive out the cold and said, 'Getting soft in my old age, maybe. I just got the impression watching you dealing with Mr Homewood that you'd gone off him a bit. Compared with how you started. Can't put my finger on it, just sometimes talking to him you were coming over a bit hesitant, like you didn't altogether trust him. And him with you too. And the only reason I could think why was you'd got a hint he knew things he didn't ought to, personal confidential stuff you hear in your tits-a-tits.'

Which she had. But not till very recently.

Alva thought she could see what had happened. Her concern at picking up signals that Homewood was developing the hots for her had caused her to introduce a measure of circumspection into her dealings with him. But eagle-eyed Chief Officer Proctor, his sensors honed by a lifetime of dealing with violent men whose mood swings could be a matter of life or death, had detected something. Detected and misinterpreted.

What was especially worrying was that this hard-headed, down-to-earth, long-serving prison officer preferred to stand out here in the freezing air rather than take the risk of talking in his own car. Or hers, for that matter. A bad case of paranoia? She looked at the man standing before her and wished she could think it so.

She said, 'When you say you think the Director's attitude to me changed too, what do you mean?'

'Little things again. Thought he started being a bit more abrupt with you.'

Meaning he'd spotted as she had that Homewood, fighting against the attraction he felt to her, started over-emphasizing that she was just another member of staff.

But Proctor hadn't finished.

'And he was always asking how you were getting on, saying he hoped I was making sure that no obstacles got in your way, like he was concerned to give you a chance to do well. But I sometimes felt like I was being asked to spy on you. Then on Monday . . .'

He hesitated. Alva pressed.

'What happened, George?'

'He called me in and gave me a spiel about having to compile some kind of report on you for the Home Office by the end of the month.'

'That in fact is true, George,' she interrupted. 'More or less. My contract doesn't come up for renewal for another two years but there is this annual review written into it. Just a matter of ticking off the boxes.'

'Yeah? Well, it didn't sound to me like the Director was thinking about just ticking boxes,' said Proctor. 'He asked straight out how I thought you were doing. Never asked me that before. What kind of effect did I think you were having on the prisoners' morale? Had it been a mistake to bring a female in? Hello, I thought, what's brought this on?'

'And you said?'

'I said I know I'd been against appointing you at the start, but now I'd had time to get to know you and see the way you worked, I thought you were doing a good job.'

This was the best unsolicited testimonial she'd ever had, thought Alva.

She said, 'Thanks, George.'

'Don't bother. I got to thinking later maybe I'd done you no favours.'

'I'm sorry?'

'Maybe if they just ease you out gently, unsuitable job for a woman, that sort of thing, no harm done to you professionally, or not much, everyone happy, that would be for the best.'

452

'So that was why you didn't want another confidential chat with me!' she said indignantly. 'You really don't want me around the place after all! Why didn't you just badmouth me to the Director in the first place?'

'Wasn't thinking, miss. But if he asks me again, I'll be ready.'

Her mind was whirling in search of a viewpoint that would bring all this into perspective.

There was no doubt that a negative report from Homewood, even unsupported by a thumbs-down from Proctor, could put her job in jeopardy. But why would he want to do that? And why should Proctor be so ready to shift his position from a reluctant recognition that she might be doing a decent job to reverting to his original attitude and wanting her out? It made no sense . . .

Unless the man was thinking there were worse ways to go than getting the sack!

But that was absurd! Wasn't it?

She said, 'You said way back when we talked in your room that my predecessor had a big row with the Director. Was that about these listening devices?'

'That's right, miss. Dr Ruskin had worked it out like you. Must be something in your training, I suppose. Makes you spot things. But he wasn't like you in most other ways. You're the calm rational sort. Dr Ruskin saw something he didn't like, he really let you know. I heard him screaming at the Director that it breached all medical ethics, it was an outrage and he reckoned it was his duty to let the whole country know how their hard-earned money was being spent.'

'And then he died. And I became his replacement. A bit of a shock for you, I seem to recall, George.'

'Maybe, at first, but when I came to think of it . . .' he tailed off.

'What?'

'Look, miss, don't be offended. At first I thought, bloody political correctness and all that garbage. Appoint a young woman and if she happens to be black, that's even better. But later I got to thinking . . .'

'What did you get to thinking, George?'

'I got to thinking if they'd just got shot of a shrink who turned out to be a trouble maker and hard to control, well, they wouldn't want another one of the same, would they?'

This was getting worse!

'You mean, they wouldn't want another independently minded, experienced, middle-aged man, they'd much prefer a young, inexperienced girl who'd be frightened to make waves, and would be more likely to get blamed than listened to if she did.'

Proctor looked rather sheepish.

'Yeah, that's about it, miss. But when I started to see they'd picked wrong, that was when I got worried.'

'Because you felt I might end up having an accident like Ruskin?'

He looked alarmed and shook his head vigorously.

'Don't put words into my mouth, miss. I'm not saying for one moment there was a connection between him handing in his notice and what happened. I mean, the state of mind he was in, he was an accident ready to happen. But when I started worrying you were going down the same road . . .'

He stopped, as if fearful he might be straying into some unmasculine area like compassion. Or maybe the black humour of his metaphor had just occurred to him.

Alva stepped in.

'And this week, after thinking about it, you came to the conclusion that maybe the simplest thing would be to go along with seeing me edged out as not up to the job, an experiment that failed? Make your life a lot easier, would it?'

The bitterness she was feeling wasn't directed at him, but she couldn't keep it out of her voice.

He said stolidly, 'That's right, miss. Pure self-interest. Seeing you on your way, safe and free, that would suit me down to the ground. Thing is, I know accidents happen, we've all got to live with that. But an accident happens twice and I'd have to speak up. Don't know what good it would do, but I'm pretty sure it would be the end of my career. I'll say good night, miss.'

He turned away and started to walk back to his car.

Suddenly Alva felt ashamed of herself.

She called after him, 'George!'

He halted and looked back.

'Yes, miss?'

'I'm sorry. I've no right to say anything to you except thanks. You've acted like a friend. I'll not forget that. But I won't mention it, not unless they use the thumbscrews.'

That brought a smile.

'I reckon they'd need to screw them down real tight to make you talk, miss. You take care now.'

Alva watched him get into his car and drive away.

We probably disagree on most of the major political and social issues of the day, she thought. But there goes a truly moral man!

Whereas Homewood, with whom she'd have said she was in almost perfect philosophical agreement, and John Childs whom she'd come to respect and admire, these two had vetted her, not because she represented a new generation of psychiatrist, young, vital, open-minded, forward-looking, but because she was a novice, easy to influence and divert, easy too to dispose of, if push came to shove . . .

Something in her demeanour at Childs's house must have warned him that she was starting to ask questions. He'd know about her special interest in Hadda from Homewood and perhaps she'd left some evidence that she'd found the photo. At the very least her prevarications when he made enquiry about the urgent matter she wanted to discuss with him must have rung false. She'd tried to pretend it was all about the danger of Homewood making an open pass at her now that his marriage was in trouble, and the problem this might cause in their working relationship. Treating him like a Lonely Hearts consultant! Jesus!

A chat with Homewood had probably confirmed his unease. Maybe Childs's queries had prompted the Director to realize he might have revealed a greater knowledge of her dealings with Hadda than he should have had.

Whatever, the very next day Homewood had started making enquiries about her job performance. He must have got a shock when Proctor hadn't given her an emphatic thumbs-down! At least it appeared they felt they could deal with the situation by terminating her contract rather than her life . . .

She pulled herself up short.

Without concrete evidence, she couldn't just make the leap from accepting Joe Ruskin's death as tragic accident to believing it was murder!

What kind of people were capable of treating human life so casually?

And in what capacity had Childs employed the young Hadda, *the woodcutter*?

I'm not cut out to be a PI! she told herself.

In fact she was beginning to wonder if she was really cut out to be a psychiatrist. She suddenly felt weary of being the seeker after hidden truths, the recipient of shadowy and sometimes shameful secrets. How much better if she'd followed in her mother's footsteps, exploring only fictional characters and wiping off their traumas with the greasepaint. Or her father's, getting your hands bloody from time to time but washing it off at the end of the day.

Suddenly she found herself fantasizing about life without Parkleigh. Walking away from the prison without looking back. Taking a long break with her family, then looking for some cosy teaching job in a university somewhere a long way from England, somewhere that they had real summers for a start!

But she wasn't going to turn her back on Wolf Hadda. She didn't know what he was planning but, whatever it was, one way or another she was involved in it.

She went back to her car. She'd left the engine running and the heater was full on.

Eventually she stopped shivering but as she drove away she felt that deep inside her being there was a coldness no amount of hot air could reach.

10

The following morning Simon Homewood called Alva into his office.

There was a severe-looking young woman there with a notepad. She wasn't the Director's regular secretary and Alva looked at her queryingly.

'This is Miss Leslie from the Home Office,' said Homewood. 'She'll be keeping a minute of our meeting.'

'That sounds ominous,' murmured Alva.

'Just bureaucracy,' said Homewood with an attempt at lightness. 'As you know, Dr Ozigbo, like everyone else on contract, your work is subject to an annual review process, and yours is due this month.'

'Yes, I know. The review happened last year too, but I don't recall this rigmarole.'

'No? Well, procedures are constantly updated, particularly in sensitive areas. So let's start, shall we?'

For the next half hour she was subjected to a barrage of questions about her work. Their tone was unremittingly polite but their unmistakable aim was to get her to admit to problems and confess difficulties. She fielded them with some ease but also with growing irritation. If they were trying to get her out, they would have to do a lot better than this!

Finally Homewood glanced at his watch and said, 'Let's take a break. Miss Leslie, perhaps you could have a word with my secretary and see if you can rustle up some coffee and a few choc biscuits to keep up our energy level.'

Miss Leslie did not look like the kind of woman who included waitressing in her job description but she rose without demur and left the room.

This is part of the game, thought Alva. In fact, this is probably where the game really starts.

She was right. But she was unprepared for just how brutal a game it was.

Homewood said, 'Alva, this is difficult, but I think we know each other well enough to be frank. Yours was always a somewhat controversial appointment and the opposition never really went away. I've always fought your corner, of course, and I'll continue to give you my full support. But sometimes in public life one has to box clever. A wise man picks his battles and only picks those he knows he can win.'

He paused. Alva had been listening with growing concern. This parade of clichés was, if anything, a greater insult to her intelligence than the unsubtle line of the official questioning. But Homewood was no fool and he was speaking with the quiet confidence of one who is certain of winning an argument.

She said, 'That may be what a wise man does. But I fight my own battles, Simon. And you ought to know, win, lose, I'll be fighting this one to the bitter end!'

She spoke with a confidence she no longer felt.

He said, 'I understand. I would expect no less. But there is something else you should know.'

She was experiencing once more the bone-deep chill that her conversation with Proctor had left her with the previous night. Now they were getting to it, the clinching argument, or threat, or bribe that would confirm her suspicions.

He had paused as if inviting her to prompt him with a question.

She kept silent and forced him to speak.

He said, 'Somehow one of the people who opposed your appointment has picked up a rumour about you and Hadda. An inappropriate relationship.'

'*What?*'

He gave her a reassuring smile.

'It's all right, I know it's absurd. But you did visit him in Cumbria. And spent the night at his house, too, I believe. I've told them I have no problem with that, perfectly under-standable in the circumstances, but these things tend to develop a momentum of their own unless halted at the start . . .'

'Then let's halt it!' she exploded. 'This is outrageous. Who's saying this? Let me meet them face to face . . .'

'I don't think that would help,' said Homewood smoothly. 'In fact, it might be provocative. Look, the point I'm making is that nobody is using this ridiculous allegation as a reason for terminating your contract. Not yet, anyway. But look at it from the opposition's point of view. Your annual review provides an opportunity for you to withdraw with honour and dignity and professional reputation intact. But if this opportunity isn't taken, who can say what kind of allega-tions might fly around? You see where it might go? An improper relationship between a prisoner and the psychia-trist who is then almost single-handedly responsible for persuading the parole hearing to turn him loose . . . Everything would be cast in doubt. At the very least there would have to be a full-scale enquiry. God knows how long that might drag on – I'm sure you wouldn't take it lying down . . .'

'Of course I wouldn't!' she exclaimed. 'I'd fight it through every court in the land!'

'I'd expect no less. And you'd have my full support. But ...'

She'd been fighting to control her feelings of outrage. That *but* did the job for her. Again she had a sense that, like the questions and the clichés, this was still a preliminary to the main event.

Now she was impatient to get to it and she gave him his prompt.

'But what?' she snapped.

'But,' he went on quietly, 'obviously, in view of the nature of the allegation, Hadda's parole would have to be revoked and until the enquiry, however prolonged, had reached its conclusion, he would be returned to custody.'

She opened her mouth to cry, 'But he is innocent.' And shut it.

The bastard was smiling at her sympathetically. He understood her dilemma. Any opposition she offered to the move to oust her was going to result in the revoking of Hadda's parole. And any protestations she made now of Hadda's innocence were just going to sound like confirmation of the improper relationship!

Homewood said urgently, 'Alva, the world of national security is a murkier place than even a criminal psychiatrist can know. Sometimes grim necessity overrides everything else: laws, loyalties, morality. I am your friend. I would have liked, as you know, to be more than your friend. That, I suspect, is going to be impossible now. But I hope something of our friendship can survive. And as a friend I say to you, there is no shame in moving on from this job. The pressures here are huge. And the external pressures you have been experiencing from your family situation can only have added to them. Spend some quality time with your father. Professionally the world is your oyster. And I promise you that any testimonial from me will do nothing but sing your

461

praises. Now, shall we have our coffee and then get back to your review?'

Alva didn't reply. It was hard for a psychiatrist to admit it, but sometimes words are inadequate, only a blow will do.

After a couple of moments Miss Leslie returned with the coffee tray.

Has the bitch been listening? she wondered.

She realized she didn't care.

For suddenly her anger was swept away by a huge surge of euphoria! It took only a few seconds to identify its source.

Without any effort on her part she was going to get what nearly every inmate of Parkleigh dreamt of, what she herself had fantasized about the previous night – release! This place with all its restraints, its fears, its secrets, its sounds, its smells, its monstrous looming presence, would be behind her. She knew she would take some of it with her, in fact she wanted to take some of it with her. But where it mattered, in her power of decision, her freedom of choice, she would be her own mistress again.

She gulped down her coffee, smiled sweetly at Homewood, and said, 'Let's get to it.'

BOOK FIVE

a shocking light

...then it befell that as they drew near safety, in the night's most secret hour, some hand in an upper chamber lit a shocking light, lit it and made no sound.

For a moment it might have been an ordinary light, fatal as even that could very well be at such a moment as this; but when it began to follow them like an eye and to grow redder and redder as it watched them, then even optimism despaired.

And Sippy very unwisely attempted flight, and Slorg even as unwisely tried to hide...

Lord Dunsany: *Probable Adventure of the Three Literary Men*

1

There had been snow off and on all through January, with particularly heavy falls in the east. At the end of the month, day temperatures began to rise and soon the wind-planed drifts that had turned the gardens of Poynters into a surreal sculpture park began to thaw to a grubby slush. The landscape that for so many weeks had something other-worldly about it now had the look of a tract of no-man's land in some wintry war.

For some reason Johnny Nutbrown associated this deterioration with Wolf Hadda's visit. His sense of euphoria after the encounter had been reinforced the following day when Pippa had taken a call from their solicitor.

Johnny was still in bed when he heard her scream of rage from below.

'Bad news, dear?' he asked unnecessarily when she erupted into the bedroom.

'That Scotch git, he's backed out of the sale!' she yelled. 'Family problems. If I could get my hands on the bastard, I'd fix it so he never had any family problems again!'

Inside, Johnny was jubilant. Good old Wolf, he'd called it right. You could always rely on Wolf.

But he took great care not to let any of this show on his face.

He had resolved not to tell Pippa anything about his meeting with Wolf, but in the end, as she went on and on about the failed sale as if it were the end of the world, he decided that describing the encounter with the stress on how well it had gone, how unthreatening Wolf had been, might reassure her.

He rapidly saw how wrong he had been.

'He was here? He was in our garden? Oh Jesus wept, you had your gun, why didn't you just shoot the bastard?'

'Steady on,' he said. 'Can't go around shooting people, even if I wanted to. Look, love, he was fine. And if he's fine, everything's fine, no need for us to sell up and head off into the sunset as if we had Interpol on our heels and we were running for our lives!'

She shook her head and said with an intensity that was worse than her screaming, 'You fucking moron. Can't you get it into your stupid head that's exactly what we're doing, and it's something a fucking sight worse than Interpol we're running from!'

After that she'd redoubled her efforts to sell the house, at the same time fixing a definite date early in spring for their move to the States, whether the house were sold or not.

As the days went by and the snow began to melt, Nutbrown found that his euphoria began to melt too. His wife's will had always been stronger than his. He'd been happy to accept this and come to regard it as a kind of protective barrier against the world's ills. Now at last he began to appreciate that if even her strength sank in face of this unspecified threat, perhaps there was something out there he ought to be afraid of too. Like a man who has never been ill, he found it hard to understand the meaning of the early symptoms of the potentially fatal disease that has infected him. Eventually, slowly, he came to recognize that for the first time in seven years he was feeling prickings of guilt at the way he'd treated his former boss and colleague and friend. Now the eight hours of untroubled sleep he'd enjoyed all his life started to decay like the snow. He awoke in the dark at one, two, or three o'clock in the morning, and that was the end of his night's rest. Fearful of waking Pippa if he lay there, tossing and turning, he took to slipping out of bed and going down to the kitchen to make a cup of tea laced with brandy and would sit there, thinking about things, till the dawn. The closed book of the past now opened to him, not as a continuous narrative, but in disconnected fragments that were sometimes identifiable as his own memories, but frequently seemed to belong to someone else. One scene that played itself again and again was of Wolf being woken by the arrival of the police that autumn dawn all those years ago and being dragged from the home he was never to enter again.

So when one dark morning early in February he heard the ringing of a doorbell accompanied by a thunderous knocking, he sat some moments longer at the kitchen table, trying to work out whether the noise originated at his own front door or in his mind.

It was the sound of Pippa yelling his name from upstairs and demanding to know where the hell he was that put the disturbance firmly in the here and now.

He stood up and went to the front door and opened it.

He was just in time. There was a large uniformed police officer standing there wielding one of those battering rams Johnny had seen on the telly. He looked disappointed at being deprived of the chance to use it.

A man in plainclothes edged him aside. He held a warrant card and some printed papers before Johnny's eyes.

'DI O'Reilly,' he said. 'Mr Nutbrown, is it?'

'Yes?'

'I have a warrant to search these premises, Mr Nutbrown. Right, lads.'

He stepped into the hallway, not quite pushing but certainly edging Johnny aside.

Behind him came at least a dozen others, some in uniform, some in plainclothes. Slushy snow slid off their shoes on to the floor. Pippa's not going to like that, thought Johnny.

He was right. She came down the stairs like St Michael descending on the dragon. Perhaps if she'd started demanding explanations or questioning the legality of the warrant, DI O'Reilly would have been able to put up stronger resistance. But her focus was entirely on the state of the invaders' footwear.

Within half a minute she had them all out of the hall and queuing up to wipe their feet on the rug at the entrance before they came back in.

Only then did she take the warrant from the DI's hand and study it carefully.

When she'd finished reading it she said to her husband, 'You'd better ring Toby.'

He said, puzzled, 'Bit early, isn't it, old girl? He's probably not up. Anyway, not sure if Toby's going to be much use here.'

She let out a snort of fury and exasperation.

'For God's sake, Johnny! Don't you understand anything?' she said, and went to the phone herself.

For once she was wrong. It wasn't just Johnny's usual disconnection from reality that was at work here.

He couldn't have given her chapter and verse on how he understood it, but understand it he did: today something was ending, and something was starting, something that not even the cleverest of solicitors was going to be able to put right, something that meant nothing was ever going to be the same again.

2

Toby Estover mounted the scaffold unhesitatingly, not because he was brave but because his legs moved independently of his mind, which was screaming, *Run! Run for your life!*

Waiting by the block with his back to him was the executioner. His right hand, which had only two fingers, was resting lightly on the shaft of his long-handled axe and he was gazing out across a wide panorama of mountains and lakes and virgin forest that somehow looked familiar.

Through his terror, Estover felt a pang of indignation. Surely his imminent execution was more important than admiring the fucking view! But he couldn't get any words out, his mouth was totally preoccupied with trying to suck into his lungs all the air that should have been his over the next forty years, all the air that should have been anybody's, all the fucking air in the earth's atmosphere, fuck everybody else, fuck global warming, fuck every fucking thing!

When his legs reached the block, they came to a halt and his knees folded and he knelt. Then his back muscles dissolved and he fell forward, prone, his Adam's apple pressing against the nadir of the block's shallow dark-stained U.

Out of the corner of his eye he saw the executioner's feet turn, he saw the shining blade rise out of sight, he saw the mountains and the lakes and the forest.

Then he heard the *whoosh!* as the blade came sweeping down.

And as he died, he woke up and was surprised to find that all the sheets and pillow were soaked with was sweat, not blood.

Two other things he eventually registered.

He was alone and the telephone was ringing.

He was not surprised to find he was alone. After a fortnight he was getting used to it.

He'd come to bed one night to find that Imogen had moved all her stuff into another bedroom, the room that had once belonged to her daughter.

The move had coincided with his announcement that he had got a new secretary, but he couldn't believe it had anything to do with this. For seven years she had seemed happy to share the large master bedroom, despite the fact that their moments of sexual intimacy had become increasingly rare. This had been due to a combination of her growing indifference and his own health problems which meant that a regular desktop servicing in the office was more than enough to satisfy his sensual needs.

There had been no warning of the move, no dispute, no debate. He guessed something had happened during her stay in Cumbria. What, he couldn't guess, and he knew there was no point in asking. This was the way that Imogen worked. No drama attended her decisions, just a quiet inevitability. He'd barged into her new bedroom one morning and found her sitting on the bed, holding a rag doll that had been a favourite of Ginny's. She wasn't clutching it to her but holding it out before her and staring at it, as if she hoped it might start talking. She didn't even glance his way and after a moment he'd left. He hadn't entered the room since.

The phone stopped. Either it had rung long enough to switch over to the answer machine, or someone had answered it.

He rolled out of bed and headed for the bathroom.

Fifteen minutes later, showered and wrapped in a monogrammed towelling robe that Imogen said looked as if it had been stolen from a particularly pretentious hotel, he headed downstairs in search of breakfast.

Imogen was standing on the half-landing looking out of the window. She had a cup of coffee in her hand and was completely naked. He was reminded of the night that bastard Hadda had chopped down the tree.

'Morning,' he said. 'What are you looking at?'

'I think it's sending out shoots,' she said.

He stood beside her.

Out in the garden in the still dim dawn light they could just make out the stump of the rowan.

After it had been chopped down, Estover had arranged for the trunk and brash to be cleared away, but Imogen had refused to let him have the stump dug out of the lawn.

'They are great survivors, rowans,' she said. 'They need to be. They cling on in places other trees would only be seen dead in. I've seen them growing out of north-facing rock faces at two thousand feet.'

'Maybe,' he said. 'But whatever it does, in our lifetime it will just be an eyesore!'

'It will still be alive,' she said. 'Wolf planted it to shelter us from evil.'

'Yeah? Well the bastard should have done the job properly when he chopped it down and dug up the roots too!' he said. 'Did you get the phone?'

'Yes.'

'Well? If you want to make me very happy, tell me it was a wrong number.'

She looked as if she might be considering the proposition, then said, 'It was Pippa.'

'Pippa? What the hell did she want at seven o'clock on a cold February morning?'

'She says they've got a houseful of policemen with a search warrant.'

'You're joking, I hope?'

She shook her head slightly.

'Jesus! What are they looking for?'

'Who knows? Pippa says she doesn't. She wants some legal advice, I think.'

'What did you say to her?'

'I said that you never gave legal advice till you'd had your breakfast. I suggested she should await the outcome of the search. Either nothing would be found and she'd be able to ring you to ask how to register a formal complaint. Or if they discovered Lord Lucan hiding in the cellar, they would no doubt transport Johnny and herself to some police station where you would join them as soon as you heard where it was.'

'Good girl,' he said. 'That's worth five hundred quid of anyone's money. Any more of that coffee downstairs?'

'I'm sure there will be. I've roused Mrs Roper to tell her you'll be breakfasting early as you may be driving to Cambridge pretty soon.'

'Cambridge?'

'That's probably where they'll take Pippa and Johnny, isn't it?'

'You seem pretty sure these cops are going to find what they're looking for.'

She said, 'In my limited experience of dawn raids, they usually do, don't they?'

473

He could think of no answer to this and continued on his way.

In the kitchen there was a pot of coffee standing on the stove. As he poured himself a cup, Mrs Roper appeared with the morning papers. The housekeeper was a hangover from the days when Wolf Hadda had been master here, and she had made it clear to Estover without overstepping any employee boundaries that she didn't reckon he was an improvement.

'Morning,' she said. 'The usual, is it?'

'Yes, thank you, Mrs Roper.'

As the woman began preparing the bacon, mushroom and scrambled eggs that comprised the usual, he turned his gaze to the pile of newspapers. It was high, containing as it did a copy of every national daily. At the office he had people who went through them all much more meticulously than he ever did. Forewarned is forearmed, he declared to his staff, and it was certainly true that a sharp eye could sometimes spot in a small para a hint of something that might ultimately affect the economy or equanimity of one of his clients. He himself liked to do a quick scan of all the headlines, or sometimes to track through the various reportings of any case he was involved with in search of misrepresentation or bias or anything else of interest.

Today what he called the *titty tabloids* were at the top, and what he saw on the front page of the third of these made him exclaim, 'Shit!'

'Sorry, Mr Estover?' said the housekeeper.

'Nothing, nothing,' he grunted, opening the paper.

It was Kitty Locksley's rag, the news editor who had quizzed him about Arnie Medler a few weeks back. That had been easy enough to field, but what he read on the front page now filled him with foreboding.

The Russian Invasion. Is there more than snow on Pasha Nikitin's boots? See Page 6 for our Exclusive Report!

He found page six.

It was full of photos of Nikitin at receptions and parties, in the company of many well-known faces from the worlds of politics, or showbusiness, or sport. The headline above them all was *WHAT'S HE TREADING INTO THEIR CARPETS?*

The main copy started on the next page. He ran his eyes down the columns with the speed of long practice and under his breath he said, 'Oh shit!' again.

Kitty's journalists were past masters and mistresses in the art of blurring the boundary between speculation and accusation. But there was stuff here that went so far beyond that boundary that they would hardly have dared print it unless they believed they had the wherewithal to back it up under a legal challenge.

The feature finished with a promise that the next day's edition would contain some *really* shocking revelations.

We'll see about that! thought Estover grimly.

He was already working out the grounds of his application for an injunction. Kitty Locksley might have persuaded her bosses that she had enough to take a run at Nikitin, but that was very different from persuading a judge that she wasn't just flying kites. And while the paper's lawyers were preparing their case for a lifting of the injunction, Estover, who had files on all the major newspaper editors and owners, would be working out the combination of threat, bribe, and called-in favour best suited to getting the whole thing nipped in the bud.

Imogen, now wearing a pale blue kimono, came into the kitchen and refilled her mug. When she sat down opposite him, he pushed the paper across to her.

She glanced over it, then said, 'Is it as bad as it looks?'

'Not nice but manageable,' he said confidently. 'I'll slap an injunction on them to put a brake on tomorrow's edition. That will give us a breathing space to wheel the big guns into position.'

'Meaning?'

'As you know, Pasha's got friends. Important friends. Important enough to make even a newspaper owner take stock of how he sees the rest of his life.'

'So, suppression not rebuttal.'

'Always less risky,' he said. 'Thank you, Mrs Roper.'

The housekeeper had placed a crowded plate before him. He reached for the tomato ketchup and squirted his initials cursively across the fry-up.

'You won't forget Pippa and Johnny?'

'I don't even know if they'll need me yet.'

'They'll need you,' she said confidently. 'And they've contacted you. Pasha hasn't.'

'That's true,' he said, raising the first forkful of bacon to his mouth. 'I'm surprised. Perhaps he's had a hard night and his people are afraid to rouse him with bad news.'

'Perhaps,' she said, as if she thought this unlikely.

He finished his breakfast at a leisurely pace, drank more cups of coffee, browsed through more of the papers.

Imogen nibbled at a slice of toast and kept up a desultory conversation with Mrs Roper.

Finally he rose, said, 'Lovely breakfast as always, Mrs Roper,' and left the kitchen.

As he dressed, the phone rang again. It stopped almost immediately.

He continued dressing. It was eight fifteen and the sky was now bright. February was generally regarded as the most dismal of months, but sometimes it held the promise of spring, he thought.

In the kitchen he found Imogen doing the *Guardian* crossword.

He said, 'Pasha, or Pippa again?'

'Pippa.'

'And?'

'They've been arrested. They're taking them to Cambridge.'

'Good God!' he said. 'What for?'

'Drugs.'

She said it so casually that for a moment he didn't take it in.

'*Drugs*? I know Johnny usually has a small stash of coke around the place, just in case he ever feels reality is beginning to break in, but I can't believe they'd do a dawn raid for that.'

'No. I think they probably did it for what, from Pippa's account, looks like half a hundredweight of the stuff found under the cistern in their attic.'

'Jesus wept! You're joking? No, you're not. What did you tell them?'

'I told them you were on your way.'

'What? Look, I can't, not till I start the ball rolling on this Nikitin business.'

'He hasn't asked you to do anything, has he?'

'No, not yet, but there's probably a simple explanation . . .'

'There probably is,' said Imogen. 'But till you hear it, you have two of our oldest friends who are expecting you. Head to Cambridge, Toby. Stay there if you have to. It might be a good idea to stay there even if you don't have to.'

He looked at his wife in bewilderment. More and more these days he felt he understood her as little as her father understood her mother. But frequently she turned out to be right.

He said, 'I'll have to call in at the office first and make sure they're up to speed if or rather when Pasha calls.'

Imogen shrugged.

'If you must,' she said indifferently. 'By the way, if you do get to Cambridge, watch out for the media. Pippa said somehow the press and TV have got wind of the raid and they're all over the place. That seemed to worry her almost more than anything else.'

'Bastards,' he said. 'State the world's in, you'd think they'd have better things to occupy them.'

This won him a faintly mocking smile, then she returned her attention to the crossword.

'I'll be off then,' he said, stooping as if to kiss her then contenting himself with a squeeze of her shoulder.

She didn't look up but said, almost to herself, 'I think you're right about the rowan. It's going to be a long time before it grows big enough to shelter us.'

He said, 'Don't worry, my love. While we've got the Law to hide behind, there's nothing that can touch us.'

Now she looked up.

'But if you chop down the Law,' she said, 'how long does that take to grow again?'

3

Alva Ozigbo also woke early on that February morning. For a moment she lay in the darkness, in that birth moment when we don't know who or what or where we are.

Then memory switched on and joy flooded her mind and body like the midday sun.

This morning she did not have to rise and prepare herself for the drive east to the Dark Tower.

Yesterday she had left Parkleigh for the last time!

Against her expectations she hadn't felt any shame at her easy capitulation. Perhaps that would come later. She could, if she'd wanted to, have rehearsed the excellent reasons for her decision to go quietly – principally the threat to Wolf Hadda's freedom and the fact that she had no concrete evidence whatsoever for her belief that the refurbishment of the prison had given Childs's people an opportunity to embed surveillance devices in every nook and cranny. But she was too honest to give them pride of place over her recognition that she was simply relieved and delighted to be giving up her job.

Know thyself is a good if not an essential motto for a psychiatrist. And she was ready to admit she knew herself a lot better now than when she'd first started at Parkleigh.

Her father had resisted any temptation he felt to say *I told you so!* when she gave him the news, but he hadn't concealed his feeling that these were glad tidings.

'Don't you be rushing into any other job,' he said. 'Give yourself time to look around. And above all, Elf, give yourself time to come up here to rescue your poor old dad from this Swedish monster who's got him chained to the wall! I'm wasting away to nothing on a diet of lettuce leaves. If she had her way, I'd spend six hours a day in a sauna, whipping myself with willow twigs. It's my birthday this month and I bet she won't even let me have a cake unless you're here!'

The 'Swedish monster' had intervened at this point to say that she hoped her daughter would come as soon as possible as Ike was now even harder to keep under control than he'd been before his heart attack.

And Alva, hearing the love in their voices and the desire to see for themselves that she was OK, had difficulty in keeping her own voice bright and steady as she promised to come up for Ike's birthday and stay at least a week.

She had put her feelings about Hadda and her concern about his plans and his future to one side during the past couple of weeks. Once the decision to go had been taken, she had no desire to hang around, but at the same time she wanted to make sure that the files and notes she left her successor were comprehensive and up to date. She thought of leaving some form of warning that the confidentiality of his exchanges with the inmates was not guaranteed. The problem was, if it were too general it would be useless and if it were too explicit, it would provoke questions she could not answer. Or did not want to answer.

She knew that in life there were some battles you had to fight even if the odds were insuperable and defeat guaranteed. This did not feel like one of them. OK, it was part of the ongoing and important debate about prisoners' rights versus the general weal. But there was no torture involved here, no physical or mental abuse. This was more like the discussion of how admissible telephone tapping should be in criminal cases. People got heated about it, but no one sacrificed their own reputation or someone else's freedom because of it.

Was this simply a self-justifying rationalization? she asked herself after her waking delight at the realization of her freedom had faded. She didn't think so, but it was almost with relief that she moved from considering that moral question to the other and more personal issue of what she was going to do about Hadda.

She was convinced he was innocent. Her duty was therefore to make public her belief, argue the case, get the investigation reopened, mount an appeal . . .

All of which sounded very straightforward if it weren't for the fact that she could not rely on any of those who should have been her supporters – Doll and Ed Trapp, Davy McLucky, Wolf himself – to stand alongside her.

And this brought her to the next, even more pressing question.

What was Hadda planning to do – and what ought she to do about it?

To hell with it – enjoy your first morning as a free woman! she told herself.

She flung back the duvet and got out of bed.

Dawn was tinting the sky an ochrous pink. London was rumbling back to full consciousness. She washed and dressed then went into her kitchen.

The room could do with a good spring clean, she judged as she sat and ate her breakfast. One way and another with all the pressures she'd endured over the past couple of months, she'd let things go. In fact the whole flat needed a good going over. Her awareness of the symbolic implications of this decision did not make it any the less a factual truth. The place had a neglected look. Leave it much longer and it would be downright grubby! She imagined what Elvira, with her Nordic standards of hygiene, would say if she walked in now.

She'd promised her parents she would drive north in time for her father's birthday. That gave her three days to set her apartment to rights. And some good hard non-cerebral work was just what the psychiatrist had ordered!

By mid-morning she had reduced the relative order of the flat to chaos, but at least it was well on the way to being clean chaos. When her doorbell rang, she was up a stepladder, dealing with a spider's web of Shelobian proportions. She thought of ignoring the bell, but it rang again insistently.

Grumbling, she descended and went to the door.

It was John Childs. He stood there, looking even more neat and tidy than usual by contrast with the confusion behind her, his sweet smile neither broadening nor fading as he took in her bedraggled appearance.

'I had pictured you taking your ease on your first day away from the toils of employment,' he said. 'Perhaps I should have known better.'

With Homewood it had been easier to maintain the pretence that her departure was by mutual agreement on reasonable grounds.

With Childs she saw no reason for such pretence.

'What do you want?' she asked coldly.

'To apologize,' he said. 'And to talk to you about Wolf.'

This, she acknowledged, was perhaps the only formula that could have got him into the flat. She suspected no matter whose door he knocked at he would always have the right formula.

She let him disinter a chair and she didn't offer him coffee, partly because she did not want to make him feel welcome, but mainly because until she shifted everything she'd taken out of her cupboards back into them, the kitchen was a no-go area.

'So, apologize,' she said.

'I am truly sorry to have recruited you to the job at Parkleigh under false pretences. I am sure that by now a combination of your own sharp intellect and the information supplied by the estimable Chief Officer Proctor will have filled in the picture. Any damage to your self-esteem from the discovery that you were recruited less for your positive qualities and more because of your youth and inexperience should be repaired by your own awareness, even more than my reassurance, that you have performed your duties in an exemplary fashion and with a skill far beyond your years. The glowing testimonial Simon Homewood will no doubt provide will be no less than the truth and no more than you deserve.'

He paused. She gave an ironic little clap that reminded her she was still wearing rubber gloves.

'Nice apology,' she said. 'Must have taken you half an hour off the Phoenicians to prepare it.'

'I'm sorry,' he said. 'I've never really mastered the art of sounding spontaneous, even when that's exactly what I'm being. I've truly enjoyed our ongoing relationship and I truly regret that it has probably come to an end.'

'Probably!' she exploded.

'Life is fuller of surprises than certainties,' he said. 'And the more I got to know you, the more I suspected you were going to surprise me. So, that's my apology. All of us are to some degree driven by grim necessity. In my job she is, alas, almost a permanent companion. Let's move on to Wolf.'

'Yes, let's,' she said.

'I assume you are pretty well au fait by now with the circumstances that led to his jail sentence?'

She nodded.

'Good. What happened was of course regrettable, but because of the way things worked themselves out, also inevitable, I fear. Had I been aware earlier what was going on, I might have been able to do something, but by the time I became involved, it was out of my hands.'

'Out of your hands!' she exclaimed. 'He was innocent, this man you feel some affection for – at least that's the conclusion I draw from his inclusion in your picture gallery . . .'

He nodded and said, 'Yes, indeed. I have always been very fond of Wolf.'

'Yet you let him be sent down for a long sentence on the most disgusting of charges! Jesus, Childs, what do you do to your enemies?'

He gave her the sweet smile and said, 'This is not the time or place to go into that. But as to those I'm fond of, I fear that from time to time in too many cases grim necessity has ordained that I should be complicit in their suffering far worse fates than poor Wolf.'

He was, she saw, deadly serious. Her head was in a whirl but she did not want to let this occasion to learn all she could about Hadda escape.

She said, 'When Doll Trapp brought him to you, what did you do with him?'

'I gave him a home and an education. He also received some special training, not that he needed much, his peculiar talent for scaling unscaleable obstacles was already highly developed. He could get in and out of almost anywhere.'

'You mean you used him as a burglar?' she asked incredulously.

'On occasion. But more often it was a matter of leaving rather than removing something.'

'Leaving what?' she demanded. She didn't want to know, but she had to ask.

'Surveillance devices,' he said. 'And occasionally, other devices.'

'Like bombs, you mean? You turned him into an assassin?'

'I fear so. Just on a couple of occasions. I did not send him in blind. He was fully briefed. On each occasion the details of the file we were able to show him on the targets were sufficiently powerful to persuade him that this was in the public good, a necessary execution rather than a wanton killing.'

Sneering is not a response that psychiatrists find much occasion to practise, but Alva managed it as to the manner born.

'You *persuaded* him! A boy, a naïve young man at the very most, in your employ, in your *care*, probably dependent upon you emotionally as well as economically! And you *persuaded* him to become a killer. I bet that called on all your Ciceronian skills!'

He said, 'If I gave you the details, I think you yourself might be persuaded that the world was a better place and our country more secure for the deaths of these men. But your reproach is not unjust. I had become very fond of young Wolf in the time I had known him. Rest quiet, Miss Ozigbo. There was nothing sexual in it, not overtly anyway. Wolf, you may be pleased to hear, is unswervingly straight in his appetites.'

He paused as if to allow response and Alva thought of bursting out indignantly, 'Why do you think I should be particularly pleased to hear that?' But she didn't. She was beginning to understand that Childs rarely used words casually.

He resumed, 'So I myself had begun to have some misgivings about steering the boy down this road. I comforted myself with the thought that it was not too late to divert. Then a third occasion requiring his special talents presented itself. Definitely the last, I told myself. And I was right, but for the wrong reasons. Things went awry.'

'Awry?' echoed Alva, tiring of his prissy language. 'You mean there was a cock-up?'

'Yes and no. The target was killed. So unfortunately were some members of his family who were not expected to be there. His wife. And two children.'

'Good God,' said Alva aghast. 'And this was down to Wolf?'

'No, as I attempted to explain to him, it was down to grim necessity. These things happen. It is not a question of choice. As I told Wolf when last I saw him, only God can claim to be independent of accident and necessity.'

'You've seen Wolf recently? And you don't have any broken bones?'

'You sound regretful, Miss Ozigbo,' he said, smiling. 'So there are occasions when you might approve violence?'

'Never approve, Mr Childs,' she said coldly. 'But I'm a human being as well as a scientist. I have emotions. So, you were telling me how you took a young boy and broke him to pieces.'

'Yes. And then as best I could, I put him back together again. I offered him the only prize that could compensate for the damage I had done. You will know what that was from his interesting interchanges with you at Parkleigh.'

'You offered him Imogen Ulphingstone,' she said.

'In a manner of speaking. He'd told me all about his reasons for running away from home. I couldn't, of course, guarantee that Miss Ulphingstone would accept his proposal, and indeed, having made a few discreet enquiries about the lady, I had serious doubts as to whether it would be to Wolf's benefit if she did. But once again I had no choice. Had I offered Wolf anything else, he would have taken off, and God knows what would have happened to him.'

'He might have been able to carve out a perfectly happy

486

life for himself!' she said. 'At least he would have been away from your malign influence!'

Childs grimaced.

'I'm sorry, I am being unnecessarily periphrastic. When I say God knows what would have happened, I am talking about details not outcome. A young man who had been privy to the sort of event I have just sketched out to you could hardly be allowed to run wild, could he? Loose cannons, if they cannot be tied down, must be tipped overboard. You must see that.'

'You mean, he would have been killed? What kind of monster are you, Childs?'

'The kind who saved Wolf's life. It was clear to me from the start that as well as huge personal charm, he had a surprising aptitude for business. In America they value these assets rather more highly than we do here and I saw to it that he received there the kind of higher education that made the most of them. Now all he needed was opportunity, and of course money. The latter was easy enough. Reward for services rendered and still to render. He returned to England a personable young man with his first million already in his account, and a great future before him. All the tests the young woman had set him he had passed with flying colours. She, alas, kept her end of the bargain.'

'You said, services still to render. Do you mean Wolf carried on working for you after he founded Woodcutter?'

'Not in the capacity you fear,' said Childs. 'But in his capacity as international businessman, he was welcome in circles that we were glad to get intelligence from. And people opened up to him in a wonderful way. Oh yes, he earned his keep. In fact, as he was soon so successful he didn't need to be underpinned by public monies, he proved to be huge value for our initial investment.'

'But you were still willing to let this valuable asset be destroyed?'

487

'Even if he had been saved, with the collapse of Woodcutter, he was considerably less of an asset. And there was no way that I could have prevented the defection of Imogen. His occupation gone, his wife untrue, he would have been as unstable as Othello. As I say, loose cannons must be tied down, and it was convenient in so many ways that the State did us this service.'

'He's not tied down now,' said Alva.

'Indeed. And after the apology, that is my second reason for intruding upon you today. The Woodcutter is running free. I am sure you have been experiencing some serious concerns as to what he may be planning to do.'

She said, 'Yes, I have. But I've no reason to believe whatever he's planning will have anything to do with his connection with Chapel. You say you've spoken to him. He must have made this clear, surely?'

'Because I have no broken bones?' He smiled. 'True. But I'm not here in my ringmaster capacity, Alva. I'm here as a friend of Wolf's.'

His use of her name was as shocking as anything else she'd heard from him. It signalled . . . she wasn't sure what it signalled, but it put her on maximum alert.

'His friend? You mean you want to save him from himself and scupper any plan he might have to take revenge?' she mocked. 'Of course it would be pure coincidence that this would probably involve protecting what sounds like another of your valuable assets, the unspeakable Toby Estover.'

'Too late for that, I fear,' he said.

The words trembled across her brain like a migraine.

'What do you mean?'

'There have been developments. You've probably been too preoccupied with your priestlike task of pure ablution to listen to the news, but if you had done so, you might have heard that the Nutbrowns' country residence was raided this morning and Johnny and Pippa Nutbrown have been taken into custody. Naturally they have summoned their solicitor, Mr Toby Estover. Unfortunately, he is nowhere to be found. His car is in its reserved spot in the underground car park that serves his office block. But of Mr Estover himself, there is not a trace.'

'Oh Jesus,' said Alva, feeling the strength drain out of her muscles.

'Please, don't upset yourself,' said Childs. 'There's no reason to think that Wolf is involved in the disappearance, not physically anyway. He works much more subtly than that, and I'm sure at this moment he is safely alibi'd three hundred miles away in Cumbria. No, the fate of the Nutbrowns and of Estover is nothing to cause us concern.'

'You're saying that Wolf has nothing to do with this?' she asked incredulously.

'Don't be silly,' he said, with the first signs of impatience she'd ever seen him show. 'Of course I'm not saying that. But whatever connection there is will not be traceable, of that I'm sure. Forget these people, they're getting no more than they deserve. And as I do not think they deserve death, I shall do my utmost to ensure their fate stops short of that.'

'How nice to protect your conscience by making such delicate judgments!' she sneered.

'No, it is not my conscience I want to protect,' he said quietly. 'It is Wolf. Eventually I have hopes that we may be able to get his convictions overturned. I am not without influence. But the seeds of doubt must first be sowed. Meanwhile the best we can do for him is make sure he draws no attention to himself.'

'You think it's still possible to get the case reviewed?' said Alva. Despite her resolve never to trust Childs again, she found she was letting him give her hope.

'Anything is possible if you have the means to make it

necessary,' he said. 'But let me speak plainly. Wolf so far has moved with stealth and care, but what I fear is that his final act might not be so meticulously planned, so remotely triggered as the first two. If Wolf seriously harms his former wife, he will certainly spend much of the rest of his life in jail. And that, I fear, might be the least of his worries. What such an act might do to his mental stability, you are better placed than I am to work out. This is why I have come to see you, Alva. I want Wolf to remain free, in body and in spirit. I think you want the same. What I can do, I have done. But I feel it may not be enough. He needs reasons other than any I can give him to stay his hand. If you think you can supply those reasons, then I beg you to make the attempt before it is too late.'

'For God's sake,' cried Alva. 'Can't Imogen be taken into protective custody?'

'To be protected from what?' said Childs. 'If the authorities get a hint that Wolf poses some kind of danger, it is he who will be returned to custody. Not that I would put money on them being able to find him if he decided to go to earth in that wilderness he so loves.'

'At least you can keep a watch to make sure there's plenty of warning if he looks like leaving home . . .'

'I don't think he has any intention of doing that. The good huntsman knows how his prey will react. He prepares his hide, and waits.'

'I don't understand,' said Alva. 'What do you think is going to happen?'

In an inner pocket of Childs's immaculate jacket, a phone trembled.

Murmuring an apology, he took it out, looked at it with distaste, then placed it close to but not touching his ear and said, 'Yes?'

He listened, said, 'I'm on my way,' replaced the phone in his pocket and stood up.

'I'm sorry,' he said. 'I must leave you. But in answer to your question, I think that in the very near future, Mrs Estover is going to find her home besieged by the media. The last time that happened she was able to take refuge at the Nutbrowns' house, Poynters, in leafy Essex. That is no longer an option, so I believe that, both because it is a good place to hide and also because I suspect that's where she will want to be, eventually she will head north to seek solace in the bosom of her family at Ulphingstone Castle. And from what I know of the lady, I would guess that Wolf will not need to go looking for her. She will come looking for him.'

4

They had transported the Nutbrowns to Cambridge Police HQ in separate vehicles with sirens ululating and lights oscillating in hope of outspeeding the media caravan. All they did of course was open up a traffic-free channel along which the motley gang of reporters and cameramen sped at supra-legal speeds a couple of hundred yards behind them.

In the station they were kept apart as they were booked in and fingerprinted.

Both refused to make statements until the arrival of their solicitor.

After two hours when Estover still hadn't arrived, DI O'Reilly rang the lawyer's London office to check if there were any known reason for the delay. He found the staff there in a state of mystified concern. Toby Estover's car was in its reserved bay in the car park, but of the man himself there was no sign.

His wife, when contacted, confirmed that her husband had set out early to the office with the intention of dealing with a pressing matter there before driving north to Cambridge to represent the Nutbrowns.

O'Reilly then informed the Nutbrowns separately that it

did not look as if Mr Estover was going to turn up and invited them to nominate an alternative, failing which they could, of course, accept the services of the duty solicitor.

On hearing this, Pippa Nutbrown gave her opinion of her absentee lawyer in such ripe terms that the DI observed drily that if he was even half those things, she was probably better off without him. Johnny Nutbrown asked what his wife was doing. In the end the man opted for the duty solicitor while the woman said that in order to get out of this shithole as quickly as possible, she'd answer just enough questions to let O'Reilly see what a dickhead he was being.

In the event, though for very different reasons, neither interview lasted long.

Pippa Nutbrown denied all knowledge of the packages of cocaine discovered in her attic. When asked how, in that case, her fingerprints came to be on the plastic wrapping, she shook her head violently and said, 'It's a lie.'

Next she was asked if it were true that there was always a plentiful supply of coke on offer at her parties.

She snapped, 'There might be the odd line for recreational purposes, but not fucking bucketsful!'

'So you're not in the business of actually dealing in the stuff?' enquired O'Reilly.

'Certainly not!'

'In that case, you'll have a perfectly reasonable explanation of your account in the Caymans that, according to my information, currently stands at something in excess of five million pounds in credit?'

And now she stopped talking altogether.

The same sequence of questions to her husband produced a rather different set of answers.

Asked about the packages found in the attic, he said, 'It's an old curiosity shop up there, wouldn't surprise me if you found Lord Lucan riding Shergar.'

493

When told his fingerprints were on the wrapping of one of the packages, he said, 'Suppose it must be mine then. Bit of a facer, finding I'd got all that gear up there when I think of the price I've been paying for a couple of bags in town.'

When asked if he supplied coke at his parties, he said, 'Doesn't everybody?'

And finally, asked about the Cayman account, he raised his eyebrows and said, 'Thought it would be more than that. Still, Pippa's a bright girl, she's probably got it spread about a bit.'

At which point DI O'Reilly enquired politely if Mr Nutbrown felt in need of some refreshment as he had a feeling this interview might take some little time.

Leaving Johnny to enjoy a breakfast-all-day from the canteen, he returned to Pippa.

'Mr Nutbrown is being most cooperative,' he said. 'Usually, in the case of co-defendants, the judge tends to look more favourably on the more cooperative.'

'Fuck off,' she said. 'Any sign of Estover?'

'I'm afraid not.'

She didn't look surprised.

'I hope the bastard rots in hell,' she said.

5

It is not often that a wish so malevolent as Pippa Nutbrown's is positively answered, but in figurative terms hell was certainly where Toby Estover had been spending the past couple of hours.

As he'd stepped out of his car in the underground car park, he was approached by a bulky figure he recognized as an associate of Pavel Nikitin. The kind of associate who fades into the background in polite society but looms menacingly in less friendly surroundings.

The man, who was definitely looming at the moment, said, 'Mr Nikitin would like to talk to you.'

'Yes, I thought he might,' said Estover. 'First thing I'll do when I get into my office is give him a ring.'

'He would like to talk now.'

'Yes, I said . . . oh, you mean face to face. Listen, there's something I've got to do, I'll ring him and make a firm appointment for later, if that's what he wants.'

Suddenly the man was looming very large indeed.

'Now,' he said.

And Estover felt his arm seized, he was spun round, marched forward a few steps, then thrust into the back seat of a car with windows tinted dark enough to hide an orgy.

In the front passenger seat sat a man he recognized. His name was Pudovkin, known familiarly as Pudo, though he did not invite familiarity. His precise function in Nikitin's entourage Toby had never discovered. Small and wiry, he lacked the intimidating bulk of the looming man. 'Make sure your bodyguards are wide enough to take the first bullet,' Pasha had once said to him in a lighter moment. So, not a bodyguard. But clearly a man of value to Nikitin who always called him Pudo and occasionally draped an arm round the smaller man's shoulders in a way that made Estover wonder if some of the services he provided might be very personal indeed. But the deference the big bodyguards showed him confirmed he was a lot more than just a best boy.

'Pudo,' said the lawyer, anger making him risk familiarity, 'what the hell's going on?'

The man turned and stared coldly at him and hissed, 'Sit still!' with hardly any movement of his mouth. Perhaps that was because his jaw was wired. Whatever, the effect was extremely scary, and increasingly, as the car sped through streets that, so far as he could tell through the darkened windows, did not lie on any route he knew to Nikitin's home or office, fear began to outweigh anger in Estover's mind.

Their destination turned out to be a riverside warehouse somewhere, he estimated, in Wapping. Pavel Nikitin was waiting for him here, seated behind a dilapidated desk in an office that did not look as if it had been occupied by anything but mice and spiders for a very long time.

'Jesus, Pasha, you're not back home in Russia, all you had to do was ring me,' said Estover, exaggerating his exasperation in order to cover his concern.

The looming man thrust him down on to a chair he would have preferred to brush with his handkerchief before settling his mohaired buttocks on it. Nikitin still didn't speak.

'Look,' said Estover, 'there's nothing to worry about, just because some gung-ho editor has a rush of blood to the head. They've all tried it before. We'll have an injunction on them by lunchtime and by the end of the week they'll be printing a grovelling apology and paying large sums to the charity of our choice.'

Now the Russian spoke.

'No,' he said. 'They have more, much more.'

'How much more? How do you know this? Have they been in touch?'

'Early this morning, just before the paper came out. They woke me to tell me what was going to be printed and asked if I had any comment. They said there would be at least three follow-ups. They told me what was likely to be in them also.'

'A bluff!' insisted Estover. 'They knew if they'd contacted you earlier, I'd have made damned sure even this first load of crap didn't see the light of day.'

Then, genuinely puzzled because Nikitin was no respecter of anyone's comfort or convenience, he asked, 'Why didn't you ring me straight away? I'd have come round, no matter what the hour.'

'Because I wanted to see you without anyone knowing I was seeing you,' said Nikitin.

For a moment the response seemed an impenetrable enigma.

Then the Russian drew an envelope out of his pocket and shook half a dozen photographs on to the desktop.

Estover stared down at them and the enigma began to dissolve.

They showed him at a restaurant table, handing a package to Kitty Locksley, the woman looking at it quizzically, the pair of them smiling as she slipped it unopened into her handbag.

'This was delivered to my house just before the paper phoned me,' said the Russian.

Professionally speaking, extreme situations had always made Toby Estover's mind go into overdrive. This was one of the reasons he was such a good lawyer. As he riffled through a client's options, he inevitably recited the reassuring mantra, 'Rest easy, there is always a way out.'

His mind worked fast enough now to grasp the implications of the pictures and the fact that nobody knew he was here with the Russian. The reassuring mantra did not seem quite appropriate, and he was saying, 'Come on, Pasha, you surely don't believe . . .' when the chair was pulled from under him and he sprawled on the floor. He cried out in alarm then screamed in pain as the looming man's foot drove hard into his crotch.

They waited patiently till he was recovered sufficiently to push himself up into a sitting position.

'Now, Toby,' said Nikitin. 'Let's us talk.'

A couple of hours later, at just about the time Pippa Nutbrown was uttering her anathema, Pudovkin said to his master, 'I think perhaps he is telling the truth.'

Nikitin nodded and looked at the photos on the desk.

'I think so too, Pudo,' he said. 'This means we must look for explanations elsewhere. Go to this restaurant. See if you can find out anything about the taking of these pictures.'

Pudovkin nodded and left.

On the floor, Estover moved slightly and let out a groan.

'So what shall we do with him, boss?' said the looming man.

Nikitin made an impatient gesture and took out his cigarette case. He lit a cigarette and frowned down at the limp and bleeding figure on the floor. One eye was invisible beneath a mass of bloody flesh, the other peered out of the remaining narrow slit like a terrified hunted mouse that has squeezed into a minute crack in a wall. On the pulpy lips a pink bubble slowly grew, then burst in a soft, almost inaudible sigh.

He knew Estover. He was soft. No way he would have held out under this pressure. So someone had set this up. The question was why? To get at Estover, or to get at him?

He finished the first cigarette and lit another. Curiously, he found himself wanting to discuss the affair with the man at his feet. Soft, the solicitor might be, but when it came to working out moves and counter moves, Toby Estover was without doubt the best in the business.

Used to be the best in the business.

One thing was clear. They couldn't just pick him up, dust him down and send him home.

The looming man was looking at him expectantly.

He stubbed out the second cigarette and said, 'Make sure he is weighted down so much he does not come to the surface in your lifetime.'

'Guaranteed,' said the looming man with perfect confidence.

And whatever god the man worshipped smiled, knowing that this lifetime had something less than ninety seconds to go.

The door burst open, there was a cry of 'Armed police!' and the looming man reached inside his jacket. Two shots rang out, and he loomed no more but slumped on the floor, not yet as bloody as, but already stiller than the figure he joined there.

Pavel Nikitin stood perfectly still, his face impassive. When the new arrivals screamed at him to lie face down on the floor with his hands behind his head he obeyed instantly. Seconds later his arms were forced down behind his back, his wrists handcuffed, and he was dragged to his feet.

A well-dressed man with wispy, almost white hair and a benevolent smile stood gazing down at Estover. A pair of paramedics came into the room, took a quick look at the shot man, shook their heads, then moved John Childs aside to start working on the lawyer.

Childs turned his attention to the Russian.

'I'm so glad to meet you at last, Mr Nikitin,' he said.

The man regarded him blankly.

'Who the hell are you?'

'A friend. I think you're going to need a good lawyer, though after the way you seem to have treated your last one, you may find it difficult to hire a substitute. Whatever, it seems likely you are going to spend several years in one of our prisons. Parkleigh might suit you very well, it has all mod cons and is very handy for London. Of course, there is an alternative . . .'

'What?'

'Under the recent human rights reciprocation agreement, it may be possible to transfer you to Russian custody so that you can enjoy the solace of serving out your sentence under the tender care of your fellow countrymen.'

'Go to hell!' the Russian spat.

'I daresay I will. But I hope we may meet again before then. Who knows? We might even find a way of being mutually beneficial. Grim necessity makes strange bedfellows, Mr Nikitin. I'm sure there's an old Russian proverb that states as much.'

The man was back in control now. He even managed a smile as he said, 'You speak very well, *friend*. But how important are you really? You are an old man and I think I know all the truly important old men in this country. Yes, soon you will find I have other friends who speak better than you. This is just a misunderstanding, a small difficulty that can easily be resolved.'

'Of course,' said Childs. 'As you resolved the small difficulty of Mr Hadda, you mean?'

That got Nikitin's attention. He looked genuinely puzzled as he said, 'What has Hadda to do with this, old man?'

'Nothing,' said Childs, regretting the impulse that had made him mention Wolf. 'I just happen to know you had a small commercial problem with him. And a small emotional problem too, I gather. Neither of which your boasted expertise was able to clear up.'

But he could see that his efforts at diversion were not working. The man's gaze moved from the recumbent figure of Estover, still being worked on by the paramedics, to the photos on the table.

Childs thought, they must have worked on Estover enough to know it wasn't him who spilled the beans to the paper. Now, because of my foolish desire to display omniscience, this bastard is making a link to Wolf.

He turned away abruptly and signalled to the armed police standing in the doorway.

He watched as Nikitin was hustled out of the room, then turned his attention to Estover. The medics had done all they could for him on the spot and were now preparing to stretcher him out.

'Will he live?' enquired Childs.

'Probably,' said one of the men. 'But there'll be long-term damage. And he won't look pretty. One of his eyes is a goner.'

'Oh dear. The whirligig of time, eh?'

'Sorry?'

'Nothing. Don't let me hold you up.'

A few seconds later he was left alone with the dead bodyguard. A fatal-shooting enquiry would follow and the corpse wouldn't be shifted till it had been photographed from every possible angle.

In death we can all become stars, thought Childs.

Of course it would have been neater if it had been Toby Estover's body lying there. The lawyer still had the capacity to cause the Chapel some embarrassment, particularly if, as was not uncommon, his near-death experience turned him into some kind of blabbermouth penitent.

On the other hand, he thought, studying the photographs lying on the desk, if the press were fed some tasty morsels about some of Estover's other clients who were then permitted to see these pictures, no one was ever going to believe a word he said again!

He slipped the photos into his pocket.

It was an ill wind that blew nobody any good, and he could either sell Nikitin to the Russians or he could bargain every last drop of useful information out of the man. And once a man had betrayed his associates, he was yours for ever.

Still, he would have to move carefully. Had this been purely a Chapel operation, Nikitin would have been rapidly removed from all possibility of contact with the outside world, but now he had entered the conventional legal system there was no way of keeping him incommunicado. The man wasn't lying when he said he had friends, both in high and in low places.

Would he among all his other concerns have time to do anything about the possibility that he had Wolf Hadda to thank for his predicament? The man Pudovkin was still free. He had been seen driving away from the warehouse not long before the police moved in. A couple of men had been sent to detain him once he was safely out of range of the operation, but they must have been careless or he had been extra alert, and he had slipped past them.

Nikitin would almost certainly get word to him of what had happened, and share his suspicions of who was behind it. Once this happened, and the attack dog was let loose, Wolf might find what it was to be the object as well as the agent of revenge.

Walking back to his car, Childs took out his mobile and dialled.

'Dr Ozigbo,' he said. 'John Childs. I wonder, if you should happen to see Wolf in the next few days, could you possibly give him a message from me?'

BOOK SIX

the world's edge

... but Slith, knowing well why that light was lit in that secret upper chamber, and who it was that lit it, leaped over the edge of the World, and is falling from us still through the unreverberate blackness of the abyss.

Lord Dunsany: *Probable Adventure of the Three Literary Men*

1

As Luke Hollins walked down Birkstane lonning, he heard the sound of an axe biting into wood. It came from beyond the house, over the boundary wall, in the Ulphingstone estate forest.

As he got nearer he could see the tall figure of Wolf Hadda swinging his axe with rhythmic ease, carving gobbets of bright white wood out of a young pine tree. The man was naked to the waist, his upper body glistening with sweat. In the reflecting sunlight, Hollins appreciated the play of muscles in his arms and chest as the axe rose and fell.

Michelangelo could have done something with this, thought Hollins as he called out, 'Hullo!'

The woodcutter's head turned slowly towards him. He wasn't wearing his eye patch and the sight of that scarred face with its one eye glaring at him turned the vicar's thoughts from Greek statuary to Greek monsters.

'I shouldn't stand there,' said Hadda, placing his hand against the trunk and pushing.

'What? Oh yes . . .'

He turned and ran backwards and sideways as the tree began to sway towards him. He could have sworn he felt the rush of displaced air as it passed close and he certainly felt the ground tremble as the trunk hit the earth. But when he turned he saw that in fact the tree had fallen many yards to the side of where he'd been standing and Hadda was grinning broadly.

'I doubt if a Cumbrian parson's moved so fast since they raided that knocking shop near Carlisle Cathedral,' he said as he strode forward, towelling himself down with his shirt before pulling it over his head.

'Very funny,' said Hollins, slightly out of breath. 'Does Sir Leon know you're stealing his trees?'

'I reckon he can spare one,' said Hadda indifferently. 'In fact, I reckon he probably owes my dad quite a few. But if he looks bothered when you mention it to him, tell him to send me a bill.'

'Even if I were inclined to act as a grass, I doubt if the occasion will arise in the near future,' said Hollins. 'I seem to have become *non grata* at the castle since Christmas. In fact, Lady Kira hasn't shown up at church for the past couple of Sundays, though that might have something to do with that unfortunate business with her Mr Nikitin.'

'Really? What's that all about then?' said Hadda, leading the way towards the house with Sneck walking at the vicar's side, trying to get his nose into his trouser pocket.

As Hollins produced the looked-for treats, he regarded Hadda sceptically. Even in his self-imposed isolation, could he really have missed the main topic of local interest for the last several days? It had got plenty of media space to start with.

He said, 'It sounds as if Lady Kira's distant cousin (the distance is increasing daily, I gather) attempted to murder her son-in-law. Surely even if you didn't hear about it on the news, you must have had journalists sniffing around to see if they could get a quote out of you. Everybody else in the parish has.'

And not everybody else in the parish is a notorious parolee who once employed the assaulted man as his solicitor and had subsequently been replaced by him in the marital bed, was the unspoken rider.

'Oh *that*,' said Hadda indifferently. 'There were a couple. Never found what they wanted. I chased them off with Sneck. Then I borrowed Joe Strudd's muck-spreader and parked it up the lonning. Next lot that came, I turned the spreader on as they were getting out of their car. After that they didn't seem to bother me any more.'

Hollis fixed on the most remarkable piece of this statement.

'Joe Strudd loaned you his muck-spreader?' he said incredulously.

Strudd, Hadda's nearest neighbour, was a Cumbrian farmer of the old school and a devout chapel-goer who regarded St Swithin's as an outpost of popish laxity.

'Aye. I found one of them Holsteins he's so proud of badly mired in Hillick Moss and I pulled it out. Someone must have seen me, but didn't want to risk contamination by actually helping me. One of your Anglican flock, I daresay. At least he told Joe, and he called round to say thanks. Would have said a few prayers too, but I told him I was already spoken for. And he said, "Aye, I can see how you'd feel more at home at St Swithin's." So you see what kind of reputation you've got, Padre!'

Hollins grinned and said, 'Yes, Strudd's usual greeting to me is "Give my regards to the whore of Babylon!" But all the same, Joe Strudd loaning you his muck-spreader . . . well, well. That's a step in the right direction.'

'They'll be inviting me to speak at the WI next,' said Hadda indifferently. 'So, to what do I owe the pleasure? I've not put in my Tesco order yet.'

They were in the kitchen now. Sneck, persuaded the treats were finished, had stretched himself out on the hearth. Hadda, having put the kettle on, was spooning coffee into the pot.

Hollins said, 'Mainly, like I say, to check you weren't being besieged by journalists, but I see I needn't have worried. In fact, you've never been much bothered by the media, have you? Not even when you first came back here. One might almost think you were under some kind of protection . . .?'

'Aren't we all, Padre? Surely that's part of your message.'

'I was thinking more of the terrestrial sphere,' said Hollins drily.

Hadda poured the coffee. He'd grown quite fond of the young vicar and it pleased him to note that Hollins's professional desire to see the best in people hadn't taken the edge off a sharp eye and a sharp ear.

'No cream, sorry. No, not really sorry. I still have hopes that I can convert you to agreeing black is best.'

'Perhaps we can look forward to a mutual conversion? Perhaps not! But on the subject of black being best, another thing that brought me here was I had a phone call from Ms Ozigbo.'

The mug paused momentarily in its arc to Hadda's lips, then he drank and said mildly, 'I'm trying to work out if that's racist or not.'

'Hardly, when it's not my intention to be discriminatory, inflammatory or offensive, any more than it's yours when you offer your little *bon mots* about the Church.'

Oh yes, thought Hadda. One might make much of the Reverend Luke Hollins if you caught him while he was still young!

He said, 'So what did Alva want? Checking up that I hadn't run amuck with my axe?'

'She told me several things. One was that she's left her job at Parkleigh.'

'Good lord. Any particular reason?'

'None given to me. She said that she was presently staying with her parents again in Manchester. Her father seems well on the road to full recovery, by the way.'

'I'm glad. Owt else?'

Hollins grinned. It was good to feel on top in a conversation with Hadda for a change. The man's effort to sound only casually interested wasn't all that convincing.

'She seemed particularly concerned to know if your ex-wife was at the Castle. I said in view of the reported condition of her husband, it hardly seemed likely.'

Hadda said indifferently, 'Don't see why not. Unless Imo's changed, I can't see her spending her waking hours sitting by a sickbed, mopping Estover's heated brow and squeezing his hand reassuringly.'

'It turns out you're right. When I checked with my church-warden, whose youngest daughter does a bit of cleaning at the castle, he said that Mrs Estover is expected there some time today.'

'You really are adapting to country life, Padre,' said Hadda. 'Impossible to survive here unless you've got a well-organized and highly motivated intelligence network. So did you relay this bit of news to Alva?'

'No. I thought it would keep till I talked to her face to face.'

That got his interest.

'Face to face?'

'Yes, she too is driving up today.'

Both your women on the road north, he thought; maybe they'll meet up for a coffee and a chat in a service station.

Hadda was regarding him sharply, as if he'd read the thought. Or maybe because he'd had it himself.

'And she's coming all this way just to see you?' said Wolf.

'She didn't indicate otherwise,' said Hollins. 'She said she had some information she needed to share with me.' He paused, counted to three, then added, 'Something to do with you, as far as I could make out.'

'So let's get this straight, my psychiatrist is driving up to Cumbria to talk with my local vicar about something that concerns me?'

Hadda sounded angry but only, it seemed to Hollins, to hide some other emotion.

'I suppose you could put it like that.'

'And tell me, Padre, why did you feel the need to share this information with me? Secret meetings to discuss a patient's state of mind are conventionally kept secret, I should have thought.'

'I expect so. But as Ms Ozigbo didn't indicate it was your state of mind she wanted to discuss, I don't think it applies here. I'm sure she will reveal all when she calls to see you.'

'But you said she wasn't going to try and see me.'

'No. I said she didn't say she was. But I would lay odds she does.'

'Oh yes? Turned you into a gambling man now, has she? So what am I supposed to do, hang around here all day on the off chance she drops by?'

'You must do as you will, Wolf,' said Hollins, standing up.

'Must I? Well, I suppose I should thank you for acting as go-between.'

'No, I'm not a go-between,' said Hollins sternly. 'Nor am I the confidant of either you or Ms Ozigbo. If you have secrets from each other, you should learn not to share them

512

with me. Not unless, of course, either of you wish to confide in me as a priest.'

'Wow,' said Hadda. 'Nice speech. I'll pick the bones out of it later. There wasn't anything in there about not being a delivery man, was there? You might as well take my Tesco order while you're here.'

He took a pad out of a drawer, checked through a list written on it, scribbled a couple of extra items, and handed it over to Hollins.

'Nearly forgot your cream,' he said lightly. 'Wouldn't like to think I was driving you off by not pandering to your fleshly weaknesses. I like a few fleshly weaknesses in my priests.'

Hollins said, 'Just as I like small acts of generosity from my sinners. Incidentally, as a matter of curiosity, what exactly are you going to do with that tree you've stolen?'

'The ridge beam in one of the barns has a bit of a sag in it,' said Hadda. 'Probably been up there for three hundred years or so. It'll last a while yet, but I'd like to have another one, seasoned and ready, for when the time comes.'

'I see. You're planning to stay around then?'

'Not for three hundred years, perhaps,' laughed Hadda. 'But I can't think of anywhere else I'd want to go. Not wanting shut of me, are you?'

'Of course not.'

'And you, you'll be sticking around too?'

'Not wanting shut of me, are you?' retorted Hollins.

'Just when I'm breaking you in? No way. They might opt for a woman next time!'

'Now that does sound sexist.'

'No. It's just that I'm out of practice with women. Now, I'd better get my tree sorted and shifted before one of Leon's foresters notices it lying there.'

They went into the yard together. As they parted, Hadda

said, 'By the way, tell Alva if she does decide to drop by and I'm not here, she should make herself at home. This time, she should light the fire.'

'I'll tell her,' said Hollins.

He made his way back up the hard rutted lonning, wondering how it was that every time he saw Hadda, it felt more and more like a meeting of friends.

2

Imogen Estover sat at the breakfast table, studying the morning paper. In front of her, hardly touched, was a bowl of muesli. Behind her the electric hot-plate on the sideboard was covered with the usual array of silver-domed dishes. The fact that the sole occupants of the castle at the moment were herself and her parents made no difference. Any suggestion that it hardly made sense to offer such a wide choice to so few people drew from Lady Kira the response, 'Why should I treat guests better than I treat myself?'

Imogen turned a sheet and let her eyes run down the next page. She wasn't so much reading the paper as grazing over it to check if there were any references to the assault on her husband and the arrest of Pavel Nikitin.

There were none. The Great British public likes its meat fresh and any successful editor knows that today's lie will always sell more papers than yesterday's truth. When Nikitin came to trial, it would all start up again, but a man locked away in a prison cell and another lying comatose on a hospital bed do not combine to generate very much of interest. Meanwhile a terrorist bomb in Paris, a premier league footballer accused of match-fixing, the suspicious death of a TV chat-show host, a scientist's claim that global warming was responsible for a plague of locusts in the Channel Isles, the first streaker in the House of Commons, the possibility of a constitutional crisis if the imminent royal twins both turned out to be male, the launch of the first solar-powered sex toy – these and many other items of similar importance competed for the headlines.

'Good morning, darling.'

Her mother had come into the room.

'Good morning, Mummy. You're bright and early.'

It was barely light outside.

'I sleep badly these days. You too?'

'No. The days are short and I thought I might go for a walk.'

'Yes, I see you are dressed *au paysan*,' said Kira, her gaze taking in with distaste her daughter's woollen socks, cord breeks and checked shirt. 'Anything in the paper?'

'Not a word. I think it's probably safe for you to go out now.'

When Imogen had arrived the previous evening she discovered her mother hadn't been out of doors for nearly a fortnight.

The upsurge in media interest in the Ulphingstones that had occurred as a consequence of what was referred to as the Wapping Warehouse Shoot-out had put the castle under siege for a couple of days. Locking the main gates gave little protection as the estate perimeter was defined by little more than sheep-proof fences and decaying dry-stone walls. Lady Kira's initial response was to stroll around with a shotgun under her arm, ready to take a pot-shot at any stranger she came across. It had taken a formal warning from the Chief Constable after a couple of near misses to persuade her that she was not entitled to kill, maim or even seriously frighten trespassers.

'Then let them roam at will. They shall not see me!' she'd declared.

Now she helped herself to a generous plateful of bacon, sausage and eggs and sat down opposite her daughter.

'How do you stay so healthy?' she asked, looking disapprovingly at the muesli.

'I wonder the same about you,' said Imogen.

It was true. In her early sixties, Kira Ulphingstone weighed little more than when she'd arrived at the castle as a young bride more than four decades earlier. Nor had she controlled her weight in any way that had visibly affected her looks. The high cheeks might be more accentuated than they appeared in her wedding photographs, but her brow was still smooth, her skin tone was good, her eyes were still bright, and her figure, clothed at least, was still as seductively curvaceous.

What did seem to have changed from those old pictures was the difference in age between herself and her husband. Sir Leon was over twenty years her senior. On his wedding day it seemed less. Now when they appeared together, the difference looked to be nearer half a century.

'Will Daddy be breakfasting?' asked Imogen.

Lady Kira shrugged.

'Who knows? These days, I do not disturb him.'

It was many years since she and her husband had shared a bedroom. In fact, Imogen could not recall a time when they had. When she'd grown old enough to notice such things, she'd been aware that from time to time her father would walk down the corridor from his room to his wife's, then return a little later. Such excursions became rarer as she got older and had long since, to the best of her knowledge, ceased altogether.

This separation was not down to any frigidity on her mother's part, Imogen was sure. In fact, probably the contrary. She believed she'd inherited her own strong sexuality from

Kira, and she guessed that, even as a young bride, she had never been satisfied by her middle-aged husband. At least, thought Imogen, with Wolf present, she had never had that problem, but his increasingly long absences had left a gap that needed to be filled . . .

She sometimes wondered how her mother had dealt with her needs, but their similarities had somehow never added up to a closeness that permitted her to ask. Or perhaps it was affection for her father that prevented her from wanting to know. It seemed to her that Leon had had a bad enough deal in life already. A wife he could not satisfy, a wife who did not care much for his friends and whose own friends he did not altogether approve, a wife who had set herself to change the traditional, easy-going squirearchical relationship between the castle and the locality to something the far side of feudal, a wife who had given him no male heir, only a daughter as wilful as her mother who, in the old phrase, had married to disoblige her family.

He did not deserve that this daughter should be privy to his cuckolding.

Her mother had no such inhibitions, it seemed.

After devouring a large forkful of sausage, Kira said, 'I am not sorry that Pasha has been found out. I always suspected that there must be something a little soiled about his money. And besides, he was a great disappointment in bed.'

Imogen felt a surprise that came close to shock.

She hoped she concealed it efficiently as she replied, 'And why do you imagine that this is of the slightest interest to me?'

'Do not be so disingenuous, dear. You know very well I had hopes that perhaps one day you and he might get together.'

'I hope you're not going to tell me that these hopes included encouraging him to try and murder Toby?'

'Now you're being silly. One way or another, it was clear

to me that you and Toby are pretty well played out. When did you last have sex with him?'

'I shouldn't have thought that you rated marital sex as an essential element in a lasting marriage, Mother,' said Imogen.

'My case is different. A title and a castle are worth clinging on to. A fat lawyer who is notorious for fornicating with his secretaries is quite another matter. Anyway, that is beside the point now. What condition he will be in, if he recovers, I dread to think. But with Pasha out of the picture, we must look to your future. No real problem. You are still a desirable woman in many ways. There will be plenty of suitable candidates.'

Imogen said, 'And do you intend to vet them all as thoroughly as you did Pasha?'

Lady Kira shrugged.

'Pasha was here, feeling as always very frustrated by the way you played with him. The poor boy needed an outlet. I needed – how shall I put it? – an inlet. Do not pretend to be shocked, my dear. You are my daughter, you know how these needs of ours work.'

'There is such a thing as discrimination,' said Imogen. 'As a matter of interest, how long have you been offering this in-depth maternal service? And who to? Good God, don't tell me, not you and Toby . . .?'

Kira waved her fork dismissively.

'A long time ago,' she said. 'He was better than I anticipated. After you and your peasant split up, I thought he might do quite nicely for you. Money, standing, a good school, an old family – there is a title, you know, but unfortunately he is at least three disgustingly healthy cousins away from it.'

Despite herself, Imogen could not restrain a small smile.

'Mother, I thought you had long ago lost the capacity to

surprise me, but I see I was wrong. Well, at least I can be confident that my first choice was tested by no one but myself. No way would you demean yourself by making out with a peasant!'

'Come now, my dear. I am sure back in the old days our ancestors felt no shame in taking their pleasure with a well set-up *kulak*. And working as a woodcutter certainly seems to set a man up very well . . .'

She smiled as she said it with a kind of significant coyness that put her daughter on the alert.

She said, 'Mother, if you're trying to imply that you and Wolf . . . I don't believe you!'

'And if I had, how would that make you feel?' asked Kira. 'In fact, how *do* you feel about Hadda? It bothers me. You don't seem to hate him as you should. And what's worse, you don't seem to fear him as you should! For God's sake, you're not still lusting after him, are you?'

'What I feel about Wolf is nothing to do with you,' said Imogen.

Lady Kira looked at her daughter with the kind of icily reductive stare that in olden days had probably set serfs thinking nostalgically of happier times working out in the fields in sub-zero temperatures till their frostbitten fingers fell off.

Then she relaxed and smiled a smile that was worse than the stare.

'Well, that's not precisely true, my love,' she said. 'Let me tell you a story . . .'

Fifteen minutes later, Kira stood by the window and watched her daughter's Mercedes go screaming down the drive.

Had that gone well or badly? she wondered. She wasn't sure, but she wasn't going to let it spoil her breakfast.

She took the congealing remnant of her first selection to

the sideboard, set it down, and began to load another plate. She was not so arrogant that she did not count her blessings. High on the list alongside her ability not to get emotional about things she could not change was possession of the kind of body that could take in almost anything by way of food, or drink, or men, extract maximum enjoyment, and then move on with very little residual damage to show for it.

She lifted another domed lid and now she did give her emotions free rein.

No black pudding!

She was really going to have to have a serious talk with those incompetents in the kitchen!

3

Wolf Hadda stood under the icy waterfall and rubbed himself vigorously with a bar of kitchen soap.

He remained there long enough for the hissing water to sluice off the suds then moved out into the shallow pool.

There was someone on the bank. Sneck was standing by, watchful, but on the whole assessing the watcher as harmless.

Hadda said, 'I didn't have you down as a Peeping Tom.'

Alva Ozigbo said, 'I wanted to see whether you really did take a shower here at the crack of dawn every day, or if you were just trying to impress me.'

'Call this the crack of dawn, city girl? It must be nearly nine o'clock! I'm coming out now.'

'So what am I supposed to do? Blush and turn my back?'

'Of course not. A man should hide nothing from his psychiatrist. But if I stand here too long being admired, I'll start to form icicles. Let's get back to the house. Do you want to walk in front or behind?'

'In front, I think. Walking behind, I wouldn't know where to look.'

'Not a problem for me,' he said, falling into step behind

her. 'Young Hollins was here yesterday. He told me you might be coming. When did you get here?'

'Last night. I stayed at the vicarage.'

'Draughty old place, as I recall. You'd have been better off here. What did his wife think about having a good-looking dolly bird from the big city landed on her?'

Why am I feeling such a glow of pleasure at being told I could have stayed at Birkstane and being referred to as a dolly bird? Alva asked herself.

She said, 'I don't think she likes me much.'

'Something else you and I have in common, I suspect.'

Something else . . .

She didn't spoil it by asking what, but led the way into the kitchen where she was glad to see flames licking out of a tall wigwam of logs in the old grate.

Hadda said, 'Excuse me a minute. Make yourself useful. You know where the coffee is.'

When he returned fully dressed, she said casually, 'Talking of Luke, I told him I was certain you'd been framed.'

'That must have been relief for him. Can't have been much fun, having to stand up for a pervert. He took your word for it, did he? No demand for incontrovertible evidence?'

'He just nodded as if I was confirming something he'd known all along.'

'Yeah, sure he did. That's why he got his canonicals in such a twist when he found the money. You going to pour that coffee or are you waiting for the maid?'

The brusque jollity confirmed what she'd felt from the moment their eyes had met at the pool. He was glad to see her! That was . . . she wasn't certain what it was, but it was certainly something.

But it was time to get serious.

She said, 'I nearly forgot. John Childs asked me to give you a message.'

'Jesus!'

That really did surprise him. Good! He needed to be surprised from time to time.

He sat down heavily and looked at her from under lowering brows.

'How the hell have you got involved with Childs?' he asked.

She told him, succinctly but not omitting any significant detail.

He listened intently and when she'd finished he said accusingly, 'Well, well. Pity you hadn't thought to mention his name a lot earlier.'

'Why should I?' she demanded.

He considered this, then relaxed and said, 'No reason. So what was this message?'

'Something about Nikitin knowing, and the man with the broken jaw being on the loose.'

'And that's it?' he said indifferently.

'That's it.'

'Very mysterious. Dear old JC always did like to speak in tongues. Knows what, I wonder?'

Alva said, 'I would guess, knows it was you who set up Estover so the Russian would do your dirty work for you.'

This was the second time she'd surprised him in a minute. A third success and she might get to keep him!

He said, 'Psychiatrists shouldn't make guesses. So all this time you've been a buddy of JC's. Got to give the old boy credit. Having your own personal prison with wall-to-wall wire, that's a real Chapel trick! Now if I'd known that, I might have done things differently.'

'You mean you might not have played your game with me?' she said, regarding him steadily over the brim of her coffee mug.

'My game?'

She said, 'Don't pretend you didn't enjoy playing me.'

He said, 'Of course I did. To start with, anyway. Who doesn't enjoy outwitting an expert? But then, I did have the best expert advice on how to go about it . . .'

He regarded her quizzically.

'My book, you mean? And I was foolish enough to feel slightly flattered when I saw it in your bedroom.'

'Sorry about that. I hadn't meant to be so careless.'

'Come to think of it, I didn't see it in your cell at Parkleigh. That was really a book-free zone. Except for *The Count of Monte-Cristo*.'

He grinned and said, 'I couldn't resist leaving that for you to find.'

'You knew I would be having a look?'

'It seemed likely if, as suggested by *Curing Souls*, you had a truly enquiring mind,' he said. 'So I rented storage space for the books I didn't want you to find from a guy in the next cell.'

'Books?'

'Yes. Sorry. Couldn't just rely on *Curing Souls*, could I? It was, after all – what was the word the reviewers used? – rather *precocious*. So I got hold of some more mainstream stuff.'

'Just as well. It would hardly have done for you to rely for your deception on the work of such a second-rate psychiatrist as I clearly am,' she said, unable to keep the bitterness out of her voice.

'Oh dear,' he said. 'And now you hate me more for being innocent than ever you did for being guilty? Don't you find that odd?'

'I don't hate you,' she said. 'I never did.'

'A child-abusing fraudster? Come on!'

It did not seem the time to tell him she'd felt attracted to him almost from the start, despite everything she'd thought

525

she knew about him, despite his appearance, despite all her efforts to analyse this troubling reaction out of her psyche. Getting this back on a formal professional level was important.

'Hate the sin, not the sinner is the first line of the psychotherapist's creed,' she said. 'You can't help where you hate. I wanted to help you. I still do.'

'Really?' he said in mock surprise. 'But now you recognize that I'm innocent, that I was set up, what's to help?'

She regarded him sadly and said, 'Wolf, after all that has happened to you, there's no way you're not damaged goods, you're too bright not to see that.'

'Damaged's a bit strong, isn't it? I've taken a few knocks, yes, but in the circumstances, I think I've come through it all a lot less battered inside than out. Look, Elf, don't take it personally. I'm sorry you were the tool I used for getting out of jail. OK, I enjoyed fooling you to start with, but as I got to know you, I stopped enjoying.'

'Why didn't you just try to convince me you were innocent?'

He laughed and gave her much the same answer as Doll Trapp.

'How the hell could I do that when every protestation of innocence was just another symptom of denial in your eyes? Even if I'd succeeded, who was going to listen to you? The parole hearing would pay you the respect due to an expert if you told them I'd responded to treatment and was now fit to be turned loose. But tell them I was innocent and all they'd see was a dotty woman who'd been duped by a manipulative sociopath.'

She resisted the temptation to say that was a pretty good description of what had happened anyway, and replied, 'OK. So the end of the exercise was to get out and look for evidence of how you were fitted up. And you got it from Medler. So why didn't you go straight to the authorities and say, Have a listen to this?'

He laughed again.

'Don't be naïve, Elf,' he said. 'They don't want me to be innocent any more than you did. Fine, they'll look into it, but while they're doing that, I'll be back inside.'

'But not for long, surely, once they hear your recording.'

'You reckon? But how do I prove it really was Medler talking? Or that he wasn't under duress? After all, the poor sod was found dead not long afterwards. There'd be plenty of people eager to point the finger at me. And there's Ed to think of. I was supposed to be staying with him. The Law Society would be down on him like a ton of bricks for covering up for me. And if they managed to prove it was Ed and Doll that fixed me up with a fake passport, what do you imagine that would do to them?'

She didn't speak for a while, just sat there regarding him steadily.

Then she nodded and said, 'Good arguments. You've obviously thought it through. But I think that, even if none of them applied, you would still have found some equally convincing reasons for not taking that recording to the authorities and asking them to take another look at your conviction.'

He grew angry now, or perhaps, she thought, unconsciously echoing Hollins the day before, he was seeking refuge in anger.

'Haven't you learned anything about the way the world works?' he demanded. 'To find evidence to support what Medler alleged, they'd have to go after Estover and the Nutbrowns. Toby's one of the smartest lawyers in the country. Pippa Nutbrown's as slippery as a sackful of snakes. As for Johnny, following his thought processes is like trying to count bubbles in a champagne glass. And remember, they'd be outside crying foul! while I'd be sitting on my arse in a cell.'

'Childs says he thinks he can help you get your name cleared officially.'

'Does he? I shan't hold my breath.'

'I just meant, with him on your side, it seems to me there's a real chance for justice to be done.'

'He let me go down in the first place,' said Hadda indifferently. 'I always knew, if I wanted justice, I had to look for it my way.'

'You call what's happened to the Nutbrowns justice?'

His expression turned cold.

'To be dragged out of your bed by a dawn raid, to lose everything you hold precious, oh yes, that sounds like justice to me.'

'And Estover?'

'I gather his professional reputation may take a bit of a nosedive, and if he seeks for consolation in the little pile of gold he's got stashed away for a rainy day, he may be in for a big surprise. So, no reputation, no money. Now who does that remind me of? Of course I'm sorry to hear he's going to lose his youthful good looks and may end up walking with a bit of a limp. Maybe we could get together and do a double act round the halls?'

This was going to be even harder than she'd anticipated. She said, 'So, an eye for an eye; that sounds a lot more like revenge to me than justice.'

'Anything they get will be less than they deserve,' he said dismissively.

'Would you still have been able to say that if Estover had died? You knew that was the likely outcome if it hadn't been for Childs's intervention.'

He shrugged.

'It may still be that Toby will come to regard that as the

better alternative,' he said. 'As for JC, I'll bottle my grati-tude till I've got enough to make a grateful tear.'

'I think that, despite everything, he's helped you because he is fond of you.'

'And the same for you, no doubt. But John's god is Necessity, and that's an idol carved out of granite. Try not to come between it and anything you value.'

'He's genuinely worried about what you intend to do next,' she said.

'He needn't be. What's the point of worrying about fate?'

'He said you might be suffering from the delusion that you were the instrument of God. Wolf, believe me, if left too late, that's a delusion whose dissipation you might find too hard to bear.'

Suddenly he relaxed and let out a hoot of laughter.

'Jesus, Elf, we're beginning to sound like two characters in an old-fashioned melodrama! What do you think's going to happen? I'm not about to mount a rocket attack on Ulphingstone Castle or anything like that, believe me. I've got most of the revenge stuff out of my system now, honest. All I want's a bit of peace and quiet so that I can watch the spring arrive.'

She wanted to believe him. She had a feeling he wanted to believe himself. But she'd had it drummed into her that the truly effective psychiatrist always gets the couch warm for the client. Or, put another way, the first job is to look deep into yourself and make sure you start with a clean sheet.

Sneck suddenly rose from the hearth and went to the door, growling deep in this throat.

Hadda rose too.

'Excuse me,' he said.

Motioning Sneck to heel, he pulled the door open, waited a moment, then slipped outside. Alva found herself once more comparing the smooth, slightly rolling movement caused by his ruined knee with the laboured limp she remembered from Parkleigh.

She too stood up and went to the door.

She saw him in the barn doorway standing by the Defender. He plucked a spill of paper tucked in behind the wipers, unfolded it and began to read. Sneck turned and looked at Alva. Not wanting Wolf to think she was spying on him, she retreated and was sitting at the table once more, nursing her coffee mug, when he came back in.

'Problem?' she said.

'No,' he said, tossing a screwed-up ball of paper towards the fire. 'Might have been a deer. Sneck and me are both getting neurotic. We had a bit of trouble with reporters.'

'Yes, Luke Hollins told me about the muck-spreader. He seemed to find it rather poetic.'

'He's a good lad,' said Hadda, resuming his seat and picking up his mug. 'Now, where were we?'

He was trying to sound the same as he did before, but something had changed.

She said, 'You were telling me how content you were to relax in your own cosy little house, far away from the world's troubles, just waiting for the daffodils and swallows to return with the spring.'

'Was I? Sounds good to me. Why are you giving me that fish-eyed psychiatrist look?'

'Because I don't believe you,' she said.

'Hang about? Are you people allowed to call your patients liars?'

'I'm not talking to you as a patient but as a friend,' she said. 'And here's what I think. I think that everything you've done since you got out, all your clever planning and scheming, all your talk of justice and revenge, amounts to nothing more than delaying tactics. You don't really give a damn about Estover and Nutbrown. You don't give a damn about proving your innocence. The only thing that really matters to you is what you're going to do about Imogen. And the truth is, you've no idea what to do, no idea what you want to do. But now, with everything else out of the way, the big moment's getting near. So what's it to be, Wolf? Have you made up your mind yet?'

For a moment she thought she'd stung him to an honest reply. Then he let out a rather histrionic sigh, shook his head ruefully and said, 'There you go, Elf. Even when you're talking as a friend, you can't stop working out interesting little mental scenarios, can you? I always suspected that all this psycho-analysing stuff came down to storytelling in the end. You plot a little narrative to take everything in, make a few adjustments to let the action flow more smoothly, offer a couple of endings, one happy, one unhappy, then tell your client to make his choice, that'll be a hundred guineas please. Well, I'm sorry, Elf. I'm no longer a character in your fairy tale. I'm very happy in my own.'

She said, '*Once upon a time I was living happily ever after.* Those were the first words you wrote for me, remember? You were a character in your own fairy tale, Wolf, not mine. In fact, you were two characters. The wolf and the wood-cutter. Bit of a conflict there. Maybe it's a good job that fairy tale's over. No way can you ever get back into it. But you're right. Even without paying a hundred guineas, you can still choose the ending.'

On the wall the old bracket clock struck the hour.

He stood up and said, 'That time already? Damn. And I was so enjoying our fireside chat. But I'm afraid I've got to go. Us licensed cons aren't masters of our lives, as I'm sure you know. I need to show my face at regular intervals, prove I'm still on the straight and narrow.'

'You mean you're driving to Carlisle to see your probation officer?'

'That's right,' he said. 'No need for you to rush off, sit here and finish your coffee. But don't feel you've got to wash up! Will I see you again before you go back down to Manchester, or are you heading off straight away?'

She looked up at him and said, 'I'm not sure.'

'OK,' he said, turning away to pluck his axe from where it stood in a corner. Then he turned to look at her, curiously indecisive. Finally he took a couple of steps forward till he was standing alongside her chair. She sat quite still, aware of the closeness of his body. And of his axe also.

He said, 'I never felt I could do this while you thought I was guilty. And now you don't, I'm finding all kinds of other reasons for being frightened of doing it. At this rate, I'll never do it! So here goes.'

He stooped, put his right hand behind her head and pressed his face to hers in a kiss that went on so long she felt herself becoming breathless, but she made no effort to break contact.

Finally he pulled away.

'For better or worse, that's done,' he said. 'First kiss? Last kiss? Who can ever tell?'

He made for the door. Sneck rose from the hearth but subsided reluctantly as his master commanded, 'Stay!'

Then he was gone. A moment later she heard the grating roar of the Defender. When that died away, the silence seemed like the silence of space.

She finished her coffee. She'd made it strong, the way she knew Hadda liked it, but far from being a stimulant, it seemed to act on her like an opiate. A strange lassitude stole over her limbs and she sat peering sightlessly and for the most part thoughtlessly into her empty mug. It was as if there were a problem she had to puzzle out, only it was so big her mind could not even begin to get to grips with it.

It was the wigwam of logs in the grate collapsing in a

gentle sigh of heron-grey ash that roused her from her reverie.

She ran her tongue round her lips.

Better or worse? First or last?

Who can tell?'

She stood up to get some more logs from the basket. Sneck looked up at her hopefully. She said, 'Sorry,' and he returned his attention to something he was licking at between his paws. As she set the logs in the grate, she realized it was the piece of paper Hadda had balled up and thrown at the fire.

She tried to pick it up. The dog bared his teeth. She went to the kitchen cupboard and got a ginger biscuit. Sneck acknowledged this was fair exchange and let her retrieve the paper.

She smoothed it out on the kitchen table.

It was a handwritten note:

Is she a permanent fixture then? I think I'll take a stroll to Pillar Rock. Who says I'm not sentimental?

She didn't recognize the writing; she didn't need to.

He wasn't on his way to see his probation officer. She should have known that as soon as he took his axe from the corner. But the kiss had diverted her mind down other channels in search of its meaning.

One thing she was certain of: the kiss couldn't mean whatever she wanted it to mean while his problems with Imogen remained unresolved.

And she doubted whether a true resolution were possible while the woman was alive. But if she died, and if Wolf was responsible, then the problem would remain frozen in time for ever, and Wolf would be completely beyond her reach, emotionally, mentally, and almost certainly physically too.

She had no idea what she could do, but she knew that

the possibility of solution did not lie in the maze of her mind but out there somewhere on the cold fell tops.

She made for the door. From the hearth came an enquiring growl.

She turned and looked at Sneck.

'Why not, boy?' she said. 'To tell you the truth, I'll be glad of company!'

4

Imogen stood on top of Pillar Rock looking down at the Liza winding its way along the valley bottom two thousand feet below and recalling the first time she had climbed up here more than a quarter of a century before.

Then she had simply trailed along beside Wolf, not certain where he was going, just knowing there was a life force in this young man that she wanted a share of.

Well, she'd certainly got her share, sucked him almost dry some might say, though he had got his fair share of all that she had to offer too.

No, not his *fair* share, because fairness didn't enter into it.

He had stepped out of his world into hers, but it had been both impossible and undesirable that he could step all the way.

Impossible because, despite all the social cosmetology of the modern democratic era, it remained as true as it had always been that the *arriviste* could never really arrive.

And undesirable because for Wolf to have completely adapted to the moral code of her circle, which was basically *do what thou wilt shall be all of the law,* he would have had to sacrifice so much of what made him Wolf that he'd no longer have been worth having.

The wind was blowing hard up here. She sat down with her back to it. She was well insulated by several layers of clothing, but its chilly fingers still probed through to her warm flesh. Suggesting the Rock as a rendezvous point had not been the cleverest idea she'd ever had. Why had she done it? In one sense it was typical of the way she'd conducted a great deal of her life, an instinctive decision made without reference to reason or consequence. But at the same time it was also atypical, a reaching out of the random in search of a pattern.

Here it had all started. Here it would all end.

How it would end, she could not foretell. Her efforts to see him at Christmas had been coloured by the assumption that she would still have power over him, based on her awareness that he still had power over her. Her sense that he was making a conscious effort not to see her had confirmed her assumption. But after what had happened to Toby and the Nutbrowns, things had moved on. A first step had been taken, and she knew from her own life how much easier a second step was.

Curiously, her increased sense of risk made her all the more determined to confront him head on. She enjoyed danger as long as it was in her face. What she didn't like was relaxing in her bath and hearing the buzz of an invisible wasp. Or to put it more poetically (she sometimes tried at poetry) all she wanted was to be able to stroll through the woodlands of her future without constantly straining her ears to catch the distant sound of an axe.

Was she a cold-hearted bitch, as a discarded lover had once called her? She'd examined the accusation closely and did not think so. Indeed, compared with her mother, she felt she was a creature of impulse and feeling. They had so much in common yet there were ways in which they were incomprehensible to each other. When Kira declared that the only thing better than having Wolf back in jail would be to have him buried deep in his grave, she was simply stating what she felt. To Imogen, neither of these was a desirable solution. What she wanted was to find a way for the pair of them to accept the collapse of their relationship and walk away from the wreckage comparatively unscathed.

There was a chance, albeit a small one, that her breakfast exchange with Kira might have provided a faint hope of finding such a way.

And another hopeful factor was the possibility that Wolf might even have something to walk away *to* as well as from. Men traditionally fell in love with their nurses, so why not with their psychiatrists?

Finding the black woman at the house again had been a surprise. When Alva Ozigbo came to the castle after Christmas, Imogen hadn't considered the possibility that she might have any interest in Wolf other than a professional one. After all, from her point of view, he was a convicted paedophile/fraudster whom she had certified safe to return to the community, so naturally she had a vested interest in keeping a close eye on him.

Now Imogen wished she'd taken rather more notice of her as an individual. She was certainly striking. Attractive? Possibly. Imogen tried to see her through male eyes. She herself wasn't too sensitive to the sexual aura of other women. In the interest of total experience she and Pippa had once spent a night together, but while there had been certain advantages in relating to a body that had the same geography and responses as your own, it had not been something she wanted to do again.

But she could see how Alva Ozigbo, with that combination of black skin, ochrous hair and fine bone structure, might turn some men on. Wolf? She wasn't sure. He had been so totally fixated on herself that she had never heard him express even a theoretical interest in another woman. She was one hundred per cent sure he'd never been unfaithful to her, even when his travels had kept him away from home for months on end. The pent-up passion released on his return had given her some of the sensual highs of her life, though after he'd been at home a while, his attentions began to make her feel a touch claustrophobic.

Had he ever suspected this? She thought not.

And she was absolutely sure he'd never suspected her of being unfaithful. His reaction would have been, to say the least, extreme. She had been very lucky for fourteen years that no malicious tongue had sought to set him straight. Perhaps his natural unself-conscious likeability had protected him. It would have been like hurting a child.

Or perhaps it had been his other defining quality, the sense of raw power seething beneath the surface and looking for an outlet, that had kept him safe. If ever there was a man whose first reaction might be to kill the messenger, it was Wolf!

But eventually, inevitably, he would have found out.

She knew her friends.

They might hold their peace for years but in the end, like the scorpion in the fable, they would have to sting, because it was in their nature.

This certainty that the marriage was living on borrowed time had been one of the factors that made it easy to go along with Toby and Pippa when they'd revealed their survival scheme. When necessity rules, regret is as pointless as resistance.

One way or another, Wolf was going to jail and the marriage was finished.

One way, she would be penniless.

The other, she wouldn't be.

Where was the choice in that?

To say she saw him condemned without a pang would have been untrue. To say that this pang kept her awake at nights would have been untruer. Only two things kept her awake and they were sex and toothache.

No, that was the kind of smart untruth she'd grown too used to pushing away people with. After Ginny died, she hadn't slept soundly for months without the help of pills or alcohol. Though, curiously, she now found that since moving into Ginny's old room, she slept like a child.

And she felt a kind of childish diffidence now as she sat on top of the Rock and wondered if he would come, and if he did, what he would do. She felt a sense of danger but no real fear. If necessity drove him to harm her, then so be it. She was confident he would not want to disfigure her as he had been disfigured. Death was another matter. He had never spoken openly about the years of youthful absence, but there had been killing in there somewhere, she was sure. In the right cause, he had the power to kill.

She stared down into the valley and saw herself slowly tumbling through the air.

Of course it wouldn't really be slow. Thirty-two feet per second, something like that, she seemed to recollect. Which worked out at a lot of miles per hour!

But how slow might it feel in the mind? Climbing, she'd often wondered about this. How many recollections and regrets could be crushed between that moment when your fingers slipped from their hold and the next when your body broke against the rocks?

Perhaps there was just time for one clear revelation, one all-illuminating insight.

Or perhaps it would go on forever. She recalled a story her father used to read to her about a thief who escaped capture by jumping over the edge of the world. She used to lie in bed after Leon had put out the light, imagining how that would feel. And the words had often played through her mind as she was climbing . . . *falling from us still through the unreverberate blackness of the abyss* . . .

Falling . . . falling . . . falling . . .

A sound reached her that wasn't borne on the gusting wind. She rose to her feet and strained her ears.

There it was again, the sound of boot on rock, from far below.

He was coming. She'd never doubted that he would.

She settled down for the last minutes of waiting.

5

Pudo Pudovkin had all the attributes of a fine chess player: a mind that could sum up several moves ahead, an ability to read an opponent, and the patience not to make a move until he was happy it was the right one. Everything, in fact, except the capacity to accept defeat philosophically. And while being a bad loser doesn't necessarily make you a bad player, being the kind of bad loser who is likely to fly into a rage and attempt to make a winning opponent swallow his chessmen tends to leave you short of people willing to play with you.

His positive qualities, plus a large infusion of the negative one, combined to make him an excellent assassin. But on this dank February morning, he found his patience was being sorely tried.

Arriving early in the vicinity of Birkstane, he had left the anonymous grey Honda he was driving parked out of sight near the head of the lonning and made his way towards the house. He took up a position on a swell of ground about thirty yards from the building where a few scrubby gorse bushes gave him cover, and his elevation gave him a view into the yard through his compact Leika binoculars.

As the sky grew light, there'd been signs of activity within the house, and smoke had begun to rise from the chimney. Then to his amazement, the door opened and Hadda stepped out into the cold morning air, stark naked except for a towel flung over one shoulder. He headed out of sight behind the barn buildings. The sound of running water revealed the presence of a stream somewhere close. Presumably this madman was going to bathe in it!

Pudovkin shivered at the thought, but it made his job easy. The only fly in the ointment was the mangy dog trotting along at Hadda's heel. It looked a vicious beast. Pudovkin did not care for dogs. He'd once been bitten by one in childhood. Later he had returned with a piece of poisoned meat and had the pleasure of watching the beast die in agony. Hadda's dog would have a more merciful death. The first shot would take care of it. A naked cripple bathing in an icy stream would hardly be in any condition to take advantage of the brief respite offered by this diversion.

He was just beginning to move forward from his hiding place when he heard a distant engine. A few moments later, a black woman had come down the lonning and into the yard. Who the fuck was she? he wondered. Maybe she would leave when she found the house empty.

She opened the door and peered inside. For a moment she hesitated in the doorway. Then she turned and went in the lame man's footsteps.

'Fuck!' he muttered. A man and a dog were do-able, but this woman complicated matters. Who was going to miss her and how soon? There might even be someone waiting for her in her car. In cleaning operations escape routes were vital, and in this fucking wilderness time was an essential part of any escape plan. Pudo wanted to be long gone before the deed was discovered. He needed at least an hour to get on the south-bound motorway. Any pursuit that started

542

sooner than that could have him road-blocked off with the peasants.

He settled back into his hide. After a few minutes he heard the sound of another car engine. Jesus, he thought. This is like Oxford fucking Street at Christmas!

Shortly afterwards another woman came strolling down the lonning. This one he recognized. It was the lawyer's wife, the good-looking blonde that Pasha Nikitin lusted after. As he'd worked on Toby Estover in the warehouse, Pudo had been satisfied the lawyer knew nothing about the newspaper article long before his boss had signalled a halt. How much, he wondered, had this had to do with the lovely Imogen? And how was Pasha going to react to the news that she was still sniffing around her ex-husband?

With great indifference, if the said ex was dead, he guessed.

But her presence was a further unwelcome complication.

As she approached the gate, there was a sound of voices and the black woman came into view, heading towards the house. The blonde stepped sideways out of sight into the hedgerow that flanked the lonning. Hadda, still naked, and his dog appeared behind the black and the three of them went inside.

The blonde woman retreated up the lonning. Pudovkin listened for the sound of a car starting up but heard nothing. Then she re-appeared. This time she passed through the gate and walked into the yard. She was holding a sheet of paper in her hand as she vanished from the Russian's line of sight into the barn, but when she reappeared a moment later, she was empty-handed.

Once more she went up the lonning, moving with an easy grace, but purposefully. This time he did hear a car start up.

Next Hadda, now fully dressed, came out of the house. He looked around carefully. Something must have alerted him, probably that fucking dog. Now he crossed the yard

543

and went into the barn. The black woman stood in the doorway watching him for a moment before going back inside. Hadda followed shortly, in his hand a sheet of paper, presumably that left by his ex-wife, which he crumpled up as he passed through the door.

Now what was that all about? wondered Pudo. Not that he really gave a damn. His only concern was that he was freezing his nuts off stuck in this gorse bush with no way of working out how long it was going to be before he could have the pleasure of blowing Hadda's fucking head off!

Much longer and he would be too cold to pull a trigger. He was sorely tempted just to head down to the house, burst into the kitchen and blast away at everything that moved. But that was just the chill entering his brain. Time to head back to his nice warm car and review the situation.

He was almost at the head of the lonning when he heard the roar of an engine starting up somewhere behind him. He scuttled sideways through the hedgerow and was able to see the Land Rover Defender bumping over the rutted surface of the lane. He hurried after it, keeping on the blind side of the hedge. Where the lonning met the narrow road, if the vehicle turned west then it was heading towards what passed for the main road in this third world county and pursuit would be futile.

But if it turned east . . .

And east it had turned.

Pudo had studied his map before venturing into this waste-land and he knew that eastward, not far past the head of the long dark lake with the suggestive name of Wastwater, the road came to a dead end. Here stood a scatter of dwellings and an inn. A man wanting to go further than these would have to go on foot.

He sent the Honda hurtling along the narrow road till he could see the Defender up ahead, then slowed to its pace.

Hadda kept going all the way to the inn and parked before it. Pudovkin brought the Honda to a halt with a light blue Merc coupé between it and the Defender. There weren't many other cars here. Big surprise. Who in his right senses would want to come here at this time of year?

If Hadda went into the inn, then he might be in for a long wait. But the big man was shrugging on a cagoule and slinging his fucking axe over his back. Pudo's jaw, still wired, ached at the sight of it. Even if Pasha hadn't sent commands, he'd have wanted to sort this bastard out on his own behalf.

Now Hadda was ready. He slammed the tailgate shut and set out past the inn.

A glance at his map confirmed to the Russian that there was nowhere to go except wilderness. This was excellent. One thing you could say for this benighted landscape was it offered the careful killer any number of good ambush positions, plus a superfluity of sites where a body could be dumped and not be found for days if not weeks.

He gave his prey a couple of minutes' start which he used to slip into a pair of trekking shoes and a fur-lined parka, congratulating himself on his foresight in coming prepared. Then he set out in pursuit.

He didn't anticipate any problem keeping pace with a lame man, and felt confident he'd have enough in reserve to overtake him when the moment and location seemed ripe to conclude the business. In his work, keeping fit was a condition of service. It could mean the difference between life and death. So he worked out daily at the activity centre when he was in London, with separate regimes for strength, for endurance, for agility. He could run for an hour, snatch a hundred and sixty kilos, and go up the climbing wall at a speed that made some of the serious mountaineering boys open their eyes. When, as occasionally happened, one of them suggested he might like to join them on a real rock face, he said, 'You must be fucking joking! I don't do this for pleasure.'

Hadda had vanished towards the rear of the inn. There was a broad stream here spanned by an ancient footbridge. Pudovkin started to cross it but paused when he could see no sign of Hadda on the open ground ahead. He glanced to his right, and there he was, still on the same side of the water.

Pudo followed. The path bore left, climbing above the stream. He lost sight of his prey but a solid stone wall to one side and a wire fence to the other cut down the chance of diversion. There were several gates to pass through. He didn't waste time by closing them behind him. The final one took him out into open countryside with the path descending into a broad valley. Now once more he could see Hadda. Despite his lameness, he was setting a spanking pace and the Russian soon had to revise his notion of being able to overtake the man at his ease.

As the path became steeper he revised it even more, discovering the considerable difference between gym fitness and the demands on your muscles made by hill climbing. He made up a bit of ground when his prey came to a halt beside a tumultuous stream and stooped to gather water in his hands and take a drink. He didn't look back. No need to worry if he had. At this distance recognition wasn't likely and the presence of another walker on the same well-trodden path was hardly going to be suspicious.

When Pudovkin reached the stream, he too paused to drink and briefly consult his map. The path crossed the stream (fittingly, in view of its spate, called Gatherstone Beck) and then bore right above it to the depression of Black Sail Pass between the mountain whose side he'd been traversing, Kirk Fell, and an even higher one ahead, named Pillar, though it didn't look to have much that was pillar-like about it.

Having no idea which of the routes on offer Hadda was planning to take when he reached the pass, the Russian forced himself to speed up. But despite his best efforts, the man had vanished by the time he got there.

Furious that all this expenditure of energy might have been in vain, Pudovkin checked out the options. To his right the track rose to what looked like a steep and rocky ascent of Kirk Fell. There was no one climbing it.

He went forward till he could see down into the next valley. He recalled its name: Ennerdale. If anything it looked even more godforsaken than the valley he had just climbed out of.

He scanned the possible lines of descent from the pass, but again spotted no movement.

He returned to the main cross path and started along it towards Pillar. Now once more he spotted his man, not on the main path but on a lower branch that skirted beneath the craggy north face of Pillar overlooking Ennerdale.

The short descent to this lower path was steep and slippery and he did most of it on his backside. His earlier notion of somehow overtaking and lying in ambush was now completely abandoned. Apart from the surprising speed at which the lame man was moving, this was a track that followed the best, indeed for most of the time the only possible line, and getting ahead of his prey was virtually impossible. So now all he could hope for was to get close enough for a clear shot.

His weapon was a Makarov PM, similar to the one that Hadda had ruined on the beach. He'd really loved that gun. It had belonged to the first man he'd killed, and he felt a sentimental attachment towards it. So though there were more efficient modern weapons available, he'd chosen to replace it with the same.

Its drawback was that to guarantee deadliness of both aim

and impact he needed to be within a range of no more than twenty metres and preferably nearer half of that. In his usual urban environment, this was fine. Out in this fucking wilderness, something with a long-range capability would have come in useful. On the other hand, closeness might bring the pleasure of being recognized. He was more than happy to shoot Hadda in the back, but the buzz of letting him know who was pulling the trigger would be a definite bonus.

The weather was changing. Clouds were gobbing up the clear blue sky, sinking low enough to obscure the mountain crests and send questing swirls of mist down the rocky slopes. Not normally a fanciful man, Pudovkin was surprised by the thought that it might be Hadda who was summoning these vapours to help conceal him, and when a huge raven swooped out of the crags and croaked mockingly just above his head, it felt like a visitation from an enemy spy.

He waved away these superstitious fancies, but they came flocking back a few minutes later when the track climbed to a prominent shoulder on which stood an imposing cairn.

Straight ahead of him, towering from the mountainside like the ruin of some ancient troll-king's stronghold was a huge jagged rock, dark and menacing, its front plunging precipitously to the valley below.

Here was an explanation of the name Pillar. The fell was named not for its height or bulk but for this single dominant feature. And it was toward this terrifying excrescence that the track was leading.

He could see Hadda clearly, striding onward at the same unrelenting pace. For the first time, doubt seeped into the Russian's mind. This creature he was pursuing was in its own hunting grounds. He was the intruder here.

Then he reminded himself that his quarry was a one-eyed cripple with a maimed hand and no weapon but a long axe. He felt the comforting weight of the Makarov in its shoulder holster and, leaving the cairn behind, he resumed his progress along the path.

Most of the snow had vanished from the track up to Black Sail but here on the north-facing flank of the fell, many of the cracks between the dark crags were still packed white, creating a savage pied beauty that might have appealed to a mind less focused than the Russian's. All he noticed was that the wind here was much stronger than it had been in Mosedale, blowing in gusts that rattled among the crags and bounced back with a resonance almost metallic. He drew his fur-lined hood up around his head. The din of the wind would conceal the sound of his approach and, even if Hadda did look round, the hood would delay recognition till it was too late.

Ahead the man was following the track up a steep slope across loose stones that scrunched and tinkled beneath his boots. Pudovkin lost sight of him in a swirl of mist. He expected to glimpse him again higher up the track but he didn't appear. Perhaps he was taking a rest. Surely there was nowhere to divert to in this rocky wilderness? This could be it, he thought, picturing coming upon his prey lying at his ease to catch what he didn't realize was his last breath.

He pressed on, but as he approached the spot where he'd last seen Hadda, there was no sign of the man. Indeed, it wasn't the kind of place anyone in their right senses would have paused to seek rest. At least while you were moving you didn't have too much time to take in the horror of your surroundings.

Above him, the track steepened up a scree slope. Up there, Hadda would surely have been in clear view. He looked for alternatives and spotted a tiny cairn. It seemed to indicate the start of a side path, not the kind of path anything but a demented sheep would follow, but he followed it anyway. It led down and round till at a bend he found himself gazing over a desolate gully that made the terrain he'd just crossed seem an oasis of calm and security.

On the far side of the gully, close now but diminished by the scale of the surrounding crags, he saw his prey again. He was picking his way gingerly up a great slab of rock that seemed to lead nowhere but the sheer face of the towering pillar above. The slowness of his movement encouraged Pudovkin to consider the possibility of a shot.

He pulled out his gun and took aim. Even as he did so, his mind was calculating the distance, and the wind, and coming almost instantaneously to the conclusion he'd be mad to take the risk. At the moment, if Hadda spotted him, he was just another idiot whose idea of fun was to risk life and limb crawling around this inhospitable place in the middle of winter. But a bullet bouncing off the rock he was clinging to would be a strong hint that there was trouble around!

He reholstered the gun. He had to get close enough to ensure his first shot at least disabled the guy.

Hadda had reached the top of the slab. He seemed to take a step down, moved a little to his right, and then began climbing straight up.

Now this was much more promising, thought Pudovkin. Get below him and he would present a perfect target with no scope for evasion.

As quickly as he could, he crossed the gully and pulled himself up on to the slab. Its angle wasn't so steep as to be much of an obstacle in itself and there were cracks and indentations that provided good footholds. But there was also a lot of ice and Pudovkin now appreciated why Hadda had been taking this so carefully.

His foot slipped and he went down heavily on his right knee.

He swore violently in Russian. His friends would have

550

taken this as a signal to stand clear. He had a full range of English oaths at his disposal for everyday use, but at moments of extreme anger, he always reverted to his native language.

He was beginning to wish he'd just shot Hadda as he bathed in the stream behind his house, and the black woman too. And the dog as well, of course. Not so easy getting off three accurate shots at different targets, but if he'd known where his pursuit of Hadda was going to bring him, he might have taken the chance.

On the other hand, as he headed back to his car, he'd probably have met Estover's wife, and she'd have had to go too. That wouldn't have pleased Nikitin. OK, he might have accepted the argument of necessity, but resentment has a longer shelflife than gratitude, and in some dark recess of the future, when all the many services Pudovkin had done for him had faded from his memory, he would still recall that his faithful servant had killed the woman he loved.

So he bottled his anger. Here was where he was, and he did not intend to leave without accomplishing what he'd set out to do.

But his heart sank when he stepped off the end of the slab and moved along a narrow ledge to the right. He'd been hoping when he looked up to see his quarry exposed on the rock face above him. Instead he was just in time to see him moving out of sight to commence the next section of the ascent.

To get to him he was going to have to follow him.

Suddenly the indoor climbing wall which he was accustomed to running up like a spider diminished in his recollection to little more than a gentle slope liberally scattered with regular hand and foot-holds.

But where a fucking cripple could go, he could go too!

Not before he had a rest, though, and some refreshment. He squatted down and pulled a small plastic bag out of an inner pocket. From it he took a pinch of white powder, set it to his right nostril and sniffed. Then he repeated the process with the left.

Now he sat for a couple of minutes till he felt strength and clarity return.

At last he was ready.

He took a deep breath, said a prayer to his birth-saint (who after so many years of neglect probably wrinkled her face and said, *Who?*) and began to climb.

6

'Hello, Wolf,' said Imogen.

Hadda looked up and saw her standing above him. She was in her forties now, but she still had the clear glowing skin and the fresh-faced beauty of a Botticelli angel.

If she wanted, she could drive her boot into his face and send him tumbling five hundred feet, give or take a bounce. End of all her worries. End of his too, and perhaps not the worst way to go, with those calmly lovely features the last thing he saw on earth.

She reached her hand towards him and he thought for a moment that maybe his fantasy was going to come true. Then she grasped his hand and hauled him up towards her.

They stood facing each other.

'So here we are,' she said.

'Again,' he said.

'Yes. Again. Only I didn't need a rope this time.'

'I don't think you needed a rope the first time.'

'But then you were worried about me,' she said. 'Funny, isn't it? All the climbing we did, we never came back here.'

'There was nothing to come back for. I mean, nothing that could be added to that first time. Not for me, anyway.'

'Oh, Wolf,' she said. 'You made a bad choice.'

'No,' he said. 'I never made any choice. Choosing didn't come into it. It was you who made the bad choice.'

She nodded gravely.

'You're right. I chose. And it was a selfish choice because I could see you had none.'

He realized he was still holding her hand and let it fall.

He said, 'Let's sit down.'

'Why? Have you brought a picnic?'

He said, 'No. I was thinking, violence is more difficult from a sitting position.'

'Ah.'

They moved away from the edge and sank on to a rib of dry rock. He'd unslung his axe and now he laid it between them. Then he reached into the pocket of his cagoule and produced a pewter flask.

'No picnic,' he said. 'But a drop of the Caledonian cream to keep the cold out. You could have frozen to death, waiting up here.'

'I'm like you, I don't feel the cold,' she said. 'And I haven't been waiting long. You must still move fast.'

'For a cripple, you mean.'

'No,' she said. 'For a geriatric.'

That almost made him smile. He unscrewed the flask and passed it over. She took a short drink. He took a slightly longer one.

'So, Wolf,' she said. 'Let's talk seriously. There's just me left, now that you've pronounced judgment on Johnny, Pippa and Toby.'

'Have I?' he said. 'I thought I'd just been sitting quietly up here in God's Own Country, minding my business.'

'That's what you were doing when you chopped our rowan tree down, was it?'

He said, 'Woodcutting's always been my business. But I

554

doubt anyone will be able to link me with whatever's happened to the Nutbrowns and your husband.'

'I'm sure of it,' she said. 'Just as I'm sure that, if you wanted, you could arrange for me to be dealt with at a distance. But you're here.'

'Justice is like sex,' he said. 'Less satisfying at a distance. That could be my explanation for being here. What's yours?'

'Oh, you know me,' she said. 'Just an old-fashioned girl who prefers most things face to face. Especially a trial.'

'So you've come to make your defence?'

'No. No defence. Guilty as charged. But I would like to exercise my right to make a plea in mitigation.'

He took another drink, offered the flask. She shook her head.

'Plead away,' he said.

'Well, first of all, I have never lied to you.'

'You're saying you weren't screwing Estover before and during our marriage?'

'No, I'm not saying that. And not just Toby. There were others,' she said. 'You did spend a lot of time away from home, Wolf. If I say it meant nothing, I would be lying. But it meant no more or less than eating. Always a necessity, only occasionally a real pleasure. Never like it was when you came home.'

'So you were just keeping in practice, is that it?' he said harshly. 'And you don't count that as deceiving me?'

'I didn't say I didn't deceive you. I said I never lied to you. If you'd ever asked, I would have told you. But you never did. Was that because you trusted me, Wolf? Or because you were frightened to ask?'

'Forget the psychoanalysis,' he said. 'I'm done with that. If I were your brief, I'd advise that your plea in mitigation is getting off on the wrong foot. When are we going to get on to the disturbed childhood, the school bullying, the dysfunctional family stuff?'

'I had all of those,' she said evenly. 'The bullying stopped when those concerned found they suffered far more than I did. As for my family, well, you know my mother.'

'Ah yes. Kira. All her fault, is it?'

'To a large extent. Didn't you wonder why she stopped objecting to our marriage?'

'I always assumed it was because I got you pregnant and she didn't care to have a bastard for a grandchild.'

'The second part of that is certainly true,' said Imogen.

She spoke so calmly that it took several seconds for the implication to sink into Hadda's mind.

He scrambled to his feet and took a few steps back from her. His fists were clenched. He had clearly realized, she thought, that sitting down wasn't such a disincentive to violence as he'd imagined.

He said, 'Now you're lying.'

She said, 'No. I got confirmation I was pregnant about a week after your return. Far too early for it to have been you. But, if it's any consolation, I didn't know about it when I said I'd marry you.'

'And when you did know, you just let me think it was mine?'

'If you'd asked, I'd have told you the truth,' she said. 'But you didn't. So I didn't. Wolf, I'm sorry.'

'*Sorry!* For what particular lump of all this shit you've piled on me, may I ask?'

'I'm sorry I connived at keeping Ginny away from you after . . . after it happened. I told myself it didn't matter as she wasn't really yours. But that was wrong. I see that now. She was as much yours as . . .'

'As whose? Who was Ginny's real father? Estover?'

'I don't think so,' she said indifferently. 'Does it matter? You were the only father Ginny ever knew. That was a pain I had no right to inflict on either of you. For both your sakes,

I should have let your letters reach her. I shouldn't have listened to Mother.'

'Ah, the bitch-queen. I knew she'd be in there somewhere. What did she advise then?'

'That now was the time to tell Ginny the truth about her parentage. I agreed because I thought it would make her feel better, less connected . . . She was very upset.'

'Jesus!' exclaimed Hadda, his face working with rage. 'Upset! You mess up her mind and then send her out of the country! No wonder the poor kid never got in touch with me, no wonder she went completely off the rails. Whatever else I blamed you for, I tried not to blame you for her death. But now . . . For Christ's sake, Imo, forget all this crap about a plea in mitigation for what you've done to me. How can you ever forgive yourself for what you did to Ginny?'

She said urgently, 'Wolf, I can't, I don't. Believe me, for a long time now, I've been frozen inside. When I melt I'm simply going to wash away. You and I are very much the same. We survive by not asking questions. We create a world we can live in because we have invented our own rules. We climb not because we want to reach the top but because deep down inside, what we really want is to fall. *We are the same!*'

Her voice had become increasingly agitated till the final words came out in a single breath. Her agitation seemed to calm him and when he replied it was in a low, even tone.

'What the hell are you talking about?' he asked. 'Don't try to tar me with your brush, Imo. All I ever wanted was to get into your world so I could have you, but it was a delusion, a madness, and I'm over it now. When I was a boy I always thought you were far beyond my dreams and now I see how right I was. But not beyond. Beneath! I thought I had to climb up to get to your world, now I see that all I did was let go of everything real and fall till I hit rock bottom!'

557

He had moved steadily forward as he spoke and now he stooped to pick up his axe.

She looked up at him and said softly, 'Oh, Wolf. It's not worlds I'm talking about. It's genes. We're sides of the same coin, that's what drew us together. You weren't the first woodcutter to feel the pull of the magic castle. Did you never wonder why we were so drawn to each other? And when we made love there was a darkness in it that made it all the better, don't say you never felt that.'

'What the hell are you talking about?' he repeated, this time more vehemently. *'The same coin? Darkness?* Come on, woman, speak plain while you've still got the chance!'

She regarded him sadly and said, 'Haven't you guessed? I thought you might have guessed long ago. We're brother and sister, Wolf. Fred was my father too.'

7

At Wasdale Head, Alva parked her car alongside Hadda's Defender. Next to it was a blue Mercedes. No way to identify it positively as Imogen's, but she recalled a similar car standing outside Ulphingstone Castle when she'd called there in January.

She took her small day-pack out of the boot and checked its contents. Waterproof, spare pullover, mint cake, isotonic orange juice, lightweight binoculars, map, compass, whistle, torch. Everything the wise psychiatrist should carry on the fells. All her Lake District walking had been done on the east side, so she opened her map to check the route to Pillar, but when she heard Sneck's bark, she realized she needn't have bothered. The dog was standing on the track that led past the side of the inn, looking back at her impatiently. As she went after him, he turned and ran ahead with a reassuring certainty.

Perhaps Hadda wasn't as far in front as she'd feared. Perhaps for some reason he'd diverted on his way here.

As she reached the main path running up the right-hand side of Mosedale along the flank of Kirk Fell, she glimpsed a figure far ahead and her heart leapt. But when she paused to focus her glasses, she quickly realized it wasn't Hadda. Just another walker, and one moving fast. She put the glasses away and settled into the long rangy stride that had been the envy of her college friends when they went hiking together. 'For God's sake, Alva, it's not a bloody race!' they'd say. But, being a student psychiatrist, she'd known that it usually was.

Sneck knew exactly where he was going and in his eagerness often disappeared from view, but always he returned as if to reassure himself she was keeping up. She thought of urging him to take off by himself in the hope that he'd catch up with his master and let him know that she was following. But what good would that do?

And while the path ahead was perfectly clear at the moment, if ever she reached a point of divergence, she'd need the dog to guide her to the right choice.

As the angle of ascent steepened, the rangy stride became harder to maintain. At the crossing of Gatherstone Beck she paused and rested for a moment, looking up the slope towards the col and seeing the other walker silhouetted momentarily against the skyline. She'd made up ground on him but this was no guarantee she'd made up any on Hadda.

What the hell did she think she was doing here, anyway? Their rendezvous on top of Pillar Rock was probably going to put them out of her reach – she was no mountaineer, and from what she recalled of Wolf's description of the climb, it posed real problems for a novice.

But she'd come this far and wasn't about to turn back now.

Carefully she crossed the stream and then began the haul up to the pass.

She knew from the map that to approach the Rock she needed to move off the main track to the summit of the fell, but it was Sneck who showed her where the diversion began. Now she found herself in an airy craggy area that made the track up to the col seem homely by comparison. The river winding along the valley bottom far below seemed little more than a blue ribbon. She felt that surge of exhilaration which is the mountain walker's true reward for effort, and normally would have paused to savour the experience. But today she was walking not for pleasure but for something that she didn't quite understand, though she felt that somehow the meaning of her future lay in it.

She increased her speed along the narrow path. Increasingly the way ahead was obscured by mist. At a large cairn with a memorial plate screwed into a rock beneath it, she paused for another sweep ahead with the glasses. As if at a command, the mist cleared and for the first time she saw the Rock. It was an awe-inspiring sight. She couldn't make out anyone on top of it but when she lowered her sights to the approach path, the figure of the other walker swam into view.

This was good, she told herself. If he too was looking to climb the Rock, then surely the presence of a stranger would inhibit Wolf from offering any violence to his ex-wife?

She was about to lower the binoculars when the man ahead halted. He seemed to be pulling something out of his jacket. Now he was pointing it ahead . . .

Oh Jesus Christ! she thought. It's a gun!

John Childs's message erupted into her mind. *Tell him Nikitin knows. Tell him the man with the broken jaw is still on the loose.*

She couldn't see what the man was aiming at but assumed it was Hadda. She tried to scream a warning but the wind drove the sound back into her throat. All she could do was wait for the sound of the shot.

It didn't come. The man slipped the weapon out of sight and a moment later he too had vanished behind a crag.

She hurried on. She was taking risks now to move at speed, but she knew it was in vain. The gunman was too far ahead. If he got Wolf in his sights as he was climbing up the Rock, that would be an end to it. Her only hope was that Wolf would reach the top unharmed and she could somehow get a warning to him. How the hell she would do this, she didn't know, but as she scrambled up the track to a point where the side path the man had been on branched off, she began to get the glimmer of an idea. This diversion had to lead round the huge crag ahead of her to the foot of the climb. The main track ran up a steep scree slope to the top of the crag and presumably thereafter led all the way to the summit of the fell. From up there it must be possible to look out directly on to the top of the Rock.

She attacked the slope ferociously. After a moment or so she realized that Sneck had opted for the path taken by his master. For the first time she felt truly and frighteningly alone. At the top of the slope the path turned along a more gently inclined rock shelf that on her right side fell steeply into the valley. She fixed her gaze firmly ahead. A mountain rescue stretcher box came into view, more of a dreadful warning than a comfort. Now the track headed up another scree slope. The Rock loomed to her right, but she still wasn't high enough to view its top.

Soon, she told herself. Soon!

But what was she going to see when she got high enough to look down at it?

She recalled the shining blade of the axe that Wolf had carried out of Birkstane with him.

But he wasn't a killer, she told herself. It had been un-necessary killing that had made him fall out with JC.

Unnecessary.

There was the rub. The death of the innocent had filled him with rage.

But the death of the guilty . . .

She pushed herself still harder.

8

As Lady Kira told her story at the breakfast table, Imogen had noticed with a slight distaste how her voice grew mellow under the power of sensual recollection.

'It wasn't long after I came to the castle,' said her mother. 'Your father, well, let me put it this way, your father had a very English attitude to making love. He was the perfect gentleman, very concerned in case he hurt me, and anxious to make what he assumed might not be a very pleasing experience for me last as short a time as possible. I tried to let him know that I didn't care about being hurt as long as I was overwhelmed, but . . . anyway, things weren't going too well, and after a particularly unsatisfactory night, I wandered out in the morning, across the lawns and into the forest.

'I heard him before I saw him. The perfectly regular, powerful crash of an axe into the trunk of a tree. A rhythm that seemed to vibrate through my whole body. I walked towards it. Then in the light of the early-morning sun slanting down through the trees, I saw him at the edge of a clearing, tall, fair, naked to the waist, already sweating through his effort though the morning air was still cool.

'I sat down on an old stump and watched him, delighting

in his strength, his vigour, his strong rhythmic movement. He paused to wipe his brow with a large red kerchief. And then, though I made no sound, he became aware of me.

'He stood and looked at me for a moment, then he came towards me. He was still carrying his axe. I remember the blade seemed huge close to my head and he himself looked like a giant towering over me.

'He said, "I shouldn't sit there, my lady. Tree 'ull be coming down shortly."

'I didn't say anything, but just drank in his closeness. His belt buckle was only a foot or so from my face. Almost without thinking, I reached up and began to undo it. For a moment he went tense and I thought he was going to pull back.

'Then he relaxed.

'And then I had the most ecstatic sex I had yet experienced.'

She'd fallen silent. Her features had softened, her body relaxed, and her eyes were focused elsewhere, elsewhen.

Imogen said coldly, 'And how was it for him, Lady Chatterley?'

Kira straightened up and was herself again.

'All right, I suppose. He didn't say. All he could do when it was over was apologize, as if he'd been the one who set things in motion! Men can be very arrogant, can't they? He stuttered a lot of stuff about his wife having a child a couple of months earlier, and things still not being right between them, and so on. What it added up to, I suppose, was he hadn't been getting any sex for some time before the birth and it didn't look as if he were likely to be getting any in the foreseeable future, and this state of frustration he offered as explanation for his unforgivable effrontery in screwing me. His main concern seemed to be that I might broadcast our encounter!

'Well, as you can imagine, I soon grew tired of this babble. I tidied myself up and said to him that I certainly had no intention of letting anyone know I'd demeaned myself with a woodcutter. And I further added that if ever I got the slightest hint by so much as a word or a look or a nod or a wink that he had mentioned it to anybody else, that would be the day he found himself out of work and out of his tied cottage.'

Imogen had stopped listening. Her mind was making calculations.

'You say this happened how many months after Wolf's birth?'

'Who said anything about Wolf?'

'The Haddas only had one child. How long?'

'Two, three months,' said Kira.

'And I'm almost exactly a year younger than Wolf . . . Christ, Mother, what are you trying to tell me? That you let me marry my half-brother?'

Interestingly the idea excited as much as it horrified her.

Lady Kira shrugged.

'Why not? In the old days, unions closer than that were winked at to keep the bloodline pure. Hardly applicable here, of course. To start with, while having no objection to you pleasuring yourself with a woodcutter as I had done, the idea of your actually marrying him struck me as positively obscene. Then you told me you were pregnant, but it wasn't his. And I thought, why not? It did mean the little bastard would have a name. And Hadda had come back to us with his manners mended and money in his pocket, and he looked to have the kind of ingratiating manner that could lead him to make a lot more. He might do reasonably well for a few years till you grew tired of him and someone better suited came along.'

Imogen said, 'But he was my brother!'

'Half-brother. And as you'd made it clear you weren't going to have any more children, I couldn't see how your possible relationship might be a problem.'

Imogen said, 'I bet it was a problem for poor old Fred though. I bet he put three and nine together and took a good look at me and saw my blonde hair and blue eyes and nothing whatsoever of Ulphingstone in me. No wonder he was so absolutely dead set against the marriage!'

'Perhaps,' said Kira indifferently. 'Or perhaps he just had the good sense to see it was an ill match. Anyway, he never said anything.'

'What could he say? *Excuse me, Sir Leon, I rogered your wife twenty years ago and it occurs to me that perhaps your beloved daughter is really mine?* And I was pregnant!'

'Oh, come on, dear. I think you're crediting the man with far too delicate a sensibility. He was a woodcutter, for God's sake!'

Not since her teens had Imogen felt frustrated enough to want to strike her mother, but the urge welled up in her now.

She'd controlled it, stood up and made for the door.

'Where are you going, dear?' called her mother.

'For a drive. Somewhere the air's a bit fresher.'

And she'd closed the door behind her with a gentleness more powerful than a slam.

All this Imogen recounted to Wolf plainly and simply, leaving nothing out, putting nothing in.

He listened, standing still as a statue, his features set in marble.

When she finished, he let silence fall like a barrier between them.

Finally he said quietly, 'So you and your family destroyed my father just as completely as you destroyed me.'

With an effort at lightness she said, 'You don't look too

destroyed to me, Wolf. Look, why don't we just walk away from this? I've got money. My share of the Woodcutter loot that Toby and Johnny squirrelled away. It's safely stored in a Taiwanese bank. We can live any way you like. Brother and sister. Husband and wife.'

'Wipe the slate clean, you mean?' he said.

'As clean as you like,' she said. 'If you want to spend the rest of your life punishing me, that's all right too. Or perhaps not the rest. Seven years would seem about right.'

'And is this what you came here to tell me?' he said incredulously.

She shook her head vigorously.

'No. Far from it. I had some silly notion of trying to clear things up between us, then I'd walk away, leaving you to the tender mercies of your black beauty. But now, after seeing you, talking to you, I can see how wrong that would be. You don't want to tie yourself to a psychiatrist, Wolf! She'd be in your mind all the time, ferreting around, trying to set things straight. Me, I'm in your blood, I'm in your genes, I'm in your soul. And you're in mine. I think I've always known it. But I never wanted to admit it. Betraying you like I did, I made excuses to myself, put it all down to reason and necessity. But all I was really doing was trying to prove I was stronger than this dependency I felt. I wanted to prove I was myself. Now I know that I can't be that self without acknowledging you are part of it too. So what do you say?'

'You let me go to jail for a disgusting crime I was innocent of,' he cried. 'You let me take the blame for frauds I knew nothing about. You divorced me and married the bastard who framed me. You helped drive our daughter to distraction and my father to despair. And now you want me to run away with you?'

'Look at yourself, Wolf,' she commanded with a matching

568

force. 'Think of the things you've done, or left undone. There's only one hard truth to hold on to in that fantasy world you built. You want me, I want you. We both knew that the first time we came here. We both know it still. Do I have to strip off like that first time and offer myself? I will if you want. Just say the word, Wolf. Just say the word!'

She looked up at him, imploringly, defiantly.

He loomed over her, holding the axe over her head as if to ward off her gaze. The polished blade mirrored her face beneath. She ripped the zip on her fleece jacket open, pulled on the buttons of her shirt till it too parted, revealing the soft white swell of her breasts.

A hundred feet away on the summit path, seeing the movement of the axe, Alva Ozigbo screamed, 'No!' but the gusting north-west wind blew the word back down her throat. She dived her hand into her pocket and pulled out her mobile phone. Somehow she had to let them know she was here. And then beyond the two figures who seemed bound together in a kind of all-excluding ecstasy, she saw the man she'd been following. He was on his hands and knees, having just pulled himself up the final few feet of the climb.

She opened her phone, sought and found Imogen's number that she'd put in there last month, prayed that its state-of-the-art technology would find a signal up here and that Imogen would have her phone switched on.

She pressed the speed-dial key.

Pudovkin pushed himself upright. It had been harder than he'd imagined. It wasn't at all like the climbing wall. All that space beneath his feet, and somewhere far below he kept imagining he could hear a dog barking angrily, like some hound of hell waiting to seize him if he fell. A couple of times he'd nearly lost his grip and even the coke he'd snorted couldn't stop him trembling. He'd need to get close to make sure of his shot.

And then he realized there were two of them. The lawyer's wife was here too. What the hell was that all about? He didn't want to kill her, but it was hard to see an alternative. At least her presence seemed to be such a distraction that Hadda was totally unaware of his arrival.

He took a step forward, gun raised.

Two things happened as he pressed the trigger.

A telephone rang.

And Hadda raised his axe.

The bullet glanced off the blade, making it ring like a bell, then rattled away among the fellside crags.

Hadda turned his one-eyed gaze on the Russian. Even safely distanced from any possible swing of the axe, and with a loaded pistol in his hand, Pudovkin felt himself paralysed. Only for a moment.

But in that moment Imogen had raised her phone to her ear and pushed herself upright so that she stood between Hadda and his assassin.

A shaft of sunshine broke through the lowering cloud as if to highlight a climactic scene.

She called, 'Pudo, it's Pasha. He'd like to speak to you.'

She advanced unhurriedly, a smile on her face, the phone outstretched.

Some part of his mind was yelling at him that Nikitin couldn't possibly know that he was up here on top of this fucking great rock with his fancy woman and her ex-husband.

Another part was registering that her jacket and shirt were open and she had really great tits.

And perhaps because of the normalcy of this reaction, yet another part assured him that the guy with the gun was always the guy in control, and he reached out his hand to take the phone.

He grasped it.

The woman kept on coming.

She wrapped herself around him in an embrace as fierce as a lover's and with an irresistible force drove him backwards.

Hadda and Alva screamed together in unconscious unison, 'No!'

Then they were gone.

Somewhere in mid air, they lost contact with each other and Imogen was falling alone, first through the bright air, then through the unreverberate blackness, as she had always dreamed.

Only Sneck was positioned to see the whole of the fall, and he, alone on the slab below, threw back his head and filled the valley with a mournful howl.

High above, Hadda turned and looked across to Alva in despair. Then he began to spin round, axe held out at arm's length, faster and faster, finally letting go and sinking to his knees as the axe hurtled so far through the air that it fell a thousand feet before landing in the valley below.

EPILOGUE

wait and hope

'Il n'y a ni bonheur ni malheur en ce monde, il y a la comparaison d'un état à un autre, voilà tout. Celui-là seul qui a éprouvé l'extrême infortune est apte à ressentir l'extrême félicité. Il faut avoir voulu mourir pour savoir combien il est bon de vivre.

'Vivez donc et soyez heureux, enfants chéris de mon coeur, et n'oubliez jamais que, jusqu'au jour où Dieu daignera dévoiler l'avenir à l'homme, toute la sagesse humaine sera dans ces deux mots:

'Attendre et espérer!'‡

Alexandre Dumas:
Le Comte de Monte-Cristo

---

‡ 'There is neither happiness nor misery in the world, only the comparison of one state with another. Only the man who has plumbed the depths of misfortune is capable of scaling the heights of joy. To grasp how good it is to live you must have been driven to long for death.

'Live, then, and be happy, dear children of my heart, and never forget, until the day arrives when God in his mercy unveils the future to man, all of human wisdom lies in these two words:

'Wait and hope!'

1

Autumn 2018: nothing changes; the world continues as mixed up as ever, the same mélange of comic and tragic, triumph and disaster, sweet and sour, as in every age since humanity hauled itself upright and put on pants.

Nine months after the drama on Pillar Rock, Wolf Hadda tasted both the sweet and the sour as he heard the Court of Appeal (Right Hon. Lord Justice Toplady presiding) declare his convictions of 2010 unsafe.

Outside the Royal Courts of Justice, bathed in the noontide sunshine of an Indian summer, he stood in mountainous silence as Ed Trapp read a short bland statement to the waiting reporters. Then, cocooned by policemen, the two men made their way through the exploding flashbulbs and the strident questions to a waiting limo that pulled away so quickly the pursuing press didn't have time to register that there was already someone sitting in the darkened passenger compartment.

Nothing was said as the car sped along the Strand. As it approached Charing Cross, Trapp said, 'This'll do me.'

'You sure?'

'Yeah. I'm meeting Doll for a spot of lunch.'

'Give her my love,' said Wolf. 'And Ed – thank you.'

The car pulled over, the two men shook hands as Trapp got out, then Wolf settled back in his seat as the journey resumed.

'So all's well that ends well,' said John Childs. 'Justice prevails.'

'Justice!' exclaimed Hadda. 'Imogen dead, Arnie Medler dead, the Nutbrowns in jail for a crime they didn't commit, Estover half-blind and crippled and facing God knows what kind of future, me winning my appeal on new evidence that was just about as dodgy as the old evidence that got me sentenced in the first place – and that's what you call justice!'

'*Exitus acta probat*,' said Childs. 'The end justifies the means.'

'Does it? You once warned me about acting like God, JC. Maybe you should have listened to yourself.'

'My way is not so mysterious. All I did to steer you to this safe haven was call in a lot of favours, so much so that the favour bin is rather empty now. I do hope you are going to behave yourself in the foreseeable future.'

Hadda laughed and said, 'Worried in case I'm tempted to accept one of the tabloid offers for my unexpurgated memoirs?'

'Well, since you were so energetic in making sure all the recovered Woodcutter misappropriations were returned to those who suffered from the crash, the money must be very tempting.'

'Sure! And the Chapel would let me live to enjoy it? I don't think so. No, I've got a job offer I'm thinking about.'

'Your late lamented father's job, you mean, looking after the Ulphingstone estate? Start as a woodcutter, end as a woodcutter. Neat, but hardly progress.'

'Jesus! I don't know why I bother to open my mouth when you could speak all my lines for me!' said Wolf. 'Yes, Leon is keen to keep me close. I really thought that after

576

what happened, he mightn't be able to stand the sight of me. Instead it seems to have brought us closer.'

'Without you he has lost everything,' said Childs. 'Though I cannot imagine his parting with Lady Kira tore his heart-strings.'

'Maybe not. I got her wrong, I think. Well, slightly wrong. She had a small stroke when she heard about Imo. But of course you know that. So she did care for someone more than herself. I only saw her once before she left for Switzerland. It was a shock. She'd put on thirty years; she looks older than Leon now.'

'Will she come back, do you think? After the clinic has put her together again.'

'Leon says no. She told him she hated the castle, and Cumbria, and England. "In the end the dreadful, drab English always win," she said, "that is the lesson of European history."'

'I'm pleased to hear that she got something from her stay with us,' said JC.

'She got Imo. She got Ginny. She's lost everything.'

'It's all right to feel sorry for her,' said Childs gently. 'Only, don't let it turn into guilt. Not about her, or anyone. No one got more than they deserved.'

'Even Arnie Medler?'

'That was an accident, Wolf. Truly. These things happen. Think positive. Think of the good that has come out of all this. The Trapps, what friendship they've displayed. The estimable Mr McLucky who would never have met the delectable Morag without your intervention. Your good friend Luke Hollins who may yet bring religion to darkest Cumbria. And, of course, the wonderful Dr Ozigbo. Most relationships end in deceit. Yours began with it, so that bodes nothing but good.'

'What makes you think there's a relationship?'

577

'Well, I know for a fact that when she decided to pursue her career in an academic setting, opportunities arose at Warwick University, and Bath, and there was even talk of Cambridge. But she's opted for Lancaster.'

'That's because it's handy for her family,' Wolf asserted firmly.

'Perhaps. But the M6 goes north as well as south. Talking of motorways, should you really drive back today? You've had a trying morning.'

'Hardly that,' said Wolf. 'Not when so many favours had gone into ensuring the outcome. No, the sooner I'm out of this rat-run, the better. I'll be home before dark.'

'If you are sure.'

They relapsed into a silence that stretched till they pulled into the London Gateway service area at the foot of the M1.

There, parked in an area marked Staff Only, stood the Defender.

'It's been cleaned,' said Hadda accusingly.

'I'm sure by the time you get back to Birkstane it will have lost its shine,' said Childs. '*Au revoir*, Wolf.'

He offered his hand. Hadda looked at it for a moment then grinned and leaned forward and kissed Childs on the forehead.

'Let's make that goodbye, JC,' he said.

Childs sat and watched the Land Rover pull out of the service area, and continued to sit, still and silent, long after it had passed from his sight.

'Where now, sir?' asked his driver finally.

Childs considered for a moment before replying.

'Give me a moment to make a phone call,' he said. 'Then, I think, Phoenicia.'

2

It was dusk when the Defender arrived in Mireton.

Wolf knew he should have taken a break on the long drive home, but a need stronger than reason had made him let the motorway carry him north till the familiar outline of his beloved Cumbrian fells became visible, and then it had seemed silly to stop.

He parked outside St Swithin's and went into the church-yard. Something had changed since last he was here for Imogen's funeral. The defensive metal paling around the Ulphingstone tomb had been removed.

As he approached the tomb he saw there'd been other changes. A young rowan tree had been planted before it, its handful of berries shining bright in the twilight.

And the inscription now read *Here lies Virginia, beloved daughter of Wilfred and Imogen Hadda, and granddaughter of Sir Leon and Lady Kira Ulphingstone.*

Daughter. That was right, whatever Imo had said. She'd been his beloved daughter all those years. Nothing could ever change that.

He stood there for a moment then turned away.

A voice called, 'Wolf.'

579

Luke Hollins was standing in the church porch watching him.

'Great news, Wolf,' said the vicar. 'I was delighted. I thought I might preach on the prodigal son on Sunday.'

'Shouldn't bother,' said Wolf. 'The talents might be more appropriate. I'll see you, Padre.'

'In church, you mean?' said Hollins hopefully.

'When you bring my Tesco order.'

He went out of the churchyard. Opposite the church the lights of the Black Dog were already burning bright in the gathering dusk. Three men were strolling towards the pub entrance. He recognized them all as local farmers. One of them was Joe Strudd, his nearest neighbour.

Strudd looked across the street and called, 'How do, Wolf. What fettle?'

'Middling. How's yourself?'

'Not si bad. Coming in for a pint and a crack?'

'Later maybe.'

'See you, then.'

The trio raised their hands in salutation and vanished into the pub.

Wolf smiled as he drove out of the village. Luke Hollins still had much to learn about his parish. They didn't go in for fatted calves round here. An invitation to have a drink and a crack was as good as it got.

The turn-off down the lonning to Birkstane came into view. He swung the Defender into it without slowing and the judder of its wheels as it bumped over the old ruts and potholes felt like a caress. The gate was open and he could see a light in the farmhouse while out of the chimney a plume of grey smoke drifted across the star-studded sky.

Home. He recalled JC's words, half mocking, half envious. *Start as a woodcutter, end as a woodcutter.* Is that what he really wanted? In fact, is that really possible after . . . everything.

He brought the car to a halt and started to climb out. The house door opened and Sneck came hurtling towards him, eyes blazing, teeth bared, as if intent on tearing out his throat. Then the dog's paws were on his shoulders and its great rough tongue was sandpapering his face.

'Get down, you slobbery lump!' he commanded.

'Is that what you're going to say to me?' asked Alva from the doorway.

Childs must have rung her. Bless you for that at least, JC! he thought.

What the future held, he didn't know. What demons lay in wait to haunt him, he could only speculate. But this moment, this place, were too perfect for such considerations.

For the rest, wait and hope was all a man could do.

He went towards her, smiling, and said, 'Well, let's see, shall we?'